THE
FERRYMAN
INSTITUTE

THE
FERRYMAN
INSTITUTE

A NOVEL

COLIN GIGL

G

GALLERY BOOKS

New York   London   Toronto   Sydney   New Delhi

G

Gallery Books
An Imprint of Simon & Schuster, Inc.
1230 Avenue of the Americas
New York, NY 10020

Copyright © 2016 by Colin Gigl

First Gallery Books trade paperback edition September 2016

GALLERY BOOKS and colophon are registered trademarks of Simon & Schuster, Inc.

For information about special discounts for bulk purchases, please contact Simon & Schuster Special Sales at 1-866-506-1949 or business@simonandschuster.com.

The Simon & Schuster Speakers Bureau can bring authors to your live event. For more information or to book an event, contact the Simon & Schuster Speakers Bureau at 1-866-248-3049 or visit our website at www.simonspeakers.com.

Interior design by Davina Mock-Maniscalco

Manufactured in the United States of America

10   9   8   7   6   5   4   3   2   1

Library of Congress Cataloging-in-Publication Data

Names: Gigl, Colin, author.
Title: The Ferryman institute : a novel / Colin Gigl.
Description: New York : Gallery Books, 2016.
Identifiers: LCCN 2016017761| ISBN 9781501125324 (paperback) |
   ISBN 9781501125331 (ebook)
Subjects: LCSH: Future life—Fiction. | BISAC: FICTION / Fantasy /
   Contemporary. | FICTION / Fairy Tales, Folk Tales, Legends & Mythology. |
   GSAFD: Fantasy fiction.
Classification: LCC PS3607.I34 F47 2016 | DDC 813/.6—dc23
LC record available at https://lccn.loc.gov/2016017761

ISBN 978-1-5011-2532-4
ISBN 978-1-5011-2533-1 (ebook)

To Kate,
for being the rambunctious kid sister
every brother should be so lucky to have.

To Tim,
for always being my best man.
This story is for you.

To Mom,
for your unconditional love and support,
and for never letting me forget
how ~~good~~ well I did in eighth-grade English.

To Carly,
for sharing your life with me.
I took on this book in an effort to impress you,
and never would have been able to finish it without you.

To Dad,
for the annotated copy of Lamb.
You hoped for a note from me in a copy of my own book one day.
Here it is, in every cover: We did it. Thank you.

I'VE JUST SEEN A FACE

Suicides were Charlie Dawson's least favorite part of the job for two reasons. The first was the inherent tragedy of the whole thing. Death was never pleasant, but there was a pretty dramatic gulf between an eighty-year-old man passing peacefully in his sleep and a young woman demonstrating her outlook on life via an exit wound blown out her skull. The second reason was that suicide assignments were never easy. There were few guarantees in the Ferryman world, but that was certainly one of them.

The young woman currently standing in front of Charlie—Alice Spiegel, according to the report—seemed awfully casual for someone who was about to call time on her life. She'd straightened up her room, changed her clothes (not that Charlie was watching, of course—or, maybe he was, but he was trying not to . . . mostly trying not to), and lightly made up her face. It was only after she ran out of mundane things to procrastinate over that she walked into her closet. She reappeared several minutes later, the handle of a silver box held tightly in her right hand. Alice set the case down on her bed, carefully lifted the top, and pulled out the implement of her impending demise.

Charlie couldn't say what type of handgun she produced, matte black and heavy in her dainty hands. He was willing to bet it fired bullets, though, which currently topped the list of things that mattered at the moment. Alice's eyes, half lidded and calm, studied how the gun nestled in her fingers, flipping her hand back and forth in the subdued light cast by her desk lamp. Satisfied, she slammed a clip into the pistol, cocked it, and flicked off the safety, all with a remarkable nonchalance.

No, tonight was definitely not going to be easy.

There was no anxiety in the way Alice carried herself across the room, no nerves on display as she sat behind her desk. Charlie peeked at his watch. Just under a minute now. With a shake of his head, he pulled out the president's envelope from inside his suit jacket. A golden seal had been pressed over the flap, an embellished key—the president's insignia—embossed in the wax. He'd been told in his initial briefing that said envelope would only open when it was supposed to . . . which, as instructions went, was about as useful as a sandwich bag on the moon. It was his first Presidential Assignment—a corporate classification he didn't even know officially existed until an hour ago—and he was in no mood to blow it.

Truth be told, Charlie was having trouble figuring out what was so special about this case. There didn't seem to be any wrinkles to it (girl gets gun, girl ends life—undoubtedly tragic, but not exactly unique), and he'd handled far more heart-wrenching suicides than this. Still, the assignment came directly from the president of the Ferryman Institute, which had to mean something. That's what he hoped, anyway.

A small pop shifted Charlie's focus back to the envelope in his hand. Unlike moments ago, the top flap now waved gently free, the seal having split and fallen to the floor in two identically sized pieces. As Charlie watched, the two halves silently disintegrated, each one fading away into nothingness.

There's my cue, he thought.

He gripped the contents of the envelope and pulled, expecting the letter inside to slide right out. It didn't. Out of the corner of his eye, Alice was bringing the gun up to her right temple. Charlie tried again with the same emasculating result. *Man, how did they stick this in here?* he wondered, all the while yanking furiously on the piece of paper inside.

Charlie's mind, masochistic as ever, began to prepare the explanation he'd inevitably have to give the president detailing his failure on the assignment. *Yes, sir, I couldn't get it out of the envelope, sir. Yes, sir, very stuck, sir. Only King Arthur would have been able to pull it out, sir. No, sir, I can assure you I have absolutely no pride or dignity left to speak of.* That sounded about right. However, just as he'd resigned himself to that humiliating fate, the letter popped free of its standard number 10 prison.

Charlie stole a glance at the time. Twenty seconds and counting.

The piece of paper inside had been folded in half. Almost immediately, it opened of its own accord. He began to read.

Fifteen seconds left.

Charlie wasn't sure what he'd been expecting, but it definitely wasn't this.

The letter inside contained nine words handwritten in big, bold letters on an otherwise blank sheet. Charlie read it, then read it again. Nine stupidly simple words, and he still couldn't believe what they said.

Ten seconds.

There was a horrifying moment where Charlie's mind seemed to shrivel up and disappear. It was as if having the ability to think had been nothing but a pleasant memory, erased in an instant by two measly sentences. Thankfully, his faculties returned quickly enough. Not so thankfully, they'd essentially taken to running around inside his head with their hair on fire.

Five seconds.

It was a wholly unbelievable choice he was being given, in the most literal sense of the word. But it was a no-brainer, wasn't it?

With a fluid but frantic swoop, his hand dove into the interior pocket of his jacket, a place it had gone many, many times before, and wrapped around his Ferryman Key.

Two seconds.

Acting purely on instinct, he drew the key out and tossed it underhand toward Alice Spiegel's desk. Charlie only realized after the key was well out of his hand that his plan (possibly a strong word for it) hinged on the need for an absolutely perfect throw. Willie Mays, Charlie was not.

Everything in that moment, time included, seemed preoccupied with his Ferryman Key as it arced through the air. Charlie felt like there wasn't a single detail that escaped him. He watched intently as Alice noticed the key in her peripheral vision. The gun dipped ever so slightly as her focus shifted to the golden object first sailing past her head, then clattering loudly against her desk. It was impossible for Charlie not to see her look of undiluted shock reflected in the mirror when it skidded to a stop. It was also impossible to miss her reaction when their eyes locked in the mirror. Without his key, she could see him now, standing behind her, staring at her, a stranger suddenly consuming the reflection. And the look in her eyes . . . Charlie knew that to be a dangerous one.

Alice screamed.

She spun around to face him with an undeniable grace. In that fraction of a second, Alice shifted the barrel of the gun from caressing her skull and instead leveled it at him.

She held it there, her body in a sloppy Weaver stance, her breath frantic, her arms trembling. Charlie needed to defuse the situation, and fast. The unfortunate truth, however, was that in his haste to come up with the first part of his plan, he'd failed to consider anything beyond that. Throw key on desk? Check. Get her attention? Check. Panic because he didn't know what to do now? Sure, might as well check that off, too.

"Uh, you have a very nice bedroom," he said, mainly because he had no idea what else to say. In terms of first impressions, it was probably not Charlie's finest work.

A magnificently loud *BLAM* cut off any follow-ups to that with a well-placed bullet straight to his forehead.

Charlie Dawson's head snapped back, his whole body tumbling with it. The instructions he was holding in his left hand went flying into the air. He caught a glimpse of the paper, now parallel to the ceiling, right before his world went dark.

Written in bold black letters on that ordinary sheet of paper were those nine, short words:

BE A FERRYMAN OR SAVE THE GIRL. YOUR CHOICE.

ONE WEEK EARLIER

CHARLIE

CLIFF DIVING

Charlie Dawson slammed into the canyon floor with a force that would have made Wile E. Coyote blush. His limbs splayed in directions they really had no business being in, like a discarded marionette with its strings cut. A particularly sharp spear of rock skewered him through his shirtless chest, piercing nearly two feet out his back.

A few seconds passed in silence before Cartwright yelled after him. "I would award the dismount top marks," he called down in his late-Victorian accent. "However, I must deduct points for the improper positioning of your toes. For my final score, I give a seven-point-five." His voice carried easily in the desert's desolate stillness.

Charlie, his face buried several inches into the earth, replied with a muted but distinctly audible *mmph*.

Several additional seconds ticked by before Cartwright called down again. "I sincerely hope you're not talking into the strata again, Charles."

A modest crunching sound filtered through the air as Charlie removed his head from the layer of sandstone it had been embedded in. "Only a seven-point-five?" he yelled back up.

"Ah, much better, thank you," Cartwright said as the words

reached him. "As to your question, I'm afraid so, my dear fellow. I would even go so far as to suggest my scoring was rather generous. The foundation for an excellent score is built on impeccable fundamental technique."

Charlie hadn't the faintest idea what he looked like after his feet left the cliff's edge, nor did he particularly care. As far as techniques were concerned, Charlie's list began and ended with *hit the ground*. But while the score was meaningless, the resulting opportunities to try and fluster the otherwise completely unflappable Cartwright were not.

"Fine," Charlie called up, "I'll take your word on my toes. Can we at least both agree that I stuck the landing?" He paused, then added, "Get it? Stuck the landing? Because I'm stuck on this rock right now?"

Awful puns were the only weakness of Cartwright's that Charlie had managed to discover thus far. They were a tenuous form of attack at best.

True to form, Cartwright continued to smile gamely and merely shook his head. "Charles, I will admit there are moments when your misguided attempts at humor make me question our friendship. Heinous wordplay notwithstanding, your score stands." Even from fifty-some-odd yards below, Charlie could see the British gentleman look out in the direction of the vanishing sun before returning his gaze to the depths of the canyon. His eyes twinkled in the last slanted rays of sunlight. "In any case, do hurry up, if you so please. It appears as if our only source of light is retiring for the evening, and I daresay I wouldn't mind doing the same. Oh, and I made tea, should you be interested in partaking." And with that, his head disappeared from view.

Charlie sighed. He'd hoped to get in one more dive before the sun completely set, but there was no stopping Cartwright when he had tea on the brain. In the many years they'd been acquainted, Charlie had known Cartwright to be an almost painfully polite and pleasant person. Yet even Charlie couldn't say for sure what unspeakable things the man might do in the name of Earl Grey. So, with a slight huff, Charlie began to get up.

It was slow going at first, but before long his body settled into its usual rhythm of self-repair. Misplaced limbs gingerly rotated back into place, broken bones set themselves, cuts and lacerations simply closed up and disappeared. In a span of seconds, Charlie's anatomy shifted from abstract Picasso to something actually recognizable as human physiology. When his body was more or less back in working order, he casually slid himself off the pointed rock and stood, dusting off his shorts and ruffling his hair as he did. Save for the flecks of dirt that fluttered out and a few new rips in his shorts, Charlie appeared no worse for wear. Not that he'd been expecting anything different.

His focus turned to the exit rope he'd affixed several hundred feet away down the canyon floor. As Charlie padded toward it on his bare feet, his hand unconsciously reached for the key nestled in his shorts' pocket. Charlie traced it with his right hand, feeling the ornate inscription carved into the shaft beneath his fingertips. He eventually pulled the key from his pocket and held it high in the fading light, staring at the word inscribed on it as if he were seeing it for the first time. *PORTHMEUS*, it read. Translated from Latin, it meant *Ferryman*. At least, that's what Cartwright had told him. Regardless of its translation, that word had changed Charlie's life. He was a Ferryman, an immortal guide tasked with leading the souls of the dead to the afterlife. A man who, in exchange for his service, had received the many gifts of immortality: perpetual youth, lack of pain or sickness, boundless energy . . .

Gifts, Charlie thought, a sad smirk pursed on his lips.

He reached the rope and began to climb. By the time he arrived at the top edge of the canyon, the sky had graduated from its rich pinks and vivid reds to be ensconced in a somber midnight blue.

"Ah, Charles. Alive and in one piece, I see," Cartwright said as Charlie hoisted himself over the canyon's lip. Cartwright was sitting comfortably in a folding chair several yards back from the cliff's edge, a well-worn copy of *Moby-Dick* cracked open in his hands. Cartwright's build—not to mention choice of facial hair— was probably best described as nineteenth-century pugilist. His lanky frame and narrow shoulders belied the cords of muscle Charlie knew were hiding underneath his loose button-down. A finely trimmed crest of slicked-back hair the color of coal rode atop his head while his mustache—that luxuriant, neatly twirled, pinnacle-of-masculinity-itself mustache—flexed on his upper lip in a never-ending tribute to an era of manliness long since past. A lacquered yet otherwise ordinary pipe was perched between his lips, a veil of hazy smoke drifting out of its bowl. To the right of Cartwright's chair sat a small, battery-powered teakettle, complete with a pair of unadorned white teacups. His full name, as introduced, was William Henry Taylor Cartwright IV, but he'd insisted from the very beginning that Charlie simply refer to him by his surname.

"If I didn't know any better," Charlie said, "I'd almost say you sound surprised."

Cartwright waved his pipe in the air to dismiss the statement, causing the smoke to trace indistinct patterns in the darkening sky. "As a friend who has watched you inflict countless acts of gratuitous violence upon yourself, I must be honest in saying I'm not. Rationally, there's no reason you shouldn't be fine." He finally looked up from his book. "But that doesn't mean a small but irrational part of me isn't always relieved to see you as you stand before me now."

Charlie took a look at himself. "Covered in dirt?" He brushed off the modest layer of grime he'd acquired scaling the canyon wall in nothing but a pair of shorts.

Cartwright sighed. "I was implying something much more profound, but I should have known better than to think you would gratefully accept such heartfelt intent."

"You're right. You should have known better, and on both accounts, I might add." Charlie wandered over and sat down on a bare patch of dirt beside Cartwright. The stars winked into existence above them as the sky grew darker.

Despite the remarkable celestial panorama—despite the cliff diving, the amusing banter with Cartwright, the sunset, despite all the things he enjoyed—Charlie's mind wandered elsewhere. A much darker elsewhere.

The elsewhere it always seemed to be these days.

He thought of last week's assignment, of the young man lying in front of him, alone and helpless. He thought of himself, standing there, waiting for the man—practically a kid, really—to die. He thought of all the things he could've done differently, of how, in the end, he'd done his job, just like he always did.

Without fail, it was always the job first. Always the job, forever and ever.

"May I ask you a slightly personal question?"

The sound of Cartwright's voice snapped Charlie's attention to the present. He turned to see Cartwright looking over at him, his book now closed in his lap. Though Cartwright's expressions were almost always perfectly neutral, Charlie couldn't help but notice the slight tint of concern in his friend's eyes. Worse, Charlie had a feeling he knew exactly what—or, more accurately, *who*—Cartwright was truly worried about.

"I have a feeling even if I say no, you're going to ask anyway," Charlie replied.

Cartwright gave him a mischievous smile. "I'm not sure I'd put it quite so brusquely . . ."

"It's fine, it's fine," Charlie said, waving him off. "Ask away with my blessing."

Even with Charlie's permission to continue, Cartwright hesitated. A moment of silence followed, after which he placed his book on the ground. Cartwright gave the stars a searching look, as if they might contain the answer to the question he'd yet to say out loud. Finally, he turned again toward Charlie.

"Rightly or wrongly, I can't shake the notion that there is something weighing heavily on your mind," he said. If his eyes had only hinted at concern moments ago, then the somber tone of his voice removed any remaining doubt.

A dour smirk flitted across Charlie's face. Cartwright had a remarkable knack for knowing exactly what Charlie's mind-set was at any given time. Granted, Charlie also had the poker face of an excitable three-year-old, so maybe that wasn't as impressive as it seemed. Regardless, while he appreciated Cartwright's concern, Charlie wanted nothing to do with the topic. There were several things he'd have to be forced to do, and talk about Charlie Dawson was one of them.

"For the record, that wasn't a question," Charlie said. It was a noble attempt at avoiding the discussion.

Cartwright, however, was not so easily dissuaded. "Your propensity for quibbling over semantics aside, I would wager considerably that you still see my point," he said.

Unfortunately, Charlie did. "It's nothing to worry about," he replied, trying to sound indifferent. He suspected it came off as anything but.

"I believe that is also precisely what the Romans said when the barbarians arrived outside their city walls," Cartwright said. "Except in Latin, naturally, but I digress." Cartwright smiled, but his eyes still lacked their playful glimmer, as if he'd seen what Charlie had actually been thinking earlier and knew he'd just been lied to. Or maybe that was just Charlie projecting. Lying always gave him a serious case of the guilt trips.

Cartwright pulled a small white towel from his pants' pocket and proceeded to clean his used cup, then absentmindedly packed up his various possessions—teakettle and cups, book, pipe—into a small suitcase before closing it shut. "I apologize if I've offended, old friend. However, in the two and a half centuries we've been acquainted, I cannot recall a time you've seemed quite so . . . distant."

The remark stung only because Charlie knew it was the truth. While he'd always believed he hid his emotions well, he was increasingly aware of lapses in the great charade. Even Charlie begrudgingly accepted that, based on recent behavior alone, it didn't take a PhD in psychology to point out what Cartwright had just alluded to. Maybe it was high time he admitted it.

Charlie picked himself off the ground and stood just as Cartwright did the same. The moon had taken the sun's place in the sky now. Though not full, it was large and bright enough to cast a pale glow, illuminating the desert in a ghostly light.

"I know." Charlie then paused, searching for the right words and coming up empty. With a shrug, he ran his hand roughly through his short crop of hair. "I know." There was a not-insubstantial part of Charlie's mind that desperately wanted to open up, to confess, to tell somebody about all the drama it was currently racking itself with. Yet he held his tongue.

Cartwright, perhaps sensing the moment had whispered away, gave Charlie his neutral smile. "Chin up, my good fellow. You are made of stern stuff, indeed, of that I have no doubt. I will not press you on the matter. A man should be entitled to the sanctity and privacy of his own thoughts. However, should you find a need to confide in someone, I am at your beck and call."

"I appreciate it," Charlie said. He initially felt content leaving it there, but then he quickly added, "Really, I'm fine. Seriously. I've just had a lot on my mind lately."

Cartwright's smile softened before he gave the hint of a bow. "A more disturbing notion I could not possibly dream of—that is to say, you using your mind."

The bow complete, Cartwright produced a golden key from his vest pocket, one nearly identical to Charlie's own. With an elegant grace suggesting countless repetition, Cartwright thrust the key through the air, twisted it, and let go. A barely perceptible *click* sounded in the night, and the key, now floating in midair three and a half feet above the ground, remained motionless. A moment later, the silhouette of a doorway appeared around it, shimmering gently in the moon's light like a heat mirage. With his free hand, Cartwright pushed forward. The outline silently swung open on invisible hinges, revealing a sterile white hallway beyond.

"'Til next we meet, Charles," he said as he plucked the key from its floating position and replaced it in his pocket. "Do take care of yourself."

Charlie gave a wave. "I will. Be good, Cartwright."

Cartwright hefted his suitcase and chair, then walked through the door. As he passed beyond the threshold, the opening swung closed, and the night air of the barren landscape was once again whole.

Charlie stood alone, out in some uninhabited stretch of the

Mojave, and stared at the stars. They seemed different tonight, as if they'd somehow lost some of their luster. He knew they hadn't—that was easy enough to see—which could only mean that *he* was seeing them differently. It was not an altogether pleasant prospect. After several minutes, he turned his gaze away and decided it was time he headed back as well. He'd ducked out unannounced again, which he was sure to catch some grief for, but the hell with it.

He took out his key and reproduced Cartwright's steps with the same deft grace, turning it until he was greeted with a *click*, then stepping into the narrow white passageway that appeared shortly thereafter. The passage was about twelve feet long and reminiscent of an average hallway in its length and shape, but strange in that its walls, ceiling, and floor were all completely devoid of color. Even after centuries of use, Charlie still found traversing *the corridor*, as he called it, a mildly bizarre experience. At the opposite end of the passageway stood a stout brown door, its surface weathered with scratches and nicks of varying shapes, lengths, and depths. It was a wholly unremarkable door, which, thanks to its surroundings, made it actually (and ironically) quite remarkable. Nailed into the door at about eye level was a small yellow plaque made from some indistinct metal or combination thereof. It, too, was simple and, like the door, had clearly seen better days. However, it carried with it a strange sense of stature, as if it had been around far longer than the wood it was attached to. Etched into the plaque's surface were the words:

THE FERRYMAN INSTITUTE

Charlie twisted the key back and removed it from the door, then began walking down the hall. As he moved past the door, it swung silently shut, and the last view of the night sky disappeared behind him.

MEET ALICE

Alice hated meatloaf. Detested it. It was the bane of her culinary existence, the kryptonite to her Superman. She wouldn't eat it in a box; she wouldn't eat it with a fox. In fact, she wouldn't eat it trapped in a box with a fox hell-bent on ripping her throat out. She stared at the piece of meatloaf as it lurked menacingly over her dollop of mashed potatoes. Okay, *maybe* she could be compelled to eat it if it meant not getting her throat ripped out, but that didn't make her feel any better about it. She knew it was childish to have such an averse reaction to dinner, especially as a quote-unquote "young adult" aged twenty-five, but there were certain things you just didn't get over in life. For Alice, it was meatloaf. And clowns. But mostly meatloaf.

"You haven't touched your meatloaf yet," her father remarked before sticking a large forkful of it into his mouth.

When Alice had come down to dinner, she was mortified to find the brick of meat sitting in the middle of the table. Having spent more than a few late nights at the office, Dad had opted to cook tonight for the first time in weeks, and she could sense he felt a certain amount of pride in his work. The last thing she wanted to do was take that away from him. Already a sense of foreboding began to build in the pit of her stomach, just below where the meatloaf would be digested if she chose to eat it. Maybe she could force herself to eat it, for his sake?

It sat ponderously in front of her, mocking her in all its meaty glory. Her stomach clenched in queasy protest. No, she couldn't. She didn't even want to poke it lest it contaminate her fork and then, by extension, the rest of her meal.

Why? Why, of all things, meatloaf? Her fork began trembling slightly in her hand. Alice immediately set it down and made a show of wiping her mouth. *Calm down*, she thought. *No reason to get all worked up. Dad probably just forgot you don't like it.*

Exactly. This was just her sitting down to dinner with an entrée she didn't like. Actually, she loathed it, but whatever—same difference. Everything was going to be just fine. So what if her mother would have never made a plate of her most vehemently disliked meal? No big deal. Who cared if she wanted to scream at that stupid, semiburned meat block until her lungs exploded in violent tatters like a grossly overinflated car tire? That was still a perfectly normal and rational reaction to this situation, right?

Alice picked her fork back up. Unfortunately, she knew the answer to that question.

"It's just meatloaf. It won't kill you." Alice's younger sister Carolyn had now joined the fray. Carolyn knew of Alice's utter resentment to anything vaguely related to the meatloaf kingdom, yet decided that it was appropriate to weigh in because that's what Carolyn did. Worse, her comment meant that she'd noticed Alice hadn't touched it yet, which just made Alice that much more self-conscious. "It's good protein, too," she added. A mass of half-chewed mush—about the same color and consistency as the, ahem, contents of a recently used baby diaper—screamed for rescue from inside her sister's mouth as she spoke.

Alice tried to send Carolyn her patented death stare, but Carolyn's consistent lack of table manners was nauseating and Alice simply couldn't bear the sight. Not that she could actually kill anyone with her death stare, but it was known to make people feel very, very guilty, and *guilt stare* wasn't all that catchy.

The end of Alice's fork found its way into her mashed potatoes, and with an exaggerated gusto, she dug in. It was a vain attempt to deflect the attention off her current eating habits, an attention she rather strongly disliked (though, to be fair, she tried to avoid any attention, eating or otherwise). Like a surgeon working near a major artery, she deftly maneuvered her fork around her plate, operating so as to avoid making contact with the hideous baked meat amalgamation.

"Is something wrong with the meatloaf?"

She looked up to see her father gazing at her, his own fork hanging limply in the air as he studied her.

"No, no, not at all. I just . . . had a late lunch." It was a lame attempt at a save, but it was plausible, so it would have to do. "Yeah, just not, you know, super hungry tonight." She pushed her plate forward for emphasis.

He raised an eyebrow. "You feeling okay?"

She felt the concern coming off him in waves. *Wouldn't you be worried, too,* she thought, *if your daughter locked herself in her room for hours on end, then didn't eat at all?* She looked again at the meatloaf. *Actually, if I had a daughter and put that in front of her, I'd probably call child services and turn myself in.*

The sad part was that he was right to be concerned—she couldn't remember the last time she'd eaten a full meal. A week ago? Longer than that. If anything, that made her hate the meatloaf more for drawing attention to what she was—or, more practically, wasn't—consuming. Alice's thoughts started to spiral downward in an unfortunately familiar pattern. She hated meatloaf—honest to goodness considered it an assault on all five of her senses—but more than that, she hated how it was making her *feel*. It was such a stupid, pitiful, downright pathetic reaction to anything, let alone food.

Wow. Can't even get through dinner without an internal meltdown anymore. Now that's *pathetic.*

Alice centered herself with a deep breath. She hoped it went unnoticed. All she wanted was to get away.

"I'm totally fine," she said. "Just had a long day of writing and a little drained from it. You know how it is." That wasn't technically a lie, though she figured most people wouldn't consider rewriting the same three lines over and over again *writing*. "But I'll have some for lunch tomorrow if you leave it in the fridge."

There were a few heavy seconds of near silence (Carolyn chomped food like a masticating cow, so no dinner was ever truly quiet) before Dad began moving his fork again, albeit warily. "Alrighty," he said. "Sorry you weren't hungry. Say something next time. I would have saved it for later in the week."

That was her cue, Alice realized. Casually as possible, she began to push her chair back and stand. All that was left to do was to thank her father for dinner. The sentence formed on her lips, the right tone built in her throat—

"Why would you eat it for lunch tomorrow?" Specks of meatloaf scattered across her plate as Carolyn spoke, her mouth inevitably full. "You hate meatloaf."

Not knowing what else to do, Alice froze, stuck in an awkward *I really have to pee, but this toilet is gross, so I'll hover above it* pose. The things Alice would have done to Carolyn right then ranged from plain wrong to too-horrific-for-Dante's-*Inferno*.

A brief wisp of anger blew behind Alice's eyes as the urge to scream at her sister clawed its way halfway up her throat. She instinctively clenched her jaw and swallowed hard.

"You don't like meatloaf? Since when?" her father asked. His voice was inflected with nearly every inquisitive and incredulous emotion humans were capable of. Alice imagined in other circumstances she would have been impressed by that, but for the moment, there were other matters at hand. Before Alice could respond with another excuse, her sister was already speaking for her.

"Alice never liked meatloaf," Carolyn said. "You haven't eaten it since— How old were you? Like, six?"

"Really . . . ?" her dad said. A tinge of hurt colored his voice. "Why didn't you say anything?"

"Whoa, time out!" Alice said, practically yelling at this point just to interject anything into the conversation. Then the words started coming, anything to avoid further questions and disappointment. "So it's not my favorite or anything, but it's not like I've never had it before, you know—I mean, I would eat Mom's occasionally—well, not really eat it, just kind of nibble on the corners. Not that yours isn't as good, Dad—completely, uh, nibble-worthy—but I wouldn't go out of my way to order it at a restaurant because it's just . . ." She had to catch her breath before finishing weakly, ". . . not my thing." She dared not rewind that explanation in her head, lest her brain commit seppuku to atone for the abomination of English language she had just unleashed on the world.

God, she was hopeless.

Her father stared at her for a second, his eyes open but unseeing. Then he put his fork down and stood up, taking her plate with him and moving it to the counter. "I'm sorry, Alice. I honestly had no idea. Let me make you something else. I have eggs, and . . . let's see . . ." He had made his way over to the fridge and began shuffling through its contents. Alice watched him give the inside of a plastic container a brave sniff before recoiling. "Ugh, well, that's no good. Oh, there's bologna—how about a bologna sandwich instead?"

Hoo-ray, from meatloaf to bologna. "Dad, really, I'm good. Like I said, I had a late lunch. Promise." She hadn't, but her plan to not hurt his feelings had already backfired—why cause more damage?

Her father's head peeked out from behind the door of the refrigerator. His long limbs and arthritis made it difficult for him to comfortably get down to the lower shelves, but there he was anyway. "Are you sure?" he said. "There's plenty of stuff. I've got fresh tomato soup from Mr. Soup Guy back here."

Alice nodded vigorously. "Positive. One hundred percent. But thank you for dinner, the potatoes were excellent." She silently pleaded with her stomach not to growl, hoping that what little sustenance she'd managed to force down would be enough to keep it quiet. "Really good. They should put that recipe on the Food Network," she added with a laugh, hoping against hope that it only sounded forced to her.

"I'm not sure they do Betty Crocker instant-mash recipes on TV," he said as he drew himself up from the tangle of limbs on the floor.

She cringed inwardly. "Well, maybe there was a little extra butter in there or something, because I've had instant mash before, and that tasted way better." Alice wasn't even sure she was making sense anymore.

Carolyn finished up her meal, walked over to the sink, deposited her dishes, and then sauntered upstairs. As always, her sister seemed oblivious to anything outside of her own world. It was a trait Alice found infuriating at the best of times, but at that moment, she was a touch jealous. Ignorance was bliss, after all. Regrettably, Alice had never received that ability, so she and her father stood there in silence for a few seconds, neither knowing what to say.

"Well . . . ," her dad finally said, "I guess I should get started on these dishes." A random assortment of mixed-and-matched cups and plates cluttered up the sink. He strode over to it, his long legs moving in an exaggerated lope before he delicately bent down to get a pair of beaten-up rubber gloves from underneath the sink.

"Are you sure? I can help," Alice said, but he waved her away.

"No, no, I'm all set here. Why don't you go back to your writing?" He shifted his weight from one foot to the other as he stood there.

"I mean, I'm not in a rush or anything . . ." She hesitated. "Why don't I just—"

"I said I've got it, Alice." He playfully waved the gloves at her. "Now get out of here before I start beating you with these." She could see the hint of a smile on his face.

"Horror of horrors," she said in an exaggerated voice as she walked toward the door. She stopped in the doorway. "If you need anything, just let me know. Please?"

"I will. By the way—"

She looked over her shoulder to find him looking patently ridiculous in his small rimmed glasses and dull yellow rubber gloves, but that was her dad.

"There are SpaghettiOs in the cabinet if you're hungry later."

"Thanks, Dad. See you tomorrow." She didn't bother telling him she hadn't eaten those since she was six, either.

Alice took to the narrow staircase quietly, daintily creeping upstairs. The door to Carolyn's room was ajar, and her sister's loud voice talking on her cell phone carried into the hallway. Alice stuck her head in the door. Carolyn's eyes looked up at the intrusion, one eyebrow raised, though her conversation didn't skip a beat.

"What the hell is wrong with you?" Alice hissed at her sister, who was lying on her stomach as she talked on the phone.

Carolyn eyed her carefully before saying "Hold on one sec?" sweetly into her phone. She pressed the mute button on the phone screen and looked at Alice. "What?" she asked in a much harsher tone.

"What do you mean, *what*? Were you trying to make Dad feel like a total ass?"

"Hey," she said flippantly, "I'm not the one who was lying to him about a piece of friggin' meatloaf. Lying to make someone feel better, or whatever it is you were trying to do there, is still lying. Honestly, the only person who made him feel bad today was *you*." She left those words to hang there before adding, "Get over yourself. Seriously."

A string of responses nearly jumped out of Alice's throat, but she swallowed them before any could escape. Arguing with her sister now would only make things worse and she knew it. With a scathing look that nearly transcended her usual death stare, Alice shook her head and closed the door, hard. A few steps down the hall and she was in front of her own room. The lights were off as she shuffled in, and off she left them. The dim screen of her computer monitor bathed the room in an otherworldly glow. Her shoulders dropped as she pushed the door shut and, with what felt like the last reserves of her strength, made her way to her bed and flopped on top of it. Alice lay there, motionless.

She'd barely eaten in weeks, and who knew how long it had been since she'd gotten even a decent night's sleep. All at once, the frayed edges of her mind collapsed. The nearly empty document open on her computer screen taunted her from across the room. Nothing was right—hadn't been for a while—and tonight was just more evidence that she was losing the ability to pretend like it was. Without any warning, she broke down. The little Dutch boy with his finger in the dike had finally given up, bringing tears that simply wouldn't stop. She felt so completely and utterly wrong.

Alice Spiegel lay on her bed and cried long into the night.

THE INSTITUTE

No matter how many times Charlie used his key to travel to and from the Ferryman Institute proper, it was always an odd feeling coming back. The door he'd entered out in the middle of the desert had brought him back to his office, a spacious room with a high ceiling and bright walls. Charlie called it his office mostly due to it being within the Ferryman Institute, but in truth it was designed to be a comfortable living space—he was just stubborn and chose not to see it that way. He strode noiselessly across the floor, the plush carpet absorbing the sound of his uncovered feet and, given the long, dark trail that marked his path across the room, also all the crud he'd accumulated.

Attached to the office was Charlie's private room, a space that was more or less the size of a large walk-in closet divided into two sections. Off to the left was a modest bathroom complete with a sink, vanity mirror, and an unassuming shower stall outfitted with a frosted glass door. To the right, two long rows of clothes hung neatly on hooks. His wardrobe was composed mostly of suits, but there were some more casual outfits mixed in, even if a few were several years out of fashion.

That was the way of it for Charlie—always a few years behind, it seemed. Granted, almost all Institute employees fell at least somewhat out of the loop as far as pop culture and current affairs went. That was pretty much a given living in the micromanaged bubble that was the Ferryman Institute. There was no way of getting news, no Internet access or the like to speak of. Not that the Institute was completely devoid of technology, just that it had all been retrofitted to be used solely for Ferryman purposes. By letting new employees use the tools they'd utilized during their previous lives, the Institute managed to establish a sense of continuity and familiarity, even for men and women thrust into a completely new way of life.

Despite its rather closed-off nature, the Institute knew better than to try and be completely self-contained. Employees were given vacation time, which—unlike Charlie—they could enjoy freely. While workers didn't have free rein to do whatever they pleased—keeping the secrecy of the Ferryman Institute intact was always of paramount concern—the range of activities was so extensive that either no employees noticed or they just didn't care. It was generally during that time that the Institute's staff caught up with the goings-on of the world. News spread by word of mouth as employees filtered back from their breaks, and while perhaps not the most efficient means of staying up-to-date, it worked on the whole.

On the other hand, while Charlie had permission to leave the premises, it came with the caveat that the Institute was to be informed of his whereabouts at all times. Strictly for emergency purposes, of course. Just in case.

Unfortunately, he quickly discovered that the Institute had a very flexible rubric for what it considered an emergency.

Charlie's officially sanctioned time away evaporated as emergency assignments piled up the moment he walked out the door. So he began stealing his time in secret when he could, sometimes ducking out to catch a quick movie (even in the medium's infancy, he'd always found an inherent escapism in film), visit a museum, or jump off a few cliffs. Standard relaxation fare. With such limited time away, he'd fallen behind the curve as far as contemporary standards went, and with a quirky best friend who felt more at home in the nineteenth century, he held little hope he'd ever catch up.

Charlie left the private room's door open as he walked in, not caring as he removed his tattered shorts, and hopped in the shower, randomly twisting the knobs until the pressure was strong. It didn't matter to him how hot or cold the water ran—being a Ferryman meant that all temperatures felt perfectly comfortable. It was originally a fun little perk—how many people could say they'd trekked across Antarctica in a Hawaiian T-shirt and flip-flops?—that Charlie now found only irritating.

He'd just started lathering up when he heard the main door to his office open and slam shut, followed shortly by the familiar cadence of three-inch heels thumping across his floor. Each small *thud* came in a rhythm he'd come to know instinctively, which meant it'd only be a moment before—

"Charlie? Is that you in there?"

The voice belonged to his manager, Melissa Johnson. If her tone was any indication, she was unhappy, and Charlie was willing to bet he knew why.

"Nope," Charlie replied casually as he ran the soap under his armpits. "Ghost of Churchill."

His comment was promptly ignored. "Jesus Christ, Charlie, where have you been? You've been gone all day."

He found it somewhat remarkable that Melissa was confounded by that. After five years of being his manager, Charlie figured she'd have moved past being irritated by his frequent disappearances. That led him to conclude she was either naively optimistic or had medium-term memory problems. For her sake, he sincerely hoped it wasn't a combination of the two.

"I've been out and about," he said. Charlie decided it was best to leave out the bit about diving into canyons and whatnot.

Melissa, however, seemed less concerned with the *what* or *where* of it all than she was with the *why*. "I called you at least ten times!" she cried, exasperated. "Why didn't you pick up?"

Charlie grabbed the shampoo. "I lost my phone," he said. This was a semitrue statement. He was trying a minimalist approach to answering his manager's questions this time around to see if maybe he could avoid some of her wrath. Based on the empirical evidence, the answer was no.

"I keep telling you, you can't just disappear like that. It's my responsibility to know where you are at all times. What if there was an emergency? And how the hell did you lose your phone *again?*"

"Well . . . ," he began, unsure of whether he should make something up or just tell the truth. He wanted the former, but his brain wasn't up to creating a plausible cover story that didn't end with him looking like an asshole. That left Charlie with the latter, which unfortunately he already knew ended with him looking like an asshole.

"I may or may not have thrown it off a cliff." In his defense, the constant ringing was getting really annoying. Charlie hated that Ferryman phones deliberately came without a *Do Not Disturb* setting, but he supposed he was also the perfect example of why they didn't. On the flip side, throwing his phone off the cliff had provided a far better reason for not calling back, so perhaps it wasn't a total loss.

A long silence followed. The last bits of dirt and detritus from his earlier adventures flowed down the drain, most likely with what little respect Melissa still had for him. When she finally replied, her voice managed to combine equal parts utter shock and complete resignation into one impressive, two word question.

"You what?"

Charlie turned the shower off, knowing full well his sarcasm was escalating to dangerous levels and yet feeling completely powerless to stop it. "I mean, it might still work," he said. "I'll be honest, though, I couldn't find enough of the pieces to check. How durable was this last one supposed to be?"

There were times Charlie was his own worst enemy.

He drew a squiggly line on the shower door. Beyond the condensation, he could make out the vague form of his manager. Her shoulder-length blond hair and long athletic legs were what most people first noticed about Melissa, but her affable personality and generally easygoing demeanor usually took center stage shortly thereafter. She was certainly the friendliest manager he'd ever had, that was for sure. Yet it was her seemingly unending supply of patience that Charlie appreciated most.

At least, that's what she was like when he wasn't busy making her job miserable. Charlie sincerely hoped her patience was actually unending.

She stood, stock-still, one arm across her chest, the other covering her face. When she spoke again, her voice had lost its edge, as if her anger had finally collapsed under the realization that she simply couldn't win. "I swear, Charlie, you will be the death of me. I don't know how, but being your manager will most definitely kill me."

Charlie noted the difficulty of such a feat, seeing as it was impossible for either of them to die. "Am I that bad to work with?" he asked.

"Worse." There was no hesitation in her reply.

"Oh." He paused. "Can you toss me a towel?" The quiet thumping of her heels marching away provided his answer.

Fifteen minutes later, Charlie emerged from his private room transformed. His hair had a look of controlled chaos about it, a step up from its previous iteration of pure chaos. It danced to its own rhythm atop his head, a wave of chestnut with a mind all its own. The shorts had been swapped out in favor of a snappy black suit tailored to his modestly broad shoulders, a conventional white button-down underneath. An elegant wristwatch wrapped around his left wrist. The final flourish, which he was fiddling with as he walked out, was a silver tie he was exceptionally fond of. An inch shy of six feet tall, Charlie Dawson possessed a casual strain of good looks that bordered on ruggedly handsome—trim but fit build, baked-in layer of stubble, and inquisitive eyes. He was no lady-killer—nor in his occupation did he have any particular desire to be—but he caught the eye when he entered a room.

Yet the silver tie wasn't the only new adornment fastened around Charlie's neck as he reentered his main office space. He could feel the albatross strung around his neck like a physical thing, forged of heavy guilt and ponderous regrets. The intervening time had taken the thin veneer of humor off the brief conversation he'd just had with Melissa. Charlie always felt guilty after he walked out of the Institute unannounced, but this time he'd blown off his manager in fantastically sarcastic, if not downright insulting, style. It wasn't the first time he'd done that to a manager, but it was the first time he'd laid it on that thick with Melissa. It wasn't sitting well with him, which probably meant it had curdled several times over with her.

She was currently seated on his couch with her legs crossed, a dainty black heel dangling from the toes of her right foot. Though he was trying to avoid her gaze, he'd caught a glimpse of the *I'm still not happy with you* look currently aimed in his direction.

"Ah, the crown prince finally graces me with his presence," she said.

Nope, definitely not sitting well with her, either.

"I, uh . . . I owe you an apology," he said, keeping his eyes focused on his tic. "I was just—"

"Stop. Right there, just stop. You always say that," she said. Each syllable she spoke was granite. "You're sorry for this, you're sorry for that. Every time this happens, I get myself all worked up and bent out of shape over your disappearing act, only for you to waltz back in here like it's no big deal. It makes me feel like *I'm* the bad guy for trying to do my job. This is not the person I like to be, Charlie. And you know what makes me even more upset? You already know that."

Charlie found himself with a sudden and desperate need to fiddle with his watch. He couldn't think of another time he'd seen Melissa this upset. Now that he really pondered the matter, though, he had been doing a marvelous job piling metaphorical straw on his manager's back for years. Putting just one more piece on top right now was, in hindsight, a really shitty idea.

He tried some more of plan A. "You're right," he said, finally looking up. "You absolutely are. And I'm sorry."

Melissa rolled over that one, too. "You say that, but what have you done about it? It drives me crazy when you do this. And yet, for some reason, I always end up forgiving you. Why, I don't know. Maybe because beyond this, everyone here loves you." She sighed, brushing her fingers through her wheat-colored hair. "Look, I'm not saying you can't leave the Institute, Charlie—believe me, I'm not. This isn't some prison. I can understand needing time away from this place. I just need to know where you are in case we need you. It's part of the job. Why is that so hard for you to do? Why can't you do that?"

The grimace was flush on Charlie's face before he could do anything about it. He tried to hide it, but he was willing to bet Melissa saw it.

Why can't you do that? That was the real question, wasn't it? All the other *where were you*s and *what were you doing*s all boiled down to that fundamental *why*. So it had been with most of his former managers—the fairly recent ones, anyway—and so it was now.

Why, Charlie Dawson, are you continually breaking the rules? Why are you being such an asshole?

The answer was simple enough, really: because otherwise he'd have to tell them the truth.

Charlie was primed to serve Melissa another heap of bullshit-laden vagaries when the office door swung open and a short, slightly round man with an armful of papers ambled in. Dirkley Dupine made it halfway across the room before he noticed that something seemed amiss between Mr. Dawson and Ms. Johnson. His eyes darted back and forth between the pair as if he were unsure which one was going to attack him first.

He cleared his throat. "Umm . . . should I come back?"

There was an exchange of glances between Charlie and Melissa—an unspoken assertion on her part that the current discussion was merely being postponed—before she slid over on the couch, patting the seat next to her. "No, not at all. We were just going over a few last-minute things."

"Oh, perfect. I have a few of my own," he said, still a bit leery of the atmosphere as he meandered over to the newly opened space next to Melissa. He plopped down next to her, shooting her a quick, admiring glance as he settled in.

Dirkley was the third and final piece of Charlie's team. All

Ferrymen worked on teams of three: the Ferryman (which, despite its gender implications, was actually a neutral term that could mean male or female; the *-man* ending was an anachronistic throwback and/or an exercise in brand management, depending on who you listened to), the manager, and the navigator. In addition to his portly build, Charlie's navigator was balding slightly, his nondescript brown hair fading away in patches. Thankfully, it would never get worse than that because, as with all members of the Ferryman Institute, Dirkley didn't age. Charlie often wondered if being stuck in a perpetual state of almost balding was Dirkley's own little curse. Then again, he also wouldn't be surprised if Dirkley never even noticed. The man's wardrobe seemed to suggest that personal appearance was rarely a foremost concern of his.

"So," Charlie said, grateful for the chance to change the topic, "how are we looking for tonight?"

Dirkley quickly riffled through some of the papers he was holding. "Not too bad. Believe it or not, the last report I received from the front desk suggested a quiet, if ordinary, Sunday night. I'm a little unsure as to its accuracy—historically speaking, the month of May is a very busy time, so I'm a little suspicious."

"Noted." Charlie looked over to Melissa. "Anything to add?"

Charlie was surprised to find her already looking at him, like there was something written on his face that she was desperate to read. It wasn't an intense look necessarily, just oddly thorough. When Charlie caught her eye, she looked away. Perhaps thinking better of that, Melissa stood up.

"Nope," she said curtly. "I'm actually going to head to the control room. Have to go organize a few things. I'll see you guys out there." Before either man could say anything, she wandered out into the hallway beyond.

Charlie watched Melissa stride away, all the while wondering if these were the last moments they'd share as a team before she inevitably quit in frustration.

With a short whistle, Dirkley extricated himself from the couch. "Was it me or did Melissa seem . . ." His right hand absent-mindedly drew circles in the air while he searched for the word.

"Agitated?"

"I was thinking more like exasperated, but that works. Maybe because of something that happened earlier? Like, say, when I wasn't in the room . . . ?"

"Beats me," Charlie replied while walking toward the door, his navigator following closely behind.

Dirkley scoffed, "Come on, Charlie. What the heck happened? The tension in there was so thick, I'm not sure how either of you could breathe."

"I guess it's a good thing we don't need to, then. Ba-dum-chi." He smiled. "Ferryman jokes never get old. And look at that— another great one without even trying. I'm on fire."

Dirkley frowned. "You're avoiding the question," he said.

This, Charlie knew, was very true, mainly because that's exactly what he was doing. Truth be told, his most recent interaction with his manager was bothering him something fierce. Melissa had seemed more agitated (or was it exasperated?) than she usually did after one of Charlie's vanishing acts. Much more, actually. That not only made him feel much guiltier, but also concerned him quite a bit. So, in a word, yes, he was casually trying to avoid the topic. Unfortunately, Dirkley was never one to accurately judge a moment, so the odds of Charlie escaping without giving a straight answer were somewhere down around zero.

"How about I put it this way," Charlie said. "What do you think happened?"

A look of focused thought consumed Dirkley's face, his head bobbing from side to side ever so slightly as they walked. "Well, it could have been any number of things. Improperly filling out your SPT report for one, or maybe the Bradley case—"

"You can stop giving me the benefit of the doubt, Dirkley," Charlie interrupted.

The navigator was silent for a moment, and then said: "You disappeared again, didn't you."

Charlie simply smiled and continued on.

"Charlie, why do this to yourself? Why make her miserable? Heck, why make yourself miserable? You try and hide it, but, I mean . . . Look, we've been together long enough, and no offense here, but you're not exactly a hard person to read."

They were about halfway down the hall when they arrived at a pair of double doors and stopped. While the other doors that lined the passage were single wooden affairs, the ones they now stood in front of were composed of thick glass with a horizontal gray stripe drawn across them. The words *Ferryman Resources* were etched neatly above the stripe, with each door taking possession of one word.

"No offense taken," Charlie said. He grabbed the handle on the door marked *Ferryman* and pulled it open. "Don't think too much about it. I need that enormous, insightful brain of yours worrying about things that actually matter."

"You say that, but—"

Charlie looked over his shoulder. "Please. Not today, Dirkley." He appreciated Dirkley's concern—he really did—but there were times his consideration only made Charlie feel that much worse.

Dirkley's eyes suddenly seemed glued to the carpet. "Yeah . . . sure. No problem . . ." His voice trailed off.

The two men entered the obnoxiously fluorescent wonderland

that demarcated the office of Ferryman Resources. From the doors, the room quickly opened into a small waiting area outfitted with at least a dozen comfortable-looking chairs, not entirely unlike a doctor's office. Across from the entrance, a long counter ran along the length of the entire room. A short young woman sat typing behind the counter, a small nameplate resting off to her right. Dirkley hung back by the doors.

As Charlie approached the counter, the woman looked up, her facial features arranged into a rather perfect secretarial smile. He couldn't tell if she was actually happy to see him or if she'd just been trained to smile like that by rote.

"Good evening, Mr. Dawson. How are you?" she asked.

Shitty, thanks for asking. "Good," he replied, smiling blithely but feeling none of it, "and yourself?"

"I'm doing great." She pushed herself away from the computer hidden behind the counter, scooting off to her left on her wheeled chair. She set about sifting through a stack of large white envelopes until she found the one she was looking for. "Here you go," she said, offering him the envelope.

Charlie took it from her hand, making a show of studying the large stamp at the top. Not that he needed to—the stamp hadn't changed even marginally in all the decades he'd been regularly receiving them: *Office of the President of the Ferryman Institute: SENSITIVE INFORMATION.*

He held it up. "Great. Thank you."

The secretary maintained her smile. "Of course. Enjoy the rest of your night!"

Charlie fixed his own smile in place, as if to say he'd do exactly that, when he knew he'd do anything but.

"Get what you needed?" Dirkley asked as he fell into step beside Charlie on their way out.

Charlie gave a weak shrug. "Something like that."

They walked the rest of the hall in silence, continuing straight until they reached its end. There, Charlie opened the doors to the heart of the Ferryman Institute.

The hustle and bustle of the control room couldn't have proved a greater contrast to Charlie's time in the desert. People quickly bounded by, some furiously talking on headsets as they marched along, others simply plodding about with their heads down. The room itself was massive—it could easily fit fifteen or sixteen commercial airplanes, twice that number if they were stacked one on top of the other—and needed practically a small city's worth of people to fill it. To the left, the area rose gradually to a raised command area that, at its highest, was about twenty feet above the ground floor. To Charlie's right, thousands upon thousands of desks were strewn about, no two quite exactly the same.

Charlie and Dirkley casually weaved their way through the throngs of people, all in various states of activity. In front of each desk, a little square section was marked out on the floor. With a steady regularity, men and women materialized into those squares in the exact same fashion Charlie and Cartwright had in the desert. Other men and women sat at the desks, writing or typing away. Most stopped what they were doing to acknowledge Charlie as he walked by, and he tried his best to do the same. The main difference between the two interactions was that they all knew who he was, while, almost to a person, he hadn't the faintest idea who any of them were.

After spending upward of five minutes winding his way through people and pleasantries, Charlie arrived at a neat, slightly weathered desk with an outdated computer, even by Charlie's standards, on top. A gold plate that read *DAWSON / DUPINE /*

JOHNSON in bold black letters sat on the right side of the desk. Dirkley moved past Charlie, dropped his papers on the desk, and hopped into the waiting chair with the sort of enthusiasm generally reserved for newborn puppies.

"Good to be back," Dirkley announced, more to himself than anyone else, Charlie guessed. While the control room always made Charlie feel a little uneasy—probably something to do with the volume of people—to Dirkley, it seemed, there was no place closer to home.

With a deft flick of the navigator's wrist, followed by a quick volley of typing, the computer hummed back to life. The machine itself bore no significance—it was merely the conduit through which Dirkley did his part for the team. As far as Charlie understood it, each navigator chose the form of his or her navigation instrument. The criteria that the navigators used to choose their particular instrument all boiled down to personal preference—the information the navigator received was the same regardless of what physical object actually relayed it. For Dirkley, that meant an original 1977 Apple II personal computer.

The machine now up and running, the navigator pulled open a drawer, removed a headset, and fitted it over his head. He turned to say something to Charlie, only to stop abruptly. His eyes widened; his jaw clenched.

Charlie didn't have to guess why. A subtle hush settled around the area as nearby employees suddenly lowered their voices, so much so that Charlie could hear the footsteps close behind him.

One. Two. One. Two. Tap. Tap. Tap. Tap. They sounded against the tiled floor like practiced breathing.

"Good evening, gentlemen." It was a male voice, not overly deep but certainly on the lower range of the spectrum. The words were crisply enunciated, to the point of being stern and emphatic, like a military salute. Reluctantly, Charlie turned to face the speaker.

Inspector Javrouche stood a few inches shorter than Charlie, but with a posture that tried to compensate for it. There was no hint of facial hair on his clean-shaven face, nor could Charlie ever remember a time when there had been. The Inspector's brown eyes were sharp, piercing things whose focus constantly shifted around the room with a keenness that suggested a fair amount of practice at such a task. In contrast, an offhanded smirk never seemed far from his lips, a snarky grin perpetually living on the edge of a sneer. The combination made for an unsettling look, as if Inspector Javrouche always knew someone's darkest secret and couldn't wait to share it with the world. It was an arguably fitting air for the Institute's foremost police authority.

"Inspector," Charlie replied, his expression completely blank. It was a talent Charlie had honed over the years for just such occasions, particularly given how lousy he generally was at masking his emotions. Dirkley merely nodded, trying his best to seem small and inconspicuous. For a man with Dirkley's disposition, it wasn't terribly difficult.

"Monsieur Dawson," he said, his eyes narrowing in a barely perceptible movement. Both his French and English accents were flawless. "I see the rumors of the prodigal son's return were true, after all."

"In the flesh," Charlie said matter-of-factly, holding out his arms in a *here I am* gesture. "When are we going to slaughter the fatted calf to celebrate?"

"Unfortunately we're short on fatted calves at the moment. That, and there were concerns your ego wouldn't fit in any of our prospective venues, so right now it's tentatively scheduled for some time around never."

Charlie scratched the back of his head. "That's exactly the sort of attitude that's going to make me think twice about inviting you."

"Wonderful. That's exactly what I was hoping for," Javrouche said. "And this whole time I thought you didn't actually listen to me. I'm flattered."

"Well, I was going to invite you as our entertainment for the evening. I'm of the opinion you'd make an excellent piñata. I think a lot of people would enjoy the opportunity to whack you repeatedly with a stick. Very cathartic, you know?"

The Inspector allowed his smirk to crawl halfway across his face before it promptly died. "And I would very much enjoy seeing a certain problematic Ferryman chained to the bottom of an active volcano, but life is so often an exercise in managing one's disappointments, isn't it?"

"Mmm," Charlie said, nodding as if he were present at an academic lecture. "Like how I find the fact you're still standing here massively disappointing."

"Yes . . . I would think you know a thing or two about disappointment, but what person wouldn't if they had to live their life as you?" Javrouche edged slightly closer to Charlie and lowered his voice dramatically as he spoke. "You know what I find peculiar, Mssr. Dawson? When the Institute is in need of its so-called finest Ferryman, he can never be found. Isn't that bizarre? It's almost as if, for all the esteem he's held in, he's actually nothing more than a childish coward who runs when he's needed most."

A sudden, impulsive urge raced up Charlie's spine right into his frontal cortex, which demanded that he punch Javrouche squarely in his throat. Fortunately (or unfortunately—Charlie couldn't quite decide which) he held himself back. It was obvious that the Inspector was trying to goad him into a reaction, and

Charlie so genuinely hated giving Javrouche what he wanted. Instead, he closed his eyes and slowly exhaled, forcing his mind to step away from the wave of anger that was now pulsing in his skull. After a brief pause, he opened them again.

"Why are you here, Inspector?" he asked. They weren't the words Charlie wanted to use, but he knew a pointless fight when he saw one. There was also the small matter of not rising to the Inspector's bait, which Charlie bet would annoy him to no end. It was a tiny victory, but a victory nonetheless.

Javrouche stood still, waiting to see if perhaps there was a delayed fuse on Charlie's reaction. But when nothing greater than a fervent stare materialized between the two of them, the Inspector wound down.

"Just dropping by to say hello, Mssr. Dawson. Occasionally I think you need a friendly reminder I exist."

"I don't," Charlie replied. "Trust me."

A smile formed on Javrouche's lips. "Then you should act like it."

Charlie gave his best plastic smile right on back. "Unfortunately, there's a limit to how much I can pretend I care what you think, Inspector. I'm only human, after all."

"I won't argue with you there, Mssr. Dawson. I just find it a shame that the rest of this institution seems to think otherwise."

Strange though it was, for once in their torrid relationship, Charlie found himself agreeing fully with the Inspector's sentiment. Not that he planned on telling Javrouche that—he had a feeling it would prove much too gratifying for the smug bastard.

Their verbal sparring now over, Javrouche produced from inside his jacket a serviceable, if clunky-looking, cell phone that he thrust at Charlie, who took it cautiously.

"Madame Johnson had a suspicion you had . . . *misplaced*, I believe was the word she used, your previous one. Hopefully, like your reputation, you will take better care of it this time."

The senior officer of the Ferryman Institute then began to turn around but stopped, turned back slightly, and said, "Mssr. Dupine," in Dirkley's general direction, then left. *Tap. Tap. Tap. Tap.*

As the footsteps receded, the sounds of the room seemed to return in their place.

"Did I mishear," Dirkley began slowly once Javrouche was well gone, "or did you just ask if you could beat the Inspector with a stick?"

Before Charlie could answer, he was cut off by a loud ring. It took a moment for him to realize it was the new phone Javrouche had just handed him. He tapped the screen.

"Charlie Dawson. How may I best direct your call?"

There was a pause on the other end before a familiar female voice spoke up. "I see your phone is magically working again."

"Yes. The Inspector delivered it to me in person. He had a suspicion I might have"—he cleared his throat—"*misplaced* my old one."

"How thoughtful of him. I wonder where he got that idea from. Maybe this one won't be thrown off a cliff as quickly as the last one was?"

Charlie smirked. "I have a feeling it won't."

The other end was quiet again, though Charlie didn't find it hard to imagine why. Despite his occasionally vagabond nature, he still considered Melissa a friend, and this game they played wasn't much fun for either side. At least, that's what Charlie hoped.

"I guess I should apologize for sending the Inspector down there," Melissa said. "You didn't deserve that, especially given the history between you two. I was . . . Well, you just put me in a bad mood today. I'm sorry."

"Stop," Charlie said firmly into the phone. "You don't need to explain yourself or apologize. I'm the one in the wrong here."

Melissa hesitated for a few beats. "That's good. I'm glad to hear it," she said. "I just worry about you, that's all. I hope you can understand that. I can't shake this feeling that there's something you're not telling me . . . and as your manager, that makes me feel like I'm doing a shitty job. I hate that feeling even more than not knowing where you are, believe it or not."

Gone was the raging Melissa of earlier, replaced with the levelheaded and grounded manager he'd come to know over the past few years. Despite their earlier exchange, he'd always carried a deep respect for his manager, even if he didn't always do a wonderful job showing it. Maybe it was because she'd stuck with him when so many others would have bailed in a huff. Charlie hadn't had much success with recent managers—few had lasted more than a year, even fewer two—yet here Melissa was into her fifth. It was a welcome change of pace.

"No, you're not. Don't even think that." Charlie sighed, long and deep, as if he was trying to expunge the events that had transpired since his return to the Institute. "How about we forget all this for now and get some work done?"

"Sure. That's what I'm hoping. Is Dirkley all set down there?"

Charlie looked over at Dirkley, who was fiddling with his own headset. Two small clipboards sat patiently on the edge of their desk. "Yeah, he's ready to go," Charlie said.

"Good. All right then, I'll leave you to it." She paused again. "Good luck out there."

"Thanks," he said. "I'll be fine."

"I know. You always are." And with that, the other end of the line went silent. Charlie took a moment to readjust his jacket and regain his composure, then walked over to the desk and picked up one of the clipboards.

"So?" Charlie looked up to find Dirkley staring at him.

"So . . . ?" Charlie replied.

"For one, are you okay?"

"I'm fine, but thank you for the concern."

Dirkley raised an eyebrow. "For the life of me, I can't tell if you're being sarcastic or not."

"No, that wasn't sarcasm. It was a genuine thank-you."

The navigator bobbed his head emphatically. "Right, right. I mean, obviously. Your sarcasm is just kind of difficult for me to pick up on occasionally."

"I hadn't noticed," Charlie replied.

"Really? I'm surprised to hear that. I feel like you have to clarify it often enough for me that you would have picked up on it by now." It took a restrained effort on Charlie's part to not roll his eyes. "Anyway—ready to get on with it?"

Charlie took a quick glance at his watch. It was a little early still, but based on the day he was having, he was eager to be anywhere but there. He gave a thumbs-up to Dirkley, who gave one back. The navigator had adopted a look suggesting that he was listening intently to something over the radio.

While Dirkley was busy listening to the Institute chatter, Charlie discreetly set about opening the envelope he'd received from Ferryman Resources. As far as anyone knew, Charlie had risen to such an esteemed level that he had regular correspondence with the president. Though Charlie was happy to let that particular rumor procreate, it couldn't have been further from the truth. As far as Charlie knew, no employees communicated with the president, mainly because no one outside of his own office had met him.

It was just another one of the quirks of serving the Ferryman Institute that Charlie had long since gotten used to. The official line was that the president's identity was kept secret so as to protect him from unnecessary bias and pressure. It made sense when viewed in a certain light, and given that the Institute pretty much ran itself, Charlie suspected most employees didn't bother giving it much thought. After all, if someone was capable of accepting they'd become an immortal guide to the dead (and Charlie had long believed that the Institute only chose those who could), then it didn't exactly take an incredible effort to subscribe to the idea that the Ferryman Institute's president was an anonymous figure. Charlie didn't necessarily believe that was the whole truth, and, as was often the case with aspects of the Ferryman Institute, didn't particularly like it. However, as a recluse himself who didn't always color neatly inside the lines of the law yet wasn't punished for it, he didn't push his luck.

At least, he didn't push it on certain things. Charlie pulled the sheet of paper out of the envelope.

Ferryman Institute Form 439-B. Standard Ferryman Transfer Request.

It was the form any member of the Institute used to request either a change in position—say, from navigator to Ferryman, or Ferryman to manager—or an authorized discharge from the Institute. There was no set required term of service to request the latter, but conventional wisdom suggested that the Institute only started taking discharge requests seriously after an employee hit their third decade.

He scanned the form, reading the returned copy, which now contained the Office of the President's official response. The first bold section at the top read *Summary of Request* and, like its name suggested, reiterated the important information from his original request for posterity's sake.

> **Employee requesting:** *Formal termination of Ferryman contract.*

It was the same thing he requested every time.

> **Years of service in role:** *2.5 centuries. 25 decades. 250 years. A hell of a long time (technical term).*

He thought the last bit was cute. Not that it mattered.

> **Reason for request:** *Losing my fucking mind.*

His eyes lingered there, just for a short time in reality that felt much longer in Charlie's head. He recognized those words for what they were: the first sign he was starting to get desperate. He'd never admitted those feelings to anyone, least of all in such dramatic terms, but he was starting to get the sense that things were coming to a head. It was the real reason why he disappeared so frequently despite the fact his managers threw enough guilt in his direction to make a Catholic weak in the knees. He hated that, too—disappointing anyone, let alone his managers—but if his choice was either a clear conscience or his sanity, it was going to be the latter every day and twice on Sunday.

There was also a difference—at least, in Charlie's mind—to admitting his concerns to some anonymous pencil pusher versus someone in his inner circle. He was too proud and stubborn to tell Melissa, or Dirkley, or even Cartwright about what was going on in his head. Rightly or wrongly, he was sure that if he spilled his guts, he'd eventually get forced over to mental services for a few months, maybe a couple years if it was that bad. Then the Institute would start to miss his talent, so, as a matter of course, they'd prop him up, stamp him with a clean bill of health, give him the requisite *Good as new!* pep talk, slap him on the ass, and throw him back into the Ferryman wild.

But Charlie couldn't do that. It was too big of a gamble, too much he could lose.

A secret shared could never be put back into the box from whence it came. He needed the freedom that the Institute begrudgingly allowed him. Even if his excursions away were limited affairs, they'd always been enough to put his life back into perspective. There was something about getting away from there—from the bureaucracy, the intensity, the sheer single-mindedness of it—and returning to the "real" world, even briefly, that kept Charlie's sanity intact. Hopefully it always would.

His eyes finally moved to the next section. A thin black line cut across the page, *Official Use Only* written underneath.

>   ***Number of employee transfer requests:*** *6049.*
>   ***Status of request:*** *DENIED.*
>   ***If denied, please provide further details:*** *Ferryman too*
>   *valuable. Service required.*

Charlie didn't even look twice at it, having seen that particular response six thousand and forty-eight other times. He folded the response in half and stuck it in his jacket to make sure no one else would see it. When he returned from the assignment, he'd go back to his office and fill out another form, stuff it in an envelope, scrawl *OFFICE OF PRESIDENT ONLY* hastily across it with a few underlines thrown in for good measure, and send it off. Then, he'd wait. Just like he always did. Eventually, he would get the response he wanted. That, or he would crack. Either way, something had to give soon, and that would be the end of Charlie Dawson, the Ferryman.

Win-win, all around.

"Sounds like you're in for a busy night tonight, after all," Dirkley said, bringing Charlie's focus to the immediate area. Dirkley's eyes never left the computer screen, his fingers typing a furious set of notes all the while.

With an understated grace, Charlie took out his key. "I always have busy nights, Dirkley. This place doesn't know how to give me a goddamned break."

"Well, being the ace of the Institute doesn't come without its downsides, I suppose. Though I like to think having a, dare I say, excellent navigator helps ease the burden a bit."

"Quiet, or you'll give away the secret to my success," Charlie said, the familiar small smile that was so often a fixture of his face once again back where it rightly belonged. Suddenly, a small green light, about the size of a Ping-Pong ball, lit up on the desk. "Aaaand there's my cue."

Charlie gave a half salute, half wave to his partner, and tucked the clipboard neatly under his arm. He thrust his key straight out in front of him and gave it a twist, opening a new Ferryman Door. Silently, he disappeared beyond it.

MR. SANDERS

Everything about the small room screamed *sterile*—the walls, the ceiling, the aseptic light that filtered down from the fluorescent bulbs. There were no windows here, just white paint on smooth, concrete walls. Mounted in the corner, a small TV soundlessly played an infomercial. Charlie watched for a few seconds, noting how the lack of sound made the exaggerated enthusiasm of the pitchman even more ridiculous. It reminded him of the first motion picture he'd seen years and years ago . . . something with Chaplin in it, but he couldn't quite catch a hold of the title in his memory.

A steady beeping and rhythmic breathing drew his attention away from the television. Charlie turned to see an old man lying in a hospital bed. The respirator rasped in place of the man's own lungs while the low *beep* of the EKG piped up every so often to confirm that his weak pulse remained just that. The elderly man looked especially gaunt in his limbs, like a poorly disguised skeleton in an ill-fitting human costume. A full tray of food sat next to the bed, untouched. At least, it looked like food—Charlie was never sure when it came to hospital fare.

The Ferryman walked over to the medical chart at the foot of the bed and compared it with the clipboard in his hand. Next to the label *NAME* was scrawled *John Sanders* in Dirkley's unmistakable handwriting. Sure enough, it matched the name on the chart.

He continued to stare at the sheet of paper on his own clipboard, which, aside from the name, was blank. This, however, was Dirkley's domain—though Charlie had been joking somewhat with his navigator before leaving the Institute, Dirkley's talent as a navigator was undeniable.

Before people passed away, consciously or unconsciously, their lives invariably flashed before their eyes. Yes, that particular cliché was actually grounded in truth. The Ferryman Institute, through some clandestine methodology Charlie wasn't privy to, managed to tap into that "feed" of memories. It was then up to the navigators to sift through memory fragments and assemble the pieces into some form of narrative. Oh, and they had to do it all in something like three to five minutes, which is how long it took for the feed to deteriorate, or *wash out*, in navigator parlance. From stories Charlie had heard, it was sort of like looking at a jumbled slideshow of a complete stranger's life and then trying to figure out who that person was from it. Sometimes the memory feed was fairly easy to piece together, while other times it took a bit of guesswork to fill in the blanks. Kind of like *Wheel of Fortune*, just with dead people. Given the extremely limited time frame navigators had to work with, the histories were often crude and vaguely detailed. Yet even the slightest bit of information—a loved one, a special moment, even a pet's name—could be the difference between a successful case and a failure.

After a few seconds of staring at the blank form on his clipboard, the first typed words began to appear. With a quiet efficiency, Charlie began reading Dirkley's work:

John Sanders. Goes by Jack. Born 1925. Served as a noncommissioned army officer in World War II and received three Purple Hearts for his troubles. The third was out in the Pacific and cost him his left leg, from the knee down; eventually fitted with a prosthetic. Married three times in relatively short succession. He had his first and only child, boy named Richard, with his third wife in '53 or '54 (tough to tell). Lost him roughly 17–19 years later in Vietnam. Son volunteered, wasn't drafted. Sanders and his third wife, Maureen (Richard's mother), lived productive if modest lives. She passed away 8 months ago. No other family. Religious beliefs: Casual Christian.

The writing stopped for a brief moment before it showed up again in a small box at the top of the form. *Estimated Time of Death: 21:37.* Charlie took a quick glance at his watch. That left him approximately five minutes. He shook his head. Only Dirkley would be able to glean all that and still leave him five minutes to spare. Say what you wanted about him—he was a hell of a navigator.

The information now in hand, Charlie moved from the front of the bed to the side, fiddling with his tie as he did. He considered it a cardinal rule to look sharp in front of the newly deceased. He undid it, retied it, undid it again, retied it again. After several moments of this, a nurse popped her head into the room. She was an older woman, slightly bent at her shoulders and a bit short in her step, but her eyes were sharp and alert. The nurse glanced down at Mr. Sanders before settling on Charlie, her eyes squinting slightly as her gaze bore into him.

"Hi," he said as he finished tweaking the position of his necktie. "Beautiful weather we're having." Charlie had no idea if this was the case, given that he really didn't know where he was, exactly. He also knew she couldn't hear him, anyway, so it was something of a moot point to begin with.

The nurse continued to stare in his direction, even leaning her head in closer from out in the hallway. Or, at least from Charlie's point of view, she appeared to be staring. From her point of view, however, Charlie didn't even exist and, without getting existential, it was quite impossible to stare at something with no eggs in the existence basket.

With a dramatic *tsk*, she waltzed into the room, whipping out a pair of worn glasses like a switchblade. "Damn screen. Only way you can read it is with your face pressed against it," she muttered to herself. "I keep telling them we need bigger screens, but what do I know, only been here thirty years." When she was only a few feet away from Charlie, he quietly stepped aside. She strode past him without even a flicker of awareness. The nurse hummed quietly as she quickly jotted down some figures from the machine buzzing behind Charlie, then briskly made her exit.

Charlie watched silently as she left, like he had done for thousands, perhaps tens if not hundreds of thousands of other people before her. His hand briefly went to the breast pocket where his Ferryman Key sat, reaffirming that it was still there.

He glanced at his watch again. The second hand ticked away. *Three . . . two . . . one . . .*

On cue, the EKG's steady beeping turned into a shrill, unending screech.

Charlie looked at his watch: 21:37, on the dot. If there was one thing he'd learned straightaway as a Ferryman, it was that death was intractably punctual.

Charlie moved to an out-of-the-way corner of the room, placed his two hands together in front of his waist respectfully, and watched the scene play out in from of him.

The nurse from moments ago reentered along with a dark-skinned nurse, who was surprisingly light on her feet, like a ballerina with a stethoscope. They skittered about, but were almost immediately stopped by a third, male nurse. He announced with the forced casualness of someone new to the profession that John Sanders was marked as a No Code. The other two quietly stopped what they were doing without any fuss, the older nurse only taking a moment to silence the EKG. They stood and waited. When the continued silence went on long enough to confirm what they all already knew, they called it. As the trio then filed out, two men entered in their place. They maneuvered the bed around and slowly, somberly, wheeled it out of the room and down the hall.

The small, sterile room was now empty and quiet.

At least, it would be to any laymen passing by. For Charlie, though, it wasn't.

Unlike the corporeal form of Mr. John Sanders, the ethereal one looked much younger—Charlie figured it was what he'd looked like when he was in his early thirties—and strikingly handsome, given how fragile he'd appeared only moments ago. While Ferryman Institute employees were stuck in whatever physical form they happened to be in at the time they became said employees, the dead tended to arrive in whatever form they felt most comfortable in during their life. The newly emerged spirit looked around the room a bit, surveying it with a restrained curiosity that suggested he was really only seeing it for the first time. His eyes traced the windowless, concrete walls; the equipment arrayed around the space where his bed had been; the tiny TV that was silently boasting about the abs they could have for only a minute a day. Finally, they settled on Charlie.

John Sanders studied the Ferryman with a furrowed brow.

"If it looks like a hospital, quacks like a hospital . . ." The spirit's voice was deep and hardy, a bit slow and with just a touch of an accent but articulate enough. His eyes landed on the plate of food that had yet to be taken out of the room. "And has shitty food like a hospital . . ." With a distracted air, he finally turned to face Charlie. "You the nurse that's supposed to give me that suppository? Son, I will tell you right now, I'm not having anything stuck up my ass and that's final."

Charlie greeted John Sanders with a smile—not too broad, a little sly, but smooth, like a Coltrane saxophone solo. "Lucky for the both of us, I'm not here to do anything of the sort," he replied, before folding his hands behind his back. His intuition was telling him to play this one slow and easy, and when Charlie's intuition spoke, he listened. That was his trick, really. Other Ferrymen often asked what his secret was, and Charlie usually came up with something that sounded meaty enough. The simple truth, however, was that Charlie just trusted his instincts. Weird? Yes. Effective? Apparently, very much so. "How do you feel, Mr. Sanders?"

The man raised an eyebrow at the mention of his name. "Jack'll do . . . though I'm afraid I don't quite remember your name," he said, "Mr. . . . ?"

"Dawson, but Charlie is fine."

"Charlie, then." He regarded himself for a moment, inspecting his freshly revitalized appearance. "I'd say I feel . . . slightly out-of-body, if that makes sense? Aside from that, I have a vague recollection of a bunch of people fussing around and then I'm pretty sure I shit myself."

Charlie pretended to fill out something on his clipboard, if only to avoid openly laughing. He and Jack were going to get along just fine.

The spirit paused for a moment, rubbing his hand down his face before really considering the room again, now realizing it for what it was, actually remembering the last few moments of his mortal existence. The man took a few unhurried steps around the room, letting his eyes linger on the walls. A small painting of a blue rowboat, wrapped in an off-white frame that matched the walls on which it hung, sat forlornly across from where Jack's bed used to be. Charlie hadn't noticed it when he entered the room. One oar of the boat lay across its width while the other sat half perched in the water. The painting was far too small for the space it was asked to fill, its colors far too nondescript, yet Charlie could see it sucking in the spirit's attention all the same.

"I've seen this before. I remember this painting . . ." Charlie waited patiently while the man's thought process began to coalesce. "And that TV with the shitty remote. I know this room. This is Mount Sinai. I had those chest pains—when the hell was that? A week ago? Two weeks ago? They brought me in here, ran some tests . . ." He began to speak, his low voice rolling along, but quieter, more contemplative than before. "This isn't a dream. I'm dead, aren't I?" he finally announced.

Charlie gave a slight nod of affirmation, but said nothing.

It was at that moment that the gravity of the situation appeared to dawn on Mr. Jack Sanders. The spirit gazed straight ahead, eyes fixed on the blue rowboat trapped in the middle of an otherwise barren hospital wall. Charlie had seen that thousand-mile stare too many times to count. Like a soldier newly returned from war, it was the look of someone trying to understand something completely beyond them. Death was such an abstract concept right up until the point when it wasn't anymore.

After nearly ten seconds of silence, the late Jack Sanders gently ran his fingers through his newly revitalized hair. "I'll be honest, I don't feel very dead. Just . . . different? Tough to find the right words; my brain feels like it's only half there." The painting finally relinquished its hold on his attention, and the spirit was again looking at Charlie. His eyes seemed to be probing the Ferryman's physical appearance for answers, but were coming up woefully empty. "Mr. Dawson, was it?" he asked.

"Just Charlie, please."

"Right, right. Now, Charlie, I must admit, I find myself slightly confused and maybe that's just because dying has a way of muddling up your head. I can't really say, seeing as this is my first time kicking the bucket and all. Either way, I guess I'm dead, or so it seems. Funny thing is, the two of us are standing here talking like we're waiting on drinks at the bar." The expression Jack wore was mostly neutral, but there was more than a hint of something—was it suspicion?—running beneath his eyes. The spirit hesitated. "How do I put this . . . ?"

"Am I an angel?" Charlie offered the question without any indication as to what the answer might be. The question caught the spirit slightly off guard, which was its intended effect. That said, Charlie was impressed by how little Mr. Sanders's expression actually gave away.

"The thought had crossed my mind," Jack answered. "I'm not much of a God-fearing man, to be perfectly honest, but I did put some stock in there being a heaven and a . . . well, a what-have-you. And, with all due respect, you don't exactly look like any angel I've ever seen. The pictures in church made y'all seem a little less business casual."

The smile came earnestly, brought on by Jack Sanders's remarkable frankness. It had been quite some time since Charlie had been treated to someone whose attitude was so forthright. As for his question, well, that was one any Ferryman dealt with all the time.

"Simply put, no, I'm not an angel. Or from the other place, for that matter. I'm a Ferryman."

That brought out a rather befuddled look from Charlie's assignment. "A . . . Fairy Man? Son, I don't even have the foggiest idea what on God's green earth you are talking about. Assuming there is a God, and that this is his earth."

"Semantics," Charlie stated matter-of-factly, as if that explained everything, then reached inside his jacket and withdrew the Ferryman Key from his pocket. He felt the engraved letters underneath his fingertips, ever present. "As for my title, I'm a *Ferryman*. As in the boat, just like in the painting over there. It's my job to escort you to your afterlife."

The neutral expression that had been the hallmark of Charlie's early conversation with Jack Sanders was quickly being replaced by one of, at the very least, mild bewilderment. "Charlie," he began, "I'm not gonna lie to ya, this is more confusing than when I tried to do my own taxes."

"All in due time, Jack, all in due time. Just bear with me," Charlie said. "A Ferryman is basically a guide. What I have in my right hand is a key. It's a very special key. This key will open a door for you and you alone that will take you to your afterlife. We say *your* afterlife because, frankly, we have no idea who, what, or where is on the other side. What we do know is that this door is unique to you. We've had some time to test that out, so trust me on it. Now, on the other side of that door could be Jesus, Buddha, L. Ron Hubbard, Gozer the Gozerian—honestly, we don't know. Likewise, any or all of them could be sipping lemonade in heaven or Elysium or Avalon—it could be anywhere or anything. I've tried more than a few times to see for myself, but all I ever see is white light."

As he was speaking, Charlie's fingers wrapped themselves

around the gilded key. When he finished, he held it out in front of him, the large letters engraved on its side glinting in the fluorescent light. He pushed the key forward through the air, stopped, and twisted it dramatically to the right. A loud *click* echoed through the room. As the Ferryman Door opened a fraction, blades of light began cascading out. Charlie looked over at Jack Sanders, who, for the first time since dying, looked genuinely taken aback. "Really bright white light, I should add."

The room went silent as both men seemed to give the moment its due. The light that radiated in the air from the open door wavered ever so gently, like sunbeams viewed from underwater.

When Jack spoke again, he had regained most of his former composure. "So you're sayin' . . . that I could be going to heaven, after all? Or I could be goin' somewhere else . . ."

There was no point sugarcoating with Jack Sanders, and Charlie knew it. "I'm sorry. I couldn't even begin to tell you," he replied.

Jack seemed less than thrilled by the response. "What's stoppin' me from staying put, right here, then?" He held out his arms to indicate the room they both stood in, then seemed to think better of it. "Well, maybe not here in this room, exactly, but I'm sure you catch my drift."

With a slow cadence, Charlie marched across the off-white tiles and approached the spirit, stopping just within arm's reach. "Nothing," Charlie said. Then, with a burst of movement, Charlie lunged forward, as if to grab Jack's wrist. However, the Ferryman's hand passed clean through. As Charlie stood there, his hand sticking through the spirit's arm like they were auditioning for a Casper the Friendly Ghost remake, he looked Jack directly in his eyes. Gone was Charlie's Coltrane smile, replaced by a look of stern compassion.

"I can't force you, Jack. No one can. That's why my job is so important. I have to convince you to make one of the hardest walks you'll ever take based on nothing but my word and a door."

The spirit returned the look. "So why should I go, then?" he asked. Gone was the hint of bravado, but the stoicism in his voice remained.

Charlie withdrew his hand and shrugged. "Why shouldn't you?"

"Because I don't know what's waiting on the other side."

Charlie took a step backward toward the door. "Isn't that why you should go?" He took another step.

Jack hesitated. "I don't think you understand, son." The irony of being called *son* by Jack despite being nearly two hundred years his senior wasn't lost on Charlie. "I've done things I'm not proud of . . . things I regret. What if I don't like what I find on the other side?"

It wasn't hard to guess what things a World War II vet might have done in service to his country, but in the gleaming light of an unknown future, Charlie always imagined the deeds, no matter how justifiable they seemed during life, suddenly lost their sheen. Cartwright had taught him that with death came insight and perspective. The deceased who were most hesitant about stepping through were the ones who saw all their mistakes and misgivings with new clarity. The ones who stepped through with no reservations had convinced themselves of their own righteousness long, long ago. There were exceptions to that, but it was a rubric Charlie saw more and more truth in after every case he closed.

"Let me shoot straight with you, Jack. The form you're in right now—your *spiritual form*, let's call it—is not meant for this world. That feeling you described as being out-of-body? That's not gonna go away. It's like an itch you can't scratch that will only get worse, and while it doesn't cost everyone their sanity, it gets to almost everyone eventually. In essence, you become a ghost. As the years go by, little by little, bits and pieces of you slowly just fade away, until you cease to exist. No afterlife, just nothingness. You simply disappear. Or that's our theory, anyway. That part's been a bit tough to prove, but we've seen enough anecdotal evidence of it throughout the years."

Sanders blinked. The look of incredulity on his face spoke the words before he did. "You're being serious right now, aren't you?"

"Well, we have a more official term than *ghost*, but yeah."

"And you tell people that, and they don't walk through that door?"

"Some people leave their physical self with very real and very tough regrets. You can't rationalize emotions. There are things that can motivate a person beyond their own promised happiness, I can assure you of that."

The Ferryman took a few more steps toward Jack's door until he was right in front of it. With the slightest nudge, he propped the opening further. The radiance that poured out of the door flooded over Charlie. To him, it was just dazzlingly brilliant light, but he knew that wasn't the case for Jack. The Institute never recommended opening an afterlife door all the way in case the subject didn't like what they saw, but Charlie rarely did what the Institute recommended anyway.

"While I freely admit that I don't know what's on the other side of this door, something tells me there are a few people waiting for you who've missed you dearly. I can think of a son and wife, in particular. But what I can assure you of, with one hundred percent certainty, is that you won't find them here. Ever." Charlie drew a deep breath. "I think it's time to go, Jack."

There was a breathless moment as Charlie scrutinized Jack's

face, waiting for some form of reaction, before the spirit's eyes went wide.

"My God . . . ," Jack said, his voice barely registering above a whisper. Charlie turned to the door behind him and looked, hoping to see something. But like every time before, he was greeted with nothing but that blinding light.

"Amazing, right?" Charlie said. He hoped the expression on his face didn't look as fake as it felt.

Jack took two slow steps forward so that he was standing in front of the Ferryman. A hint of amusement tugged at the corner of his mouth. "You're a terrible liar, son."

Charlie stepped out of the way of the door. "Eh. It pays to be bad at some things."

"I'm sure," Jack replied. He moved to take a step forward, but stopped. "I wasn't going to ask if you were an angel, ya know."

"Really?" That genuinely surprised Charlie. He had been sure that was Jack's question.

Jack Sanders shook his head. "No. It was obvious you weren't from the get-go. Charlie is a damn stupid name for an angel. Everybody knows that."

Charlie shrugged, but with a little laugh. "I guess it is."

The ethereal form of Jack Sanders took one more look around the room. His eyes lingered on the muted television, the patterned tiled floor, and, finally, the small blue rowboat. He turned back to Charlie, who stood patiently next to the door. "Thanks, Charlie. Hopefully we'll run into each other again someday, somewhere," the spirit said.

Before Charlie could help himself, he said, "Yeah. I hope so, too."

With that, his assignment strode with confidence through the white light. As Jack crossed the threshold, the light began to dim and, as if by some hidden automatic motor, the door began to swing closed.

A pang of jealousy briefly flowed through Charlie as the radiance slowly disappeared, the outline of the door with it. He stood alone in the hospital room for a few moments longer, his gaze stuck on the blue rowboat.

Eventually Charlie turned his attention to the clipboard in his hand. Near the top of the page, in the upper right corner, was a small check box with a label. It read:

Assignment successfully ferried

Charlie watched as a large check appeared in it, just like it had thousands and thousands of times before. Then, he headed home.

MARTYRDOM

We're talking six easy cases in a row, Dirkley. What are the odds on that? I haven't had six easy cases in the past hundred years, let alone the same day. Has anyone been outside recently to check if the world is ending? I think it might be."

Charlie sat perched on the end of Dirkley's desk as his navigator finished the form with a small flourish. Jack Sanders had been the hardest of the bunch so far, and even that was easy by Charlie's standards.

"Maybe it's your lucky day," Dirkley replied. The navigator moved the microphone on his headset from its stowed position above his brow back in front of his mouth. "Navigator to tower, Ferryman has successfully returned, over." After he spoke, he looked over at Charlie—"I'm going to put her on speaker"—which he then followed with a series of button presses on the desk.

There was a momentary pause before Melissa's voice came over the air. "Copy that, Navigator, request status of transfer, over."

Dirkley leaned back in his chair as he spoke. "Transfer of subject complete, over."

A small whoop came over the radio. "Nicely done, guys! I thought Ethel might have tripped you up a little bit there."

Charlie snorted at that, mostly because he considered it a bald-faced lie. "I don't believe you for a second," he said dryly into the speaker. "That was one of the easiest cases I've had in decades. No, centuries. Actually, no, wait—ever."

Even to a Ferryman with Charlie's experience, the Institute's operation was almost completely a mystery. He didn't know how its death-prediction system worked—not that he particularly cared, really, but the best answer anyone had ever given him on the topic was the three-word response of *It's magic, dumbass*—but he knew assignments were sorted first by estimated time of death (more commonly abbreviated as the ETD), and then by a difficulty ranking. Assignments were divvied up based on their ranking, with the lower-level teams choosing their cases first, thereby allowing the harder cases to filter to the top. An aspiring team could choose something slightly above their designated grade level (which was how they moved up in rank) at the discretion of their manager. How the Institute knew what cases were going to be tough, he couldn't say, but Charlie was aware that only easier assignments came with some information attached—names of people, places, that sort of thing. If Melissa knew his most recent assignment's name was Ethel, then she'd probably gotten it from the assignment notes. If that was true, Ethel should have been too low a case for Charlie's grade level. The only reason Charlie usually had names to work with was because Dirkley was so damn good at figuring them out.

"Whoa, hold on a second." Melissa's voice had taken on a tone defensive enough to be used as a fortification. "When that case came over the wire, she had all the makings of a crazy cat lady, and you know how difficult they can be."

"She was *far* from a crazy cat lady," Charlie replied. "I mean, sure, she lived with a half dozen cats. That's above-average cat ownership, I'll give you that. But I'd barely gotten to cat number three and she was already ready to go."

"Seven cats," Dirkley corrected, "and the two parakeets." When Charlie looked over, he raised his arms sheepishly. "What? She really loved Snowflake and Rosebud. They were important birds to her."

Dirkley's unerring precision was endearing at times. Emphasis on *at times*.

Melissa weighed back in. "Either way, it was a good job. You guys are making it look easy out there tonight."

That's because it was, Charlie thought. "Out of curiosity, Melissa, what was the grade on that last assignment?"

The mild hum from the speaker droned on as the voice on its other end fell momentarily quiet. "Hmm," she replied. "You know, I don't remember off the top of my head. I'll go back and take a peek after I finish this write-up."

Charlie stared at the speaker. Something wasn't right. Melissa rarely forgot the grade of a case and, now that he thought about it, hadn't ever forgotten a recent one. In fact, two weeks ago he'd asked her about a case from her first year as his manager. Not only did she remember the grade (an S10, S being the third most difficult rank overall and 10 being the lowest difficulty grade in that level), she'd casually rattled off the grades for the entire day with a stupefyingly sharp memory.

Dirkley's voice interrupted Charlie's train of thought. "Right, let us know about that, Melissa. We're going to get a head start on the next assignment. Temporarily signing off. Thanks." Dirkley immediately flipped a switch on the desk, the quiet hum from the speaker fading away. Charlie realized belatedly that, not only had he completely spaced out, but Dirkley was now staring intently at him. If that wasn't enough, the fact that Dirkley had effectively hung up on Melissa—something he never did—was proof enough the navigator felt something was up.

"You all right?" he asked Charlie.

Charlie, who was only gradually coming back to reality, replied: "Yeah. Why?" The words felt robotic coming out of his mouth.

"Well, your eyes sort of glazed over and you had this weird look on your face just now. Like . . ." He pantomimed a drooping motion with his hands. "I'd say you looked sick, but clearly I know that's not the case."

Dirkley continued to study Charlie cautiously. His eyebrows met at an almost exact V, something that really only happened when he was in navigator mode. "I'm not one to pry—well, maybe that's not entirely true," he added quickly after Charlie rolled his eyes, "but is this . . . um, how should I put it . . . *female*-related?"

"No," Charlie said. "Not even remotely."

Despite Charlie's unequivocal response, Dirkley continued undeterred. "Well, I only ask because I know that before you were a Ferryman, you had—"

For a brief moment, Charlie had a vision of her two brilliant green eyes, as if their irises were brimming with molten jade. Half-imagined laughter whispered in his ear, soft and lilting. But just as quickly as the memories came, they were gone again, an all-too-fleeting glimpse of what felt like—if not actually was, in a very real sense—a former life.

"Not girl problems, Dirkley," Charlie said, cutting him off. He left no doubt in his voice this time that this particular topic was off-limits.

"Right, sure," Dirkley replied, quickly moving on in the conversation. "I just wanted to throw out there that we're here for you—me and Melissa are. Well, the whole Institute is, I'm sure. They generally like you. Well, except for the Inspector, but he probably didn't like his own mother. But seriously, if you ever need to talk, you can tell me anything. You're not the most, shall I say, *open* person I've ever met, so I—we—" He gestured at the control room around them. "We worry about you sometimes."

It was easy to tell that the concern was genuine, even if Charlie found it strange that Dirkley was suddenly so talkative. "Don't let me worry you. I'm fine. Just a bit distracted, that's all. Glad to know you've got my back. I mean that."

Dirkley gave an almost carefree, goofy smile at that. "Not a problem. It's the least I cou—"

"DAWSON?! IS CHARLES DAWSON HERE?!"

Both Dirkley and Charlie looked in the direction of the commotion. Just over the heads of several groups of Ferryman employees, Charlie could see a young black man in a shabby gray suit running in their direction, a flow of dreadlocks trailing in his wake. "MR. DAWSON!" His voice rose above the general din of the room as he spotted Charlie. The man mouthed something into the headset he wore—what it was, Charlie couldn't say—before picking up speed. He arrived at Charlie and Dirkley's station looking like he had ten things to say and time for only one.

"Thank God you're still here. Ms. Johnson told me you have an assignment coming up, but . . . well, just damn glad you're still here. Agent Campbell," he said, offering his hand. But any warmth in his facial expression was being smothered by the air of urgency surrounding him.

Charlie shook the agent's hand. "Pleasure. No, we haven't started on the next case yet, but we were about to."

Campbell hesitated, but only for an instant. "I need your help, Mr. Dawson. It's an emergency."

The corners of Charlie's mouth went flat. Bad things always followed that word. It was never an emergency surprise party, or emergency free cupcake day.

"Did you clear this with Melissa?" When Campbell's face indicated he didn't recall the name, Charlie added, "Melissa Johnson? You know, our manager?"

Campbell's expression turned to one Charlie would have described as half sheepish, half devil-may-care. "I . . . haven't," Campbell said.

When Campbell offered nothing else, Dirkley chimed in. "You know there's an established protocol for this, Agent Campbell. The request has to go—"

"I know, Mr. Dupine." Though he'd interrupted Dirkley, Charlie noted it sounded more out of desperation than annoyance. "But my team is in a situation that's . . . It's bad."

"How bad are we talking here?" Dirkley's expression had turned stern.

"Bad. We've got practically no info—my navigator can't make heads or tails of the memory feed and it's just about washed out. We know it's a young woman, and that's only because our Ferryman on the ground mentioned it when she called in to ask for assistance."

"That's it?" Dirkley said. "*Young woman* is all you've got? No age, occupation, family members?" Agent Campbell said nothing. "Name?" Dirkley continued, bemusement creeping into his voice. The agent simply shook his head. "You're joking! Did your Ferryman at least say what the cause of death was?"

"Car accident. An ugly one," Campbell said as he pulled out a form from his jacket pocket. He turned to Charlie. "My Ferryman—her name is Jennifer Smalling—she's a rookie, Mr. Dawson. I spoke to her on the phone and she's in bad shape. She's panicking and I think she's barely keeping it together. If someone doesn't go in there, we're going to lose her *and* the assignment. We've got an ETD in five minutes and—"

"No," Dirkley interrupted. "Absolutely not. No way. Get your Ferryman out of there, but please leave Charlie out of this. We've got assignments of our own to take care of. Someone dropped the ball somewhere, and shame on them, but there's no way we can pull this one out of the hat. I'm sorry, but no."

Charlie glanced over his shoulder in moderate shock. Five minutes ago, he would have classified Dirkley being curt to someone in the same realm of impossibility occupied by the Cubs winning the World Series and honest politicians, but now he'd done it twice.

Campbell frowned but gave a surprisingly even-tempered reply. "I understand what I'm doing is out of line. I'm not proud of this. But the Ferryman in there is my friend. Maybe slightly more than a friend. I convinced her she should take this case, and right now, the fact that she's completely in the shit—that's on me. But more importantly, there's a spirit who's about to be denied her chance at the afterlife unless someone does something. So with all due respect, Mr. Dupine, if you were in my shoes, wouldn't you ask the only person in this entire Institute who's *never* failed an assignment to try and rescue yours?"

Dirkley said nothing. Charlie, however, had already made up his mind. He knew who Jen Smalling was, had talked to her a bit about random things recently in one of his better moods— welcomed her to the Institute, gotten a sense of her past, that sort of thing. She was a pleasant girl, had only been a Ferryman for a year or two, which was almost nothing in Ferryman time. Not that it mattered. Even if she'd hated his guts, it wouldn't have changed Charlie's decision.

"Give me the form."

Both Dirkley and Campbell immediately turned to Charlie. "I'm sorry?" the agent said, clearly not anticipating that request.

"The form, the form," Charlie said, waving his hand toward himself. "That's the form for the case, right? I need it." As soon as Campbell offered it halfway, Charlie whisked it from his grasp. "Here's what I need from you, Campbell. Call in the code and tell them I'll be assisting. Get someone to cover my next assignment. Also, get medical on standby, particularly someone who can do a psych eval. Got that? Jen's probably going to be shaken up when she comes back."

"Hey, Charlie—" Dirkley began, rising out of his seat now.

"Call the code in, Campbell," Charlie said. The agent scrambled to get his headset mic back over his mouth. Scurrying a few steps away from Team Dawson's area, he began speaking at a rapid clip.

Dirkley, however, wasn't having it. "Charlie. Charlie! Hey, stop!" People turned to look, and realizing that, Dirkley quickly lowered his voice. The sharp tone, however, remained. "What the hell are you doing? There are other Ferrymen here—ones certainly more than capable of taking this on, might I add."

Charlie, meanwhile, was stuffing the form into his jacket. No time for a clipboard on this one. "He didn't ask *other Ferrymen*, Dirkley—he asked me. It's a little crazy, I know, but how could I say no to that?"

"Great, it's crazy—glad we can agree on something. As for saying no, it's easy: you just say no! Why are you doing this?" Dirkley demanded in the same hushed but increasingly strident voice.

"Any information you can get, I need it relayed to me. I know you're working in a nearly nonexistent time frame, but anything at this point is better than nothing. A name would be great, for starters." Charlie took a step away from the desk, but stopped. Dirkley looked completely helpless at the situation unfolding before him. Charlie, who had reached inside his jacket for his Ferryman Key, replaced it momentarily and turned to face his partner. "Look, I can't help it, Dirkley. I know I can do this. I don't *know* if someone else can. Does that make me an arrogant son of a bitch? Maybe. Probably. I don't know. But tell me I'm wrong, Dirkley. Go ahead. Tell me."

"This isn't the time for sarcasm," Dirkley replied. His face was a revolving door of expressions: horror, resolve, concern, horror, resolve, concern.

"It wasn't," Charlie said. He didn't have time for this. He needed to get going, to see what he could salvage, if anything. But as he turned to walk toward the Ferryman Door, Dirkley spoke up.

"Is it that hard to see we're worried about you, Charlie, or do you just not care?"

Charlie stopped walking.

"When you disappeared after the Bradley case last week, for the first time, me and Melissa weren't sure you'd come back. Isn't it obvious that's why she was so hard on you earlier? I know you've already figured out that we're giving you easy cases tonight. And yet here you are, ready to be the martyr again." He sighed. "I'm just . . . I'm afraid if you keep this up, we're going to lose you." He'd been holding his hands out in front of his body, like some protective ward shielding him from Charlie's reply, but now they fell to his sides. "There. I said it."

There was a disconcerting moment where Charlie realized he didn't have anything to say. Maybe it was brought about by the realization that for all his feigned stoicism, this job—the constant dealing with death, with misery, with the pleadings of honest people who were genuinely afraid to die, all of it—was not only eating him alive, but that the people closest to him knew it, too.

Dirkley was exactly right. Charlie was playing the martyr, because that was who he felt he needed to be. It didn't matter to him that he'd been at this for two hundred and fifty years—far longer than the thirty to fifty most Ferrymen tended to put in.

He did it because of one word. One they used in situations like this, one that was far more dangerous than *prodigy* or *genius*, because it was the one word he actually cared for, the one that he secretly wanted everyone to whisper in hushed tones when he walked by.

Hero.

To Dirkley's point, there was no argument for Charlie to make, no brilliant repartee stored away in the back of his head. Charlie knew what he was going to do because this wasn't up for discussion.

"I've got a clear head right now, Dirkley, and it's best that we make use of it. I'll be back in one piece. I promise." He looked at Dirkley with an earnestness that he hoped his partner could understand without asking—one that he tried to express as *I hear you. You're right. But not now. Please, not now.* "I need to go. Did Campbell get the code in?"

Dirkley hesitated, weighing the options Charlie had left on the table. To be honest, Charlie wasn't jealous of the position he'd put his navigator in. After an eternal moment, Dirkley quickly but awkwardly sat down at his desk and banged on his keyboard a bit. "Yeah, the code's in."

The key that felt so familiar in Charlie's hand was out again, nestled in his palm. He was already twisting it in midair. "Good. When Melissa asks, please tell her this was all your idea."

"Not a chance in hell," Dirkley replied. His entire attention was locked on his computer screen, his fingers flying around the keys in front of him. "Be careful out there, all right?"

The Ferryman Door was already swinging closed.

THE FIRST SOUND Charlie heard on the other side was the unmistakable wail of someone in an extraordinary amount of pain. The second was the soft whimpering of a woman who seemed to be on the edge of absolutely losing it. The words came in one long string: "OhGodohdearGod," muttered over and over again.

A dark stretch of dreary country road snaked out before Charlie as he exited the Ferryman Door. Above, the treetops formed a twisted web of scraggly branches, obscuring any light from the moon. The only meaningful illumination came from the car up ahead. Its interior lights were on, along with the taillights and one of its headlights. It looked like a sedan, but it was tough to say, given that it was currently wrapped around a very sturdy oak tree about ten feet off the road. The car was miraculously still running, though how, Charlie didn't know. The whole left side of the car was a hodgepodge of crumpled plastic and crushed metal. If there were airbags in the car, they had very clearly failed to deploy; the deep scarlet bloodstains splattered across the beige dashboard gave little doubt of that. A long set of tire marks showed a dramatic swerve that led up to the scene of the accident, but Charlie could only see where they ended.

Through the shattered windshield of the car, her body now a mangled wreck all its own, was the as-of-yet-unnamed young woman of the assignment. The amount of visible blood on display was nigh incomprehensible. Charlie was no doctor, but he'd been around blood enough to know it was unbelievable she was still conscious. He couldn't see her face clearly from where he stood, given the angle and lack of light, but he wouldn't bet there was much of it left. Her left arm was nearly gone at the shoulder, probably only being held in place by what was left of her blouse sleeve. Her body convulsed in a short spasm before erupting in another agonizing cry.

Fucking hell, Charlie thought. *Gruesome* didn't even begin to do this justice.

Off to the side of the car, more than a few steps back from the accident, was a petite young woman who looked on the verge of bursting into tears. Her black skirt and unremarkable heels were covered in dirt. She hesitantly took a step toward the car, but withdrew immediately when a fresh howl of agony ripped through the night.

"Jennifer!" Charlie yelled as he ran over to her.

The bewildered Ferryman turned to Charlie. "Mr. . . . Dawson?" She moved a few steps away from the accident, her eyes darting between him and the screaming woman. "I . . . I . . . I don't— She, she was just . . . ! And then . . . the screaming, and, and . . . I mean, look at her!" She shook her head and took a moment to compose herself, but she was well beyond that point now. He could see the tears welling up in her eyes, her lips a thin, hard line as she fought to hold them back.

Charlie didn't want to be a callous jerk, given Jen's emotional state, but he knew he needed to move quickly if he was going to make this work. "Are you okay?" he asked.

She nodded profusely and attempted to say something, but the words refused to come out. After a couple deep breaths, she eventually collected herself. "Yes," she managed to croak out.

Not much, but it was a start.

Charlie placed his hands firmly on both her shoulders so he could look at her squarely. "Listen to me. You have to leave. That's not a suggestion—grab your key and get out of here. Go straight to Agent Campbell when you get back to the Institute. Do you understand? Go to Campbell."

The empty look Smalling returned answered that question rather quickly. "I—I can't, though. This is my case. I have to stay. Those are the rules."

He squeezed her shoulders gently. "This is going to sound harsh, and it's not meant to be, but you can't help me right now. Jen, you need to leave—just go back before we lose any more time. Yes or no, do you understand?"

Standing helplessly rooted to the ground, her eyes darting back and forth between the accident victim and Charlie, Jennifer Smalling said, "No, I can't. Protocol says I have to remain on the scene until the end. Besides, I can help you. I'm here, let me—"

Charlie resented what he was about to do. With a small jolt, he yanked her close and looked directly into her face. "Jen, seriously, so help me, you will get the fuck out of here right now!" His voice, a pale whisper when he started to speak, rose to a demanding shout as he finished. He hated the yelling, and hoped that Jen wouldn't hate him in kind, but at that point, he needed action.

To Charlie's disgust and relief, Jen cringed back from the outburst, then immediately began searching for her key, eventually succeeding in pulling it out. The loud *click* of her newly opened Ferryman Door echoed among the trees. She pushed it open, and with one last look over her shoulder, said, "I'm really sorry I fucked this one up," and nothing more.

As her door soundlessly closed behind her, one singular thought crossed Charlie's mind: *This assignment was meant for me.* He'd seen the sense of failure in her eyes, as obvious as the tears that had marked their corners. He could tell she wanted to say more before she left, maybe something to atone for what she believed was her fault. The truth, however, was that Jen should have never been here.

No, she should have been the one soothing Ethel the cat lady, and Charlie should have been here, not the other way around. Whatever way he looked at it, he didn't see a way in which he wasn't to blame. If he'd just managed to hold himself together longer or, failing that, at least not make it so stupidly obvious that he couldn't, then this would have never happened. No Ferryman to save, no spirit on the brink of missing out on the afterlife. None of it.

But the damage was already done.

He shot a burst of air through his nostrils while he shook his own shoulders loose. Much as he wanted to, he didn't have time to dwell on it, especially as now came the tricky part. He dove into his jacket pocket and yanked out Campbell's form. He needed something, anything, to connect with this woman.

Charlie stole a glance at his watch. Two minutes until ETD.

Brutal, shocking deaths (e.g., the woman in front of him) had a tendency to create abnormally confused and uncooperative spirits. If his unnamed assignment died and he had nothing for her, Charlie was almost certain he'd lose her. He said a quick prayer to whatever gods, goddesses, or benevolent flying spaghetti monsters were listening, and opened up the sheet, hoping that Dirkley's familiar Apple II font might be waiting for him on the page.

It was blank.

Charlie's heart dropped. Without any information, he was dancing in the dark to music he couldn't hear. It would be no mean feat to reason with a spirit Charlie knew nothing about, especially in the state he was imagining her arriving in. Possible, but about as far from ideal as he could get.

He started to fold the paper back up when he noticed it wasn't actually blank; he'd missed something in the gloom. There in the upper right corner—small letters that he could barely make out. With a quick snap, the Ferryman pulled out his cell phone, using it as a makeshift flashlight to illuminate the form. They were words, and in Dirkley's barely legible handwriting, no less. If ever there was a sign that Dirkley was operating completely under the gun, it was that.

Melissa Marissa Martha Matilda

All women's names. More continued to fill the page before his eyes.

Media Matia Mary Marie Maria MARIA

Suddenly, the writing stopped. Then, in the middle of the page, where Dirkley usually provided a wealth of information, a word was quickly scrawled out in huge letters: *MARIA*. Underlined twice, then circled.

Charlie shook his head in wonder. Even for Dirkley, it was impressive. The more agitated a person was before their passing, the more erratic their last memories would be. Moreover, the memory feed was probably just about washed out by the time Dirkley even got to it. How Dirkley had managed to come up with a name, Charlie couldn't even begin to guess, but now he had something. Granted, it wasn't much, but a name—even just a first name—at least gave him a shot. Charlie unexpectedly noticed more words appearing on the page. He held his phone over them.

Sorry, but that's all I've got. Feed is too far gone. Smalling made it back safely. You do the same.

—Dirkley

Charlie put away the phone and the form. *First name will have to do, then*, he thought. He considered looking at his watch, but his internal clock told him with relative certainty that there was only about a minute left before he came face-to-face with the spirit of Maria and he didn't want to waste another second. As if the woman could read his mind, she let out a piercing howl. Her body rocked perceptibly on the car, though the scream was quieter and shorter in duration than her previous one. He could hear her crying now, slowly, softly.

His eyes settled on her and her broken body. And then, just like that, the idea was in his head.

His feet carried him quietly across the road. As he walked, his right hand instinctively reached for the Ferryman Key stored inside his jacket, just to be sure it was still there. He stood in front of the car, marveling at the completely decimated state of the hood. Then, he carefully took a seat on it next to the woman named Maria.

She was whimpering now, her breath coming in quick, ragged spurts. A hacking, weak cough disrupted her breathing pattern, and it wasn't hard to see why—having passed through the windshield, she had a large shard of glass embedded in her chest, just above her sternum. Also, given how dramatically her head had twisted (*The Exorcist* immediately jumped to Charlie's mind), it was pretty obvious she'd broken her neck. She faced away from him, looking off into the dense forest, and he was glad for it. As it was, the scene before him would have been enough to keep him well stocked in nightmares for quite a while (had he needed to sleep, which, given that he was going on two and a half centuries without so much as a power nap, either made it patently obvious he didn't need to or explained why he was cranky all the time). No need to make it even worse.

There was something that was bothering Charlie, however. Mainly, his own head. His instincts were telling him to make a play that, for the first time in his career, he was hesitant over. It was risky. Very risky. But when had his gut ever let him down?

Quietly, sitting next to a woman on the verge of death, Charlie did something he'd never done before—he reached inside his jacket, pulled out his Ferryman Key, and placed it neatly on the hood.

The Ferryman Key was a wondrous thing: it allowed a Ferryman to reach destinations all over the globe almost instantly, it opened the door to an assignment's afterlife, and it made the possessor completely invisible to humans. It was the linchpin of Ferryman secrecy, the key (for lack of a better word) to keeping mankind blissfully ignorant of the Institute's existence. Charlie didn't know how it worked, only that it did. Now that he'd removed his key, however, it meant that anyone—human or spirit—would be aware of his presence.

Charlie, as was often the case, opted for a very loose interpretation of the word *plan*. Without his key, the assignment (*Maria, her name is Maria*) would be able to hear him. If he could calm her down enough before she passed, there was a chance he'd end up with a more cooperative and understanding spirit. In theory, it could work. The only downside rested in the whole violating-one-of-the-Institute's-most-sacrosanct-laws bit.

That's how Cartwright had described the idea when Charlie pressed him on the topic several years ago. They'd been camped out on the Mediterranean Sea at the time, tucked away among the rocky shores near a small Italian sea town, watching as the water rose and fell like a living thing, each small wave plowing ahead toward points undefined.

"Mind you, my good fellow, that I am no authority on the

topic. However, there's a reason it is considered one of the three cardinal rules of the Institute, second only in severity to interfering with a subject's death. I will admit, I don't quite remember all the finer points, but if the Ferryman Institute's existence was ever exposed, the repercussions would be . . . hmm, how to phrase it . . ."

Charlie had been tapping his Ferryman Key lightly on the slick rock next to him, *tink*-ing away in some atonal rhythm. "Would be sang to the tune of 'It's the End of the World as We Know It'?"

"Precisely!" Cartwright had said with a clap. "A potential human-extinction-level event, I believe is the recognized terminology."

"But that's what I don't get. If humanity knew about the Ferryman Institute and Ferrymen in general, wouldn't that make our jobs easier? Kind of prepare them for when they finally kick their respective buckets?"

Charlie remembered Cartwright smiling in that cryptic way he sometimes did, that half grin that suggested he knew something Charlie didn't. "Ah, but you forget something rather important in all this."

Charlie asked the obvious follow-up—*What?*—with his eyes.

"Human nature, Charles. If the Institute were revealed to the world, the world would try to take advantage, and even then I believe I am rather understating it. There are two types of men in this world, my dear friend: those who fear death, and liars. We Ferrymen succeed because, at a human's most vulnerable moment, when the soul is very literally bared to the world, we are there. We are comfort. We are hope. But if you remove that weapon from our arsenal, we are disadvantaged. Compromised, if you will. That would make us a liability, and Death does not employ liabilities."

With a final *tink*, Charlie had ceased tapping his key. "But we're not exactly the only organization in the soul business," he said, which was true. With 114 people dying every minute, that meant more than enough croaking for groups competing with the Ferryman Institute to have their death cake and eat it, too. "Couldn't they just take a bigger slice of the pie?"

"They could, but I feel confident in saying it would be an exercise in futility. The Ferryman Institute is a soul-processing behemoth—the original and most successful. The other organizations would be overrun in short order by the sheer mathematics. And when that last group should fall . . ." Cartwright had leaned back against the rocks, his eyes suddenly looking across the water at something Charlie couldn't see. ". . . so, too, I fear, does the curtain fall on humanity. Which is why, my friend, we must always ensure the play goes on."

Back on that desolate stretch of road, Charlie sat unmoving, staring as his key lay freely on the hood of the miraculously still-running car. The last words Cartwright had said filled his ears like the roar of an oncoming train. While the stranger he knew only as Maria ticked inexorably toward her death, Charlie arrived at a somewhat startling realization, one he hadn't expected.

Right then, he simply did not give a fuck about the rules.

Yes, not a solitary, itty-bitty, quark-sized fuck to spare for potentially ending mankind. Unbeknownst to the entire Ferryman Institute, Charlie's perfect record of two hundred and fifty years wasn't his goal, as most thought. In actuality, the record was merely a by-product of him wanting to be the *H*-word (four letters, two syllables, rhymes with *zero*). Charlie saw a woman in front of him who needed saving, and he was going to make it happen, simple as that.

Even so, this was a clear step further than anything he'd ever done before. For decades, he'd made a habit of toeing the line when it came to the rules, even nudging it forward a bit from time to time when no one was looking. This, however, was a bounding hurdle over it (one small step for Charlie, one giant leap for . . . well, still Charlie). It was a uniquely dissonant form of terror: terrifying that he could end it all, terrifying that he didn't care.

He gently placed his hand on Maria's. She twitched. Apparently, even though her neck was broken, she felt his touch, which meant she wasn't paralyzed. Charlie thought that, for once, the alternative would have been kinder.

"Helb . . . helb ee . . . ," she moaned. "Pweaaa . . . my chil'en . . ." Her words were thick and fumbling, maybe the result of a broken jaw, or maybe even damage to her tongue, but she spoke clearly enough for Charlie to understand. A gentle breeze wafted through the air, shaking the boughs above. He could feel her trying to move, trying to roll over to face him, but her body did nothing more than quiver.

Charlie presumed that the hand he held was now cold, but he squeezed it gingerly anyway. "I'm here for you, Maria."

When she heard her name, she tried to speak again, but instead of words there was only a long but excited gurgle. It was followed by a vigorous cough, which freed her voice. "Helb ee . . . doan wan . . . eye. I ave a . . . amily. A aye-ee. Icks unts old. Pwease . . . ay-ve ee." Help her, Charlie—she didn't want to die. Had a family. A baby, six months old. Save her, Ferryman—save the goddamn girl. Another fit of coughing set her rattling.

When she finished, Charlie began to speak. The words simply fell out of his mouth like autumn leaves carried over a rushing waterfall. In a very real sense of the phrase, it felt like a speech from the heart.

"Maria, my name is Charles Dawson, but everyone calls me Charlie. I'm a Ferryman. Most people don't know what that is or believe me when I tell them, but basically my job is to make sure you find your way to the afterlife, to *your* afterlife. It sounds crazy, I know. It still does to me and I've been at this for over two hundred and fifty years. Frankly, I'm not sure I'll ever get used to it. I didn't think, after all these years, I had any heart left to break. How wrong I was.

"I can't even begin to express how truly, utterly, and sincerely sorry I am to see you in these circumstances. I can't. If there were anything I could do to change things, I would. Believe me, I absolutely would. But I can't. I'm so sorry, but I can't. The only thing I can offer you is a doorway to finding some peace. It may not seem like much, but beyond it is comfort. Hope. Love. I promise you that.

"Some people call me an angel, or the Grim Reaper, or even God, but I'm telling you that I'm not any of those things. I'm just a guy in an expensive-looking suit who wishes more than anything in the world that I could go back in time and stop this from happening. You're going to die soon, Maria. When you do, please don't stay here. Don't slowly lose your mind and become nothing but a vengeful spirit, preying in mindless agony on unsuspecting strangers. Don't forget the face of your child, of your husband, of anybody you've ever cared about. I know what that's like. I'm living it right now."

He looked up at the sky, but there was nothing to see beyond the tangle of tree limbs. "Don't be afraid of death like I was. You'll only end up alone, wishing you could take it all back. Don't make that mistake, Maria. Don't be like me."

When he finished speaking, he sat in silence, unsure if that all had really just happened. It belatedly occurred to Charlie that, at some point during his speech, Maria had stopped breathing.

"Why do you think it was a mistake?"

Charlie spun around to see the source of the new voice, quickly clutching his key as he did so. Standing behind him, with her hands folded neatly in front of her, was the spirit of Maria, last name unknown. She was pretty in a girl-next-door way, with wide, curious eyes, each filled to its depth with an unbridled sadness.

"How long have you been standing there?" he asked, momentarily caught off guard.

Her face turned timid at the sharpness of his reply. "Just past the beginning of your monologue, I think."

The ETD. Charlie had been so caught up in the moment that he'd completely forgotten about it. That had never happened before—Charlie never missed the ETD. It was an amateur mistake.

You're slipping, Charlie boy.

"I'm so sorry, I had no idea you were standing there. For whatever reason, I got carried away talking and—"

"Don't apologize." She looked past him, eyeing the still body that she had once called her own. "After it all happened—you know, as I was lying there . . . even though I couldn't move, my mind was running on overdrive. All I could think about was how scared I was to be dying. Who was going to find me out here? No one. No one was going to find me. I was going to die alone."

The spirit somberly shook her head. "Then, I felt something on my hand. I heard your voice, and though I was really afraid—I mean, I still am—things started to feel like they'd be okay. So I sort of just . . . let go." Even though spirits didn't shed tears, Charlie could tell she was crying.

He unhurriedly lifted himself off the car. "Yeah. It *is* going to be okay," he replied. He didn't know what else to say. Charlie felt as taken aback by her as she did by him. He plunged his key forward into the air. The light of the great beyond leaked out from the edges of the new door, illuminating stretches of the road.

Maria marveled at it despite herself, though her attention promptly returned to him.

"This is the door to my afterlife?" she asked. Her voice was quiet with awe. "The one you were talking about?"

"Yes. All you have to do is walk through," was all Charlie said. In truth, it was all he could say. He wanted to say more—something profound or heartfelt, anything really—but was suddenly having a hard time keeping his emotions together himself.

They stood in silence for a few moments more until she abruptly took a step forward, approaching both him and the door. "So, if I go through it . . . that's it? I can't come back?"

To that point, Charlie's plan had worked relatively well—she'd left her body lucid and much calmer than he otherwise would have expected—but he could already see the gears turning over in her mind. That was not a question asked without a reason, and he suspected he knew exactly where this was heading.

"I wouldn't look at it that way," Charlie replied. He nudged the door open farther with his toe, hoping the brilliance of the afterlife might derail her train of thought.

Maria's gaze was completely captured by the opening as more radiant light tumbled free. She stared at it, her eyes so focused that it looked as if her consciousness was being drawn out of them and pulled through the doorway. And yet somehow, a moment later, she wrenched her attention free from it and turned to Charlie. "I really . . . I really need to say good-bye to my family. I need to see them one more time. Please. Is there any way? I promise I'll leave after, but I just need a little more time. I'll be quick, I swear."

She was bargaining. Not a good sign.

Maria was close—very close by Charlie's estimation—but clearly she wasn't quite there yet. Even worse, Charlie had the distinct sense that he was running out of time. Every door to the afterlife was different (another factor that determined the difficulty of a case), but they generally didn't stay open for very long. Always a few minutes at least, but not necessarily longer than that. If the spirit hadn't crossed by then, that was it. As far as the afterlife was concerned, there was no such thing as a second chance.

Though it pained him to deny such a heartbreaking request—always had, for that matter—Charlie shook his head. "I'm afraid this door isn't going to stay open much longer. You need to walk through it, Maria. I know how difficult this must seem, but please, remember that this isn't good-bye. This isn't the end."

"But it is," she said. Though her eyes repeatedly flicked toward the door, Maria kept her attention on Charlie. "If I leave now, I'm going to miss my daughter's entire life. *All* of it. What's the point of meeting her again in the next life if I don't even know who she is? But if I stay, if I stay—"

"You will end up regretting it every second of every day for however long you end up having left. You will dream of her even though you never sleep, and you will wonder in those all-too-brief moments what could have been." Charlie spoke the words simply, with neither humility nor conceit, each one painted with the haggard assurance of a man who hadn't earned that knowledge unscathed. That was his last card, his final gambit. If she didn't come around now, well, that was it—end of the line.

Maria's eyes stopped shifting, her sole focus now on Charlie and Charlie alone. The shimmer of light played gently across her face. "Like you?"

Charlie breathed a single, quiet note of laughter, its melody in a key both sad and true. "Yeah. Like me," he replied.

She edged slightly closer to him. "Why didn't you cross over?"

Charlie closed his eyes, and for a moment, he swore he could smell the sea. "I was in love. I thought I was doing the right thing," he said, and as he opened his eyes, the scent vanished, replaced by the pungent stench of gasoline. "But I never saw her again. And I never will."

She stared at him a moment longer, and he stared back, eyes unwavering. Finally, she looked away, her eyes pulled to the ground. "That's horrible," she said quietly.

All at once, Charlie wasn't worried about completing the assignment anymore. No, Maria would be just fine—she'd made the connection between her own situation and his, just as he'd hoped. What he was worried about now was keeping his own composure.

"What would you tell your husband to do if he were in your shoes right now?" he asked.

Her eyes were back on his, and he could see the genuine sadness in them, floating just beneath the surface. Yet somewhere along the way, they'd picked up hope.

"I'd tell him to meet me on the other side," she said, her voice low.

Charlie smiled feebly. "And he'd listen, because that's what all good husbands do. Assuming he had the good sense to ask for directions first, obviously."

It was, by every human standard, a horrible joke, but she humored him with a small grin anyway. It was a pitiful excuse for one that disappeared as quickly as it came, but Charlie had seen it and that was enough. Without saying another word, he made the few steps to the door and pulled it open. Dazzling brightness tumbled out as the door swung around on its invisible hinges. Charlie stepped away from the opening as the luminescence flowing out began to pulse with a steady throb.

"It's time to go, Maria," he said.

After she took another set of ungainly steps toward the door, she stopped and looked at Charlie, studying him. "Good-bye,

Charlie. If you ever see my family, please tell them I'm waiting." Then, she put one foot in front of the other and slowly, painfully, walked to the entrance of the door and beyond. The light enveloped her, and Maria was gone. The door closed soundlessly behind her.

Charlie stood alone again as he placed his key back in his pocket, the only sound coming from the idling engine of Maria's car. From inside his jacket, Charlie pulled out the Ferryman form he'd been given by Campbell. He stared at it, his eyes gravitating toward that one line—*Assignment successfully ferried*—the blank box next to it suddenly filling itself with Charlie Dawson's customary checkmark.

"Sure," he said to no one, "I'll tell them." And maybe one day he would, when Maria's husband or daughter drew their last breaths. Maybe it would be his assignment, and he'd be standing there, watching their final moments, key in hand, just waiting for them to die. Because that's what he always did, and always would do. That was Charlie Dawson.

He ripped the form into a hundred tiny pieces and tossed them to the sky. He watched as each fragment vanished almost instantly after leaving his hand, like the small cloud of paper was nothing more than a cheap trick of filtered moonlight.

As he kept his face turned to the obscured sky, Charlie realized that, for once, Dirkley was wrong. Charlie wasn't a martyr.

Martyrs only had to sacrifice themselves once.

With that thought firmly entrenched in his mind, Charlie's palm found his key, and he headed back to the Institute.

LIFE DOWN THE RABBIT HOLE

lice Spiegel wanted it all to end.

A week had passed since the meatloaf incident, and her mental stability was only getting worse. She looked at the grim expression staring back at her in the mirror. Her eyes, swollen and puffy from crying, were encircled by rings that also betrayed a lack of sleep. Her skin seemed to be paler than ever (no surprise, really, given how infrequently she left the house these days).

She was tired of it all.

Alice looked away from the small vanity positioned on the edge of her desk and focused her attention on the sheet of paper in front of her. *Write down how you think other people view you on the left side, and how you currently see yourself on the right*, her therapist had said. If it weren't for her respect and genuine fondness for the doctor, Alice would have patently ignored the idea outright. Still, she had nothing better to do—a recurring theme of late.

She began to write. On the left: *Bright, intelligent, witty, compassionate, funny. Miserable, depressed, demoralized, cowardly, broken* on the right. *Alice Spiegel in ten words*, she thought glumly. *Actually, I can probably cut that down to five.* She summarily crossed off the entire left side of the paper. *There, much better.*

Alice violently shook her head. With a grunt of disgust and frustration, she crumpled up the paper and stuck it in her mouth. She chewed on it gamely for a few seconds, then spit it out abruptly when she started tasting ink.

My God, what is wrong with me?

That was the worst part: she knew she was a functioning mess, but it was disturbingly evident how hard it was to uphold the *functioning* part of that equation. She couldn't help it, though—her brain just wouldn't turn off. It was such an easy thing to be told, *Well, don't think about it*, but nobody ever told you what to do if that was impossible. What if she physically couldn't stop thinking? What then? It was like her mind had become this horrific carousel where her thoughts spun in endless circles until their familiar melodies warped and distorted into some sort of Stephen King–inspired nightmare.

She could feel it starting again as her brain began to twirl around with her strapped into the ride, helpless. It wasn't one single thing that had so derailed the course of her life. Far from it. However, she had come to believe that the whole chain of events had been set in motion by a single error. That's where the carousel ride picked up, as it usually did.

It was an innocent enough mistake, really; a senior in college, aged twenty-two, Alice had made the tragic blunder of tempting Fate. Sitting at her desk, having just read an e-mail from her parents, she had looked over at Marc, her boyfriend of more than two years, with his sort of lopsided but still handsome smile, and said, "My life is perfect."

To be fair, it certainly seemed that way at the time. A steady guy, plans for a trip to Disney World in the works, a successful college career nearing completion in just a few short weeks, a couple screenplays in the works. After much deliberation, Alice had decided to move home after graduation, with her parents' blessing, to pursue her dream of writing for the silver screen (though, worst come to worst, she'd also settle for a few prime-time comedies). It was admittedly a long shot, but her professors universally admired her work, and in the microcosm that was her small liberal arts-fueled bubble, that was more than enough validation for her. It would also provide her an opportunity to reunite with her mother and two younger sisters, Carolyn and Kaitlin, whom Alice had seen far too little of during her college years. From there, the sky was the limit. A family with Marc, sunny California, the world of movies and celebrities, puking from the edge of the Hollywood sign after one too many appletinis with Jennifer Lawrence—it would be perfect.

What Alice had failed to realize in that truly wonderful moment was that Fate happened to be a grumpy and vindictive old bastard. Now, that's not to be confused with fate as a collective, which is a somewhat neutral thing—a little good here, a sprinkling of bad there, and off you go. *Fate*, though—the one with an ominous capitalization that generally bespoke terrible and nasty things . . . now *it* was one nasty motherfucker.

Having heard the overflowing contentment in Alice's voice as she spoke those four accursed words—*My life is perfect*—Fate realized it had to act quickly before too many good things happened. And so, just a few weeks later, after graduation, the cracks of Alice's undoing began to open.

It was Memorial Day, just after dinner. Alice's parents told her and her siblings that they had something important to talk about, maybe it would be best if they all sat in the den. Seated on the family couch that Alice had gravitated to since they bought it twenty years ago, they broke the news of the divorce. It had been in the works for a while, apparently; it was a testament to her mother and father that they had revealed nothing of it to their children the whole time. It was the first blow to Alice's perfect little world—the parents she so adored, whom she was so proud of, the people she held up to the world and said, *This is the example of love and marriage I aspire to achieve in my life!* . . . gone.

But Alice wasn't averse to a bit of adversity. It took her a few days, but she adjusted. Heck, she even began taking the new reality in stride. It was difficult, but she tried to help both her mom and dad as best she could. *Everything will be fine*, she told herself, so much so that it became her mantra: *Everything will be fine, everything will be fine.* Over and over, ad infinitum.

Though Alice was doing rather well given her somewhat introverted sense of personal responsibility, Marc provided support when she needed a bit of propping up. He seemed permanently affable and easygoing, even at the worst of times, and had an innate sense for when Alice needed someone to pry a little bit, forcing her to open up about things she would otherwise bury inside. It was a fairly symbiotic thing—Alice occasionally venting about the frustrations that built up around the edges of her family life, Marc listening and playing the role of pseudo psychologist that he so enjoyed. But when August rolled around, he was off again to school, settling in for the second and final year of his master's in mathematics at the University of Connecticut.

Since she'd spent the past four years going to school in Connecticut herself, it took her a while to adjust to not living in the same state as Marc anymore. Thankfully, her writing schedule at least allowed her the ability to visit for a short stretch of time once every so often. Sure, the drive from New Jersey was a little pricey on gas, and sure, Connecticut drivers on I-84 drove like half-blind grandmothers in a blizzard, but it was worth it. It was an escape for Alice, as her parents were starting to openly display the vitriol that had apparently been flying behind the facade of their perfect marriage. Alice and Marc played house together, in a sense, using Marc's tidy apartment as a sandbox to test what a future life together would be like. She would bring her laptop and write while he was gone, either at class or TA-ing. They would cook and clean together, watch *Jeopardy!*, spend inordinate amounts of time snuggled on the couch. Lord, did it feel good.

Fate, however, had apparently been biding its time, waiting for that opportune moment to reintroduce itself into Alice's life with a bang. After Christmas, in late February, just when Alice was beginning to think things really *were* going to be all right, it snuck in the dagger blow.

Her mother, now living with Alice and her two sisters after Dad had moved to a condo of his own, came home from a routine physical that she'd been putting off for months. Too busy taking care of her girls, she'd said. She felt fine, she'd said.

Cancer, the doctor had said.

Caught a month earlier and her chances would have been great. Unfortunately, it was not a month earlier. The cancer had rapidly metastasized, the word *aggressive* repeated with a frequency Alice didn't care for. The twist of the knife, however, was the X-ray of her mother's chest: Christine Spiegel's lungs, once the pivotal organs of a five-time New York City Marathon finisher, were littered with bright spots, like a brisk New England snowfall. That, Alice learned quickly, was bad. Very bad.

Still, Alice plugged on. She had a completed screenplay and was actively revising it. She immersed herself in it, trying to block out the real world with one of her own devising. Marc read through the script several times, offering good advice and notes along the way. But every time he read it, he seemed to finish a little less interested. Alice kept revising, adhering to a wholly unrealistic level of perfectionism. When Marc suggested Alice shop it around, she flinched, and began revising the script again, from the top.

Marc, meanwhile, was making moves of his own. Several weeks prior to his graduation, he accepted a position at the IRS just outside of Washington, DC. It wasn't anything particularly glorious, but it was money—a fact he pointed out to Alice, who wasn't exactly swimming in cash—and a start to a career. She was excited for him, but when he made the not-so-subtle suggestion that she come join him, even offering her a potential place of employment at a family friend's small law firm as an office assistant, she reluctantly refused. No, the time wasn't right yet. She just needed a few more months, just a bit more time to help out her mom, her sisters, her dad. That was all it would be, she promised, a few months. They'd talk again in September. It was May, and she watched proudly as he graduated, thinking, *He'll make a great father one day*, and believing it wholeheartedly.

Two weeks later, just before Memorial Day, Marc started the move down to DC. He was oddly radio silent most of the time as he got set up down there, but Alice chalked it up to the move. He finally texted on Thursday and asked to see her the next day. She already knew what was going to happen—it was burning in the back of her mind when she went to bed that night.

Fate wouldn't have it any other way.

When he showed up at Alice's house, she climbed into the passenger seat of his hybrid SUV, but he made no effort to drive anywhere. He looked at her, his eyes no longer affable and friendly, but sad and perhaps a touch spiteful, and confirmed her worst fears.

We're just heading in two different directions, he'd said.

The brave smile she had grown accustomed to lugging out over the past year was adopted again, frayed at the seams though it was. She understood; she was upset, but she'd manage. Busy with

Mom and helping out her sisters and all that. Good luck, God bless. And then, he was completely gone from her life, almost exactly one year to the day of her parents' divorce announcement. Fate loved coincidences like that.

It became evident almost instantly that Marc had been not only her boyfriend, but also her best friend and primary confidant. Alice was, for better or worse, the receiver of grief from most of her admittedly small circle of friends. Now that Alice was single, she found that she felt remarkably uncomfortable sharing her own feelings of anger and sadness to anyone who wasn't Marc. To make matters worse, she certainly couldn't vent to her mother, the only other possibility. Despite Mrs. Spiegel's brave face and apparent optimism, the woman was an absolute wreck between chemo sessions, physically and mentally. Alice's dad was there for support, but her mom rarely let him come around, despite his wishes to the contrary, and Alice was too wrapped up in herself to go over there, either. There were Carolyn and Kaitlin, but they were both struggling with the crumbling of their collective family life, with varying degrees of success. In that sense, Alice couldn't burden them with even more baggage courtesy of her own problems. Her father urged her to see a therapist, but that was another idea she rejected out of hand. *I'm tough*, she told herself, *and that's what my family needs right now. I'll be the rock. Everything will be fine. I'll be the rock.* Over and over again in her head.

But, like a cat who's found the end of the ball of yarn and run away with it, things were already unraveling. She couldn't work on the screenplay anymore—it reminded her too much of Marc. There were days that fact drove her to a near-frenzied rage, and others where it simply sapped the life from her. Her eating habits deteriorated, and she found solace in food. Her mom wasn't cooking anymore, too tired from extended trips to the hospital. Alice imagined having poison pumped through your body was one way to quickly ruin a day. To compensate, McDonald's and Ben & Jerry's were often nearby and, in addition to a new lethargy that was invading her lifestyle, it began to show. Her once toned soccer body stopped fitting so nicely into dresses, then jeans, then even sweatpants. Size two became four, then eight. She watched with a detached dismay as her rear ballooned out behind her, her hips widened, her muscular thighs atrophied and began to touch, her arms jiggled ever so slightly when she found the willpower to actually write, her newfound potbelly occasionally poking her desk.

There was money, too, to be aware of. Agents weren't exactly knocking down her door to read her script, partially because she refused to show it to anyone, and typing out words didn't translate to money in the bank. To compensate, she coached soccer in her free time, then supplemented that with some freelance copywriting for websites. It was enough to live off of, even if her parents were still paying the majority of her bills.

Four months later, though, and her parents were no longer paying her bills. Just her parent, singular.

Her mother had fought to the bitter end, all the doctors had assured her. They had done everything they could. She had given it her very best, they had given it their very best—everybody under the sun had given it their very circle-jerking best, apparently. If only they'd caught it sooner. If only, if only . . .

In the end, Fate won. Alice was a wreck. She moved in with her dad to his cramped three-bedroom condo in the middle of New Jersey. Her appetite disappeared, slowly but surely, as did the pounds she'd put on, until she weighed less than she ever had in her adult life. She finally agreed to start seeing a psychiatrist at her father's behest and was diagnosed in short order with situational depression. A prescription for Seroquel followed—a small dose, just to even her out and help with her newfound insomnia—but after a few weeks, Alice began flushing the pills down the toilet. Sure, they took the edge off her lows, but they took the edge off *everything*—she felt emotionally inferior to their toaster when she was on her meds. The talking helped, which was nice, but it only acted like an emotional Advil—it would dull the pain for a while, maybe a day or two, but the emptiness always came back.

Such was her desperation that she briefly tried confiding in her father, but it was a short-lived experiment. Jonathan Spiegel was a kind man—Alice would never suggest otherwise—but he was aloof to a fault. There was bread to be won, especially as a single parent, a fact Alice sometimes suspected served as a convenient excuse for him to stay away. Who could argue with a few late nights at the office? Not that she blamed him—her mother had always been the one truly immersed in the lives of her girls. For her father to suddenly have to inherit that . . . well, talk about a stranger in a strange land.

Yet even if his emotional contributions were lacking, financially he continued to support Alice and her sisters, just to differing degrees. Kaitlin, the youngest, was still in college, but putting herself through with scholarships (naturally, Alice had opted to attend the ridiculously expensive private liberal arts college that offered little in the way of financial aid), while Carolyn had just accepted a job as a sales associate at a small ad tech firm in Manhattan. It wasn't much by way of money, but it was a salary and benefits—enough to provide her with, aside from living arrangements, self-sufficiency.

Alice, on the other hand, was the true leech, relying on her dad to pay her bills, her insurance, her rent. She felt like a failure, and every day that her writing fell short of earning her a living felt like one more pound of weight placed on her weakening shoulders. It was crushing her, try as she might to hold on. The happiness, the laughter, the optimism she showed the outside world was all empty bravado, a ruse to fool the masses and perhaps even herself.

Fate had won, all right, a cruel and uncompromising victory. She felt like a defenseless boxer being pummeled against the ropes, and despite the resounding, sickening blows that Fate continued to deal her, the ref refused to stop the fight.

As Alice flopped onto her bed, the taste of ink still ruminating annoyingly in her mouth, it dawned on her, with a strange and sudden clarity: there really was only one thing left to do. She had flirted with the idea, but now she understood instinctively that it was time to throw in the towel. Time to make the ref stop the fight. Lugubriously, Alice raised herself off of her bed and sat quietly in front of her desk again.

Tonight, she thought.

She didn't want to face tomorrow. Not when tomorrow marked 365 days since her mother's death.

Tonight.

She took a blank sheet of eight-by-eleven paper from the loading tray of her printer, grabbed a pen from the zombie mug that adorned her desk, and placed the sheet on top of her desk. Then, she began writing.

> *Dear Friends and Family,*
> *This note will be labeled something I'm not all that comfortable calling it. Instead, I would rather call it my final "thank you" letter to you all . . .*

Tonight, she thought as the blueprint assembled in her head. The pen glided across the paper in effortless strokes, hardly making a sound.

THE FALLOUT

don't know, Cartwright. Two hundred and fifty years is a long time." Charlie was lying on his back, letting his feet dangle over the cliff while the sun once again sank below the Mojave's horizon.

"Well," Cartwright began, "that is relatively speaking, of course. I suppose for a normal human lifespan your supposition has merit. However, if we imagined ourselves as the bit of rock we're sitting on, then no, a quarter of a millennium would be but the blink of an eye. Quicker than that even—extraordinary, if you think about it. The marvels these specks of dirt must have borne witness to . . . But to be able to share in a fraction of those memories!"

Charlie rolled his head slightly so that he was looking at Cartwright instead of straight into the sky. The British gentleman cleared his throat. "Of course, relatively speaking, I would concede that it is a long time, yes."

It had been a week since Charlie's last case, and he'd spent most of that time doing exactly what he was doing now: thinking about that night.

CHARLIE RETURNED to the Institute with no fanfare, no bustling crowd waiting to burst into applause at another remarkable performance. The employees in the immediate area were going about their business in typical worker-bee fashion, blissfully ignorant of the events that had just transpired. There was the odd side-glance or discreet whisper—something Charlie had gotten used to from the teams in his vicinity—but nothing he would consider out of the ordinary. The only indication that anything unusual had just happened were the people milling about his area—Jen Smalling was staring at the floor, shaking her head slowly, Melissa was firing accusations at Campbell, and Dirkley was sitting on the corner of his desk in the middle of it all, arms across his chest. He was the first to notice Charlie's reappearance, immediately getting to his feet as Charlie shuffled out of the doorway.

"Well?" he asked as he hurried over.

Charlie, for his own part, had spent the majority of his return to the Institute distracted by his own thoughts and, as such, was caught completely off guard by the question. "Well, what?" Charlie asked. The other three were following close behind.

A beat passed before Dirkley said, "Did she cross?"

Charlie nodded dumbly.

"Thank God," Dirkley said, then, before Charlie could react, wrapped him in a bear hug. "Are you all right?" Dirkley asked as he broke the embrace. "You don't look all right. Jesus, Charlie, I've seen craps that look better than you. No offense."

"Stop, you're making me blush," Charlie replied in a complete monotone. He sighed. "In all seriousness, I'm fine. A little unnerved, mostly relieved, but otherwise fine." He himself was somewhat surprised at the unexpected candor of his response.

The clacking of Melissa's heels preceded her arrival. She

looked abnormally flustered. "Charlie, are you okay?" She turned sharply toward Dirkley. "Is he okay?"

"Does he look okay?"

Her eyes narrowed. "No, that's why I'm asking you."

"Guys, I'm standing right here." Charlie's mood was darkening at the same rate his patience was running out.

Melissa released Dirkley from her gaze and turned back to Charlie. "You sure you're all right? How are you feeling? Should I get someone from the medical team over here?"

He inhaled sharply through his teeth. "No," he replied. "Again, I'm fine."

But Melissa pressed him further. "Are you sure? A quick exam couldn't hurt."

"I don't want to be examined, and I don't *need* to be examined. The case is over, nobody died that wasn't supposed to, everybody's happy, the day is saved, hip-fucking-hooray."

Both Melissa and Dirkley seemed taken aback by Charlie's harsh tone, which he immediately regretted. "Sorry, that was uncalled for," he said. "I'm just . . . tired."

"Of course," Melissa said. Charlie caught her shooting a quick glance over at Dirkley. It wasn't hard to guess the unspoken message between them. "Leaving aside the numerous protocol violations along the way, which for once weren't really your fault"—she paused to shoot Campbell an icy glare—"you did amazing. You really did. We're very proud of you—everyone is very proud of you. *You* should be proud of you."

"Thanks," Charlie said softly. He looked around the room. A pack of employees still lingered around their team's area. He could feel more eyes on him now, some nearby Ferrymen undoubtedly wondering what the minor fuss at his station was about. He never asked for the attention—he really just wanted to be left alone. But when did Charlie ever get what he wanted?

"She's right, Mssr. Dawson." *Tap. Tap. Tap. Tap.* "Another remarkable job."

Case in point.

Javrouche was walking over deliberately, his hands squeezed tightly together behind his back. "It's amazing what things you can do when you're actually here to do them. To 'save' another Ferryman and successfully complete a—" He stopped walking and looked in Jen Smalling's direction. "Which was it again, Mme. Smalling—a completely impossible assignment or a definitely, completely impossible assignment?" Jen initially opened her mouth to respond, but instead averted her eyes to the ground. "My goodness, she's speechless. So it was that difficult? And here I thought we didn't deal in impossible cases. To think I've been wrong all these years."

Melissa took a few hasty steps forward and began walking next to Javrouche as he continued to march toward Charlie. "All right, Inspector, we're just making sure he's fine. I really think—"

But Charlie found himself in no mood for their obligatory verbal cut and thrust. "Let's skip the bullshit, Inspector. What do you want?"

The senior officer of Ferryman Institute initially appeared surprised by Charlie's attitude before his lips curled ever so slightly in anticipation. "Well now . . . someone seems a bit touchy tonight." He stopped abruptly about five feet in front Charlie. "Feeling a pinch of guilt, perhaps, Mssr. Dawson?"

A curt laugh popped out of Charlie's mouth. "For what? Pulling off the impossible tonight? Again?"

The Inspector surveyed the room as he considered Charlie's reply. There was a glint in his eyes that Charlie instinctively didn't like. "Yes . . . pulling off the impossible. You are the great Houdini of Ferrymen, aren't you? After all, I've never met a man who could vanish when he's needed quite as easily as you. And I'm sure you intended to make this evening's trick even more astonishing by sending the other Ferryman away from the scene of the assignment. Make your only help *disappear*. Bravo, monsieur. Clearly you missed your true calling in life as an awful magician."

Charlie knew where this was heading and opted to remain silent. He'd hoped for a chance to organize his thoughts before the inevitable meeting with Javrouche, but apparently his luck was passed out in a gutter somewhere, nowhere to be found.

Taking Charlie's silence as a response, the Inspector continued. "Are you aware, Mssr. Dawson, what Code III, Section 4, of the Ferryman Laws states?"

For a brief moment, Charlie considered not taking the bait, but ultimately decided against it. "*No Ferryman in an emergency situation shall refuse the assistance of another Ferryman, prior to or during the course of such action as is deemed necessary.*"

Javrouche applauded with mock approval. "Amazing—there is more than god-awful puns stored in that brain of yours. So if ignorance isn't the issue, why did you choose to blatantly disregard the rules?"

Charlie's right fist tightened to a degree only a man incapable of pain could manage. "I believed the assignment had a better chance of success with only one Ferryman. I was right. It's shocking how often that happens, isn't it?"

"Come now, monsieur. Just because you completed the assignment doesn't make you right. For all her speech difficulties, Mme. Smalling seems a more than capable Ferryman—who's to say your combined efforts wouldn't have made the assignment as simple as hello?"

"Whether you agree with my decision or not seems irrelevant now, particularly in light of the successful outcome," Charlie said. "With all due respect to Ms. Smalling, I made a judgment call at the scene, determining that she was mentally unfit for duty at that moment, and that her continued presence would be a hindrance. Incidents like that are hardly without precedent."

Javrouche took a step closer. "And what gave you the authority to make that decision, Mssr. Dawson?"

"Intuition. Experience. My record." He let that last one linger for a bit, knowing it was a particularly sore spot. "What gives you the authority to question decisions I make out in the field, Inspector?"

An electric tension buzzed through the air. "My position does, Mssr. Dawson, and you'd do well to remember that. I'd suggest you tread lightly when you walk on thin ice."

"And I'd suggest you remove the massive iron rod shoved up your ass and stop being so uptight. Though while we're on the topic: Does it tickle your brain when you sit? I've been dying to know that one for years."

Javrouche actually chuckled. "You are adorably predictable. My job is to enforce the laws that guide this Institute, not grovel at the feet of its false savior."

Almost everyone nearby was watching now—some with half an eye, others with their full attention. Charlie couldn't see them all, but he knew it to be true, their curiosity powered by the same primitive human instinct that fueled rubbernecking and viral videos. And yet to Charlie there was no crowd, no murmuring voices, only himself and Javrouche. He suspected his counterpart felt the same way.

As if sensing the building pressure, Melissa physically stepped in between the two men. "How about we all just take a deep breath and discuss this in a more private setting?"

Charlie, however, had other ideas. "I know you didn't come down here to say *thank you*, so why don't you tell me what you really came here to say, Inspector. Go ahead. I know that's what you want to do."

Javrouche's eyebrows narrowed into dangerous points. "You removed your Ferryman Key, didn't you? You sent Smalling away so you could remove it without anyone knowing, give yourself an edge, all at the risk of exposing our entire operation to the mortal world. *That's* what I'm accusing you of, Mssr. Dawson."

Charlie was already marching toward Javrouche as the Inspector let his accusation fly. The Ferryman almost walked past the Inspector, but stopped when they were a mere foot apart.

"I acted in the best interests of this Institute, of the general human populace, and of the friends and family of that woman. I succeeded in the assignment. If you want to bring me up on charges, fine, go right the fuck ahead. Just know that this place needs me a hell of a lot more than I need it right now."

Javrouche buried his gaze into Charlie's own. "Does it? I think my son would disagree with you there, monsieur."

Charlie clenched his right hand even tighter. "No matter how many times I've apologized, it always comes back to that with you."

"For good reason," Javrouche replied. "It's a poignant reminder that you can't be trusted."

"I made a mistake. Nothing more."

"You're a danger to the Ferryman Institute, which makes you a danger to all mankind."

Charlie glanced over his shoulder as Campbell discreetly put his arm around Smalling's waist. Both were looking in his direction. "Have you told the two of them that?" Charlie asked. "They'd probably beg to differ."

"Maybe. Maybe not. Let me ask you this: Why did you take their emergency assignment, Mssr. Dawson, when you've disappeared for so many others? Did you do it after you heard the subject was female? I hear it gets lonely being a Ferryman . . . How's a dying woman supposed to say no, after all?"

The sound of Charlie's index and middle finger popping out of their respective sockets from tightening his fist punctuated Javrouche's words. Charlie leaned in closer.

"For the record, Inspector—if you ever suggest anything like that again, I'll kill you."

Javrouche seemed intrigued by the proposition. "Such a shame, Mssr. Dawson, that you can't."

"Oh, I can," Charlie said, "just not permanently. Which is good, because I don't think once would be enough. Inspector."

Charlie didn't wait to see Javrouche's reaction. He strode out of the control room and down the long hallway back to his office. After throwing a pair of shorts and a T-shirt over his shoulder, he opened the door to the desert and was gone.

"THE INSPECTOR has a point, I'm afraid. Those are rather serious accusations, indeed," Cartwright said. "However, it is my understanding that they are based on nothing more than hearsay and conjecture, in which case you have nothing to be concerned with."

Charlie dolefully shook his head. "But that's the problem, Cartwright. I did exactly what Javrouche thinks I did, though not as deliberately as he seems to think. I *did* break the cardinal rule."

It was a revelation of fairly magnificent proportions, but if it seemed that way to Cartwright, he certainly didn't show it. Instead, he scratched his chin thoughtfully and said, "I see."

"I don't think you do. *I removed my key*," Charlie continued, as if Cartwright's reply wasn't enough. "I put it down so I could talk to her before she died, to try and calm her down, reduce the shock of things when she eventually did. I figured if I could just make her understand what was happening and that it was all going to work out for her in the end, I'd have a better shot of making sure she crossed over. I don't know. It seemed like a good idea at the time. I mean, it worked, so I guess it was. But yeah, I've never done that before. I've never gone that far."

"Charles . . . I understand. You needn't say any more. You did what you thought was right and, in doing so, accomplished the assignment. An avant-garde methodology to be sure, but a successful one, nonetheless."

Charlie absorbed Cartwright's meaning, but it didn't quite help with his current dilemma. "So, what do I do now?" Charlie asked.

Cartwright gave a few puffs on his pipe. "With regards to?"

"Everything."

"Ah, *everything*. Quite a noble question, indeed. Have you ever considered meditation? Or perhaps a good cup of tea?" Cartwright took a sip from his white teacup as if to emphasize the point.

Charlie ignored the comment and continued on with his own line of thinking. "I mean, I signed a contract, so I can't just leave the Institute. I'm immortal until deemed otherwise by the president. A guy, might I add, that apparently no one I know of has ever seen or spoken to. I could deliberately start sucking at my job, but then who knows how many innocent people would have to suffer. How many failed assignments would it take for them to give up on me? Ten? Twenty? A hundred? And even then, what's to say they'd let me go and not bring me up on charges of treason?"

"Mmmm." Cartwright set his cup down on a small table next to his chair. "That is quite the . . . Dear me, what was that phrase again? The Catch-22? Apologies, I have trouble remembering all these new phrases that are entering the lexicon. I still have trouble remembering that *knickerbockers* has gone rather profoundly out of fashion. A shame, I must admit—'twas a personal favorite of mine."

A lone vulture circled overhead. Charlie didn't think the bird was waiting on him—his Ferryman Key was sitting in his shorts pocket, after all—but he found the symbolism appropriate. "You do know that *Catch-22* was published almost sixty years ago, right? I'm not sure that qualifies as *new*."

"Was it now? I must say, my memory is going to pieces these days. Well, more credence to my theory that time is, in fact, relative." He took another long sip of tea.

"I can't be the only Ferryman who's had thoughts like this."

"Far from it, my dear fellow. The difference, however, is that those Ferrymen were allowed to transfer out of the Institute when their feelings came to light. I'm afraid your situation is rather unique in that regard. There appears to be a reluctance on the Institute's part to let their golden goose fly away, if you'll pardon the analogy."

"Maybe I could just leave," Charlie mused.

"Certainly a possibility," Cartwright said, "though I imagine that might not end with the most satisfactory conclusion, what with pesky contractual obligations and such. I have a notion that the Institute would frown upon such a course of action. The life of a fugitive is no glamorous thing, I assure you."

"Well, what else can I do? I feel like this is my . . . fate, I guess? Does that make sense? Like I'm going to be doing this until either I lose my touch or the world ends, and there's not a goddamn thing I can do about it." With a slow and haggard effort, Charlie sat up. "How do you do it?"

Cartwright turned to Charlie. Though it was a look devoid of expression, Charlie knew he was being studied. "Do what, pray tell?" the man asked.

"*Exist. Live.* Not be miserable. Not have the sudden urge to jump off a cliff. Okay, I take that one back—cliff diving is actually pretty enjoyable." A light wind kicked up, whistling gently as it worked its way through the canyon below. "But seriously, you've been around longer than I have. What keeps you going? Why does William Henry Taylor Cartwright the Fourth get out of bed every morning?"

Cartwright paused, his teacup poised halfway between his lips and its accompanying saucer in his other hand. "Hmmmm. Well . . . I do quite enjoy tea. And an engrossing story."

"That's it? Books and tea?" While Charlie didn't find that answer terribly surprising, it wasn't exactly the profound response he was hoping for.

Cartwright thought for a moment. "Sunsets. I feel I have a special affinity for a spectacularly setting sun. One can almost understand why the Greeks considered it a glorious chariot drawn across the sky by magnificent steeds. I must admit, it's why I find this particular locale so enchanting. Absolutely marvelous sunsets, quite so." He took another sip of tea.

As the sun steadily slid farther from the evening sky, Charlie stood up. His shadow stretched behind him in a long, funhouse silhouette, almost as if it were trying to reach the opposite horizon by itself. "Don't you get tired of it, though? Don't you get tired of the death? Doesn't it all get old? The loneliness? Forgetting faces, forgetting people who were important to you, forgetting what things felt like? I can't remember what being hot feels like, Cartwright. I laid out in the sun for an entire week and not once was I uncomfortable. Cold, hunger, pain—I don't remember what they feel like at all anymore. My God, what I wouldn't give to feel sore after a hard day's work. What human in their right mind would ever wish to feel pain? But that's just it, isn't it? I don't *feel* human anymore. Maybe I'm not. Maybe I haven't been for a while."

The words hung above the canyon. They wafted through the air, carried gently on the wind. Charlie faced the sun and, like Atlas before him, stood, shoulders hunched, the weight of the world upon them. Then, without another word, he fell backward onto the ground and resumed staring blankly at the darkening sky.

Charlie recognized the familiar *ting* of Cartwright setting his cup down. When he looked over, the man was delicately twirling his mustache between his fingers.

"My dearest friend," he began slowly, "the empathy that resides in my heart for you is simply impossible to express in words. I value your companionship more than all the tea leaves that ever were and will ever come to be on this astounding planet of ours. To see you in such straits is excruciating." Cartwright looked down at Charlie. "It appears that fate has given you an interesting lot in life, as it is wont to do. You traded certain death for eternal life, and it was granted to you when you agreed to the contract that now binds you. I fear it is a gift you cannot spurn so easily. However, I find it wide of the mark to also suggest that you don't feel human anymore. Physically, perhaps, but I would argue that in an emotional sense, you feel all too human."

Charlie nearly laughed at that, but wasn't in the mood. Besides, he'd known Cartwright long enough to at least give him the benefit of the doubt. "And how exactly does that work?"

There was always a playfully deviant edge to Cartwright's smiles, like he knew something Charlie didn't, and so it was right then. "It's rather simple, actually: I believe you empathize too much," he said. "You internalize your cases' suffering and make it your own. You treat them not as a form waiting to be completed, but rather as people with lives they are leaving, most unwillingly. It is that sentiment, my dear friend, that makes you more human than most. You asked me if I was tired of the death. I take it that thought has crossed your mind, then?"

A small gust of wind ruffled Charlie's hair. "Maybe."

"I find that rather curious," said Cartwright. "You of all people should understand that death in the human sense is only the first step to the next phase of being. The baptism for the afterlife, if you'll excuse my poor analogy."

Charlie sat up. "But that doesn't make it any less sad, though, does it? It doesn't mean they still aren't leaving loved ones behind. What if they don't like their afterlife? Maybe they're too attached, too afraid to listen to us. What if they never even make it to the afterlife? What if we fail them? What then?"

The pronoun Charlie had used was *we*. The one he'd meant was *I*.

In the sun's wilting light, Cartwright's eyes neither shone nor twinkled. They regarded Charlie with an alien curiosity, and perhaps justifiably so. They were seeing a new side of this Ferryman after all—one that Charlie was sure Cartwright had suspected of existing, but had never met.

"I certainly agree with your assertion that the system is far from perfect. There exist too many gaps, too many holes for innocent men and women to fall through. But whether or not you actively believe in its policies, surely we can agree that mankind might not exist in its current state if not for the Ferryman Institute. Who can say what life was like millennia ago, a world where the vengeful spirits of every man, woman, and child who'd passed on roamed the earth as wandering souls? If things hadn't changed, would humanity have ever reached the place it occupies today?

"We serve a necessary purpose, Charles. Perhaps, to your view, a necessary evil. I dare not impugn the purity of your feelings, for it is quite plain to see that you live with them to your detriment. When I look at you as you sit now, I feel as if I can almost see those doubts nipping at your heels like a pack of hellhounds. But part of me wonders if perhaps those hounds are fettered to you with chains of your own creation. You are not the turtle meant to hold the world on its shell, old friend."

The wind whistled through the canyon while, off in the distance, thunderheads began to form. They mixed with the darkening sky, roiling thick and heavy with the promise of sound and fury.

"She had a six-month-old baby, Cartwright. Six months. She carried that baby longer in her womb than she did in her arms. How many special moments were taken away from her by that car accident? How about her child? Her husband? What about them?" He looked out beyond the canyon, watching as a bolt of lightning crashed to the earth. So far away, out amid the flat stretch of desert, out where it barely seemed real. "And what if things hadn't worked out with that assignment? I got lucky. I missed the ETD by at least a minute. She could have run off into the woods and not looked back and I'd have never been the wiser. No chance of getting to the afterlife. No chance to ever see her child again."

Charlie ran his hands down his face. For all of the perks of being a Ferryman, he felt mentally exhausted. With his pride and thickheaded stubbornness worn to a nub, it was in that moment that Charlie finally broke down and told Cartwright the truth.

"I *am* tired of all the death. I've seen more people die in tragic circumstances than I can count. On their wedding day. During childbirth. The day before their twelfth birthday. Even if you guaranteed me that every single one of them was going straight to the afterlife version of Disney World, it wouldn't take any of the sting out."

"Such is the way of the world, I'm afraid," Cartwright said softly, almost as if he were forced to say those words, but well aware they were no consolation.

From some dark alcove in Charlie's mind came a memory of one of his earliest assignments—specifically, the remark the young woman had made moments before stepping through her door to the afterlife. It was a line he never forgot. *"Time marches on while mothers weep, each one wondering why the world hasn't stopped to mourn.* Right? I don't know how other Ferrymen see things like that and are just so . . . accepting of it, you know? There they are, these people, these *assignments*, almost every single one scared or confused but universally vulnerable, and then there I am, the man who knows he is the only thing that can make their death mean something. And it scares the ever-living shit out of me." A dour smirk propped up Charlie's lips. "Get it? Ever-living? Ha-ha?"

Cartwright sighed. "Through no lack of effort on my part, I shall ignore your last remark." He poured himself a new cup of tea and took a long, drawn-out drink. "You're familiar with the story of the Ferryman Council?"

"Of course," Charlie said. "I'd be shocked if there was an employee who hadn't heard it at least a dozen times."

Just as mankind had its collection of creation myths—Adam and Eve, Gaia, Yggdrasill, and so on—the Institute had a collection all its own. They all revolved around Charon, the first Ferryman.

Despite what he'd told Cartwright, Charlie was a bit fuzzy on the finer points, but he remembered most of the salient details.

Something about Charon being an unequaled warrior in both strength and cunning who wished to live forever, which Charlie always thought made the guy seem like kind of a jerk. When Mr. Unequaled himself finally kicked the bucket, he goaded Death into a duel in an attempt to win immortality. An epic battle ensued, with mountains being sundered and rivers being cleaved in twain (as should be the case in any epic battle worth its salt), with neither side able to take the upper hand. However, since he'd been locked in conflict, Death had been temporarily unable to perform his day job. In order to return to his work, Death struck a deal with Charon—in exchange for a truce, he would grant Charon his coveted immortality, but Charon would then be responsible for guiding the souls of the dead to the afterlife—an undertaking spirits had otherwise been tasked with completing on their own. Of course, being the immortality-coveting jerk that he was, Charon agreed.

For many years, Charon worked alone until the day that Death sent him the soul of Virgil. Stuff happened—there was a long interlude at this point during which Charlie always zoned out, but it had something to do with the seven hundred trials of Virgil or something—until Charon and Virgil eventually befriended each other and together founded the Ferryman Institute. They then collected six more worthy souls, whose names escaped Charlie, formed the Ferryman Council, created a bunch of laws, fought a bunch of dragons (though he was probably mixing that up with another myth), and finally, after deciding the Ferryman Institute was a success and they were no longer needed, left this world for the great beyond as their reward. Or was it outer space? Charlie couldn't remember which.

Maybe he didn't remember quite as much of the whole thing as he'd originally thought.

"Do you happen to recall the last trial Charon asked of Virgil?" Cartwright asked.

Oddly enough, that was the one detail Charlie vaguely remembered. "Yeah. Charon tells Virgil that, in order to pass his final trial, he must convince Charon they are equals with a single sentence. Right?"

Cartwright nodded. "Do you remember Virgil's response?"

Charlie thought for a moment. "Uhhh . . . Always drink your Ovaltine?"

Cartwright sighed. "*I cannot, for I have no desire to be an equal, only a friend, and a fellowship is never equal, but always greater than the sum of its parts.*"

Cartwright hesitated for a moment, his gaze suddenly transfixed by the horizon. "It is those same words I give to you. I care little for the technicalities of our small Ferryman world, and I care even less for your record, only to the degree that I feel it demonstrates your concern for others. Regardless, your most important role to me is not as an equal, or a coworker, or a protégé, or any of that nonsense. You are my truest and dearest friend, Charles. If there's one thing you take away from today, I hope it's that. By all accounts, you are a remarkable Ferryman, but that does not mean you are required to be invincible. Though I'm afraid I cannot simply make your problems disappear, I sincerely hope that, having been taken into your confidence, I can provide an extra shoulder to carry your burdens."

And just like that, Cartwright made Charlie feel like a complete jackass for never opening his damn mouth about his feelings. He was so worried about so many stupid things, when all the while he had a great man waiting in the wings to be called on for help. Though Charlie was sure he'd beat himself up over it later, Cartwright's words were the panacea he'd needed for quite some time.

They sat in silence, watching the storm as it seemed to slink away in the night.

"Do you think I could be having a midlife crisis?" Charlie finally asked. "Does that happen to Ferrymen?"

"Not that I'm aware of, though it does present quite an interesting question: When does a man who never dies reach the halfway point in his life?"

"Am I supposed to answer that?"

"Do you have an answer?"

"Wouldn't it be never?"

"Aha, one would think—but to that, I pose this: Does a man who never dies never age?"

Charlie said nothing for a moment. "When we have conversations like this, I think I can actually feel my brain liquefying in between my ears."

Cartwright grinned playfully in response. "A nimble mind is an extraordinary gift. To be able to ponder the quandaries of life is to ponder oneself."

With another heavy sigh, Charlie picked himself up. "I almost hate you sometimes. You're like one giant riddle." He hastily brushed off some of the accumulated dirt that had gathered on his legs, arms, and clothes. "I'd like to apologize for being so . . . I don't know. Glum, I guess."

Cartwright held up his hands. "I insist that you think nothing of it and, even more so, do not let apologizing cross your mind again. I merely hope that I have been able to mitigate even a fraction of your burdens."

Charlie smiled earnestly for the first time since leaving the Ferryman Institute a week earlier. "You have . . . more than you could ever know. It's refreshing to be able to come here and just speak my mind."

"I couldn't agree more, my good fellow. Having this sanctuary to ourselves is a remarkable blessing." Cartwright performed his usual ritual of cleaning and packing away his tea accessories in his small suitcase, then folded both the table and chair he'd brought with him. "I must admit, I would never have anticipated that my day would involve no cliff diving of any kind, but it appears that is the way of it. I can only hope next week you may be more receptive to entertaining an easily amused gentleman such as myself."

"I had no idea you found that even remotely entertaining."

"I am full of surprises. Now, if I may, I'd like to offer a final thought for your consideration. I have not the words to voice it, I fear, so forgive me for borrowing once more from the tale of the Ferryman Council." Cartwright cleared his throat. "*With his final trial finished, Virgil stood before Charon and said, 'Fate hath delivered me unto thee, my virtues proven, my destiny now complete.' Yet Charon laughed. 'No. Let not Fate assume the glory of thine triumphs nor the pain of thy defeats. Thou hast delivered thineself unto me and writ thine own destiny. The man who searches longest for the strings of fate often finds them, while the man who seeks them not knows himself to be free.'*"

The last ray of sunset broke through the bank of storm clouds and glinted off Charlie's Ferryman Key. "I'm normally daydreaming through that part, so if that's supposed to mean something to me . . ."

"It will," Cartwright replied, "in time." He bowed. "Until we meet again, my dear friend."

Charlie saluted back. "Take it easy, Cartwright."

Keys in hand, they each opened a Ferryman Door and vanished into the fading light of the evening sky.

It was the last time they would ever meet in the desert.

HOT DATE

*C*harlie returned to the office somewhat more at peace with himself, a feeling he'd been missing for the entirety of his self-imposed exile in the desert. In fact, talking to Cartwright had given him a bit of his swagger back. However, his plan to build on that feel-good mood with a quiet night was rudely interrupted almost as soon as he'd set foot back.

"Come in!" he yelled at the sharp knock to his door. The words had barely left his mouth when a very astonished Melissa entered.

"My God, you're back," she said, her tone of voice caught somewhere between *I just won the lottery* and *Jesus Christ has risen from the dead.*

"So I am," Charlie said as he took off his desert-stained T-shirt. He flicked his head toward the office bathroom, indicating for her to follow. "Your timing is freakishly good. I literally just walked in the door." He threw the T-shirt into his hamper and began to take off his shorts and underwear just as Melissa turned the corner into the room. She averted her eyes a second too late.

"Come on, Charlie! A little heads-up wouldn't kill you," she muttered.

"Obviously not, because nothing can kill me. Ba-dum-chi.

Anyway, it's what you get for stalking me," Charlie said as he climbed in the shower. He randomly twisted the knobs until the water pressure was coming out hard and fast. He then spoke loudly over the water: "I bet you were camped outside my door for a week, waiting to pounce the moment I walked in. Mission accomplished. In recognition, I'm awarding you the coveted 'Most Stalkerish Manager I've Ever Had' award. It is an honor most can only dream of. Congratulations. Ceremony is next week."

"But that's the thing, Charlie—I wasn't stalking you. I got a call from someone. More specifically, a representative of the president. He told me you'd be here."

There was a dull *thud* as Charlie dropped the bar of soap he was holding. That wasn't quite what he expected to hear. "Sorry, run that by me again?" he said.

The blurred visage of his manager appeared in the frosted glass of the shower stall. "About five minutes ago, I got a call from someone claiming to be a representative of the president of the Ferryman Institute itself."

Now this was unexpected. Were they finally going to grant him his Ferryman transfer request?

"Verified?" Charlie asked before picking up the soap.

"Not initially, but he gave me an Institute ID number to run. It checked out, though all his information was redacted. All I know is his first name—Gabriel. Anyway, after I run this guy's ID, he tells me that I'm going to receive a special package from the Office of the President and that the passcode for it would be *your* Ferryman ID number."

"Okay . . . ," Charlie said as he ran the bar of soap under his armpits. He was attempting to keep his intense level of interest from showing, but he wasn't sure how much success he was having on that front.

"While I'm still on the phone with him, I get a delivery. Metal case with a five-digit dial on the front. I'm then told that the assignment begins in fifteen minutes and the details were in the case. I tell him to slow down because no one has even seen you in a week—and thanks again for that, by the way—and that I can't get in touch with you. The guy laughs and says, *He'll be in his office. And one final thing: this is all strictly classified, confidential, top secret. As far as anyone is concerned, this assignment doesn't exist. We'll contact you after the assignment is complete. Good luck.* Click—conversation over. Naturally, I think this guy is full of it, but . . ." Her words trailed off as the implied part of the message—*here you are*—sank in.

It certainly didn't take a whole lot of imagination to be stunned when, though you've been gone for an entire week, somebody knew the instant you were going to walk through the door. Charlie quickly turned off the shower.

"Towel?" he asked politely. After a moment, a white one flew over the shower door. "Thanks."

There were rumors that the president occasionally contacted teams for special assignments, but Charlie had always considered them complete BS. He was supposedly the top Ferryman, after all—if the president was going to get in touch with anyone, it would be him, right? At least, that's how his train of thought went.

"What kind of assignment are we talking here? Did he say?"

The fuzzy version of Melissa shook her head through the glass. "I would imagine it's something out of the ordinary, but who knows. All I was told was that the instructions are in the case."

"Can I see it?" Charlie asked as he stepped out of the shower with the towel around his waist. "And where's Dirkley?"

Melissa handed him the metal case. The carrying handle *clinked* as it rapped against the top cover. "On his way. He was in the library reading up when I got the call."

Charlie swiftly inspected the case. True to his manager's description, it was an ordinary metal box, its only remarkable feature a set of five individual zero-through-nine number dials set where the top and bottom part of the case met. Charlie got down on his haunches and placed the case on the floor, too fascinated to even bother putting on clothes. With a steady rhythm, he spun the dials. As he entered the final number, there was a barely audible *click* and the case lid unlatched.

"Open sesame," he mumbled. He exchanged a brief look with Melissa, who neither moved nor spoke. With a nimble flip, he popped open the case.

Inside was a nondescript sheet of paper and a letter held closed by a gold wax seal. He gingerly lifted the letter and examined it. There, impressed in the wax, was a Ferryman Key. It was the same emblem that adorned every presidential memo Charlie had ever seen at the Institute. He tried to open the envelope with a quick, forceful tug, but it wouldn't budge. Charlie gave it a few more pulls before he noticed a little note, typed out in black ink, just above the seal.

"It says, *Will open at 20:29:30. Assignment instructions inside.* What the hell does that mean? And what time did your mysterious Deep Throat say the assignment started?" he asked Melissa.

Melissa glanced at the watch on her wrist. "Well, that was around five minutes ago, which was eight fifteen. So, eight thirty?"

"So this should open about thirty seconds before the special assignment starts. That's not exactly a lot of time to read the instructions, but fair enough." Charlie replaced the letter in the case and picked up the sheet of paper. It was a standard eight-by-eleven page that clearly had been composed on a typewriter. There wasn't much on it, so it didn't take Charlie long to read the whole thing.

Subject: Alice Spiegel
Age: 25
Mother recently deceased. Living with father. Struggling writer. Going to commit suicide. ETD at 20:30:00.

Charlie read the line again. "Oh, shit . . . ," he whispered. His mind raced. He had ten minutes to get prepped for a case he knew almost nothing about. In an instant, he was on his feet, dropping the towel around his waist as he did.

"Dammit, Charlie! I know we're a team, but do you really need to keep showing me your man bits? If you're trying to impress me, it's not working," Melissa called after him.

Charlie ignored the slight against his manhood. "It's not just a special assignment, Mel—it's an *actual* assignment. We've got ten 'til the ETD!" he called back.

Melissa yelped something in reply, but Charlie was already too busy looking for his favorite silver tie.

THIS IS THE END

The piece of paper was slightly translucent held so close to the lamp, but it was how Alice preferred to proofread. She found it darkly amusing that she was putting so much effort into proofreading a suicide note, but she was unapologetically OCD about grammar. It was easier for her to come to terms with rotting in the pits of hell for all eternity than having some forensic examiner say to his partner, *Hmm, she used "your" here instead of "you're." I'm telling you, it's all this new technology* . . . Two discarded copies of her letter had already been ripped to shreds, and she was trying not to add a third. She justified it as the literary equivalent of wanting to have clean underwear on for her autopsy.

Alice lifted the waistband of her sweatpants. *Yeah, I should change those, too.*

She set the letter in the center of her desk and maneuvered her flexible lamp so it shone directly on the paper. She fussed around the room, straightening things out and tidying up a bit. Alice was no stranger to a mess—if Einstein didn't need socks, then what difference did it make if she left her wardrobe scattered across her floor?—a characteristic that had driven her late mother to near homicidal rage on occasion. *What a wonderful daughter I am*, she thought. *"Hey, Mom, great to see you in the afterlife. Yeah, I know I just offed myself, but at least my room is finally clean. Aren't you proud?"* She snorted to herself. *God, I am pathetic.*

Sufficiently satisfied with the state of her room, she quietly changed her outfit, underwear included, opting for a plain T-shirt and jeans, then sat down at her desk and lightly did her makeup. Her vanity mirror had served her well for many years—she was sure either Kaitlin or Carolyn would take it when she was gone. Or maybe they wouldn't. It might be too painful for them to use. A pang of guilt trickled up her spine, but she quickly shook it away.

Done being vain for the moment, Alice found herself wandering over to the closet, the one area she'd been deliberately avoiding. The overhead light inside made a familiar *click* as she pulled the string. She rummaged around in the back, behind her collection of shoes—small though it was, she certainly couldn't knock her dad's place for lack of closet space, as her shoe collection could attest—bundling over a few old boxes of school papers in the process, until she found what she was looking for.

There was a large, squat gray safe sitting in the corner of her small walk-in. Alice had thought long and hard about how she would go about ensuring a quick and effective good-bye. Ironically, it was her ex, Marc, who'd provided both the answer and the means. Despite being a relatively laid-back guy, Marc was, through no fault of his own, still a guy. That little Y chromosome often meant a variety of things: farting, cursing, sports, testosterone. However, more importantly for her current circumstances, it had meant Marc loved shooting things.

Alice opened the safe with a couple of well-remembered twists of her wrist. The gun box within was a light silver color and about as basic and simple as they came. She carefully opened the top. Lying inside, still in the pristine condition she'd left it, was her all-black 9mm Beretta 92FS. Marc had given it to her as a pseudo gag gift for their anniversary after she had displayed a natural aptitude for putting holes in things—*In case I ever do anything stupid* was what he'd written on the inside of that particular card. Alice wondered if, since their breakup, he had ever worried about her making good on that. She did find it somewhat amusing that she would end up being more grateful for this gift than any other he'd given her.

This, Alice had decided, would make things absolutely final. There would be no one finding her in the nick of time to have her stomach pumped, no bandaging the wound enough so she didn't bleed out. Nope, this was it. Messy? Sure. Loud? You betcha. Lethal? In the right spot, undisputedly. She realized with a little sadness that it would probably undo the effort she'd put into her makeup (she was relatively certain that, despite how lovely the mascara made her eyes look, the gaping bullet wound would probably be more noticeable), but she chalked it up as one of the many recent missteps in her life.

Now was the time to do it. Carolyn was out to dinner with Dad—Alice had stayed behind under the pretense of not feeling well—while Kaitlin was away at college, leaving Alice alone in the house.

Mechanically, she loaded a single round into the clip, then picked up the gun. As soon as she held it in her hand, the mechanics all came back. Check the chamber. Run the clip home. Cock it. Safety off. Gun is hot. *Like riding a bike.* She couldn't help but smile at that.

Preparation now complete, she walked over to her desk and sat down. Rethinking her position vis-à-vis her lovely note and potential blood, if not brain, splatter, she rolled her chair back a few inches, then scooted back a bit more.

The gun felt slick in her hands. Her heart seemed to be banging up against her rib cage. Alice shouldn't have been so nervous—she had more butterflies now than for junior prom when she'd somehow scored Craig McHagert as her date—but maybe it was natural. Then again, she'd never tried to kill herself before, so how should she know?

You're procrastinating. Carolyn will be back with Dad in an hour. Focus. You can finally end all this misery. Let's do this.

Alice inhaled deeply. It was time.

Thanks, Marc—who knew your gift would come in so handy, she thought, but then shook her head. *No, that's not a good final thought.*

She chewed her lip while the gears in her brain engaged, presumably for the last time. *It needs to be good . . . something profound, slightly tragic, ingratiating yet remorseful, and deeply apologetic.* Her eyes caught the last line of her letter before the closing. "*It's been real*," she read out loud.

Good enough.

Alice looked in the mirror as the girl in the glass pressed the barrel of the gun into the right side of her head and ever so slowly pulled back on the trigger. It was coming, the end was coming, just around the corner, yes, any moment now and then—

An indistinct golden object tumbled past her head and skittered across the top of her desk. She nearly squeezed the trigger accidentally from being startled, but caught herself at the last second. Movement in her mirror. Her eyes fixed on the man who was suddenly standing behind her.

Alice screamed. Before she even realized what was happening, she was facing him, arms trembling. His mouth was moving, but her brain had gone blank, her muscle memory taking over as she instinctively lined up the shot.

She pulled the trigger.

I SHOT THE SHERIFF

"Oh my God . . . Oh my God. Ohmygod ohmygod ohmygod . . ."

The gun landed with a heavy but muted thud on the carpeted floor. Alice reflexively covered her mouth with both hands as she leaned against the chair for support. She'd meant to blow someone's head off tonight, but this wasn't quite what she had in mind.

The past minute had proceeded in a blur that she was still coming to grips with. Having been a whisper of pressure away from ultimately ending her life, she was now standing twelve feet away from a man who'd just had his cranium ventilated. She hadn't meant to shoot him, but she had been so scared that when he spoke, her finger automatically squeezed the trigger.

The man lay sprawled out on her bedroom floor, not so much as even twitching. Questions buzzed frantically around in her mind. Who the hell was he? How had he gotten in here? And what the hell was that thing that flew past her head?

The urge to run screaming from the room seized Alice, but she resisted. *He might still be alive. God, I hope he's still alive. Unless he's going to try to rape me, in which case I take that back, and I hope he dies. Okay, maybe not* dies, *but mostly dies. So God, if you're listening, that's dead to the point of not really dying, but not alive enough where he can perform sick sexual fantasies on me in an act of revenge for shooting him in the face. Thanks. Amen, or whatever.*

She picked the gun up off the floor and held it in the ready position, her hands shaking violently, and approached with the gun aimed directly at the motionless body. The gun was out of bullets, true, seeing as she'd fired the only one she'd bothered to load into its clip (in fairness, she'd had it on good authority that she'd only need the one), but if this man was still alive, he wouldn't know that. A lump moved down her throat. Assuming the bullet had gone where she thought it had—namely, just off center on his forehead—she was in for a gruesome sight. She tiptoed across the floor, her entire body coiled and ready for action, even if that action happened to be vomiting profusely.

After two agonizingly slow steps, things already weren't adding up.

Alice was now standing at an angle where she could see the bullet wound perfectly; it was a few inches above the corner of his left eye, just about where she thought she'd put it. However, there was a big something missing—namely blood, and lots of it. It should have been everywhere, with a bit of brain matter and gore thrown in for good measure. However, there was nothing; a nearly perfect circular hole in his forehead was the only evidence that this man had been shot. Still, he wasn't exactly moving and he certainly didn't look like he was breathing. His eyes, a deep green, were open and staring at her off-pink ceiling. Alice took a step closer.

Something seemed odd about the entry wound. It was only a 9mm bullet, so it wouldn't leave a massive hole, per se, but the hole was still far smaller than it should have been. Actually, it sort of looked like the hole was . . . shrinking?

Ah, a case of bullet-hole shrinkage. Now, where had she heard about that before? That's right—nowhere, because it was fucking impossible.

Within a few seconds, there was no evidence whatsoever that she'd shot him. She inched a bit closer and leaned over the body so she could get a better look at his face.

"Well, that was unexpected," he said.

Alice leapt back with an earsplitting scream. The gun flew from her hand as she ran across the room and dove into her closet. She cowered in the far corner behind a rack of old shoes, on the verge of hyperventilating, when, with a growing sense of panic, she realized that not only had she lost her only means of protection, but the undead stranger was now situated perfectly between her and the only exit save the third-story window. She was trapped.

"You're . . . you're not dead . . . ," she mumbled breathlessly, mostly to herself. Maybe this was the start of the zombie apocalypse. Or, hey, maybe she had just finally lost it, and none of this was actually happening. Maybe she was tied down to a bed in some asylum while her brain fed her crazy dreams as it slowly dissolved into mush.

"Neither are you," he said casually as he moved into an upright, seated position. With a small *huff*, the stranger stood, taking a moment to brush off his dignified coat and slacks.

"Whatever you want, just take it!" Alice yelled, hoping belatedly that she wasn't the object in question. From the rack in front of her, she grabbed an old stiletto, wishing it was of the knife variety and not the heel.

"About that . . . ," the stranger said as he scanned her bedroom. "I actually came for you."

Oh. Perfect. Alice gripped the shoe a little harder. "Why? What do you want?!"

The man stopped his inspection of the room. "You know, that's a really good question. I don't know." He stroked his chin. "In my defense, this wasn't supposed to happen, so I wasn't expecting to be having this conversation."

"How are we having *any* conversation!? I shot you!" she yelled back, her mouth spitting out what her mind was thinking. *Nice one, Alice—remind the stranger who apparently doesn't die about that time you tried to kill him. That will surely lead to wonderful things.* She retreated even farther behind the door.

If her tone bothered him, though, it didn't show. He picked up a small piece of paper that he had dropped after she shot him. "Can't really argue with that. However, I didn't intend on getting shot tonight, either. Not to sound insensitive, but I believe that was originally your plan."

Her eyes managed to somehow widen a bit farther. Had he known that was her plan all along, or was it a lucky guess? On second thought, there probably wasn't much luck involved in guessing what a solitary young woman with a gun pressed to her head was about to do. Still— *When in doubt, deny. If it does not fit, you must acquit.* Well, one of the two applied, anyway.

"I have no idea what you're talking about," she said defiantly.

He looked over at her, curiosity evident on his face. He appeared calm, if a bit confused himself.

"You are Alice Spiegel, correct?" he asked.

Okay, this was getting weird. Actually, scratch that—things had already been pretty fucking weird.

"No," she said quickly, "I don't know anybody by that name."

"Really?" He took a few steps toward her desk and picked up her letter in his free hand. With a surprising delicacy, he held it in his hands and gave it a cursory glance. "Do you sign all your suicide notes with a pen name?"

Alice's brain worked desperately to try and make sense of a situation it had no business being in and came up empty. "Who the hell are you? How did you get in here, and what do you want?"

With a sigh, the man plopped down into her desk chair. "Listen, Alice. What I'm about to tell you is going to sound pretty unbelievable, but it's the truth. You may not get it, but after shooting me in the head, I hope you'll at least give me the courtesy of listening. First of all, I'm not going to hurt you, so you can stop hiding." When she didn't move, he rolled over to the gun, picked it up, and gently tossed it in front of the closet. It cartwheeled twice before stopping a mere two feet in front of the door. "There. Not that shooting me again will do anyone any good, but if that'll make you feel a little better, then fine by me."

She darted out and grabbed the gun like a mouse snatching an errant cookie crumb before retreating behind the door again. She cradled it against her chest.

"Better?" he asked.

"If I shoot you again, will you die?"

"No."

"Then no, I'm not feeling better."

Alice peeked out again, pointing the gun in his direction from the closet. He was leaning back in her chair, reading through her suicide note. If it weren't for the downright creepy fact that he seemed to have magically appeared in her room, she would have admitted privately that he was a fairly handsome guy. She had a brief internal debate about whether she should be mortified or relieved that she was checking out a guy who could turn out to be a serial rapist/murderer before moving on to the important question: Who the hell *was* he? Despite his familiar tone of voice and casual usage of her name, she didn't recognize him at all, a fact he certainly didn't seem bothered by. To make things that much stranger (if that was possible), he seemed even less bothered by the fact that he'd just taken one straight to the dome. He stopped reading her note and looked up. Their eyes met for an instant before she recoiled back into the closet.

"In that case, please accept my sincerest apologies. Anyway, your questions: My name is Charlie Dawson and I'm what's called a Ferryman. It's my sole purpose to lead recently deceased individuals to the afterlife. As a result of my given profession, I also happen to be, fortunately or unfortunately, impervious to death, though I have a hunch you might have figured that part out by now. Normally, we wouldn't be able to talk to each other like this, as I'm invisible to the world at large, but, to cut a long story short, my key, which is not only how I got in here but also the trick to doing that, is sitting on your desk right now."

Alice could hardly believe her ears. Ferryman? Immortality? Invisibility? Dead people? *My God*, she thought with compounding horror, *this is like a bad made-for-TV movie.*

"This is crazy," she mumbled to herself. "*I'm* crazy. I have definitely lost my mind. This isn't real, this isn't happening, there isn't some well-dressed guy sitting in front of me who magically showed up out of nowhere. I'm obviously doing some crazy Freudian dream therapy and soon I'll wake up blabbering about penis envy."

She caught his raised eyebrow from across the room. "Did you just say *penis envy?*"

"I did—now hush, you figment of my imagination, before you ruin my perfectly well-constructed justification for all of this."

The man calling himself Charlie looked briefly amused at that. "Honestly, right now I'm just as confused as you are."

She barked a short peal of laughter, which she found a little surprising, given the situation. "I highly doubt that, Mr. Fairy Man."

"*Ferryman*. I don't collect teeth." He switched his focus to the other sheet of paper in his hand—the one he'd originally been carrying—and began studying it intently. After a moment, he frowned slightly, which told Alice he either hadn't found what he was looking for or he hadn't liked what he'd read. "I'm not going to waste my time trying to convince you—believe it if you want, it really doesn't matter to me because . . . well, because you're not dead, which means I can't do anything anyway. It's just—" He paused, his eyes gravitating toward the ceiling as if he hoped to find the right word written there. "This has never happened before. You were supposed to die tonight, Alice, but here you are, very much not dead. Granted, I might have had something to do with that—"

Pockets of fear were slowly being burned up by a welling anger as this guy continued to talk about her supposedly unavoidable death, the heat of her growing rage mostly fueled by the shame of not actually being dead. There was an intrinsic embarrassment in botching this one final thing that would have taken all the pain away. Though she tried to steel herself, she could hear her voice waver on the verge of tears as she interrupted him.

"All right, you know what? I'm done talking about this. I'm really sorry you came here for nothing, buddy, but as you can clearly see, I'm not dead. Now, you have ten seconds to leave before I call the cops." Alice desperately wanted to wake up in her bed, sad and alone, but generally in good shape. She screwed her eyes shut and tried to force herself to wake up.

"Whoa . . . Wow. I mean, that's warranted and I'm sorry—I really am—but you don't understand—" Charlie began, but Alice cut him off again.

"Of course I don't understand! Why the hell would I understand?! What is there for me to fucking understand?!" The anger had well and truly taken over now, the crippling fear relegated to just a distant whimper in the back of her mind. She stood and stepped out of the closet, seething. "I don't care who you are or how you got here, but please leave before I decide to test whether or not a second bullet wouldn't have a much different effect than the first."

She looked into his face and realized that he was very taken aback by her outburst. Not angry, not afraid, just . . . surprised? He sat still in the chair, observing her with a mix of pity, shame, and burning curiosity. He looked down at the two sheets of paper in his hands again, one of them her note, then sidelong at her. With a fierce glare, she consumed his glance. A moment later, he was standing up as well.

"Sure," he said, "that's a good idea." He took a few measured steps that brought him to her desk, then set both pieces of paper he'd been holding down on top of it. He started to reach for a golden key that was sitting on her desk—*Was that what I saw a minute ago?*—but stopped.

"I don't mean to pry," he said, "but by any chance, did your mother pass away a year ago tomorrow?"

The flicker of surprise momentarily swept across her eyes; she felt it fly by, barely there, but there all the same. She hastily replaced it with cold indifference. "What does it matter to you?" she asked.

He shrugged. "To be honest, I already know your mother passed away." The Ferryman reached inside his jacket and held up a different piece of paper, a small paragraph no more than a few lines long adorning the top of the page. "Says on the sheet. Just figured I'd ask for the sake of conversation."

"I don't want—"

"Conversation, I know. I know a lot of things. Part of the job description," he added. "But that's not why I brought it up. You just remind me of someone I met about a year ago. Somebody who was pretty tough to forget. If I'm honest, you two look so damn alike it's kind of scary, so I figured maybe there was a connection."

Alice's breath caught in her throat. How many times had she heard that line before? *Alice, you look just like your mother did when she was your age. You two could be sisters!* Her determined defiance remained, though. "Great, so you've stalked other members of my family. Do you watch my sisters take showers, too?"

The dig didn't bother him, she noted. In fact, he didn't even seem to notice it. He responded without missing a beat, as if Alice hadn't spoken at all. "When she passed away, she was bald. I remember, because her spirit had this absolutely gorgeous, flowing head of brown hair, and there was such a striking juxtaposition between the two that it was hard to believe. She had a birthmark, right here." He gently tapped the right side of his neck with two fingers, a few inches down from his jaw. "And it was . . . Well, as Ferrymen, we're trained to talk things out—to form a connection as quickly as possible. However, when she passed, we stood there in silence for a solid minute, at least. I don't know why, but we just did. Standing there, not saying a word, was one of the most nerve-racking things I've ever done in an assignment. It was like we just looked at each other, and I knew that she knew, but something told me I needed to wait. Finally, I asked her if she was ready, and she said yes, could she just have a moment to say her good-byes. I said sure. That never happens, which I think is why I happen to remember it."

His voice seemed to flow from word to word in a way that had her spellbound. Some of what he said made no sense, but the mention of the birthmark in particular had caught her attention. Lucky guess? What would the odds on that be—two different, older bald women with noticeable birthmarks on the right sides of their necks who died almost exactly a year ago? It wasn't impossible, but at the same time, her heart was willing to accept the other possibility, the one that suggested that maybe this guy wasn't totally full of shit. Like the greatest magicians, he'd earned just enough credibility for her to start wondering if he was actually for real.

Before she even realized it, her eyes had softened dramatically and were now intently focused on the man in front of her.

"What did she say?" she asked, and though Alice had intended for her voice to maintain its stoicism from moments ago, she found it replaced by an uneven tenderness. As soon as the words were out, she cleared her throat.

He smiled at her—a broad, disarming grin in all its glory. There were two things she immediately noticed in that moment. The first was that his smile was just incredibly striking. The second was that, for all its breadth, it betrayed a depth of sadness that she simply couldn't even begin to fathom.

"I don't know," he said with a shrug.

She opened her mouth to reply, only to taste something salty on the edge of her lips. Tears? When did she start crying? But she knew why—she desperately wanted to believe that this man had known her mother. Had met her. Had remembered her. She wanted that *so badly* that she was willing to entirely suspend her disbelief for those few moments. So, instead of biting back with the arsenal of sarcasm at her disposal, she pressed her lips together and said nothing.

Alice knew he could see this—it wasn't hard to trace the lines of guilt on his face.

"I've said too much. I'm sorry about everything," Charlie finally said. "Trust me when I say I didn't mean to upset you, but for what it's worth, this whole thing has thrown me for a loop, too."

Alice composed herself by clearing her throat several more times. "Don't worry about it . . . I'm pretty convinced this isn't real anyway. Actually, I'm not sure which would be worse—if this is or isn't real." She took a moment to look over her suicide note from afar, trying to make out her fairly neat handwriting. "And, um, sorry for shooting you in the head, I guess."

"No worries," Charlie said. "I feel bad you wasted a bullet on little old me. There's nothing in here anyway," he joked, knocking on his skull.

"So that's your secret," Alice said. "Now that I would believe."

"You and me both." He reached out his hand to shake. "Thanks. For this. It was—"

She pointed the gun at him. "Please get the hell out of here before I really do call the cops."

His laugh that followed caught her completely off guard. It seemed honest, so loud and cheerful, like he'd been holding on to it for years. He seemed nice enough, even if he'd entered her life with all the subtlety of a steam locomotive bursting through her bedroom door. Yet there were other things about him—things she couldn't quite put her finger on—that didn't scare her, per se, but made her . . . curious. That laugh, for one. It was always slightly off-putting to be around someone who was laughing at something that you weren't a part of, doubly so if you had a gun leveled at them.

A knowing smirk appeared on his face, a true debonair twist of his lips. "Sure," he said. "It was a pleasure meeting you, Alice." He gave a short two-finger salute, then picked up the key off her desk. As soon as his fingers touched it, he disappeared in a blink. Poof—gone, just like that. Alice's mouth fell open. When, after two minutes, he failed to reappear, she lowered the pistol. Her fingers went weak, slowly unraveling themselves from it until it fell from her hand. Then, like the gun, she, too, crumpled to the ground.

She sat on the floor, legs splayed out underneath her. "What the fuck just happened?" She said the words aloud, but there was no one else there to hear them.

HOME FOR THE LAST TIME

What the fuck just happened?

For the umpteenth time since leaving Alice Spiegel's room, Charlie ran his fingers through his hair. He walked with a slow, deliberate pace down the hallway that temporarily connected her room to the Ferryman Institute. Even allowing for his sluggish pace, the journey felt much longer than normal. The reason for that was obvious enough.

Save the girl . . . He certainly hadn't been expecting that, not even in his wildest imagination. He never saved the girl. *Watch girl get hit by bus* or *watch girl drink herself to death*, sure, but never *save the girl*—shit, it was never *save* anything: save the date, save your money, save the fucking whales.

Except in this case.

That wasn't completely right, though. The assignment had specifically read, *Be a Ferryman or save the girl. Your choice.*

Charlie glanced down at the sheet of paper in his hand. For the first time in his career, there was no check mark in the box labeled *Assignment successfully ferried.*

He'd always known this moment would come eventually. Two hundred and fifty years was too long to go without messing up at least once. It was bound to happen sooner or later . . . *law of averages, nobody's perfect, you'll get 'em next time, Tiger, yada yada.* Now that it had happened, however, it didn't feel anything like Charlie had imagined. Maybe that had everything to do with the circumstances—after all, it wasn't like he'd failed the assignment. Plus, the mounting pressure for him to succeed was always an internal drive stemming from what failing would mean for the subject of his assignment. In this case, though, Alice was still very much alive. No reason to feel guilty, nothing to beat himself up over. On the other hand, maybe the reality of being perfect minus one just hadn't set in yet. It was certainly too soon to rule that out, but for the moment, Charlie found himself far more concerned with the array of questions bouncing around his head.

Why had the president of the Ferryman Institute given him this assignment in the first place? On top of that, why even give him a choice? Was it some kind of test?

And why Alice Spiegel? With all due respect, Charlie hadn't found her even remotely remarkable. Interesting, maybe, but in addition to being punctual, Death had always been unequivocally impartial. At least, it used to be; now he wasn't so sure.

The most important question, however, was the one he was continually asking himself but was as of yet unable to answer.

Why had he saved her?

Truth was, he didn't know. The timing of everything had been so incredibly fast that his brain had just shut down and instinct had taken over. It was like some dormant part of him had been waiting for that moment, completely prepared to act in the unlikely event of such a scenario. And act it had. He'd willingly committed what was widely considered to be the most heinous violation of Ferryman Laws possible. The "death penalty" didn't exist in the world of Ferrymen—if it did, a wayward employee determined to get out of their service could simply commit a reprehensible crime and then be rewarded with the desired escape. That was why Purgatory existed. Though rarely used, it turned a Ferryman's greatest asset—immortality—against them. It made solitary confinement—the human kind—look like child's play, a punishment prize package capable of leaving even the most gratuitous masochist in tears.

Even with that hanging over his head, Charlie had saved Alice anyway.

The strangest part of it all? He didn't care. In fact, he felt *good* about it. God, when was the last time he'd said that after an assignment? Actually, had he *ever* said that after one? Was this the start of something new, something worthwhile? Were things maybe, just maybe, starting to turn around for him?

The answer, it turned out, was a resounding no. He opened the door back to the Institute with a firm push, only to find Fate, eternal bastard that it was, gleefully waiting.

"Welcome back, Mssr. Dawson."

Javrouche's coldly articulate voice slid through the air as the door swung open to reveal the Inspector's smiling face about six feet away. Charlie needed no other sign to know straightaway that something was wrong.

At least two dozen men clad in body armor had surrounded his work area. Four of those men, possibly more, were holding capture rifles—weapons specifically designed by the Institute to detain employees who had wandered outside the bounds of good behavior. Capture rifles, like their smaller Taser cousins, were specially designed to interrupt the electric signals that power the human body's motor system, but at a much higher amplitude and for a much longer period. It was the first time Charlie had seen them in person, and frankly, he preferred the immediate past where he hadn't.

"Thank you. Did I forget my birthday again? You know how awful I am with dates," Charlie said. Though his typically understated sarcasm sounded intact, his shifting eyes betrayed the gnawing unease in the back of his mind. Something told him the timing of Javrouche's appearance wasn't a coincidence, and that didn't bode well for his future.

The corners of Javrouche's lips twisted at Charlie's response. "Close. This is actually your surprise going-away party. I thought it appropriate, seeing as you're going to be gone for a very long time, Mssr. Dawson, and I wouldn't want to send you off without a proper gathering first. Still no fatted calf, though, I'm afraid." He turned around and motioned to one of the armored personnel standing nearby. "Could you find Koroviev for me and tell him Mssr. Dawson has returned?"

A few seconds later, a young man arrived and stood next to the Inspector. Charlie recognized him as Begemot Koroviev, Javrouche's long-standing lieutenant. A calm, if disinterested face sat upon his shoulders. His hair was short and bristly, not dissimilar in consistency or color to a black cat's fur, while his eyes, though keen, seemed perpetually half lidded. He and Charlie hadn't interacted much over the years, but his position as the Inspector's right-hand man made him guilty by association as far as Charlie was concerned.

With his second-in-command now present, Javrouche once again turned his attention to Charlie, who was busy fighting back an overwhelming urge to pummel the Inspector's pompous face in.

"Well, now that we're all here, why don't we get started?" The Inspector straightened his stance, his authoritative voice rising triumphantly as he spoke. "Charles Ronald Dawson, Ferryman Number 72514—I hereby place you under arrest for multiple violations of the code held as law by the Ferryman Institute."

It wasn't news to Charlie that Javrouche had it in for him. However, the cadre of guards—he assumed it was the detention unit, or at least part of it—and the formal charges? That in itself was worrying, but it was Javrouche's overwhelmingly self-satisfied attitude that put Charlie especially on edge.

Despite his reservations, Charlie tried his best not to show them. He held up his hands in his best mea culpa and said, "All right, I admit it. I shouldn't have suggested I wanted to kill you. I sincerely apologize. There's just something about your face that instills homicidal urges in me."

Javrouche didn't rise to the comment, and Charlie knew then, beyond a shadow of a doubt, that something was terribly, horribly wrong.

"Keep digging that hole of yours, Mssr. Dawson. He who sows the wind reaps the whirlwind."

Charlie's mind immediately kicked into overdrive, simultaneously trying to figure out a way to stall the conversation while attempting to discern what the Inspector knew. He had a bad feeling the answer was *too much.*

"Fine. No more jokes. What am I being charged with?"

"Koroviev, if you'll do the honors," Javrouche said.

Koroviev cleared his throat, then began in a slight Russian accent. "The first: two counts of removal of one's Ferryman Key during the course of an assignment. The second: two counts of revealing sensitive information to unauthorized Institute personnel."

Bewildered, Charlie tried to interrupt—"What are you talking about?" he cried—but Koroviev continued.

"The third: one count of deliberating sabotaging an assignment to prevent the designated death of the subject. This charge qualifies as treason and is therefore punishable with admission to Purgatory."

Purgatory? Did he really just say *Purgatory*? That was bad. Very bad.

Charlie could practically feel the adrenaline coursing through his bloodstream. "I said, *what are you talking about?!*" He advanced a step from the door. In immediate response, the guards standing at ease behind the Inspector snapped into a ready position. Several capture rifles were now pointed directly at Charlie. He held his ground, half in, half out of the Ferryman Door.

"Mssr. Dawson, you insult me," Javrouche said. "You have no idea what we're talking about? I doubt that. Just admit it and save us all some trouble."

It was taking a Herculean amount of restraint on Charlie's part, but he remained still. "Bullshit," he growled.

It was a trap.

The Inspector reached into his jacket and pulled out his phone. He pushed a button, then held it high in the air. A recording started playing.

"*But that's the problem, Cartwright. I did exactly what Javrouche thinks I did, though not as deliberately as he seems to think. I did break the cardinal rule.*"

Charlie's voice was unmistakable even through the poor quality and crappy acoustics of the control room. He knew right away that the jig was up. Checkmate, game over, thanks for playing, we have a great parting gift for you. Javrouche *really* had something this time, and there was nothing Charlie could do to stop it. But how was that possible? And if they had him saying that . . .

Javrouche pressed a button on the phone and the recording

went silent. "Should I continue? I'm willing to bet you know what comes next."

Charlie refused to answer. His mind was reeling, trying to slow things down. Javrouche, however, was clearly aiming for the opposite. He had Charlie on the ropes and he knew it.

"No witty comebacks for us?"

Charlie again said nothing.

"Ah, Mssr. Dawson, your silence speaks volumes. Very well, next question. Answer carefully now, as you're failing rather woefully at the moment. Who is William Henry Taylor Cartwright the Fourth?"

"Where did you get that recording?" Charlie asked instead. He was suddenly finding it difficult to stay silent. His breath was coming in long pulls.

"Me first. Who is Cartwright?"

His mind whirling, Charlie struggled to come up with the answer to what was a simple question. "He's my mentor," Charlie finally said. "He's a former Ferryman, now doing office work. We've known each other since I first started here."

"Interesting. Did you know, Mssr. Dawson, that there is no record of a William Henry Taylor Cartwright—the Fourth or otherwise—ever having worked for the Ferryman Institute? In fact, there is no record of anyone with the surname Cartwright having served here, period. I don't want to sound alarmist, but it would almost seem as if that person doesn't exist."

The world seemed to swim in front of Charlie. What the hell was Javrouche talking about? Of *course* Cartwright existed—they met all the time. He was Charlie's only confidant. What was being proposed right now . . . "That's impossible."

"Wrong again, Mssr. Dawson. Impossible is you treating your position and this Institute with any amount of respect. Possible—

and very real, I should add—is you revealing Institute secrets to a man with no association to the Ferryman Institute whatsoever."

Charlie blinked a few times, just to make sure that yes, this was reality. "You can't be serious."

"I have every reason to believe this Cartwright to be a spy for a rival organization. Though I can't prove it just yet, I imagine I'll be able to soon enough. So what does that mean for you? Apparently you've divulged an unquantifiable amount of our secrets to an outside party—secrets you were sworn to protect. That, Mssr. Dawson, is very, very bad. And how unknowingly you revealed that information is also a matter of considerable debate."

This was all a mistake. It had to be. Cartwright, a spy? Ridiculous—the man pretty much embodied everything the Institute stood for.

Yet, as absurd as the idea sounded, it gave Charlie some doubt to chew on. While espionage wasn't exactly a common occurrence, he hadn't forgotten the havoc caused by the Zoroastrian debacle of 1833. Needless to say, there'd been a spy or two involved there, and it had almost led to the end of humanity as everyone knew it.

Cross-organization spying had only arrived recently (relatively, anyway) to the world of the Ferryman Institute, mostly because the Institute had been the sole proprietor of soul-to-afterlife guidance for the majority of humanity's existence. There was no one else *to* spy on them. For millennia, the number of people dying and the number of cases the Institute pulled in were one and the same. At some point, however, the numbers stopped going hand in hand; more humans were dying than the Institute was handling.

Apparently, Death had started outsourcing.

The Institute had made contact with a few groups over the years, like the Sisters of Valhalla or the recently met and altogether screw-loose People's Temple, but others were out there. Similar to Ferrymen and their keys, each group had its own methods of crossing people over to the afterlife—the Sisters rode their souls away on horseback, for example. Though it was impossible for a Ferryman to outright switch allegiances to a rival FILO (Ferryman Institute–Like Organization), as they were called, that didn't necessary preclude a rogue employee from passing over valuable information. However, these organizations were small. In fact, most Ferrymen would go their entire service without running into a member of one.

So it was less the FILO numbers that frightened parts of the Institute's workforce and more their simple existence. No one at the Institute understood why Death had recruited more groups to do the Ferryman Institute's job, and anyone who claimed they did was full of more shit than a constipated hippo, but there it was—competition for the soul market. Why did Death need those other outfits? Did that mean Death was unhappy with the Institute's performance? Was Death trying to phase out the Institute? If the Ferryman Institute disappeared, then so did its employees—or so went the conventional wisdom among the ranks—and most employees wanted no part of being disappeared. Anything outside of diplomatic contact with a FILO during an assignment was strictly forbidden by the Ferryman Institute

And if Javrouche was to be believed, Charlie was doing just that.

Charlie continued mounting a defense, but the ramparts were quickly being overrun. "But Cartwright brought me to the Institute . . . he's the reason I'm here!"

"Interesting you mention that." Javrouche held up a file for Charlie to see. "I was able to procure your official record from the Office of the President. I'm sure you could imagine my disbelief when I found the information detailing your recruitment was missing. Isn't it strange how you claim to have been brought here by a man we don't believe to exist and, even stranger, you can't prove he did?"

Charlie stood rooted to the ground, his mouth hanging open like a feeding whale. *What the hell is going on here?* he thought.

"How did you get that file?! Those files are never supposed to leave the main office of records!"

Javrouche appeared just as surprised as Charlie to find Melissa yelling at the Inspector, but there she was, storming the perimeter in her heels, Dirkley following dutifully in tow. Charlie was well versed in Melissa's knowledge of the Institute's more obscure rules—for whatever reason, that was her God-given talent as a manager—but he was rather shocked she was so willingly putting herself in the line of fire.

"Good evening, Mme. Johnson," Javrouche said as she strode directly to him. Though the guards near him shifted into more ready positions at her arrival, Javrouche signaled for them to stand down. "I was just explaining to your Ferryman the numerous reasons why we're arresting him."

Melissa's eyes went wide. "You're doing *what*!?"

"Arresting him." Javrouche sighed. "Does anyone on this team listen to me?"

When Melissa moved to speak again, Koroviev clamped his hand over her mouth. She initially struggled, but gave up after he whispered something in her ear. Given the expression on her face, Charlie imagined it couldn't have been pleasant.

"Thank you, Koroviev. Now, if all that weren't enough, we've been monitoring your most recent assignment. One with a Mademoiselle"—he consulted a separate report—"Alice Spiegel." The Inspector shook his head. "Words fail me, Mssr. Dawson. To deliberately intervene and prevent the death of your assignment . . . I consider myself your harshest critic, and even *I* never figured you capable of something like this."

The word *how* circled around inside Charlie's head. He wrestled with it briefly, letting go only when he finally convinced himself that, right then and there, it didn't matter. He needed to stand his ground, at least get a foothold back into this conversation. For the moment, *how* was irrelevant.

"I had orders from the president himself," Charlie said.

Javrouche shook his head. "You expect me to believe that the highest authority here, whose primary purpose is to lead the souls of the dead—emphasis on *dead*—to the afterlife, ordered you to save the life of a random girl?"

"I wasn't ordered, but given a choice. I have proof," Charlie said. The assignment letter might not be bulletproof evidence, but with the presidential seal, it would hopefully be enough to at least raise reasonable doubts about his present circumstances. Charlie reached into his jacket, but it occurred to him rather quickly that he had a problem. Namely, the problem of nothing being where the letter should have been.

"Misplaced your proof? How inconvenient. I'm sure it's that, and not that it doesn't actually exist."

Charlie's options were disappearing at an alarming rate.

There has to be something, he thought, his brain whining in protest as the overtaxed gears inside were pushed beyond their limits. If it were an assignment, there would have to be a record of it somewhere, probably in the president's office. Even if Javrouche dragged him away, Charlie could request it, bring it to the attention of a Judicator, or really anyone who could put the brakes on this runaway train.

But then he remembered, with a horrifying, dawning clarity,

Melissa's recounting of her conversation with the president's representative: *As far as anyone is concerned, this assignment doesn't exist.*

As soon as his brain processed that, one by one, the gears in his head ground to a halt, and his brain, wheezing and smoking, eked out a final prescient remark in its dying moments.

You're fucked, amigo.

Charlie's hand fell to his side, the obstinate swell in his chest blown out like a candle. He tried to maintain a semblance of quiet dignity, but the realization that Javrouche had finally won squeezed out what little he had left.

"I assume I don't need to explain the severity of your actions to you, Mssr. Dawson," Javrouche said.

Charlie's lips pressed together in a thin line. He knew full well what a charge of treason meant: Purgatory, the highest form of punishment available to the Ferryman Institute, for the longest term possible. It was, in many ways, a fate worse than death.

Charlie stared at the Inspector. "How the hell do you know all this?" he asked, his voice trembling with an alchemic mix of pure astonishment and budding scorn.

"And we're back to this question, I see. It was your phone, Mssr. Dawson." Charlie's eyes flashed. "A week ago, I met with your manager to discuss another one of your disappearing acts. She lamented the fact that there was no way of knowing where her aloof Ferryman was gallivanting off to. In response, I authorized a Privacy Consultation Override, which, among other things, let us track your every move."

"No!" Melissa yelled. She'd somehow managed to shake her mouth free from Koroviev's grasp and was currently fighting back his attempts to regain control. "I never gave you permission to do that!"

"Technically, you're correct—you never specifically *asked* me to bug Mssr. Dawson's phone. However, I felt, given the circumstances and your implied consent, a PCO was in order. And look where we stand now. It appears I was right to trust my instincts."

"That's horseshit!" Melissa exclaimed. "Any additional security measures have to be approved by the president's office!"

Javrouche looked back at the manager, who was now being held by an additional guard and struggling against both men. His perpetual grin melted away, leaving his eyes to consider her with obvious disdain. "What makes you think they weren't? You should be thrilled, Mme. Johnson, that we've managed to stop your Ferryman from any more illicit activities, yet I'm getting the distinct feeling you're not."

"Thrilled!? You're arresting my Ferryman without even consulting me! I should have been the first person notified, Inspector! This is fucking absurd!"

"Absurd?" Javrouche turned to face her. "I'd watch your tone, madame—"

But if Melissa cared for what Javrouche thought, she didn't show it. "Fuck you! You can't do this! I *know* you didn't get the president's approval! This is *clearly* a personal vendetta against Charlie. I'm shutting this down right now! This is absolute—"

"I don't care what you think!"

The silence that settled afterward reminded Charlie of the way sound vanished in the wake of thunder. When the Inspector spoke again, his voice had returned to its articulate and regulated self, but a terrible undercurrent of barely controlled fury ran just beneath it. "I. Don't. *Care.*"

Before another word could leave Melissa's lips, the Inspector grabbed a capture rifle from the hands of the nearest guard and put a round straight into her chest. Her body, racked by thousands of volts of electricity, seized and convulsed for five agonizing seconds before she went limp in Lieutenant Koroviev's hands. Dirkley, who'd practically been a statue up to that point, gasped in horror.

Javrouche flipped the rifle back to the guard he'd poached it from as if he'd just borrowed a broom for a quick sweep.

"Very sorry for that brief interruption," Javrouche said as he turned back to Charlie. "I believe we left off at the part where we formally take you into custody now."

"What the hell did you just do?!" Charlie shouted. His attention flicked from his manager back to the Inspector.

"I took care of a distraction," Javrouche replied.

It wasn't until after the unconscious form of one Melissa Johnson registered in his mind that Charlie realized he'd been pinning some vague hope on her saving his ass. Her knowledge of Institute procedure was first-rate, her negotiating skills excellent, her general approach to life pragmatic (at least, when Charlie hadn't pushed her to the brink of insanity). For all the hell he'd given her, she was unerringly reliable, and he'd believed in her ability to somehow sort this whole mess out. Now, much like his future prospects, she was nothing more than a twitching dead weight in the hands of the enemy.

Charlie took a step forward, which was instantly greeted with the forefront of the detention unit acting in kind. Time to play his last card. "I need to speak with the president. You can come with me, arrest me the second I'm done talking with him if you want. But he can vouch for me. We can get this all straightened out." There was nothing he could do to keep the desperation out of his voice.

Javrouche merely shook his head. "Request denied."

"This is your payback, isn't it, Inspector? After all these years, you're finally getting what you wanted. How does it feel? The man you once considered your idol brought down by your own hands, and for what? Revenge? Damning the Institute because you feel slighted?"

The two men stood only meters apart, yet were separated by the ocean of mistakes in their past. Charlie's words clearly struck a nerve, as undeniable truths long buried often did. The look of effusive superiority that Javrouche had been maintaining with relative ease fell off like a broken mask, revealing a face of pure contempt hiding just behind it.

"You really can't handle the fact that you're finally being punished, can you? I'm simply doing my job, Mssr. Dawson. I wish I could say the same for you."

Charlie could feel the last tenuous grip on his composure slipping, each one of Javrouche's digs having pushed it further away, until finally he was lost, screaming at the top of his lungs. "You want to know something, Javrouche?! I saved that girl today, and in two hundred and fifty years, it stands as one of the proudest things I've ever done! I saved her *life*! And if I have to be punished for that, then so fucking be it! But you can't take that away from me! No one can take that away from me!"

There was silence. And into that silence, painted on the face of Inspector Javrouche, bloomed one of the most horrible, shit-eating smirks Charlie had ever seen.

"Au contraire, Mssr. Dawson. You're right—as much as I'd like to, I cannot go back in time and change what you've done. But I can change the result. Just think . . . you can spend every moment of your sentence knowing that I'll have stopped at absolutely *nothing* to ensure that the Institute's secrecy is preserved. If that means the death of Alice Spiegel, then *c'est la vie*. At least then you, too, can finally feel what it's like to have something you tried to save slip away."

Charlie reached into his pocket and fished out his phone, the instrument of his downfall, and hurled it at Javrouche's simpering face. It whizzed through the air, spinning end over end like a touchscreen-enabled shuriken. Javrouche simply twisted his shoulders and the phone sailed past.

"I thought I asked you to take care of that phone," Javrouche said. He spoke with the unhurried cadence of a museum tour guide. "Maybe you'll learn to follow directions better in Purgatory. Now then: Koroviev, if you'll do me the honor, please arrest Mssr. Dawson."

The perimeter of armed guards began to move in; the lieutenant, after carefully laying down Melissa, leading the way. Two of them crouched down and took aim with their capture rifles.

So this was the end. Charlie could see it all—his impending arrest, being hauled before a Judicator, subsequently convicted, and finally thrown into Purgatory indefinitely. There he would rot, not physically but mentally. Javrouche would see to that. What a shitty way to go.

A flurry of movement raced toward him, but Charlie ignored it. He wanted his last free moments to be focused only on the Inspector.

At least, that was the plan, until a pair of hands hit Charlie hard in the chest.

The force knocked him off balance, causing him to stumble backward. Charlie lost his footing and landed on his back with a dull thump. The stark white walls of the connecting passageway— the one he'd used to return from Alice Spiegel's bedroom— greeted him as Charlie found himself staring at the ceiling. He quickly sat up.

There, standing above him, was Dirkley.

Given Dirkley's general demeanor, it wasn't hard to see him

going relatively unnoticed by the rest of the assemblage. In the ensuing commotion, he'd managed to rush over and shove Charlie back into the passageway. With an awkward wriggle, Dirkley removed Charlie's key from the Ferryman Door, briefly holding it with an air of reverence. Charlie could see the guards racing toward them. Javrouche's voice rang out in the background with righteous fury.

A smile crossed Dirkley's face. He met Charlie's dumbfounded eyes, then slammed the door shut in Charlie's face.

A moment of blank incomprehension slowly gave way to realization. Without his key, Charlie wouldn't be able to enter the Ferryman Institute again. However, the passageway to an assignment—in this case, from the Institute to Alice's bedroom—stayed open only as long as the Ferryman Key happened to be at the end of it. Now that the door on the Institute end had been closed with the opening key on the other side, the passage had essentially been sealed shut. No one would be able to chase him using it. But Dirkley . . .

Charlie couldn't remember how long he yelled at the door. He banged and screamed at it, pounding away with an animalistic determination. At some point, tears began to roll down his cheeks, striking the floor with as much usefulness as his fists. Finally, he gave up and let himself fall onto his back against the ground. The white floor of the passageway was solid, and had he been able to feel it, Charlie imagined, it would have been very cold. He closed his eyes, and tried to remember what cold felt like.

He couldn't.

Obviously there had been a mistake. What else could it be? Just a small mix-up, a failure to communicate. Charlie would serve his punishment, but they'd clear everything else up for sure. All he had to do was leave, contact the Institute, arrange for a pickup, and sort out this mess. In due time, he could have his career back, his perfect record, his admiration. In the long run, it would probably only cost him Alice Spiegel's life.

He didn't know how long he lay there. Eventually, Charlie picked himself up and began walking, shakily at first but with increasing determination, toward the door at the other side of the hall.

Fuck it. He was going to save the girl.

FUGITIVE

I'm crazy. *I've gone crazy.*

Alice lay facedown on her bed. She'd spent the past thirty minutes considering every conceivable possibility and the one she kept returning to was insanity.

Men didn't magically show up out of thin air and talk about your dead mother, even if what they said made you all teary-eyed and nostalgic and sad and oddly . . . No, she didn't even want to think about that part. There were only two possibilities: it was a dream—*It has to have been a dream!*—or she was officially crazy. Maybe she was crazy *and* dreaming? That was a new and exciting possibility to consider, actually.

She lifted her head up slightly and looked at the palm of her hand. The spent bullet casing flashed in the light of her room. Next to it, slightly dull by comparison, was a fired nine-millimeter bullet.

Alice pressed her face back down into the bedspread. *I really, really should have just pulled the trigger the first time*, she thought.

The sound of a door opening immediately caught her attention. Her throat nearly closed when she realized that she hadn't cleaned up her room at all since the incident—her gun was still out, the room reeked of gunpowder, and the crumpled suicide note lay casually on her desk. If her dad walked in the room right then, she was, in a word, fucked.

Four years of creative writing practice at one of the finest English departments the United States college education system had to offer whirred into action.

Raccoon came through the window. Happened to be cleaning my gun for kicks. Startled me and fired at it, but it escaped. Bullet must be somewhere in the backyard. Sorry, long day, wasn't thinking. Play Mom card. Done and done. Flimsy, but not bad for two seconds' notice. She turned toward her bedroom door.

It was closed.

The sound of a door slamming shut caused her to whirl around. Behind her, the clearly frazzled face of Charlie Dawson once again greeted her.

She screamed.

It lasted for a good five seconds, which Alice found impressive, given how easily she became winded these days. It was the little things in life.

"I thought you left," she hissed.

"Surprise. Guess it's your lucky day," Charlie said with all the monotone enthusiasm of a root canal patient. "So, random question: You have a car, right?"

The sheer randomness of his question completely threw Alice. What was originally self-righteous indignation sputtered into a confused "I mean, yeah, but—"

"Good, I'll drive. Also, do you have a cell phone? I'm going to need to make a call while we're on the road."

"I'm sorry, but what are you—"

He walked over to Alice and put his hands on her shoulders. There was a distinct look of urgency in his eyes. "I know how absurdly cliché this is going to sound, but I don't have time to explain. That's the cliché part—not having time to explain. Whatever, you're smart, you know what I mean. True or false—you're alone in the house right now? I'm assuming true based on what you were about to do half an hour ago, but maybe you're indifferent about doing that sort of thing with people around."

Alice had no idea what was going on. It was like her mind had simply said, *Fuck this shit*, and caught the last train to Clarksville. Honestly, she wasn't sure she blamed it. Plus, who needed rational thought, anyway? Complete and utter mental fantasy was where things were at nowadays.

When she failed to provide anything by way of answer, Charlie seemed to read between the lines. "I'm gonna go with true. In that case, we need to make sure no one comes back here. This is where they'll come looking for me first."

Alice forcefully stomped her feet, which jogged some of her mental faculties. "Stop! Just . . . stop!" She was desperately trying to get a grip on things.

"Hate to say it, but that's not an option. I've already wasted too much time feeling sorry for myself. We need to get moving."

Alice looked at Charlie, his calm if slightly pensive face an undecipherable mix of emotions. "What do you mean, *we*? Why do you—"

"Look, I promise you two things. One: I'll explain everything in the car. Two: what's happening right now is very, very real. Now, I need you to trust me." He offered his hand to her while she was still sitting on her bed.

This isn't happening, she thought. *Right?* Might as well test the waters. "You're not real," she said. Now that she'd said it out loud, she felt a little stupid. What was he going to say back: *Shucks, you caught me*, then disappear? Well, a girl could hope.

"I am the realest unkillable random stranger you will ever meet. The problem here is that the people who will be trying to find me—and, rather unfortunately, you—are just as real and unkillable. I don't know how much time we have, but I know we're wasting it." He reached out his arm. "Come on. We need to go."

Alice sat perfectly still on her bed as Charlie stood there in front of her. With a haggard sigh, he looked around the room.

"That your purse?" he asked. He pointed to the medium-sized beige Coach knockoff sitting next to her desk.

". . . No?" she ventured.

Charlie walked over to it and scooped it up.

"Hey! Put that down!" Alice yelled.

He opened the main pouch and frenetically searched through it. Her car keys jangled as he pulled them out. He then found her cell phone hiding in plain sight on the corner of her desk, threw it unceremoniously inside the bag, and proceeded to zip the whole thing shut. Finally, he strode over to Alice and, with a smooth motion, hoisted her up on his shoulder.

She felt the blood rush to her head as her world flipped upside down. "Oh my God! Put me down! *Put me down!*" She pounded on his back, tore at his hair, and scratched at any exposed skin she could find. Her captor didn't so much as flinch.

"I think you're forgetting the magic word." The purse looked ridiculous hanging from his shoulder, but maybe being wrong side up had something to do with that.

"*Please!*" she begged.

"Better, but still no," he said serenely, and left the bedroom.

Alice tried to break free, but she was already weak from another night without dinner (in her defense, no one ever said you couldn't kill yourself on an empty stomach). The best she could do was wiggle about as he quickly carried her down the staircase. Her hair acted like a curtain and obstructed her vision, but she could tell they were headed to the front door. Just as they reached it, Charlie stopped. Alice continued to wrestle against being taken against her will, but her efforts were having little—okay, who was she kidding—*no* effect.

"Let. Me. *Go!*" She pounded against his back with renewed vigor. "I am not that fucking girl from *King Kong!*"

"Fay Wray?"

"Do you honestly think I know who the hell Fay Wray is? And why do *you* know that?"

"I saw it in theaters when it first came out. Great thing about being invisible all the time is that you never have to pay for a movie." Since his return, Alice noticed, his voice hadn't risen above being glibly sardonic. The true implications of his statement only occurred to her a few seconds later.

"Wait . . . *King Kong* came out like a hundred years ago. How old are you, exactly?"

He paused for a moment. "Old enough to wish I was only that old."

Her body was being jerked around as he examined the room for something. A bit of whiplash later and he'd apparently found what he'd been looking for. After three short *beep*s, Alice quickly realized it was the cordless phone next to the living room couch.

Alice struggled some more, her thrashing growing desperate. She was getting increasingly light-headed, what with all the blood pooling in her cranium, but he was remarkably strong. Or she was remarkably weak. Tough to tell, really. She could hear the phone ringing faintly through the speaker in the phone before it clicked.

The feminine voice that answered sounded tinny and distant, but it was instantly familiar. "Nine-one-one, what is your emergency?"

This is it! This is my chance! "Help me!" she screamed as loudly as she could.

"Listen," Charlie calmly said in the receiver, but with the slightest hint of terror in his voice, "my friend Alice has been badly hurt—"

"No! I'm fine! He's lying! He's kidnapping me!"

"—to the point where I think she's getting a little delusional. I'm rushing her to the hospital now. She's bleeding profusely out of the side of her head. Also, I think there might be a gas leak here, so you should keep everyone away from this address. Could blow any second."

"Please! He's taking me!"

The voice on the other end of the phone sounded very startled, not that Alice blamed her. "Sir, can you please—"

"No," Charlie interrupted smoothly, "I can't wait until help arrives. I'm leaving now, otherwise she might not make it. Please trace this address and send help as quickly as you can." Alice heard another *beep*, and the call was gone. "Maybe it's me, but if I didn't know any better," Charlie said, "I'd say it seems like you're not very grateful that I'm trying to save your life."

"Grateful! Are you shitting me? You're kidnapping me!" Alice yelled. Maybe there was a cop nearby and someone would be there soon. Her vision blurred slightly and the dizziness began to kick in. Just when her sight began to tunnel, Charlie plunked her down on the couch. He held both her arms tightly against her sides, preventing her from moving.

"Listen to me." His voice had taken on a slightly forceful edge. "Your life is in danger, all right? That may not mean anything to you right now, but it does to me. I'm being chased by other Ferrymen—people just like me—for all the wrong reasons. Well, some wrong reasons. Anyway, my team is going to be torn limb from limb for helping me. Until I can figure out how to clear this up, I need to get you someplace safe, because if I leave you here, they will hurt you—that much I can promise. With the cops and other emergency personnel around, they won't touch your family, but they still might go after you. If you're gone, the police are more likely to keep everyone here under a protective watch. I don't want anybody else getting involved in this, least of all your family. We're taking your cell phone with us and I promise you can contact them as soon as it's safe.

"Now, as compelled as I feel to just take you for your own good, I'm not going to. I realize that I'm putting you in a ridiculous situation, but someone important to me recently told me something that's suddenly starting to make sense. This is your choice, Alice: come with me or stay here. It's your call."

God, it all felt so real . . . his expressions, the force of his hands against her arms, the warm breath that played across her face. The light in his emphatic jade eyes danced frantically as he searched for an answer in hers.

He let go of her arms, but extended his hand again for her to take. "Care to take a chance on a complete stranger?"

This was real. At least, it seemed that way. Was it, though? God, this was confusing.

Without thinking, she nodded slightly.

"Good enough." He removed the purse from his shoulder and set it in Alice's lap. She gingerly took hold of it, only to be whisked away as soon as she had a decent grip on the handle.

Alice didn't know what to do. She had to admit, his little impromptu speech sounded rational, albeit in a completely irrational sort of way, but when push came to shove, she was still letting herself be kidnapped. Even so, what could she do? He was certainly stronger than she was and apparently impervious to destruction. That limited her options for escape somewhat drastically.

Yet even as she told herself all that, a voice whispered in the back of her head: *But then why did you agree to go with him? Do you want to trust him?*

She ignored it.

They shot through the front door and into the street. Alice's two-door silver Jeep Wrangler (her mom had nicknamed it the Silver Surfer before passing away) was parked neatly next to the curb. Charlie began pressing buttons on the keyless entry, then almost ripped the driver-side door off as he yanked it open. Alice numbly settled in the passenger seat. Her mind was in a bit of a haze. Dream? Reality? Dream? Reality? Which was it?

"Wait, time out," she said as some of the shock began to wear off. "Why are you driving?"

"Because I know where we're going." He searched the area around the wheel for the ignition, without much success. "I thought that'd be pretty obvious."

"Said every man in the history of forever. Have you even driven a car before, Mr. King Kong?"

"Sure, plenty of times. Well . . . I've never driven a regular car before," he said. "Race cars, on the other hand, I've been behind the wheel on more than a few occasions." The SUV roared to life as he turned the key in the ignition.

"So that's pretty much the same thing, I think," she said. Actually, Alice had no idea if that was true or not.

Charlie stared at the Jeep's shifter. He tried to put the car in reverse but overshot it. "I guess I should warn you," he said nonchalantly as he missed again, putting the car back in park, "I wasn't very good at it, but then again"—he missed again, sending the car into neutral—"I wasn't really trying to drive in the conventional sense." Finally, he had the car in reverse. "It was more of a *how horrifically can I crash?* type of thing. It's what you do when you're bored and can't die."

"Oh." Alice put on her seat belt.

On the plus side, if this was real life, it didn't appear that she was going to have to suffer through a long stretch of it. In fact, it looked like she was going to die tonight after all. *Hooray for small favors.*

"Good thing you put on clean underwear, right?" That charming but increasingly irritating smile again, which she caught out of the corner of her eye.

Alice began to mockingly laugh, then suddenly stopped. "How the hell do you know I put on—"

The words in her mouth quickly transformed into a howl of abject terror as Charlie reversed the Jeep, smashing into the car behind them. Without even hesitating, he threw the car in drive and took off down the street, the sound of burning rubber their exit song.

INTO THE WILD

He's not answering."

Charlie held Alice's phone limply in his hand. The third attempt to reach Cartwright had been as unsuccessful as the first two. With a sigh, he dropped the phone into his lap. Charlie wasn't sure whether it was a good idea to call Cartwright or not, but he wasn't exactly drowning in options, either. Mostly, though, he just wanted to know the truth. Actually, he didn't want that—he only wanted Cartwright to be who he'd always been. And if that wasn't the truth . . . ?

He frowned. *Dammit.*

The streetlights lit up Charlie's face in intermittent beats as the Jeep rode steadily through the night. Was it possible that Javrouche was lying about Cartwright not being in the Institute's records? It was nice to think the Inspector had made up the accusation, but ultimately it was bound to be true. Javrouche was vindictive, sure, but he was no fool—if he didn't have the evidence to support the charges, there wasn't a chance he would have made them, no matter how much he hated Charlie.

As for what that all meant, Charlie had no idea. In Charlie's mind, Cartwright was the Institute's ultimate ambassador, the one who had made Charlie a Ferryman to begin with two hundred and fifty long years ago. It seemed completely beyond comprehension that the Institute didn't know who the guy was. There was no way Cartwright could have snuck Charlie in, all the while leading a double life. It just wasn't possible.

Right . . . ?

"So, what now?" Alice asked.

Charlie kept both eyes on the road as his attention turned to the passenger next to him. Despite a few narrow misses and some flagrant traffic violations, she'd given up on getting Charlie to relinquish the driver seat. To be fair, they were currently driving in New Jersey, so traffic laws were more guideline than law anyway.

"First order of business is getting away from your house. If my phone was bugged, they probably know its location from when I dropped in the first time around," he said.

"So we're fleeing the scene of the crime. Interesting. Are we going to be on the lam for a while?"

He could see her looking at him anxiously from the corner of his eye. "I have absolutely no idea what that's supposed to mean."

"You know—fugitives, on the run, pulling a Bonnie-and-Clyde."

Charlie stole a glance at her before returning his attention to the road. "You sound disarmingly excited about that prospect."

It was true. She did appear oddly chipper about the whole thing. If Charlie had to guess, he would have put it down to shock or adrenaline. After all, she had just cheated death, and in rather unconventional style to boot.

"Well," she said, "it's either that or I hysterically lose my shit, which I'm trying desperately hard not to do. But if you don't have a preference—"

"Status quo is fine by me." Charlie made a hard right onto a highway ramp he thought would put him in the right direction. "In response to your question, no—being fugitives is about the last thing I want. We're going to get this sorted out as soon as possible. Regardless of what I may or may not have done, *you* had nothing to do with it, and I intend to make sure that the Ferryman Institute knows that's the case."

It was a plan Charlie was admittedly cobbling together as he went, but even an improvised one was better than nothing. Unfortunately, said plan's success hinged on a meeting with the president of the Institute—a person he had no idea how to find. Still, if—and it was a big if—Charlie could find him, it'd be his best chance at sorting out the tremendous clusterfuck he'd tangled them in. It was a long shot, but crazier things had happened. Exhibit A, everything so far that night.

Even without looking over, he could feel Alice's eyes on him again. "So we're headed where then, exactly? Not for nothing, but I didn't think you could take the Garden State Parkway to the afterlife, though that would explain a lot about the traffic," she said.

A wry expression co-opted his face. "No, but you can take it to New York."

"Hold up. Are you implying that your dead-person tour guide club—"

"That's not even close to what the Ferryman Institute is," Charlie interrupted.

"Fine, whatever," Alice said. "Back to my question. Are you saying your base is in New York?"

"No."

Alice frowned. "So we're heading to New York, then, because why, exactly?"

"Because even if the Ferryman Institute doesn't physically *exist* in New York, there are still ways to enter it from the city.

Without getting into the weeds on this, the Ferryman Institute isn't just this place you can go to. I've been told it's between worlds—this world and the afterlife. Before you even ask, I have no idea what that means in terms of precisely where it is. Parallel dimension or something like that."

Alice didn't reply immediately, instead sitting in silence for several seconds. Then, she said, "Somehow, things are making less sense as this explanation goes on."

"The important thing to understand is that, generally speaking, the only way you can get into the Ferryman Institute is with a special key," Charlie said.

"Like the one you threw at me in my bedroom?"

Charlie sighed. "I didn't throw it at you, I threw it near you. But yes, that key."

"What's stopping you from using that again?" Alice asked.

"I don't have it anymore. That means if we're going to get back, we're going to have to do it another way. There are a series of secret portals the Institute's hidden in various places—sort of like heavily monitored public entrances—and I think there are a few in New York. We just need to find one. After that, it's a simple matter of getting everything straightened out and then everyone can leave happy."

Despite the assurance with which Charlie outlined the plan, he felt none of it, namely because he had no idea if any of his suppositions about Institute public entrances were actually true. He'd heard rumors of the so-called Institute portals, but never in anything approaching an official capacity. Even if they did exist, who knew what—or who—would be waiting on the other side of them. Still, Charlie wasn't exactly swimming in ideas, not to mention the last thing he wanted was to give Alice any more reason to suspect this wasn't the finely honed exit strategy he'd let on. At the very least, New York was an easy place to lie low for a while, Institute access or not.

"Portals. Right," Alice said. She went silent, gazing out the windshield, unblinking. "I swear to God, if the next thing you tell me is that Elvis is alive, I'm leaving through the window."

"Don't worry, he's not." All things considered, she was handling this better than expected. At least, it seemed that way. "Amelia Earhart, on the other hand . . ."

"Shut. Up," she said. "No she's not. You're fucking with me right now."

"Nope, true story," Charlie replied. He was enjoying blowing her mind. Figuratively, of course. "One of the best employees currently at the Institute."

"You're joking."

"From what I hear, she's a great manager. Just don't ask her for directions. She gets a little lost sometimes."

Alice stared at him blankly. "Was that a joke? That was a joke, wasn't it?"

Charlie shrugged, keeping his eyes on the endless supply of repeating white lines on the road ahead of him. "It could have been," he said. "Were you going to laugh?"

"No," she replied. "Hang myself with this seat belt, maybe."

He frowned. "Just the *no* would have sufficed."

Alice croaked a harsh laugh. "Right. Just remember—you're the invincible one here. As a mere mortal, my body can only take so much of the torture that is your sense of humor."

It was a weird situation Charlie found himself in. Usually, he only had to deal with an assignment for a few minutes, tops. With Alice, however, he had no idea what time frame he was looking at. Keeping her happy, not to mention in one piece, felt like a tough ask for even a few hours, particularly as her penchant for sarcasm seemed fueled by the sort of limitless energy source that had thus far eluded scientists. But what if it was days, weeks, maybe? This was uncharted—and mildly terrifying—territory no matter what way he sliced it.

"Can I tell you something, just in the interest of, you know, full disclosure?" Alice said.

He managed to sneak a look in her direction, and in that fleeting moment her eyes looked brilliant, filled with a light that he'd seen tumble out of countless Ferryman Doors. Then it vanished, and he realized that it had only been the reflection of the highway streetlights.

"Sure," Charlie said. "I'm always good for a listen."

"All right." Alice inhaled—*one, two*—then exhaled, almost as if there were an imaginary stethoscope pressed to her chest. "So, just because I decided to tag along with you doesn't mean I'm happy or grateful or anything that you"—she looked out her passenger window quickly before turning back to him—"temporarily postponed the inevitable. I never asked you to, uhh . . . intervene, let's say, so when I decide I've had enough of this little"—she drew a few circles in the air with her index finger—"whatever this *thing* of ours is, that's it. I'm out. You only get to stop me once. *Capisce?*"

Charlie took that moment to mentally reorder his list of priorities vis-à-vis Ms. Alice Spiegel. Needless to say, keeping her happy no longer topped the list.

Keeping her alive, on the other hand . . .

Alice's eyes were studying him again, but when he turned to face her, they were impossible to read in the dark, the streetlight reflections no longer able to reach them. As Charlie looked back to the highway, a small chuckle escaped his lips. It shouldn't have been funny, but given the circumstances, he just couldn't help it. He'd finally rescued someone from the very brink of death itself, and—go figure—she was annoyed at him for it. Evidently he was single-handedly paving the road to hell.

He quietly drew a deep breath and closed his eyes, making sure there was no traffic around him first. Despite her sharp remarks, they meant nothing—the improvised plan was still in effect. In fact, the basic principle of what he was doing was the same as what he normally did with any Ferryman assignment, only this time, he wanted the subject to walk *away* from the light. Hell, when he thought of it like that, the whole thing seemed downright easy.

If only he knew how wrong he'd be.

"I hear you," Charlie replied, "but, also full disclosure, I just might choose to completely ignore you. I can be remarkably selfish sometimes."

Normally, Charlie was a better match for a little inane banter, but his mind continued wandering back to his recent confrontation at the Institute. He promised himself that as soon as he sorted things out with Alice, he would find his team and set things right. Maybe it wasn't even an issue anymore—maybe Melissa had managed to smooth things over in the interim. She did have a knack for that sort of thing.

Well, when she hadn't been electrocuted into unconsciousness, anyway.

Did he feel guilty that he wasn't riding to his team's immediate rescue? Of course he did. Was he worried about them? Very much so. But Charlie knew where his priorities lay. While everyone at the Institute was very much immortal, Alice was very much not.

"Jeez, dude, lighten up a little bit," Alice said. "You look like I just ran over your cat or something."

"In my defense," Charlie said, "you did just tell me you'd prefer being dead over spending time with me. If you're trying to boost my self-esteem, you may want to consider a different strategy."

The start of a tiny grin seemed hidden somewhere in the corner of her lips. "Look, I'm not happy about the fact that I'm still alive, per se, but I'd be lying if I said I wasn't a little curious about where this is heading. I haven't been out of the house much lately. Plus, no offense, but if I really wanted to be dead right now, I've had ample opportunity to roll myself headfirst out of the car."

Charlie looked over at her. He promptly locked the doors.

He could practically hear her eyes rolling in their sockets. "Hilarious. The point, Mr. Fairy Man, is that I didn't expect you to be so sensitive about it. I thought you dealt with dead people all the time. What's one more dead flamed-out failure to you?"

A lone car zipped past them on the left as Charlie gave a short, harsh laugh. "Is that really how you think of yourself?"

"Before you even think of giving me some *It's a Wonderful Life* speech right now, I'd like to remind you that I have a power-lock button on my side, too." The *ker-clunk* of the doors unlocking emphasized her point.

"Duly noted. And yes, I guess you could say I'm a little sensitive when it comes to . . . that sort of thing."

"Apparently," she replied. From the corner of his eye, he could see her playing with the tips of her hair, gaze focused out her passenger window. "So what year were you born?"

The question came as a surprise only because he'd gotten the sense that Alice would prefer the conversation be over with. She was proving to be a very difficult person to read. "Come again?" Charlie asked.

"You mentioned before that you saw *King Kong* when it was in theaters. It doesn't exactly take John Nash to figure out that means you've been around for a while, so I was wondering when you were born. If you were actually born, I guess, and not created in a lab. Or by aliens. Or both."

He gave equal consideration to both dodging the question and laying it on thick, but given her apparently volatile nature, he decided it best to go along. "September twenty-first, 1732."

"Wow," she said. "That's, uh, a few years ago. You don't sound very eighteenth-century-ish."

He laughed at that, the green mile markers ticking by on the side of the road. "Just because I was born then doesn't mean I've warped through time to get here. My speech has evolved along with everyone else's."

"Makes sense. I think. Where were you born?"

The steady rhythm of disappearing and reappearing streetlights bathed the interior of the car. The engine of the car hummed quietly as cruise control kept the speedometer just under seventy. "You've got a lot of questions all of a sudden," he mused.

Alice gave a laugh at that. Charlie noted that it was still of the cynical variety. "One, apparently you know *all* about me, including what underwear I'm wearing right now, so we don't really need to talk about me—"

"Let's not exaggerate too much," Charlie interjected. "I know a few bits and pieces, and the underwear thing was a joke."

"—and two, *I'm* not the mysterious guy with the bulletproof noggin who swears on his grandmother's grave that he's abducting me to quote-unquote 'save me' from a mysterious organization seeking to do terrible, terrible things to me on account of me *not* blowing my brains out. This all seems a few yards to the left of patently outrageous, so if it weren't for the fact that it *really* looked like I shot you before, I don't think I'd believe you. However, since that did happen, and loath as I am to admit it, I'm also a little scared, so the less we're sitting here in silence, the better. That work for you, Superman?"

Evidently it was his turn to be surprised by her honesty.

"Boston," he said, repaying that belief in kind. "I was born in Boston, but left for London on my seventeenth birthday. I hopped aboard a whaler out of Howland Dock almost as soon as I set foot in England, stayed there for twelve years, then went on my last expedition in 1762."

"Really? You were a sailor?"

He raised an eyebrow. "Is that so surprising?"

"I don't know . . . maybe? You don't look manly enough to be a sailor." Charlie scowled, but she continued unabated. "So you were a sailor. Why'd you stop? Get tired of it?"

Suddenly, he was beginning to get the feeling that Alice was having a little too much fun with this. Not that he minded, necessarily—it was better than her fighting him every step of the way—but he did find it slightly disconcerting that she abruptly seemed such a willing participant in their newfound adventure. Then again, her actions hadn't followed any predictable pattern up to that point, so maybe this was the new normal.

"No," Charlie said, leaning back into his seat, "because that's when I became a Ferryman."

"Ohhh, how mysterious. And how did you 'become' a Ferryman, exactly?"

Charlie felt his lips tug into an uncomfortable line as he fought off a knee-jerk reaction to grimace. "Long story," he replied.

Alice tapped the plastic clock in the middle of the console. "I'm assuming you're going to take the Lincoln Tunnel, whether you know it or not, and we've got about thirty minutes until we get there. How about you try me? I'm a good listener, too."

There was a tone of hopefulness in her voice that Charlie found surprising. Be that as it may, it didn't seem right to be sharing so much about himself—that just wasn't how things worked. It was his job to know about his subjects. Having the roles reversed just didn't feel right.

"I'm not a big fan of bringing up the past," Charlie said.

"And I'm not a big fan of being kidnapped by immortal strangers, but beggars can't be choosers, I guess. I think I'm owed this story."

"You really want to know, huh?"

"No, me and all my other Ferryman friends were just talking about it the other day. Of course I want to know. Come on, keep your hostage happy, Charlie."

Charlie. It was, he realized, the first time she'd used his name. Whether that was a good thing or not, he had no idea. It also occurred to Charlie that only one other person knew that particular story—the same person who was presently and inconveniently not answering his phone.

With a final, drawn-out sigh that signaled his admission of defeat, Charlie began. "It happened on what was supposed to be my last whaling expedition . . ."

WHITE WHALE

W e've lost the mizzenmast!"

The explosive cracking of the timber was all but lost in the roar of the tempest, the rain splattering across the deck in a near-impenetrable curtain. Massive waves barraged the deck, rolling over the ship with such force that they'd already claimed the lives of two sailors who couldn't find purchase anywhere before being carried off into the sea. The wind swirled and danced like a vengeful Roma, blasting into the sails of the foremast and mainmast until they snapped at their riggings, the cloth pulling taut with explosive snaps that rang out like musket fire.

The crew was working in nearly impossible conditions to bring the sails in, having already lost the third sail. The mizzenmast had snapped about halfway up its length, sending it careening down into the black void of the ocean.

The *Canterbury* had been caught off guard by the sudden turn in the winter weather. Though the clouds had been ominously gathering in the distance, the captain, Barnabas Shipley, had decided to press onward, convinced they could outpace it in the middle of the Atlantic. During the night, however, the storm had arrived, an assassin in the dark.

The foremast rigging had been secured, and the mainmast was just about there. The first mate, Crowley, threw his voice into the raging gusts. "Come on, Dawson, ye whoreson dog! Get that knot tied!"

Charles's legs had gone numb minutes ago—he was using all the strength he could muster to keep his body wrapped around the spar. His fingers, also moving without feeling, fumbled with the ends of the rope. Even with his eyes well adjusted to the darkness, the lashing rain made seeing a difficult prospect. He just needed to tighten the last knot, and the sail would be secure.

As his fingers moved with automatic precision, his thoughts drifted back to London, back to home. He could hear Crowley bellowing below, but another gust of wind carried the words far across the ocean waves. Charles liked the first mate; tough, crass, and fiercely loyal, the man had more than proved his worth aboard the vessel. Captain Shipley, on the other hand . . .

"Dawson!" boomed Crowley's voice.

With a final, fierce tug, Charles finished the knot. "It's done!" he cried. A rogue wave—nearly impossible to spot in the gloom of night—slammed into the side and set the ship shuddering. Charles nearly lost his grip as the ship rolled slightly to starboard, but he held on. He waited for the whaler to right itself before clambering down into the netting. The ropes were slick with freezing spray, and Charles struggled to get any solid hold as he descended. Carefully but gracefully, he worked his way down until the deck floorboards were underneath him once more.

"There's a good lad!" roared Crowley. His voice went silent as another gaping wave rolled across the face of the ship, knocking men off their feet and sending others scrambling. When the water had slid off the sides of the deck, it was Crowley's laughter that broke through the fury around them. "Well now, who fancies a voyage with Davy Jones tonight, eh?! Which one of you devilish lot brought this cursed storm upon us?! Come now, I'll have no liars!"

The ship's carpenter, Stevens, yelled over the bedlam: "You should check with your own son-in-law first—perhaps he hasn't been treating your precious flower as delicately as you would!"

Charles, exhausted from the battering he'd taken having been exposed to the full brunt of the storm, still managed a wry grin. "You're an evil man, Mr. Stevens, casting me into the fire like that! Isn't having our esteemed first mate as a father-in-law punishment enough?!" Gallows humor at its finest, he noted miserably, but both Crowley and Stevens found the gem of laughter in it as well.

Elizabeth had appeared in Charles's life five years ago, when he'd made port at Howland Dock after another successful expedition. When he first laid eyes on her, she was standing nervously by herself, waiting patiently in a dress too fine to blend in with the chaotic rabble of merchant vessels. He watched her closely from aboard the *Manitoba*, his heart slowly being reeled in by her gentle beauty. Finally, as he departed the ship, Charles worked up the courage to approach her.

"Excuse me, miss? Are you lost? I couldn't help but notice that you look a bit out of place here," he'd said, with the best manners he could manage after several months at sea. The compliment was implied.

She smiled at him warmly—a smile that immediately crystalized in Charles's memory, bound to be remembered for centuries to come—and said, "I couldn't help but notice the same of you. You look a bit sissy to be a sailor."

It was not the way Charles planned on starting a bright and wonderful romance, but so it was.

After a dutiful combination of persistence and dry sarcasm, he managed to convince her to meet several days later. When he'd arrived at her house, he quickly figured out why she'd been waiting at the dock earlier that week. Standing outside, dressed exponentially more elegantly than he'd ever been on the ship, was Oliver Crowley, the first mate of the *Manitoba*.

Despite every misgiving Charles had upon laying eyes on Crowley's hulking form that day, he learned quickly that Elizabeth was as witty as her father was boorish—a trait Charles found wildly endearing. The courtship proceeded smoothly, and a year and a half later, the two were wed. Charles took up work as an apprentice cartographer, pursuing his fascination with maps, and the two lived happily for several years. They'd been unable to conceive a child, but it was something they were working at, God bless them.

Except it was never to be.

One day, Charles's father-in-law came around looking for a competent ship hand to complete the ranks of a new vessel, the *Canterbury*, which was preparing to set sail for the Atlantic. Elizabeth pleaded with her husband not to go, repeatedly stating she had a bad feeling about the business. Her father could shove off, for all she cared. However, Charles knew something she didn't. Around the shop, he'd gotten wind that Mr. Crowley had placed a rather sizable investment in a ship—the *Lady Lucifer*—that had disappeared somewhere off the Cape of Good Hope. Though Crowley would never openly admit it, the man was desperate for work. If he couldn't fill the crew of the *Canterbury*, there'd be no expedition, as it was late in the season to be whaling already. Charles couldn't turn him down.

Now, however, with the fierce gale cutting the ship into pieces, he desperately wished he'd listened to his wife.

"If I didn't need the pair of you scullies to see to it that this ship doesn't carry us all straight to hell, I'd throw you o'erboard myself!" barked Crowley. "Now get below deck, both of you—no reason to make any more widows tonight!"

With narrowed eyes, Charles surveyed the deck. "Where's Shipley?!" he yelled over the wind.

Crowley said nothing initially, instead looking at Stevens. "Our gallant captain," he finally said, "has decided his expertise is best served from his cabin. I have been left in complete command until the end of this 'mild weather.'"

Stevens spit on the deck. "If this is mild weather, then I'm the bloody Prince of Wales. A pox to the bastard!"

"We'll see it through, God willing. Keep your wits about you and your sinful thoughts far from your heart."

"Aye," Charles said. Crowley lifted the door for the two to go down. "Wise men first!" Charles yelled to Stevens, even though he was standing mere feet away from him.

"A true gentleman you are, Dawson. Wish I could say the same about your father-in-law!" the old carpenter called back as he ducked below the ship's deck. Charles laughed and looked over to see Crowley's reaction.

Instead of the first mate's squat face, he was greeted with a wall of black water.

The wave pounded Charles into the wooden floorboards as his body was swept across the deck. For an eternal few seconds, he tumbled underwater until he slammed into the ornate railing. His back cried in pain as the hard wood abruptly stopped him. His hands flailed in the darkness, grasping for anything to hold on to, but his already depleted fingers slid over everything they managed to touch.

Suddenly, he was weightless.

A firm tug on his arm nearly tore it out of his socket, but it arrested his fall. Finally given a second to catch his bearings, Charles realized he'd been flung over the rail on the complete opposite side of the ship. It was only a tremendous grip that was keeping the ship hand from plunging into the frigid water below.

"Hold on now, I've got ye, I've got ye!" Crowley yelled as he held on to Charles's left wrist with one hand. His other hand, wrenched around the back of a nearby cannon, was the only thing keeping the two from barreling into the sea. From between the banisters in the rail, Charles could make out Stevens and another man, Dawkins, racing up from below deck.

Charles said nothing—his feet pawed at the side of the ship as he tried to find some sort of purchase to propel himself back up. He looked up desperately into Crowley's eyes, each one standing out against the vivid darkness of the storm. Stevens wrapped his arms around Crowley's waist and tried to pull him back, bringing Charles up as well, but with no surface to steady him and the ship rolling to and fro, Stevens only managed to stabilize the first mate. Dawkins raced to an errant rope that was dangling over the side and worked to rein it in.

The feeling had left Charles's hand long ago. His strength was already gone. Unless someone could pull him up, he realized, he was done for.

"Don't you dare let go, Dawson! For the love of God almighty, *don't you dare let go!*" Crowley bellowed down at him. Dawkins was rushing back with the rope, preparing to fling it overboard.

The wave smashed into the side of the ship and plucked Charles from his dangling position in midair. His body receded with the wave, back into the ocean. The sheer intensity of the freezing water stole the air from his lungs and ripped like knives at his skin. A newfound instinct to survive coursed through Charles's body, and he kicked with all his might until he breached the surface. He whirled around, looking for the giant whaler fighting through the sea. The oppressive rain made it difficult to see anything. After a few seconds, he spotted its hulking shape behind him, perhaps a hundred yards away—the current must have whisked him off. A half dozen or so small lights emerged across the deck, the lanterns flitting like fireflies as ship hands searched for Charles in the sea.

Despite the burning in his arms, he rallied his limbs, and with stroke after well-practiced stroke, he powered toward the ship. He wasn't the best swimmer on the crew, but he was no slouch, either. The fire in his muscles was slowly being replaced by a deadly numbness, but still Charles drove on.

He swam without stopping, his mind only daring to think of his next stroke. After what felt like five minutes, he moved to tread water, hoping that he wouldn't have to go much farther to get into range of the *Canterbury*'s ropes. He looked up.

The ship was a fraction of its size, the lantern lights now floating like distant embers as Charles found himself even farther away than he had been only moments ago.

He knew it now in his heart: he was a dead man. It wouldn't be long before his limbs would lose what remaining strength they had in the frigid water. His head would sink below the waves, his last breath fighting to last endlessly. He would drown soon after, another sacrifice to Davy Jones.

He was utterly alone. Inside his head, his teeth chattered uncontrollably.

A glint of bright white light flashed in his periphery. His stiff limbs struggled to turn his body in its direction within the violent current. With a final effort, he managed to swing his body around to find the source, hoping it might be an unseen ship nearby. But as he finally came around, Charles gasped, inhaling a mouth of seawater instead.

Sitting in front of him, floating in midair above the waves, was a door. The entrance opened to an almost blindingly white hallway beyond, and what looked to be another door far off in the distance. A grinning man was perched in the entrance, his legs dangling just beyond the tips of the waves. He sat, absentmindedly stroking the Vandyke beard below his slightly curved mustache. He seemed like a man borne out of the past, but given the circumstances of his appearance, it was hardly the least peculiar aspect of the situation.

I'm either dead already or I've swallowed too much water, Charles thought.

He was so stunned that, for a moment, he forgot to speak. Almost immediately, though, he regained his senses and yelled, "Help me! Please!"

The man's eyebrows arched dramatically at the sound of Charles's voice. "What ho, good fellow! Can you truly see me?"

"Yes!" Charles's head was plunged under a wave. His clothes were getting heavier by the second. He popped back up sputtering. "I don't know who you are, but for the love of God, please, help me!"

The man clapped in delight. "Marvelous! I suspected you had something special about you, and it would appear my suspicion has been proved correct. Unfortunately, I must ask in the name of complete diligence: You are not presently deceased just yet, are you?"

Another rough wave rolled over Charles's head, but he fought against it. "No, but if you don't do something, I will be!"

The man checked a pocket watch, then laughed quietly, or at least it looked that way—it was tough for Charles to hear over the roar of the ocean. Yet much to his surprise, he had no trouble discerning the man's next words. "Very well. My name is William Henry Taylor Cartwright the Fourth, though Cartwright will do well enough, and I am a Ferryman—an attendant to the souls of the departed. It is entirely possible for me to preserve your life, Charles Ronald Dawson, but it will not come without a price."

"Help—!" Charles began, but his words were cut off as water poured into his mouth, the rest of his statement reduced to a fit of coughing and sputtering.

The man stood up in the doorway. Despite Charles's struggles, he continued his explanation unabated. "Immortality for your service to the Ferryman Institute. That is the covenant I offer. But I warn you, sir. This gift should not be accepted if you possess even the slightest of doubts about this opportunity. You will work until the Institute deems it sufficient. Nevertheless, I proffer you this choice, to guide the spirits of this world to their next life. Do you accept?"

Charles tried to answer, but couldn't get his mouth above the waves. His arms lethargically pushed through the water as he willed them for one last thrust. He didn't want to die—he couldn't. He was so young, his life was so promising, there was so much to do . . .

"Do you accept?!" roared Cartwright, his eyes glittering with excitement.

Charles's head sank below the water. There, swallowed as he was by the ocean, he saw Elizabeth. Her smile. Her eyes. Heard her laugh, whispering like traces of moonlight. Felt her lips, teasing his neck. Saw her as no one had or would ever see her, as only a man on the brink of death can.

He needed to see her again. If that meant following this stranger into something Charles still didn't quite believe, then so be it. Whatever it took.

With one last agonizing push, Charles threw his body above the churning sea.

"*Yes!*" he cried before his body sank again below the surface.

He had lost all of his strength. The ocean had stolen it, replacing it with a paralyzing cold that seeped into every pore of his body. The surface slowly floated away from him, the cacophony of the storm muted beneath the calm water. He drifted downward, slowly, slowly downward toward the bottom of the sea.

Without warning, a strange sensation rippled through his body. The iciness disappeared from his limbs. His lungs, which moments ago had burned with the agony of a man on his last breath, suddenly ceased to ache. Energy flooded back into his arms and legs.

He was alive.

With a few powerful strokes, he rose above the surface again, cresting it with ease. The water no longer bothered him, nor did the wayward gulps of seawater send him into coughing fits. The look on Charles's face must have betrayed his thoughts, as Cartwright unexpectedly burst into laughter.

"Surprised?" said the man.

Charles's stunned silence spoke for him.

"Come," Cartwright said, offering his hand to the still treading sailor. "A whole new world has just been opened to you."

Charles grabbed it and was pulled up beyond the threshold of the floating door. Cartwright closed the door to the violent ocean, and with a small click, the roaring noise disappeared. The pair stood in a perfectly blank hallway, its walls and ceilings so devoid of anything that it was impossible to tell where one ended and the other began. Across from the entranceway Charles had just been pulled through—the one that had moments ago been suspended above the Atlantic—was another door, squat in shape and dull brown in color with a surface marred by scratches and nicks. A small plaque sat affixed to the center of it.

Charles surveyed his new surroundings, and came to the rational conclusion that absolutely nothing going on made any sense whatsoever. "I don't understand," he said.

There was a faint air of amusement to Cartwright's expression, or at least that's what Charles thought. "Shall we start with a question in particular, then, and proceed from there?" Cartwright asked.

"I'm alive," Charles replied.

Cartwright laughed. "So you are, even if that wasn't a question in the literal sense."

His heart raced at the idea that somehow, in the most unbelievable circumstances, he'd cheated death. Or had he? Was this all a dream, or perhaps the beginning of the afterlife in its own right? Charles rubbed his face. He could feel his fingers kneading into his flesh, yet as he pressed harder and harder, he experienced no discomfort. With two fingers, he pinched the skin on the back of his hand. Nothing.

"I don't feel any pain," he said. The thought was both exhilarating and terrifying.

"Nor should you," Cartwright said as he took a step toward the far door. "You're a Ferryman now. That is one of the many benefactions granted to us, immortality being another, as you can clearly see. Now, if you'll follow me to—"

But before he could take another step, Charles grabbed him by the arm. "My wife. I need to see her."

As the words reached Cartwright's ears, the vague glow of humor disappeared from his face. "Your wife?" he asked.

"Yes! Elizabeth Dawson. I have to let her know I'm alive. When can I see her? It has to be soon—if we wait too long, she'll assume the worst. I can't do that to her."

"I'm afraid . . ." Cartwright paused, deliberately averting his gaze. "I'm afraid I have some bad news for you."

"You have . . . bad news? What of it? Is she hurt? Sick?"

"Good heavens, no. At least, not so far as I know. Now, where to start . . . You see, Charles—may I call you Charles?—a Ferryman is rather special. We are neither living nor dead—not completely man, not completely spirit. Ferrymen exist between worlds, acting as guides to show the recently passed to their next life. Do you understand?"

"No," Charles said, "not at all."

Cartwright ran his fingers through his mustache. "Well, I certainly appreciate the honesty. What it means, my good man, is that this life—this new life—is no extension of your past one. There are rules, I'm afraid—rules we must abide lest we bring about the end of mankind."

"What are you saying, sir?"

Cartwright hesitated, and as the silence stretched from one beat, to two, then three, Charles loosened his grip. He sensed what was coming next, before Cartwright even said it.

A pained expression lurched across Cartwright's face. "I'm saying you cannot go back to her, Charles. I'm truly sorry."

"No . . . ," Charles said, his hand falling to his side. "I thought . . . No, but you saved me. Why am I still here if not to see Elizabeth?" He shook his head. "You're mistaken, sir. This place you speak of will understand my cause. I'm sure of it."

Cartwright put his hands on both of Charles's shoulders, grasping them tight. "They may very well—love is indeed our noblest and purest pursuit. And I do not mean to suggest you will never see your wife again. Do not lose that hope. However, that you are here evinces that you have been called to serve a higher cause." Slowly, he released his grip, turning one hand behind Charles's back to better lead him toward the battered brown door.

"Do you say true?" Charles asked.

"Humility aside for a moment, I am skilled at many things, Charles. I do not place lying on that list. But there will be time to discuss everything. For now, let me say this . . ." As they arrived at the door at the far end of the hall, Cartwright slowly wrapped his fingers around the handle. The fascinating glimmer in his eyes had returned, his gaze fixed on Charles.

"Welcome to the Ferryman Institute." Cartwright swung the door open.

Though Charles certainly felt overwhelmed not only by what but also by how fast everything was happening, he couldn't deny that there was something that felt incredibly *right* just then. It was as if his previous life had been a droning chord hampered by one note faintly out of key, but now—now, with the door open—it was finally ringing true. For that moment, his sense of loss melted away, replaced by something entirely unlike anything he'd ever felt before—like this door had been waiting for him, and him alone, to arrive.

Without a word, Charles followed Cartwright's footsteps, and the two of them entered the Ferryman Institute.

BAD COP, BAD COP

ssr. Dupine," Javrouche began, "you appear to be a reasonable man. Can I ask—what on earth possessed you to push Mssr. Dawson through that door?"

The navigator wriggled against the taut rope that held him in place, but found it devoid of even the slightest bit of slack. That was intended, of course—his wrists, upper arms, thighs, and ankles were tied fast against the steel chair. Aside from a bandana tied across his eyes and the rope, however, he was completely naked. The Inspector had arranged for that as well.

"You do realize that we now have to classify your partner as a magnitude-zero threat: a Ferryman, believed to be a traitor, location unknown. It doesn't get worse than that, I'm afraid. Given this development, I hope you can understand that time is a commodity I can ill afford to squander. I need answers, Mssr. Dupine, and quickly."

When Dirkley made no effort to reply—whether out of defiance or sheer terror, Javrouche couldn't say—the Inspector sighed dramatically. "Talkative one, aren't you? Remove his blindfold, Koroviev."

The blindfold was taken away, revealing just what Javrouche

had planned for Charlie Dawson's navigator. The chair hung about fifty feet in the air, suspended above a giant vat filled with a perfectly clear liquid. The vat itself was easily twelve feet tall, with an inner lining composed of one smooth and continuous metal surface. Underneath the blindfold, Javrouche had attached a device that forced both of Dirkley's eyes open at all times. It looked similar to an eyelash curler, only one invented by the Spanish Inquisition.

"A nice-looking bath, don't you think? I'd heard rumors that you've been neglecting to clean behind your ears. Fear not, Mssr. Dupine—I won't allow you to fall victim to poor hygiene. Cleanliness is next to godliness, after all." Javrouche slapped the side of the vat several times, each reverberation of the dull metal echoing loudly in the large room. "Although I suppose it's worth pointing out that the liquid inside this vat isn't water. I figured we needed a cleaning agent with a bit more *oomph* to it."

From a personal standpoint, Javrouche had nothing against the navigator, aside from his close association with Dawson, at least. He was a quiet, unassuming man who'd earned high marks in all of his performance reviews. Unfortunately, he now held information Javrouche needed. With the Institute's security at risk, dehumanizing insults were the tip of the iceberg.

The Inspector stared fiercely into the unblinking eyes of Dirkley Dupine, but still the navigator remained silent. "Koroviev, am I correct in saying that we didn't tie down Mssr. Dupine's tongue?"

An old catwalk hung near the massive ceiling in the room, snaking its way around most of the warehouse. From the area near Dirkley's chair, the lieutenant poked his head over the rail. "That's correct, sir."

Javrouche nodded thoughtfully at that. "I thought so. Can you think of any other reason why our good friend Mssr. Dupine has suddenly gone mute? Some rare Ferryman-specific disorder that I might be overlooking? Or perhaps he's so terrified that he's evacuated his vocal cords out his bowels?"

There was a brief pause while the Russian lieutenant evidently considered the Inspector's question. "I don't think that's possible, sir."

"I didn't think so, either. In that case, there are two ways we can play this, Mssr. Dupine. You can tell me everything you know about our current predicament—your details on Mlle. Alice Spiegel, why Mssr. Dawson saved her, where they're headed, so on and so forth—or I can explain to you not only what you happen to be suspended above, but why you are suspended above it."

Dirkley stirred in his seat, then, half whimpering, said, "I don't know. I'm sorry, but I don't know anything."

The Inspector shook his head in disappointment. He'd hoped to avoid this part of the game, but such was life. "You don't know. Of course you don't. No one in that chair ever does." Javrouche made a signal, and with a sudden, awkward lurch, the chair began to descend.

The navigator didn't appear to like this new development very much. "Honestly, I don't know!" he shouted, panic woven into his voice.

"*Honestly*, Mssr. Dupine? Why *honestly*? Were you lying to me before?" The words came sweetly from Javrouche's mouth, his face fixed with a look of interest as the navigator sank lower and lower.

"N-n-no! I don't know!" Dirkley yelled again.

With another wave of Javrouche's hand, the chair came to an immediate stop. It swayed gently back and forth, creaking mildly with each small swing.

Javrouche had been many things in his former life—he simply had to be, given the poverty he'd been born into. Yet, ironically enough, the skills that had been his greatest asset as the Institute's police authority all were acquired from his time as a thief. His ability to read people—the drunken baker, the violent constable, the naive bourgeois girls—was a hard-won talent that had saved his life on more than one occasion. He trusted it intrinsically. And there, standing beneath the cowering form of Dupine, it told him the navigator was telling the truth.

Logically, however, that made no sense. Dupine had to know—the alternative was unconscionable. Right now, he was Javrouche's only lead, and the farther away that Dawson got from Alice Spiegel's bedroom, the harder he would be to track down. There were answers Javrouche needed, and he needed them immediately.

"So option number two it is, then. Now, I know what you're thinking—what could I possibly do to torture you? We can't feel pain, after all. I could proceed with a form of mental torture, but I'm in a bit of a hurry. Answers, Mssr. Dupine—that is the magic word. That being the case, I've prepared something unique to immortals. Consider it a Ferryman original.

"The vat you happen to be hanging precariously above is filled with one of the most corrosive substances known to man— hydrofluoric acid. It penetrates the tissue, enters the bloodstream, and from there, it can wreak all kinds of havoc, including cardiac arrest. But that's of no concern to immortals like us. However, hydrofluoric acid is unique in that it is an incredibly penetrative substance. It will seep deep, deep into your tissue. From there, the fluoride cations mix with the calcium in your bones, which causes the calcium to dissociate. Do you know what the means?" Javrouche didn't wait for an answer. "It essentially means your bones slowly liquefy inside you. Then it's only a matter of time before the rest of your body follows suit. You will, in essence, melt."

Javrouche signaled again with his hand, and with a sudden jerk, the chair Dupine was helplessly strapped into once again teetered downward. His feet dangled just above the fluid line of the vat.

"Imagine that, Mssr. Dupine—what it must be like to watch yourself simply dissolve into a glorified puddle. I've heard it can be quite psychologically scarring. What's worse, though, is what happens after your head is submerged and your eyes begin to liquefy into soup. After that, everything goes black. No sight, no sound, not even the feel of your own body—just you and your thoughts. That is how you will remain until we drain the vat and the magic of the Institute begins to reassemble you. However, if your answers remain, shall we say, unenlightening, then there's a chance 'until we drain the vat' becomes '*if* we drain the vat.' A month is an agonizingly long time to be left alone with only your thoughts to keep you company. Now imagine that, but over a quarter of a century."

It was a mostly empty threat, whether Dupine knew it or not. Even stretching his expanded authority in emergency situations to its absolute limit, Javrouche had no authorization to do that. The acid bath was, by and large, a big show. If a subject was going to talk, they'd start soon after their big toes began dribbling away, if not well before.

Yet these were extraordinary times. There was a growing voice in the Inspector's mind that was preaching to do whatever it took to protect the Ferryman Institute—authorized or not.

Dupine squirmed anxiously in his bonds. Javrouche would have bet the navigator's eyes would have been just as wide without their restraints.

"I—" Dirkley croaked. "I told you I don't know. It was a special assignment. I wasn't . . ." He swallowed hard, an action that didn't escape the Inspector's attention. "I was at the library when it came in. I only joined the case when it was in progress. I–I don't have any notes. I didn't even know the subject's name until you said it. I swear it. I don't know where Charlie is right now. Please believe me."

Javrouche frowned. He began pacing beneath the hanging navigator. "Really? You have *no* idea what's going on?"

Dupine shook his head violently.

Javrouche could feel his patience evaporating. "Koroviev, bring out Mme. Johnson, please."

The Inspector had suspected early on that while Dupine might shrink away from threats, he wouldn't bend to them—that was clear enough given his act of self-sacrifice for Dawson earlier. However, what if the Inspector turned that selflessness against the navigator?

There was the clanking of chains as another seat slowly began to lower from the ceiling. Melissa Johnson sat in an identical metallic chair, bound in almost exactly the same fashion as Dupine. The only additional measure to her restraints was a simple gag placed in her mouth. She struggled ferociously against her bonds as she descended. The Inspector watched with a detached ambivalence as Dupine renewed his own struggle against the ropes.

"You wouldn't," he said with a mix of seething rage and abject horror.

It was exactly the reaction Javrouche had been hoping for. Now all there was left to do was turn the screw. "You give me too much credit, Mssr. Dupine. Call me barbaric, but with Mssr. Dawson's disappearance and therefore the continued existence of mankind hanging in the balance, I hope you'll forgive me for not giving a shit."

He stood directly in front of Dupine and stared into his eyes. "In my former life, I had a child. A son. His name was Henri, the son of a whore I'd paid to sleep with me using what little money I had. Unfortunately for her, giving birth to that boy was the last thing she ever did. I don't even know if he was mine, but I took him in for reasons I will never quite understand. You have to remember, Mssr. Dupine—in addition to his questionable paternal lineage, there was the very practical matter of barely being able to support myself at the time. But despite it all, I came to love that boy. He was my son."

For a moment, Javrouche fell backward in time, slipping into memories long forgotten. There they stood, side by side, backs pressed against the bakery wall, smiling despite their meager shelter from the deluge blanketing the back alleys of Paris. His son was laughing—something to do with the monkeys they'd just seen at the Jardin des Plantes zoo for his birthday—the large birthmark on his cheek standing out despite the mud smeared across his face. Their bellies were full—a welcome change—and the air was warm even with the rain. It felt like, for once, the universe had decided to briefly smile on them.

Then the memory slid through his grasp, an ethereal strand of silk too fine for him to hold for more than an instant, and disappeared.

Melissa's chair lowered steadily, the *clink* and *clank* of its chains filling the momentary silence that had ensued. Slowly, the Inspector picked up his words again.

"And do you know what that boy made me realize, Mssr. Dupine? That sometimes you need to use whatever means necessary to protect something you love. My son is gone now, has been for too long. This place is all I have left. And unlike with my son, I plan to do whatever is necessary to save it."

The acerbic tone had fallen away, his voice strangely quiet. For a time he said nothing, shrouding himself instead in introspective silence while a fighting Melissa was lowered down until her chair was aligned evenly with Dupine's.

"As you can see, Mssr. Dupine, your manager is in as much trouble as you are. Now, here's what's going to happen. I will be back in ten minutes. If you haven't come up with a better answer to my questions by then, I will leave it to my friend Koroviev to demonstrate all those wonderful things I explained to you on Mme. Johnson. And you will watch every single second of it. Mssr. Dawson has already cost me one dear thing in my life. I won't allow him to do it again."

The Inspector was already walking out of the room, the *tap tap* of his feet muffled by the shabby concrete floor. When he reached the exit, he stopped. Slowly, he turned, his expression blank. "Whatever it takes, Mssr. Dupine. Whatever it takes."

He left the room, played out by the familiar clanking sound of Melissa's chair slowly beginning to drop.

UNDER ORDERS

Begemot Koroviev walked briskly down the hall with the file under his arm. The sound of the metal chairs clanking loudly as they finally reached the bottom of the acid-filled vat followed his footsteps, echoing dully against the concrete passageway. He had tidied up a few other loose ends while he was at it, just to be safe.

Suddenly, his cell phone sprang to life. He didn't bother looking at the caller ID—he had a very good idea who it was.

"Koroviev," he stated. He listened intently, his footsteps never wavering, as the voice on the other end talked quietly and quickly. "It's been taken care of. Yes, both of them. That's right . . . Yes. Yes, I passed on the information to the Inspector. He's acting on it now while I head back to coordinate . . . I understand. Thank you, Cartwright."

Koroviev ended the call. The door at the end of the warehouse hallway creaked as he pushed it open and walked out into the night air. It had been some time since he'd been outside the Institute's walls—long enough that he couldn't quite remember when his last visit had been. Perhaps that was why the stars seemed so bright just then, glittering so shamelessly above. He longed to stay just a few minutes more, but there was work to be done, unfortunately.

He sighed. It was going to be a long, eventful evening.

LEARNING THINGS

ow. That's . . . Wow," Alice said. She had breath-lessly listened to Charlie's story, and now that he was finished, she didn't have the faintest idea what to else say.

Apparently, he didn't either. "Yeah" was his only reply before lapsing into silence. She looked over at him, but he continued to stare out the windshield as he guided the Jeep along. She could practically see in his long-gone stare how far away his mind was then, his dry sense of humor buried by the mess he'd made digging up the past. What thoughts were tumbling around behind those green eyes of his? What mix of emotions had she just stirred awake? And, perhaps most surprisingly to her, why did she feel so bad now about asking him? Maybe it was early-onset Stockholm syndrome, if that was such a thing.

"I had no idea that you died," she finally said. "Well, sort of. Mostly, maybe? It's kind of like that part in *The Princess Bride*—have you ever seen that movie? *He's mostly dead!* Do you know what I'm talking about?"

Alice knew she was rambling, just like she always did when the silence became too stifling for her to bear. He looked over at her with a sidelong glance, his lips curling just a touch, then returned his gaze to the road ahead.

"So you were married, huh?" Alice said, barreling on. "Can't say I saw that one coming. I had you pegged as bachelor material."

Charlie didn't react initially, but eventually he gave her an indifferent shrug. "It was a very long time ago. I've changed a lot since then, I'm sure."

The silence began to creep back in, but Alice was loath to let it take hold. "Did you ever see her again? Your wife, I mean. After you became a Ferryman."

"No," he said harshly. Alice was slightly taken aback, and evidently Charlie was as well. "I wasn't allowed to," he quickly added. "Deliberately visiting friends or loved ones as a Ferryman is considered one of the three gravest offenses of the Institute. Treason, basically. We have to protect the secret of our existence at all costs, which is why they're coming after you."

Ah. Well, that explained it—Alice had become the not-at-all-clichéd *girl who knew too much and must be eliminated*. While that would have been a stark revelation a very short time ago, she currently found herself more concerned with Charlie's past. Namely, one aspect in particular.

"So even though you agreed to become a Ferryman so you could see her again . . ." She left the thought unfinished.

The remark brought a cynical shape to Charlie's face. "I was young and stupid back then. Naive. They told me I couldn't see her, and I listened, but I continued to dumbly believe that destiny would bring us back together somehow . . . two star-crossed lovers whose bond was so strong even death couldn't break it apart, or something like that. But I never saw her again. I asked around, but never heard a word about my wife from anyone else at the Institute. To this day, I still have no idea what happened to her after I became a Ferryman."

Alice leaned forward in her seat. "Wait, you never found out what happened to her?"

"No," Charlie said, "and it haunted me for a long time. I tried to convince myself that there was nothing I could do. It's much easier to accept the regrets of your life when you believe the outcome was already written. Except that's not how the world works—at least it hasn't for me—and I've only recently come to see that. Sometimes, you just have to fight for the things you believe in. Given the chance today, I would break that rule in a heartbeat. But I don't have any friends or loved ones from my old life to see now . . . and I haven't for a while. It's just me."

Alice once again found herself at a loss for words. It seemed there was quite a bit more to the man than she'd originally allowed for, and she wasn't quite sure how to feel about that realization. After running through a laundry list of responses in her head, she settled on the only one she found appropriate for the situation. "I'm so sorry," she said quietly. "I can't imagine what that must be like."

Her words seemed to bring the Ferryman back from himself. He drew a deep breath, and forcefully exhaled. "Don't be," he said. "In fact, if there's anyone who should be apologizing, it's me. I didn't intend on turning what was otherwise a wonderfully upbeat car ride into the last half hour of *Titanic*."

Alice felt a smirk brush across her lips. "Look at you. An old geezer at two hundred and however many years old and you're rattling off pop-culture references like they're going out of style. Color me impressed." Alice considered changing the topic, but his relating of his past had stirred up one last question in her mind, one begging to be asked.

"Do you miss her?" she asked.

She wasn't sure why she felt comfortable asking him, of all people—it wasn't the type of question you generally asked someone you hardly knew—and yet, the way he'd spoken about his own life moments ago, she had the sense that maybe she was asking for him as well.

He laughed, though Alice had a hunch it was more to himself than anything else. "You can't possibly enjoy talking about depressing stuff this much."

"Your thinly veiled attempt at avoiding the question is noted. Your hostage is displeased."

Charlie sighed. "I'll answer the question, but only on the condition that you stop referring to yourself as my hostage."

Alice made a show of thinking about it before answering. "Deal."

His eyes seemed to focus farther down the road. "Do I miss her?" Charlie said. "The idea of her, yes. But do I miss *her*? That's a tougher question. Honestly, I feel like I don't even remember her. I can't picture her face anymore. It drives me crazy sometimes when I sit and really try to see it in my mind. It's like . . . I can only remember certain things about her. She had these vivid, green eyes—almost the same color as mine, but a million times more beautiful. I used to joke about that. I told her that's why we fell in love, because really, when we looked into each other's eyes, we were just looking at ourselves."

"Like the story of Narcissus and the lake," Alice said. Before she could do anything, the words were out of her mouth. Almost immediately, though, she realized he might take that the wrong way. *Good one, Alice. Call your invincible kidnapper a narcissist.*

However, he seemed pleasantly surprised by the observation, given the excitement in his voice that sprouted in its wake. "Exactly. Anyway, one day I told her that I was serious, and when she asked me why, I told her that only I could possibly understand myself as well as she seemed to, so really, we must just be the same person living in two bodies physically, but bound by love as one. That, I do remember." A broad grin spread across his face, fueled by his reverie, but he shook his head slowly all the same. "Everything else is fuzzy, though. They say that happens to you when you become a Ferryman. I will never forget those eyes, though. Never."

It took Alice a moment to realize that she was staring at him. A half-remembered scene of her and Marc lying naked together was playing in her mind, his gentle whispers teasing her about her overly flowery, cutesy language, their giggles wrapped tighter around themselves than the sheets they'd kicked off the bed.

Charlie caught her gaping before she had a chance to look away. "Why don't we stop talking about me for a while?" he said. "It's a pretty lousy topic."

A sign for the Lincoln Tunnel passed overhead as the scene in her mind faded away, leaving in its wake the hollow sensation of things lost forevermore. "Only as long as we don't have to flip the spotlight onto yours truly."

"Why's that?"

Alice couldn't help but laugh at that, turning toward her window as she did. "Asks the guy who almost had a front-row seat to my last moment on planet earth. Let's call the life of Alice Spiegel a sore subject." There hadn't been a whole lot of time for self-reflection since she'd put a gun to her head earlier—not that it was something she particularly wanted to do. However, if there was one thing she'd learned about herself, it was that her mind seemed to do what it wanted, regardless of what she asked of it.

"Any reason for that?" he asked. She could see him looking at her from the reflection in the passenger-side window.

The casualness with which he asked the question—as if he were a close friend, a confidant, someone even remotely trustworthy—went over like a fart in church.

"So in addition to trespasser and kidnapper, I should now add therapist to your many titles? No, thanks," she replied with a touch of bitterness. When she turned back to look at him, a smirk was fluttering at the edge of his lips. The sight of it caused a red streak of anger to filter its way through her veins. "I'm glad you find this all very amusing. I really am."

"I think you would, too, if you had any idea how amazing it is that you're still alive right now."

"Who fucking cares?! I know I don't care!" she barked back, her restraint snapping like an overtaxed cable. Who did he think he was, acting like he had any idea what it was like to be her? "I'm not supposed to be here right now, and the fact that I even am is your fucking fault!"

Charlie didn't respond right away. When he did, it was with a steady and measured tone. "I care. A lot, actually. Do you honestly regret having a second chance at this?"

"So one, fuck you and your caring because I don't need either, and two, you really think I want life advice from some degenerate kidnapper?" And yet the fire was gone as soon as the words left her mouth. She'd deliberately avoided his question, which she found odd. Alice felt like it should have been easy to answer. Now . . .

Was she actually glad Charlie had shown up so unceremoniously in her life, the proverbial white knight coming to save the damsel in distress? Maybe that was exactly what she'd wanted all along—someone to just show up in her life and give a damn. How many hundreds of times had she prayed asking for that very thing before she'd given up? Or was she just romanticizing what was otherwise an absolutely ludicrous situation?

"I'm not sure I believe you," Charlie said. His voice was soft.

Alice pressed her fingers to her nose, a sigh falling from her lips as she did. The New York skyline rose in the distance as they took the exit for Route 3 East. "Yeah, well, you should," she replied.

"Are you mad at me?" he asked.

She looked at him again, trying to read something from that placid face of his. She hadn't been expecting that question, nor had she expected to see him so genuinely interested in her answer. At least, she thought he seemed interested. It's not like she was really any good at reading facial expressions, so maybe that was just her projecting things onto him. Those green eyes, though . . .

"I don't know. I really don't know what to make of you," she said, shaking her head. The anger was gone, tamped down by the realization that maybe, just maybe, Charlie was being sincere. "If I'm glad of anything, it's that you weren't necessarily the last man to see me naked."

Charlie's sigh arrived as the shallow exhale of a man knowing he couldn't win. "Have I mentioned that I wasn't looking? Because I wasn't looking."

"Bullshit. And you're a married man, too. For shame, Charlie."

"*Was* a married man," he corrected. "Widower now."

"Okay, *was*, fine, whatever. Either way, you should be ashamed of yourself. I thought eighteenth-century men were supposed to be gentlemen."

"The very fact you're even considering the possibility that I'm not a gentleman suggests you don't know me well enough to draw that conclusion," Charlie replied.

"Yeah, sure. Whatever you say, hombre."

Maybe it really all was a dream, though it seemed increasingly unlikely. Even if it wasn't, was that a bad thing?

A blinding light suddenly exploded into life behind them. Fog lights? Alice squinted into her side-view mirror, trying to make out the source. It looked like a large SUV, only it had a spotlight mounted on the side. Was it the police? There were no flashing lights or sirens, only the hand-controlled beam next to the driver-side door. She couldn't make anything else out, as the light was far too bright.

"Shit," Charlie said under his breath. She looked over at him. His face was blank.

A booming loudspeaker voice abruptly cut through the night. *"Charles Dawson! You are under arrest! Please, pull over immediately. No innocent bystanders need to be harmed!"*

Alice looked at Charlie, and he right back at her. Their eyes connected for a soul-searching second.

"So remember everything I said about being a fugitive and being excited by it?" Alice said. "I take it all back."

CHARLIE

CARMAGGEDON

"Hang tight!" Charlie yelled as another SUV, nearly identical to the one behind them, moved up on their left. They were already in the right lane—if another one caught up and pulled in front, they'd be boxed in. He slammed the accelerator to the floor and the car responded with a burst forward. Had he been alone in the car, he would have driven with a death wish, knowing full well that it wouldn't matter. However, having Alice next to him changed things. Charlie had never been directly responsible for another person's death before and he preferred to keep it that way.

They'd gained some distance from their pursuers, probably having caught them off guard with the sudden acceleration, but the two SUVs were already gaining the ground back.

"How do I make this thing go faster?" he cried over the revving engine.

"It doesn't go fast! It's a Jeep, not a Ferrari!" she shouted.

He glanced furiously between his side-view and rearview mirrors. "But really, make it go faster."

"Well, when you put it that way, let me just flip the emergency turbo-boost switch!"

He looked over at her. "Seriously?"

"No!" she yelled back.

One of the SUVs was nearly on his bumper while the other moved into the blind spot on Charlie's left. Charlie considered trying to cut off the blind spot SUV, but it was tight—if his estimations of each car's positioning were even marginally off, they'd definitely get clipped. At their current speed, that would mean bad things for his passenger. On the flip side, if he didn't do something fast, their pursuers might take that option into their own hands.

An orange *Road Work Ahead* sign whizzed by on the right. About a thousand feet ahead, the lanes shifted tightly to the left in a small *S*. A line of cones stood nearby, tracing the start of the curve and blocking off a straight corridor lined with concrete barriers that ran for at least a quarter mile.

The plan occurred to Charlie from completely out of left field. In actuality, calling it a plan was being more than a little generous. *Suicidal last-ditch effort* was probably more accurate.

"Hold on," Charlie said. "This is going to be a little on the tight side."

"What are you doing?"

"Improvising."

"Improvising?" There was a moment's pause before Alice evidently caught sight of the orange cones. "No, no, no. That isn't a road! Cars drive on roads!"

"Yes, hence my use of the word *improvising*."

In Alice's defense, she had a point. The pavement over in the work zone looked completely ripped up, with chunks of asphalt lying about like land mines. Unfortunately, Charlie wasn't seeing much in the way of alternatives.

"I hope I don't need to remind you that only one of us claims to be immortal."

Charlie smiled wryly. "Good thing the other doesn't care about dying then, right?"

"Gee, thanks, Clarence, I really hope you get *your fucking wings!*" she screamed as the work zone loomed ahead of them.

The lane began curving to the left. Charlie initially began to follow it, just long enough to steer the other two SUVs into that course. Then he threw the wheel hard to the right, aiming for the work zone corridor. If he took the turn too tight and the brakes too hard, he would roll the car. Not enough and their journey would end with the concrete barrier—and abruptly at that.

Charlie knew better than anyone that life and death were often separated by very fine margins. He was willing to accept that, in this case, even he was pushing his luck.

The tires squealed as Charlie struggled to keep the car under control. Both he and Alice snapped against their seat belts as the whole chassis shuddered in its arm-wrestle against physics. Alice was screaming, having built it up in a gradual crescendo that was just now reaching its peak. The passenger side of the car kissed the concrete divider and kicked back to the left before coming to a full and complete stop. Somehow, aside from some dings in the paint, they were sitting in one piece. The trailing SUVs sailed past them before stopping on their own about three hundred feet down the road.

"Holy shit," Alice said in stunned exasperation. "I don't even . . . I can't believe . . . What the fucking fuck just . . ."

"Couldn't agree more. You all right?"

She looked at him, visibly shaking, but Charlie could see no obvious bleeding or misplaced bones. Generally a good thing, that. "Almost, uhh . . . spilled some water on my pants. Other than that, peachy."

"You're doing great," Charlie said as reassuringly as he could,

given the circumstances. He had already popped the car into reverse and was backing out onto Route 3. A stray car or two had
sailed by slowly, obviously wondering what was going on, but none
of them stopped to help.

He could see the reverse lights on the SUVs up ahead. If he
got into a street race with them again, he'd inevitably lose. He
needed to buy himself a little space. He continued to push the Jeep
backward along Route 3, and with the SUVs following in the same
fashion, it seemed like the cars were going to simply resume the
chase in reverse. However, as soon as Charlie was sure the coast
was clear, he whipped the car around in a 180-degree spin.

"What the hell are you doing now?!" Alice shouted. Apparently she didn't much enjoy driving into oncoming traffic.

Charlie didn't reply, focused solely on his rearview mirror. He
floored the Jeep, hoping that the other two SUVs would buy it.
"Come on," he whispered to himself. "Come on . . ."

As the speedometer clicked past forty, Charlie got his wish.
Both the chasers turned their respective cars around and quickly
accelerated. Good—that was the first part of his revised plan. The
second part would be just a touch trickier.

"Just a heads-up, this is about to get a little crazy," he said.

"Oh, good, you mean it wasn't already?" The car picked up
speed. "This is it!" Alice yelled. "This is how we're going to die!"

"Correction—you'll die. Immortal, remember?"

His passenger did not seem amused. "You know, you picked a
helluva time to start cracking jokes, smart-ass. Did it ever occur to
you that maybe—just *maybe*—I don't want to die in a horrific car
crash?"

"Look at that. Sounds like we're making progress already."

"I *meant* that I don't want to die in excruciating pain, you asshole, not that I don't want to die!"

Charlie eyed the approaching underpass. He'd made a note of it before, back when they'd been driving in the proper direction. Now it was his best shot at losing their tail. A car whizzed by on the right, its blaring horn no doubt a poor substitute for the creative string of profanity the driver was yelling inside.

Just beyond the underpass to Charlie's left of the highway was an exit ramp—a short, forty-five-degree uphill slope that ended with a stop sign. Across from the stop sign was an entrance back onto Route 3, allowing cars to get off and then right back on again. Charlie maneuvered toward it, the SUVs flying behind, closing in.

As soon as Charlie passed beneath the underpass, he threw the emergency brake and yanked the wheel to the left, causing the Jeep to drift in a tight arc. If Alice had a follow-up to her previous statement, it was abandoned in favor of screaming bloody murder.

While it was an impressive piece of driving by all accounts, it wasn't quite perfect. Charlie had overshot it, spinning the car more than the 180 degrees he wanted. The Ferryman cursed under his breath as he ripped the wheel back around to the right and crushed the pedal to the floor. The wail of burning rubber filled the air. The now oncoming SUVs seemed to figure out Charlie's course of action—they, too, swerved to their left, one sliding in behind the other to act as a safety net in case Charlie was bluffing.

The Jeep's wheels continued to spin, kicking up a plume of smoke as they floundered. "Go, goddammit!" Charlie bellowed as he pounded the steering wheel with his fist. As if waiting for that cue, the Jeep leapt forward, engine racing. The lead SUV barreled toward them, no longer attempting to get in front of them but instead trying to stop them head-on. Charlie ground his teeth as he kept his eyes on the onrushing car, his mind trying to gauge the distances. It was way too tight to call.

"HOOOOOLLLL—" Alice yelled in one long string. Their front wheels were on the ramp, but the black SUV charged on. Time seemed to stretch out like an elastic band being pulled to its limit. Charlie was no physicist, but if there was any contact now—even the slightest tap—it would surely end with them becoming intimately familiar with a concrete wall.

A deafening crash resounded through the night.

Charlie waited for the Jeep to spin, roll, flip, or otherwise explode in a blaze of glory, thereby signaling the ultimate termination of this little adventure of theirs. But then another second ticked by with the sky very much above, the ground very much below, and the car very much not destroyed. Charlie's brain had to gently remind him that—while grossly unexpected—those were all good things. He chanced a glance in his rearview mirror to see the lead SUV finish crushing itself into the wall behind them. The front driver-side tire went flying past his window as car parts flew through the air like steampunk confetti. The entire front of the car was decimated, the body crumpling in on itself like a mechanical pancake.

Charlie knew that the passengers inside would be fine, at least eventually—they were immortal, after all—but there'd be no way to get them out of that kind of wreck without assistance. The question was, would the second SUV stop to provide it, or would it continue the chase?

Alice hollering *"Charlie!"* snapped his attention back to the road.

They were nearly at the top of the ramp now, approaching the stop sign at fifty and climbing. A souped-up Honda Civic was speeding across the overpass, tracking an unintentionally perfect intercept course. There wasn't enough room to stop, given how fast they were both going. Without thinking, Charlie punched the horn and kept his foot pressed to the floor, urging the Jeep on.

Tires shrieked like banshees as the Civic locked its brakes. With mere seconds to spare, the Civic veered to the left. The Jeep caught air as it crested the ramp, the front driver-side wheel missing the oncoming hood by inches. Charlie and Alice flew over the street before landing on the opposite side. Charlie slammed on the brakes, causing the Jeep to slide to a stop where the ramp met the highway.

The pair sat for what seemed like a long while, Alice's heavy and somewhat irregular breathing the only noise. Finally, they looked at each other, turning at almost the exact same moment. Charlie let out a playful exhale of relief. Alice looked ready to puke.

Fine margins and all that.

"So," he said, "that just happened."

Alice's eyes had temporarily turned to glass. Her head swayed slightly from side to side. "Next time, can you just let me blow my brains out? I think it would be a lot less stressful than the heart attack you're trying to give me."

"That's the weirdest way someone's ever thanked me for saving their life—again—but you're welcome." Charlie accelerated back onto the highway, repeatedly checking the mirrors. For the moment, they appeared to be alone.

"And again, I didn't ask for that *or* this. Just so we're clear." The quaver in her voice was slowly dissipating, though a trace of it remained.

It was a tough point for Charlie to counter. Despite the noble overtones, something about what he was doing for Alice felt selfish. He cared about the girl's life—he wanted to be clear on that—

but in a way, it was more symbolic than personal. He'd saved her because he was given the choice to do so. Because he finally wanted to be on the other side of the universe's perpetually balancing scales of life and death. Because someone had given him an opportunity and, consequences be damned, he'd chosen the path he'd always wanted to take.

Even with her protests, his objectives hadn't changed. Charlie was going to make sure she was protected from the Institute, like it or not. Maybe that made him naive, an anachronistic holdover from a bygone era. Hell, maybe it made him just plain stupid. Didn't matter. Charlie was going to see the girl safely on. If the moment she was released she wanted to step in front of a bus, well, that was on her.

"We're clear. Very clear," came Charlie's reply.

Alice hesitated. "Good," she eventually said. She made to say something else, but apparently thought better of it. The settled hum of the Jeep rolled on.

Music suddenly filled the car, the staccato pluck of violins punctuating every beat. Then the lyrics came, the beginnings of a story woven through them, framed by the acute loneliness of the melody.

The sound was so unexpected that, had it not been for his seat belt, Charlie would have had a good chance at putting his head through the soft-top roof. His eyes immediately began scanning the mirrors again for signs of trouble.

Alice, however, was already furiously searching the car for something. "It's my phone, my phone! Where the hell is it?"

That made a bit more sense. Charlie looked down at his lap—its previous location—but the cell was gone. Not surprising, given the stunts they'd just pulled. "It was on my lap, but I don't see it anymore." Then it dawned on him. "That might be Cartwright!"

"More likely my dad." She was searching the floor by her feet. "Check by your feet, would you? It should be lit up."

"I'm doing eighty on a highway meant for fifty. For your sake, no."

Alice's phone rang on, the ringtone still playing, the namesake woman in it waiting, waiting, but for whom, the song wondered.

Charlie shook his head. "You have a very depressing ringtone," he said, trying to keep one eye on the road and the other searching the interior of the car. Without warning, Alice was climbing over the shifter, sticking her head in between Charlie's legs. "What are—"

"Don't crash right now and kill me, please and thank you," was all she said as she scurried onto the driver-side floor.

Her body pressed against his as she slid farther underneath the seat, the sense of urgency clearly overriding any of Alice's demure sensibilities. First her stomach, then her hip, finally her thigh all snaked along his right leg while she spelunked deeper into the cave of underdriverseatopia. Though he'd eased off the speed, Charlie still had the car doing sixty—more than enough to kill her should they get in an accident. Charlie was desperately trying to keep his eyes on the road, but Alice's butt was waving around in front of him, like that of a regal house cat in heat. He opened his mouth.

"So much as a word right now and I will rip your tongue out," she said. Apparently, Alice had assumed the worst of Charlie. He was about to tell her how offended he was by that when she preempted him again. "I see it!"

There was a subtle key shift as the chorus arrived, another minor chord, the very barest hint of urgency wrapped around the lyrics as they asked a different question now.

"Got it! Stupid thing was facedown." With a triumphant grin

she clambered out from underneath him with an impressive amount of dexterity and dropped back into her own seat. She stared at the phone while fumbling with her seat belt. "Blocked number?"

Of course it would be—if Cartwright was calling, that made perfect sense. "Answer it, before he hangs up."

The last bars before the chorus, the same question about to be asked, the string quartet building—

He could make out her eyes on him in his peripheral vision, no doubt wanting to ask a question. Instead, she slid her finger across the phone's touchscreen and placed it against her ear. "Hello?" She listened. Her eyes widened slightly before relaxing. "Yes, this is Alice Spiegel. I'm sorry, who is this? Uh-huh. And how did you get this number?" Charlie motioned for her to put it on speaker, but she was staring at the floor. She was listening again. "No, I'm afraid I don't want to do that. Listen . . . yes, listen, I don't want to. I don't care. I'm sorry. Good night." Alice lowered the phone.

Charlie blinked. He couldn't believe it. She'd just hung up on Cartwright. Who else could it have been? It wasn't conceivable that Cartwright wouldn't call back.

It had to have been Cartwright.

Right?

His anger bubbled just below the surface as his brain forced him to entertain the possibility that Alice—egocentrically suicidal Alice—had just deliberately sabotaged his attempt to save her. He liked to think that would be out of character for her, but in reality, how well did he really know her?

"Please tell me you didn't just hang up on Cartwright." He was careful to maintain a relaxed tone, but his knuckles whitened around the steering wheel.

Alice looked over at him, evidently confused. "Cartwright?" Then, realization hit. "Right . . . Cartwright." She hesitated. "That depends. Does Cartwright call himself Stephanie, give away free, all-expenses-paid cruises, and sound like he's mainlining nitrous oxide? If yes, then you have my sincerest apologies."

Before he even realized what he was doing, Charlie ripped his eyes from the road and glared at her. *God help you if you are fucking with me right now*, they said, very clearly. The thought raced through his head in all its malevolent splendor, his sense of humor razed in the wake of the phone call's implications. Though his thought went unspoken, Alice heard every word through his eyes. She shrank back slightly into her seat.

"I swear to God I'm not lying," she said. "I'm sorry, Charlie."

Charlie held the edge of fury for a moment longer before it deflated like a busted blow-up doll. A neutral observer would probably have pointed out that Cartwright could call any second now, but Charlie, removed from such an enviable position, knew the truth. How, he didn't know, but he was so completely sure of it that it frightened him.

There was no phone call coming. Though a small part of Charlie certainly had wondered about Javrouche's accusations, he mostly had held on to the belief that it was all a misunderstanding, that Javrouche was somehow terribly mistaken. That conviction now disappeared. It was a mirage, just the shimmer of heat playing on the sand while Charlie struggled through the desert.

The truth, it seemed, was that Cartwright had abandoned him.

Charlie was on his own.

THE DEATH OF YOUR HERO

"Dawson! Mr. Dawson!"

It was initially the sound of the high-pitched voice, thick with a Manhattan accent and a slick cadence, rather than its words that caught Claude Toulouse's attention. A young man—a boy, really, probably no older than seventeen or eighteen when he'd been recruited into the Institute's ranks, by the look of him—was scrambling through the mob of people bustling around the control room floor.

"Mr. Dawson, can I get a quick word with you? It's an emergency!"

It was only after that particular outburst that Claude noticed the other man, the one the youngster was trying to stop. He recognized the Ferryman immediately.

Charles Ronald Dawson. In the flesh.

Despite his sixteen years of service as a Ferryman, Claude had never actually run into the Institute's most legendary employee, let alone met him. Even with their nonacquaintance, to say that he admired the man was to understate it somewhat severely. He'd gone through and studied almost all of Dawson's cases—the Benderman Affair in 1793, his pioneering work with young children during the mid-1800s, and even his recent work handling celebrity cases. Dawson was a revolutionary, and Claude wanted to emulate that as closely as he could.

From his very first days in its employ, Claude had immersed himself in the world of the Ferryman Institute with a gusto that bordered on fanatic. He worked at his trade with zealous dedication, seeking the pinnacle of the craft clearly marked by where Charles Dawson stood. Though most saw his ethic as excessive, if not slightly frightening, it was perhaps understandable when viewed as the long-sought dream it represented for him, now finally come true: it was in almost every sense a new beginning. The place had come to be his paradise, his Avalon. The Institute had unveiled itself as a fresh start for Claude, and with that came the chance to finally mold himself into a person whom people admired and respected.

What better person, then, to choose for the template of his new life than the universally revered Charles Dawson.

Even if Claude hadn't met him personally, the Ferryman record Dawson had amassed was nothing short of extraordinary. It was impressive even to the average employee, but to someone well versed in the difficulties of Ferryman service, as Claude fancied himself, it was positively staggering. But while he'd heard much about Charles Dawson's exploits—he'd been the Institute's crème de la crème for over 175 years, so what employee hadn't, really— the man himself was notoriously reclusive. Yet here he was, heading directly toward Claude at a brisk pace.

The facial expression the Ferryman currently wore seemed slightly bemused, but it was clear the look was an overlay hiding his true feelings underneath.

"I'm sorry, but I just finished for the day," Dawson said as he continued walking on, his pace picking up just enough to be noticeable. A few people turned to look at him as he brushed by but most ignored or, more likely, didn't recognize him.

The young man chasing him, however, wasn't so easily turned away. "I understand, but like I said, it's an emergency. Please! I need your help."

Just as Charles Dawson made to walk past Claude, who was standing idly by his own desk, being done for the day as well, he stopped and turned to face the young man. For an instant, Claude swore he saw a look of utter dismay cross the Ferryman's face, but perhaps not.

"Listen, sport," Dawson started, beckoning the other man closer, though he still spoke loud enough for Claude to overhear. The tone was conciliatory, but urgent. "I can't, all right? I just came off my tenth emergency shift tonight as it is. I'm sorry, but you'll have to find someone else." As the words left his mouth, he started marching away.

"But you said you were off duty!" the man called after him, his accent cutting in with the same inflections as a low-grade gang-ster. "The law says you're supposed to gimme a hand!"

Dawson stopped midstep, and then slowly, deliberately, turned back around, his head cocked slightly to one side. The look in his eyes was one of dejection, as if he couldn't bear to hear those words but couldn't stomach carrying them out, either. He shook his head sadly and turned away. In that moment, Charlie Dawson seemed so very tired to Claude, so very . . . human.

"Come on, Dawson! Help me out!" yelled the young man.

But the mob was starting to close around the elusive Mr. Dawson, who merely wandered on without turning back.

Claude couldn't believe what he'd just seen. Despite the laws strongly holding that any Ferryman should assist if available, the mythic Charles Dawson had just turned down such a request and walked away. The stories that passed from employee to employee all said he worked tirelessly, never turning down anyone. But then again . . . hadn't he heard whispers of this new attitude several months ago? At the time, Claude had dismissed it as rubbish, but now . . .

The young man, who up until then hadn't even noticed Claude, looked him up and down. "The hell you looking at, buddy?"

Claude shrugged. "The man who was going to save your case walking away, apparently," he replied.

Much to Claude's surprise, the young man's face brightened at that. "Quick tongue. I like that. You a Ferryman, chief?"

"Yes. Claude Toulouse"—and he held out his hand. As the man took it, Claude sensed an opportunity that hadn't existed before. If it was true that Dawson was beginning to shirk his duties, then what if *he* became the Ferryman who took on the emergency work? It would take some effort, but surely he'd make a name for himself, and quickly at that. "Sixteen years of service, twelve stars of commendation. I also happen to be off duty now, so should you be requiring—"

Before he could even finish, the other man had already grabbed his wrist and started dragging Claude in the direction he'd come.

"Sure, whatever, pal. Clock's ticking, so you'll have to do. Toulouse, was it? Nice ring to it. Good to have you on board, Frenchie. Keep your ears open because I'm gonna walk and talk"—*wawk* and *tawk*—"and you're gonna listen real good, understand?"

With a sharp tug, Claude extracted himself from the man's grip and adjusted his coat before falling back in stride. "I believe I can handle that, Mssr. . . . ?"

"Vanderducken. E. B. Vanderducken. Rhymes with Bandershmucken. Now, I know what you're thinking, and don't think it, champ. I know I look a bit short in the tooth such as I am, but I've got more than twenty years under my belt here—that's better than most of the nincompoops pissing around this joint, and that includes you." Vanderducken barely looked over his shoulder as he threaded his way through the waxing and waning crowds. "Here's my problem. I've got a new kid under my wing with a lot of talent who gave me the royal treatment for a higher-ranked case. I figured I'd throw the pup a bone, but it seems like he's got a bit more bark than bite and now he's bitten off more than he can chew. No nuances to this one, Joe—I'll give you the lowdown, you go in, rescue our adorable young twit, push the ghost to the other side of town, and then you two make tracks back here. Follow?"

Claude wasn't sure he understood half of what Vanderducken was saying, but he thought he'd connected enough to get the gist. "Get your Ferryman out and secure the spirit's passing to the afterlife. Have I got that right?"

Vanderducken shot a sharp glance behind him. "Of course, that's what I just said. Keep up with me, would ya?" he said, snapping his fingers in a quick rhythm as he continued to zig and zag away.

"Anyway, here's the good news. The kid might be wet behind the ears, but the navigator I've got is aces. I swear, that gal could reassemble *War and Peace* from the opening line and a fragment of the title page. She's put together quite the note package for the assignment, so listen up and I'll give you the dress rehearsal." Vanderducken reached into his vest and produced two haphazardly creased sheets of neatly typed paper. After giving them a rough smooth over, his feet still whisking him around groups as they plowed on, he began to read.

"*Subject's death: beaten by a small group of 'La Resistance' outside a bar in Paris and strung up as an example. Group discovered that he'd sold information to the German SS about several Jewish families in hiding. Also revealed key Resistance figures and hideout locations."* Vanderducken lowered the paper for a moment. "What I'd tell ya? Doll's good, no doubt about it. Anyway, based on what the kid said when he radioed in for help, subject's gone wacky thanks to the way he kissed off. Serious regrets, by the sound of it. Snitching on your pallies for some greenbacks will do that you."

News in the Institute often arrived by way of Ferrymen, similar to how Claude imagined it used to travel from sailor to sailor before telegraphs. Often it came in bits and pieces, little snippets of observation by the men and women on the ground, as well as tidbits from the subjects of assignments themselves. The Second World War, however, arrived with all the details of an intricate novel, mostly thanks to all the extra souls that started pouring in—a common occurrence in times of war. Claude had heard that Germany had occupied France a year ago and now briefly wondered at the future of his former homeland.

"So the subject is unstable due to the circumstances of his death. That's unfortunate," said Claude. He removed a small notepad from inside his jacket and began crafting an outline of what he knew so far. He didn't always need it, but it had become part of his process. Every Ferryman had their own style, and Claude, for his part, preferred knowing everything he could about a subject. "Any other pertinent information you have on the assignment?"

Vanderducken stopped for the first time to allow Claude a chance to compose some notes, but the look of impatience on the man's face suggested that thoroughness might have to give way to a slightly more ad hoc approach. "We don't have time for this futzing around. My Ferryman's already given up on trying to get that stool pigeon's spook to the afterlife. He's stalling until we can get you in there to do just that."

Claude frowned, but accepted that, for future emergency cases, he'd have to operate slightly differently than his usual well-prepped method called for. "I'll take the highlights, then."

With a dramatic sigh, Vanderducken returned to the two sheets of paper. "If it were up to me, I'd have your face halfway to France by now." He scanned the pages, flipping back and forth between the two as he sought out the relevant details. Claude stood ready with his pen.

"Born and raised in France. First Paris, then several other cities, including Marseille and Nice in his teenage years before returning to Le Paree. Ran with a gang for most of his life. Deserted the French Army last year. Never met his mother, who died giving birth, and his father passed when he was young. Nickname is Porto, given for the port-wine stain on his right cheek. Date of birth: October nineteenth, 1918."

The pen had been scratching furiously across the page when Claude let it fall to the floor. "Give me that date again," he said. The words came out, yet they sounded somehow unsure of themselves.

"October nineteenth, 1918," Vanderducken replied. He seemed prepared to follow that with some flippant commentary, but as he looked up, Claude was already in the process of grabbing him around the collar.

"His name!" Claude barked at the man. "What is this man's name?!"

"Settle down, slick, I'm getting—"

But Claude pulled the man's face even closer. "*Tell me!*"

"All right, already," Vanderducken said, his face a mix of bewilderment and amusement as he consulted the notes again.

"Guy's name is Henri. Last name has changed a bunch, but my navigator says his father's family name was . . ."

He stopped speaking immediately, the twinkle of amusement in his face vanishing in a wink.

". . . Toulouse."

Claude released his grip and took off back in the direction of his desk, his feet churning at what seemed like an impossible rate. The words Vanderducken shouted after him never reached his ears. The world around him fell into a subtle hush, like someone had lowered the volume on Claude's life. In that extraordinary moment, all of Claude's previous ambitions stood vaporized, blown into dust by the revelation Vanderducken had inadvertently unleashed. A single repeating thought reverberated in his skull, over and over:

Dawson can save this.

His son. The assignment was Claude's own son.

Claude couldn't go in to assist now. He'd be useless, worse than that.

But if Henri didn't cross . . . Good God, if he didn't cross—!

Dawson can save this.

He'd promised Henri on his deathbed that they'd meet again, and Claude now longed for that eventual day even more than he had then. He had no reassurances about what constituted the afterlife or who would meet him there, but Claude truly believed that once he was released from his service, he would tell his son what a great man he'd become, the souls he'd helped to the after-life, the trying cases, the accolades.

All of it was earmarked for the next life.

Dawson can save this.

It had to be Dawson. They'd wasted so much time—the

chances were so slim now. Yet Dawson's assignment history was riddled with cases that he'd rescued, impossible circumstances that he'd managed to turn in his favor.

Claude frantically scanned the crowd as he bolted past his desk. Dawson could still be nearby.

"Dawson?!" he yelled, his booming voice stopping groups of employees where they stood. *"Charles Dawson?!"*

Eyes turned to him, a few accompanied by shrugs, others mild distaste, some simple curiosity.

He shouted again. *"Charles Dawson! I need to see Charles Dawson!"*

Claude searched the throngs, his old thieving skill of seeking out a mark returning with little effort. Countless faces with as many expressions, almost all of them now staring at him. But still no Dawson.

"For the love of God, I need him! Please, anyone?!"

Nothing.

"What do you need Charlie for?"

The voice was approaching from his left, a look of concern evident on her face. Neatly cropped brown hair pushed out around her head in tight curls while her pale blue eyes intently studied Claude.

"It's an emergency, I need him—"

"I get that," interrupted the woman. "What for, specifically?"

"A case," Claude said. "An emergency assignment." His eyes continued to search the crowd around him.

"He's had ten of those already today," she replied, apparently unimpressed.

Claude whirled around to face her.

"How do you know that?" he snapped, trying hard not to lose what little control he still had over his temperament.

She responded with a lackadaisical smirk, perhaps amused by the sheer intensity of his reaction. "Because I'm his manager."

The final word had barely left her mouth when he raced over to her, his anxious expression rising several levels to on-the-verge-of-meltdown. His voice spilled out in spastic, stunted clips. "Call him! Please! The subject of the assignment is my son. He's in danger of not crossing over. I need to see my son again. I need to know he's made it!"

The desperation in his voice slapped what little amusement there was off of the manager's face. In fact, Claude thought she looked more than embarrassed about it.

"Jesus," she said as she pulled out a large, handheld radio transceiver. It looked comparable to the current "handie-talkies" being used in the war, except the Ferryman version was slightly more compact. "I actually just ran into him—he was on his way to his office. He looked a little run-down, but given the circumstances I'll get him over here as soon as possible." She placed the receiver next to her ear and spoke quickly but firmly. "Switchboard, it's Vanessa Miller, authorization code 8171984. Connect me to Ferryman Charles Dawson, ID 72514. Urgent."

They waited.

After the longest minute of Claude's life, he watched Dawson's manger frown. "Well then, ring his office phone."

Another minute passed in silence, and quickly succeeded the previous one as the longest Claude had ever experienced.

"Can't be reached?" Now even Vanessa seemed concerned. "What do you mean . . . ? He has to be on-site somewhere. All right, keep trying. Contact me if you get ahold of him." She replaced the receiver in a special sling vaguely reminiscent of a pistol holster attached to her leg, and started walking toward the exit of the Ferryman control room.

"What's going on?" Claude asked, following closely behind. "Where is he?"

"I don't know." The slight hitch in her speech confirmed it as the truth.

They marched out, precious seconds ticking away. Through a maze of hallways they wandered—left turn, right turn, left again—until they reached a small set-off section with a single door at its end. A lounging security guard sat at its entrance, his hands folded behind his head. He instantly perked up as Vanessa approached.

"Well now, if it isn't Ms. Miller. Been a while since you've come round these parts. I was just saying to Charlie—"

"Not now, Barney," Vanessa said, promptly interrupting. "Did he come through here?"

Despite being slightly put off by Vanessa's crude interruption, Barney said, "Just walked through not two minutes ago. Looked right sore, so he did."

Vanessa pushed past the guard, who made as if to speak but ultimately said nothing. Claude followed closely in tow. She threw the door open, its handle banging against the wall on the other side.

"Charlie?" she asked the room, her voice rising. "Charlie!"

No answer. It was empty.

Just as quickly as she'd entered the room, Vanessa strode out. "I thought you said he was in here!" she barked at a startled Barney, who nearly fell out of his chair.

"He is!" Barney responded. "At least, he ain't come back this way since he went in there."

"You're sure? You're *absolutely* sure?"

"I never lie to a pretty face, honey. Swear on my grandmother's Holy Bible, so I do."

Vanessa stood in the hallway, unmoving. As the silence stretched on, Claude looked between the pair. Barney, for his part, affected a look of absolute befuddlement.

"So, where is he?" Claude asked. When his question was greeted with no response, he asked again. "Madame—where is he?"

Vanessa slowly turned to him, a look of clearest dread slathered on her face. "He's gone."

Claude stared at her, unsure of what to say. "What do you mean, *gone*?"

That was impossible. If Dawson had entered his office, he still had to be in there. Unless he had used his Ferryman Key outside of the control room . . . but that was a clear violation of the Ferryman Laws. He would *never* do that. Charles Dawson was the hero of the Ferryman Institute . . .

"I don't think he's in the building anymore," Vanessa said.

"But . . . the assignment . . . ," Claude whispered. "My son . . ."

"I'm sorry." She hesitated, then shook her head, clearly avoiding meeting his eyes. "I'm truly sorry." She paused again, then started walking away. "I have to go find my Ferryman. I'll keep you and your son in my thoughts." And then she strode off, her hand coming to cover her mouth as she disappeared down the maze of halls through which they'd come.

Barney looked at Claude, who now stood shell-shocked in the hall. The security guard did not seem a very prudent man, and yet even he sensed the dejection of the moment and wisely said nothing. Claude slowly returned down the halls, numb to the eventuality he faced.

Charles Dawson had not saved him.

Charles Dawson would not save him.

Charles Dawson was going to let his son slip away.

Claude arrived at Vanderducken's desk in just enough time to see the manager's Ferryman, the previously discussed "kid," return. The check box on his form—the one labeled *Assignment successfully ferried* in the upper right corner—remained blank.

———————

CLAUDE SPENT the next seven nights locked in his office. His manager, hearing of the incident, placed him on administrative leave until he was ready to return to his Ferryman duties.

He never would.

At some point, Charles Dawson had evidently stopped by to extend his apologies and condolences, but Claude remained where he sat, staring at the only thing hanging on his otherwise barren walls. It was a painting, a copy of a portrait by Pierre-Auguste Renoir of his close friend Claude Monet gazing down intently into an open book, one errant page fluttering seemingly of its own accord. How the Institute had managed to procure or even produce a copy of the piece, Claude couldn't say, but it had been his only request after becoming a Ferryman, and the Institute had obliged. The picture had been Henri's favorite—they'd seen it on a tour of the artist's work after his death. For whatever reason, the boy had fallen in love with the piece, enamored by the pipe jutting out from Monet's bushy, unkempt beard. Claude himself derived a small piece of satisfaction from the knowledge that he shared a name with the subject of the painting. He'd sought it out almost immediately after his introduction into the Ferryman Institute, eager to hold on to one well-regarded connection to his past. Now it hung on his wall, and while nothing about the painting itself had changed, he knew it would never look the same.

On the eighth day, Claude stirred, his course of action finally decided. He bathed quietly, taking his time in the tub, running over every detail in his mind as he soaked. When he'd finished, he shaved off the chaotic layer of patchy facial hair that had sprung up and put on his finest suit. Only then did Claude emerge from his office and proceed directly to Ferryman Affairs. He gathered a collection of forms, eyes seeing but not truly comprehending, and filled them out, one by one, until he arrived at the final paper. *You acknowledge that you will be legally bound by this name henceforth (subject to appeal by a review board),* read the sheet's final paragraph, *and that all Ferryman Institute documentation will be transferred to this name. If you consent to this agreement, please present your new signature below.*

It was one of the few things Claude had determined with clarity during his mourning. He once again found himself in need of a new beginning, a symbol of his new path. The answer had arrived unexpectedly, springing to life in his mind without any prior thought—had he been a religious man, it would have been tempting to call it divine intervention. It was a name, born out of two from the only story he'd ever loved. The young street urchin, raised on the streets of Paris in poverty, and the man of the law, bound so deeply to it that he'd take his own life before breaking it.

With a final flourish, Claude signed the name that would now become his own. The one the entire Institute would come to know in the years to come.

Javrouche.

––––––––––

THE INSPECTOR sat motionless in his solid oak chair, hands folded neatly together in front of his face as he waited for news on Dawson. The initial recon unit consisting of two pursuit vehicles had failed, with one of the vehicles reported as utterly destroyed.

He was unconcerned. The recon detachment was, in essence, little more than a diversion anyway. As Dawson approached the tunnel, the plan would enter phase two. There was no entrance or exit to the tunnel Javrouche had not covered. It was the perfect ambush.

So, with only time to pass, he sat and waited, staring at Renoir's painting of Monet, listening for the approaching footsteps of justice.

TO LIVE AND DRIVE IN NJ

The look on Charlie's face said it all, really. Getting them to the Lincoln Tunnel had taken a backseat in his mind, replaced by a million thoughts that Alice would never be privy to. She had questions all her own—even more than she'd had a couple of hours ago—but Charlie seemed to have left for lunch, please come back in an hour. Nevertheless, she tried him.

"So if my memory serves me correctly, Cartwright was the name of the guy who made you a Ferryman, right?" she asked.

He nodded. "And my most trusted friend, too. At least, I think he is. Or was?" Charlie shook his head. "I'm not really sure anymore."

"That's a weird thing to not be sure about."

"Well, it's a weird situation now. It seems he's not the man I thought he was . . . and I mean that quite literally."

"Oh." Alice wasn't quite sure how to react to that, so she said nothing.

The car rolled on in silence. For once, the quiet didn't bother her, perhaps because her thoughts were elsewhere, busy being absorbed by particular questions that were bothering her. Like just about everything else that'd happened so far that night, these, too, were questions she hadn't been expecting. Unpredictability was the new norm, evidently, and life had forgotten to cc her on that.

When did she start caring so goddamn much about this crazy situation she'd somehow become a part of?

Why was she upset that it hadn't been Cartwright on the phone?

Why was she suddenly so invested in what this guy—this mysterious, ridiculous guy with his mysterious, ridiculous story—was thinking?

These couldn't be normal questions, not under her circumstances. Sure, she'd told him she still wanted to die, but her feelings didn't necessarily follow that same desire anymore. It was funny an hour ago when she was ironically diagnosing herself with Stockholm syndrome. Not anymore.

Was it because it made her feel important? That was an interesting thought, and the more she rolled it over in her brain, the more it took on some sense. Clearly there must be a reason Charlie was going through all this trouble. Maybe there was something special about her after all?

There was something else, though—more specifically, something about Charlie. What did sportscasters always call it? *Intangibles*. Something that couldn't be measured in numbers or stats. He was just . . . different, and like it or not, that intrigued her. It was like he was looking through the world rather than at it, like he could see the same gray world she did, but could also somehow see where all the colors belonged . . .

. . . and how beautiful it would look with them in it.

"I'm sorry," Charlie said suddenly, "about all of this. You shouldn't be in this mess, and it's my fault that you are." He hesitated, maybe wondering if he should continue and ultimately deciding not to.

In the pantheon of things she hadn't expected this man to say, Alice would concede that those words were near the top. For a moment, she fell into old habits as a line of sharply snarky retorts queued up in her head. But they didn't feel right, not in that moment. She'd relied on them so much over the past few years that they felt as natural as a crutch. That wasn't quite right, though—it was more like a mask. *How can I be sad when my rapier-sharp wit is this honed?* her witticisms said to the outside world. But it was a disguise she hid behind, too afraid to show how beaten down she really felt because she was just too damn proud.

No. She was too *afraid*.

She tried to look through Charlie the way he seemed to with her, in a way that she hoped would somehow give her access to his mind. Who was this man, really? Why had he saved her? Why him? And why her? So many questions, and no answers. Not knowing . . . that was another annoying thing about life she wouldn't have missed. *Bang.* Should have been easy. Should have been . . .

He remained a closed book to her. But in searching the Ferryman to her left, Alice found something in her own mind she hadn't expected to find. It was the truth, inexplicable though it was. Lying there at the bottom of her mind like Hope had in Pandora's box, she found her reply.

"Don't apologize. I hate to admit this, but in a really bizarre way, it's been kind of . . . fun."

Was it terrible to think that, somewhere in that sadistic brain of hers, she was enjoying this? Maybe not on the same level as, say, riding Space Mountain, but enough to be noticeable. Was that really a bad thing? Weird and probably not healthy, sure, but *bad*?

She closed her eyes. There was fear waiting there, just behind her eyelids. A fear that this would all be fleeting, that at some point minutes, maybe even seconds from now, she would lose this feeling, never for it to return again. She tried to savor it anyway.

"You all right over there?" Charlie asked, concern woven into his voice.

"Yeah," Alice said, eyes still shut. For the first time in who knew how long, she meant it.

BOTTOM OF THE HELIX

Who was this girl, and what had she done with Alice? She was smiling softly, Charlie noted out of the corner of his eye. How could anyone in her position possibly seem so content at a time like this? There was only one explanation. *I did it*, he thought. *I've broken her. She's finally gone off the deep end.*

"You sure you're all right?" he asked, not certain if this was a road he really wanted to start down, but morbidly curious nonetheless.

Her voice never faltered when she answered. "No," she said, "I think there's a good chance I've completely lost my mind, but I'm going with it for the time being."

At least they were on the same page as far as sanity was concerned.

They took the exit for the Lincoln Tunnel, Charlie slowing down only enough to keep the Jeep from pitching over in the fairly steep turn. It was a half mile to the entrance, which meant a mile stood between them and what Charlie hoped were answers at the Institute. With everything that had happened so far, he felt nothing could surprise him at this point.

Which was exactly when the pair of glaring headlights burst into life behind them. They blazed just outside the rear windshield, so close they might as well have been in the backseat. Though it was tough to see, given their sheer intensity, Charlie would have bet the house that it was the second black SUV from earlier.

Alice turned in her seat, shielding her eyes from the beams. "Man, what did you do to piss these guys off?"

"Forgot to send them Christmas cards last year," he quipped automatically. He took the Jeep into another steep turn, hoping that he wasn't going too fast. The hook continued to sharpen as they entered the aptly named Helix that led to the tunnel's entrance. The wheels cried in protest as the cars pushed the laws of physics, racing around the giant curve like dueling vehicles in an automobile ad.

"Interesting. I would have figured Ferrymen were more of a Festivus crowd."

He peeked over at her. "You are being scarily calm about this situation right now, and it's kind of freaking me out." Sad but true. Her newfound Zen-like attitude was off-putting, to say the least.

Alice shrugged. "I've been watching you drive. I've got faith." She paused. "Please don't make me regret saying that."

A quick glance in the mirror confirmed that the SUV was tight to their bumper, Charlie doing just enough to hold their lead. However, even with his nose in front, he didn't want to take this particular chase into the tunnel. There were too many variables, too many things that could go wrong. He needed a plan B.

As they finished coming around the ring of the Helix, Charlie noticed a small, coned-off section between the leftmost and middle tube of the Lincoln Tunnel's three entrance/exits—two reserved for entering and exiting New York respectively, the third switching from one to the other based on time and traffic. It looked to be an official area of sorts, complete with two parked utility trucks, probably for emergency crews to clean up any accidents or breakdowns that might occur in the tunnels. Behind the area was a simple white garage door. It looked like it could fit a small truck comfortably, but not much else. Though Charlie didn't know much about the architecture of the tunnel itself, he suspected there was some form of connecting passageway inside from one end to the other, be it for maintenance, ventilation, or otherwise. If they could get inside . . .

Charlie had concocted a lot of crappy plans already that night. This one, however, took the shit cake.

Already in the far left lane, Charlie quickly slammed on the brakes and yanked the steering wheel hard to the left. "Hold on!" he yelled as the car demolished the first cone. A crescendo of wailing came as the car tipped onto two wheels and spun 180 degrees. With a tremendous crash, the rear passenger side of the Jeep slammed into the front end of one of the parked service trucks, immediately stopping the car. The other SUV was completely caught out by the maneuver and flew into the entrance of the tunnel, its own brakes howling. Though it disappeared from view, the sound of two cars meeting at high speed reverberated from inside the tunnel moments later.

Charlie immediately looked over at Alice. To his relief, she was already undoing her seat belt.

"You okay?" he asked.

She seemed a bit shaken up, but overall looked no worse for wear. "So, the next time you plan on deliberately crashing my car, do you think I could get a—I don't know—one-second heads-up? That half second was just a little too short." She popped open her door, jumped out, and made a beeline for the garage door.

Charlie quickly unbuckled his own seat belt and followed after her. "So I'm assuming *yes*, then?"

As he hurried to the door, Charlie realized that the middle tube of the tunnel was currently serving outbound traffic. The sound of a droning car horn drifted out, the way cars do endlessly after they've collided with something, and Charlie had a good feeling he knew what that something was. Just as he started to pat himself on the back for another perfectly executed bit of Charlie Dawson genius, two men wearing body armor—members of the Ferryman Institute's detention unit, no doubt—burst out of the tunnel with their legs pumping furiously. It didn't take Charlie long to figure out who they were chasing. He pulled up next to the entrance door where Alice was standing, her breath coming in short huffs now.

"Now what?" she asked.

Charlie looked at her quizzically. "Um, we open the door?" His mind was already trying to figure out how many seconds they had until the guards arrived.

"Let me rephrase that." She tried to push open the door. Nothing happened. "It's locked. What the hell do we do now?"

Admittedly, Charlie hadn't accounted for that possibility. In his glorious plan B, the door opened easily from the outside— where he currently was—and locked even more easily from the inside—where he currently wanted to be.

"Oh, for fuck's sake," Charlie muttered under his breath.

He could hear the shouting now over the steady clamor of the car horn. "*Dawson! You're under arrest! Stay where you are!*"

"Charlie," Alice said, emotion creeping back into her voice, "we need to do something!"

The Ferryman jumped down from the small landing in front of the service area door to the large garage door next to it. "Yup,"

he called back, "I couldn't agree more." The men from the detention unit were rounding the corner of the tunnel. Charlie crouched
down in front of the garage door before sliding his hands as far
underneath as he could.

Charlie licked his lips. *Here goes nothing.*

He put everything he had into trying to lift the garage door.
His body shook under the tremendous force, yet the door didn't
budge. Alice jumped down beside him, but he was so focused on
the door that he barely noticed. Charlie stopped, readjusted his
position, and tried again. "Open sesame, you stupid piece of shit!"
he yelled as he poured every ounce of strength into lifting.

The detention unit officers closed the gap with each pounding
step. It wasn't going to be enough, they were going to run out of
time, they were going to—

Suddenly, the door rose up three feet. Charlie lost his balance,
accidentally toppling backward in the process. A mustached face
poked out from under the opening of the garage door.

"Quickly now," Cartwright said.

Alice apparently didn't need to be told twice as she scurried
under the door. Charlie looked over to his right. One of the officers was sprinting, a look of cold determination frozen on his face.

"*Charles!*" barked Cartwright from under the door.

Spurred into action, Charlie quickly scrambled to all fours like
an ungainly bear cub. The lead officer dove at the Ferryman with
outstretched arms. Charlie tucked and rolled as fast as he could
through the small opening.

Just when Charlie thought he'd cleared the door, his body
came to an abrupt stop. Charlie whipped his head around and
found himself staring into the eyes of the detention officer who'd
gotten ahold of Charlie just below his biceps.

The rest of Charlie was inside the garage—only his arm was

pinned down against the ground, half in, half out. Charlie tried to wrench himself free but only managed to cause the officer's grip to slip down to his wrist. The other officer closed in, clearly aiming to slide underneath the door.

Then, with a dramatic crash, the garage door came careening down to the ground.

Cartwright stood over Charlie as he swiftly locked the door. A loud *thud* resonated from outside the door, followed by the sound of a fist pounding against it. "They've locked us out!" came the muffled voice from the other side.

Charlie lay there, unmoving.

"Cut that one a little close, don't you think?" he said to Cartwright, an amused smile tripping over his lips. For that brief moment, the accusations disappeared from Charlie's mind. It was damn good to see Cartwright again. There was also the small matter of him pulling Charlie and Alice straight out of the fire, which certainly didn't hurt the man's reputation.

The moment was short-lived, however, only partially because Alice chose the next second to start screaming.

"Charlie, your arm!" she shrieked, visibly cringing as she pointed.

Charlie looked down. Sure enough, his left arm from the elbow to his hand was gone. A tiny portion of his jagged stub poked out from beyond his rolled-up sleeves, the bone in his forearm jutting out a few inches.

He held it up to his face, then shrugged. "It'll grow back," he said.

She looked at him, her face a mix of wonder and disgust. "Wait, what?" she asked.

This should be fun, he thought.

Within seconds, the end of the Ferryman's left arm began to

stretch like a sentient piece of taffy. Muscle fibers lengthened, braiding together at the ends as they became long cords. The open wound closed off immediately, leaving behind a completely inconspicuous nub. A small bubble began to form at the end of his reconstituted arm, growing outward from his wrist. When it was about the size of a fist, it suddenly sprouted five thin outgrowths, which almost instantly began to flex into fingers. Charlie opened and closed his hand several times.

He caught Alice looking at him. Both her hands were covering her mouth, and she quickly turned away, gagging. After a few dry heaves, he could hear her mutter, "Ugh, gross."

A clap drew Charlie's attention. Cartwright stood with his hands pressed together, looking just as he always did, his twirled mustache finely spiraled in on itself. He bowed to them both.

"Please accept my sincerest apologies for the rather precise margin of timing. I assure you I had every intention of arriving sooner, but tonight has been a rather chaotic night." Charlie opened his mouth to speak, but Cartwright was already walking to a back room. "This way, if you please. I have the utmost faith in that door, but I'm afraid it shan't hold our undesirable guests forever. I believe a smattering of privacy would be most welcome indeed." He opened the door and beckoned the pair in.

The room was a closet. Not in the figurative sense of it being a small room, but in the literal one of it being an actual closet. Motor oil, several extra car batteries, jumper cables, a mop. All else being equal, it would certainly give them some privacy, but it wasn't much for comfort. Charlie could see a narrow passageway off to his right, which he assumed led farther into the tunnel, namely what his original plan had called for.

"Uh, is there a reason we're going in here and not following that tunnel over there?" Charlie asked.

Cartwright's oh-so-familiar, all-knowing smile arrived on cue. "Of course" was all he said.

Forthcoming as always, Charlie thought with a grimace.

Reluctantly, he followed Cartwright's lead, shuffling in behind Alice as they filed into the cramped space. When they were all inside, Cartwright reached into his breast pocket and produced what Charlie always considered his Ferryman Key, then moved aside a box of windshield wiper fluid. Curiously, carved in the wall behind it was a small opening. With casual indifference, Cartwright flipped his key around so that the barrel and key bit were facing away from the hole, holding the key essentially backward, and slid it into the wall. There was a *click*, and just like that, the wall was sliding open.

Cartwright looked at them, a twinkle in his eye. "Contingency plans. You simply cannot have enough of them."

Beyond the now-open wall was a softly lit room roughly three or four times the size of the closet. There was a small wooden table in the center, complete with four chairs situated around its four sides. A lazily steaming teapot sat in the center of the table, three teacups placed nearby. An open doorway stood beyond the table, its long passageway quickly bleeding into darkness. As Charlie crossed into the room, the last of their threesome, the wall behind him began to close and, within seconds, had sealed shut.

In all his years of service, Charlie had never seen anything quite like it. Yet it felt strangely familiar, his skin buzzing ever so slightly as he crossed the threshold—much like it did whenever he used his Ferryman Door.

Alice looked around, obviously surprised that such a space appeared to exist next to the Lincoln Tunnel, of all places (Charlie knew the feeling). "Did we just walk into a secret passage, or is it safe to say I'm now in Narnia?"

"Not that particular universe, precisely, but a not altogether dissimilar idea," Cartwright said.

"So, as of right now, I'm not on earth anymore?" she asked. "One small step for man and all that jazz?"

"How to explain it . . . yes and no. Ferrymen operate between worlds, as it were, an existence betwixt the mortal world and the afterlife. It gets complicated rather quickly, and I regret to say I don't quite understand it all that well myself, so unfortunately that explanation will have to suffice. Now then, I daresay I will find it nigh impossible to excuse myself for such inordinately rude behavior. I haven't even given you the common courtesy of introducing myself. William Henry Taylor Cartwright the Fourth, at your service." He bowed, and took her hand.

Something very important occurred to Charlie just then. "Hold on a second. If you're holding your key, how can she see you?"

That was Ferryman 101. Even without his key, Charlie would still be able to see Cartwright—such was the way of the Ferryman. It had been explained to Charlie as a necessary precaution should any Ferryman lose their key and need assistance. However, as an outsider, Alice shouldn't have been able to. In fact, Charlie had witnessed her inability earlier in the night when he'd arrived in her room. With his key, she couldn't see him. Without it, she could.

Cartwright, who at the moment was leaning toward Alice's hand, stopped. "Magic, my good fellow," he replied, then proceeded to gently kiss the back of Alice's hand.

She looked over her shoulder at Charlie. "Now *that's* a gentleman," she said, a touch of impish delight drawn on her lips.

Charlie's brain, however, was too busy trying to process everything to notice. Secret doors that were opened by Ferryman Keys; Ferryman Keys that didn't make their Ferrymen invisible;

Ferrymen—or men who claimed to be Ferrymen—who somehow knew all about this . . .

Jesus, what the hell is going on here?

"You must be Ms. Spiegel, I assume?" Cartwright asked politely.

"Yes, Alice Spiegel," she said, apprehension coloring her response, "though I'm a bit curious as to how you know that . . ."

"My apologies, I had absolutely no intention of alarming you. However, without divulging too much, I have been reliably informed by various sources as to who you are." Charlie's eyebrows shot up. That was news to him. "Regardless, and I pray this isn't too forthright, I am positively delighted to make your acquaintance, Ms. Spiegel. I must say, you have a positively intoxicating smile." Alice's mood instantly brightened at the compliment. "May I offer you some tea? I would offer Charles some, but his rejections of such offers generally end in ill-advised attempts at comedy. I would imagine you are now quite familiar with his unique sense of humor as well, for which you have my condolences."

With a giggle, Alice followed Cartwright to the central table and sat with him. Charlie, however, stayed standing where he was. He ran his fingers through his hair, completely at a loss for what to do next. Javrouche's revelation was exactly the type of problem he'd normally go to Cartwright for, except that was an obvious nonstarter in this situation.

Hey, Cartwright. Listen, I just had a quick question . . . Let's say I have this friend who, hypothetically speaking, knows a guy who might actually be a spy for some clandestine operation that for all he knows could directly or indirectly lead to the end of humanity as we know it. Any tips on how I—I mean he—might approach his friend about that? Without hurting his feelings, of course.

That was sure to go over well.

Did Cartwright even know about Javrouche's accusations? If he didn't, then how did he know about Alice? Even more mind-boggling than that, how had he known where to find them? The maintenance garage of the Lincoln Tunnel wasn't generally the place old acquaintances coincidentally ran into each other. There had to be something else at play—it was simply inexplicable otherwise. And if Cartwright did know about his own apparent lack of existence, why was he acting like . . . like . . .

". . . all is right with the world."

Charlie looked up at the sound of Cartwright's voice. "What?" he said dumbly. Only after Charlie had opened his mouth did he realize that Cartwright had been talking to Alice, though both were now looking squarely at him.

"I was just relating to your new acquaintance my particular fascination with Earl Grey tea. A cup of it paired with some fine reading can make it seem as if all is right with the world, or something to that effect. Where was I? Ah, yes. Ms. Spiegel, would you be terribly offended if I had a somewhat personal discussion with Charles in your presence? Under normal circumstances, I would no doubt ask for some privacy; however, present circumstances being what they are, it would seem that option is currently un-available." He gave a broad gesture to signify the room they were in to finish his point.

Alice took a sip of tea before responding. "First, just Alice, please. Second, it doesn't sound like I have much of a choice. But I mean, hey, go for it. Pretend I'm not even here." She gave both men a meaningful look before returning to her teacup, peering over the brim at them like a scheming cat. Though she was trying her hardest to seem put off by the whole thing, Charlie caught the now familiar glint of excited curiosity in her eyes.

"Splendid," Cartwright said, finally turning his attention to Charlie. In contrast to the buoyant tone of his voice, Cartwright's face seemed . . . off. It appeared a little worn at the edges, far from its usual picture of serenity. "So then, Charles, where should we begin?"

Ah, yes—the million-dollar question. What to ask first? If questions were ammo, Charlie was sitting on a stockpile large enough to outfit a platoon. However, with Alice present, Charlie was beginning to think a somewhat guarded approach might be warranted. Actually, what if Cartwright knew Charlie would take a more restrained line of questioning with her listening in? What if Cartwright's inclusion of Alice was a deliberate ploy to subtly manipulate the context of the conversation? The man knew Charlie well enough, that was for sure. Unfortunately, Charlie didn't feel qualified to say the same. They'd been together for centuries, and yet Charlie knew practically nothing about the man. Well, that wasn't entirely true. He knew *things* about Cartwright: his favorite city (London, specifically the northern end), his favorite tea (Earl Grey), the number of times he'd read *Moby-Dick* (forty-eight, not counting his latest read-through)—he just didn't feel like he *knew* Cartwright.

And that, quite neatly, summed up Charlie's problem: his distrust in Cartwright was beginning to snowball. Every thought Charlie had about the man now cast long shadows in his mind.

Like a chess player assessing various moves, Charlie remained a statue of composure, contemplating his next play with deliberate care. Finally, he shifted away from the wall, careful to keep a moderate distance from his companion. Gathering his courage, Charlie hoped he knew what the hell he was doing.

"Are you aware of the accusations Inspector Javrouche made against you earlier tonight?" Alice's intent expression told Charlie he should tread carefully when it came to detailing the various transgressions of the night lest he have to explain his own.

Cartwright sipped his tea with delicate precision. "I am," he said before setting the cup on the table. He offered nothing more.

"Are they true?"

Cartwright was not the type of man to hesitate. So when the curl of his lip dipped in the slightest bit of indecision, Charlie braced himself.

Cartwright took a deep breath. "I'm afraid I cannot say."

Put diplomatically, that wasn't the response Charlie had been expecting. Put more colloquially, it was bullshit. The fact Cartwright was avoiding a question that should have had an easy answer instantly left Charlie jumping to conclusions.

"I don't understand," Charlie said. "Why not?"

"That, too, I cannot say. There will come a time when I can explain everything, but it cannot be now. Forgive me, old friend."

Old friend. It was, in a way, a surprisingly fitting turn of phrase. The last hopeful holdouts in Charlie's brain—the ones that continued to believe that Cartwright was Cartwright, that this was all some hilarious misunderstanding—were quietly dropping their weapons and hoisting the white flag of surrender. The walls had been breached. The city was lost.

"I fully understand that there is very little I can presently say that will earn your complete trust again. No words could possibly express how deeply sorry I am. This is, in no small part, my fault." He sighed. "The comedy of it all is that we are quickly running out of time, and now I must ask you to blindly trust me. I will not begrudge any decision you make to ignore me, but I beg of you to please listen to what I have to say. I swear on my honor that I have been as open with you as I can be—perhaps even more so—but your next steps are crucial."

The paranoia raced through Charlie's head, the errant snow-ball picking up speed down the hill. How about all the times over the years that Cartwright had said things in passing that were just a touch too . . . convenient. Subtle things—little cues that Cartwright seemed to spring on Charlie after a rough case or the like. Charlie had always chalked it up to his being an easy read, but what if that wasn't actually the case? How did Cartwright know those things, then? Or did it just seem that way? Was Charlie trying to find a pattern that wasn't there? Which was it? Why wasn't Cartwright answering the question? What was he hiding?

Who the hell was William Henry Taylor Cartwright?

"You're doing that look again. The *someone just ran over my cat* one."

Charlie looked up in surprise at Alice, who was staring right back at him. There was an air of disappointment in the way she gazed across at him. She held her cup in front of her face with both hands, obscuring her features aside from those piercing eyes. He hadn't been expecting her to say anything, and given the expression on Cartwright's face, neither had he.

"Look, Charlie, I'm no life guru. In fact, I'm probably the shittiest person to take advice from on this side of the Mississippi. However, I'd like to remind you that you told me Cartwright was the only person in a long time you've considered a trusted friend. If at the end of this crazy little adventure, you lose out, wouldn't you rather it be because you believed in the guy who's always been there for you instead of doubting him the one time he's asking for a little faith?"

A singular thought simmered in his head: *Who the hell does she think she is?* What did she know about the Ferryman Institute? About friends? About Cartwright? About him? Nothing. She was just another cocksure, arrogant kid, not having spent even thirty years on this planet yet convinced she knew it all. Didn't she real-ize that if he chose wrong here, it would be *her* head on the block?

Then Alice set her cup down and said: "I trusted you—*trust* you. I'd say it's worked out okay so far. Well, except for that time you saw me naked." Alice finally broke the eye contact she'd been sharing with Charlie and looked over at Cartwright. "Take a chance. Worst come to worst, we end up getting captured and ex-perimented on or vivisected or something. And if you think about it, that really only matters to me, seeing as I'm the only normal one of you weirdos, and I'm fine with it." A short smile crept across her lips before she nodded in Cartwright's direction. "That, and he kind of reminds me of Gandalf, and Gandalf is *awesome*."

In the silence that followed, Charlie tried and failed to come up with anything even approaching an adequate response. The Ferryman bore a certain pride in the small number of times he'd been caught speechless throughout his extended life. It paid trib-ute to his quick wit, a facet of himself he probably cared a little too much about. Yet, what she'd said was so audacious, so ridiculous, and so unexpected that the sheer outrageousness of it had short-circuited Charlie's accumulating anger and left him with a clear head. Saying that also took real courage, and, strange though it was to admit, he was proud she hadn't held back. With the dan-gerous red filter removed from his consciousness, he heard her words objectively for the first time, recognizing them to be some-thing he was absolutely not expecting: sound advice.

Charlie trusted Cartwright implicitly, had for decades. Things were a little screwed up right now, but maybe there was a reason for it. The man had brought Charlie into the world of Ferrymen and had thus far shepherded him through it. Even if things had taken the proverbial wrong turn at Albuquerque, Cartwright was remarkably still there, still pledging his help. If the man had spent two hundred and fifty years pretending to be a friend just to set Charlie up, then fine. In a sense, Charlie was willing to concede defeat to something as monstrous as that.

"I'm listening," he said. "Just keep in mind that if this is some weirdly elaborate ruse involving tea or something like that, we're leaving."

There was a disconcerting moment where Charlie became convinced that Cartwright was going to cry. He didn't, but Charlie could've sworn he came pretty damn close.

"Thank you," Cartwright said. "I presently find myself at a loss for words. Thank you. Both of you."

He took a moment to recompose himself—a sip of tea, a check of his watch—before he spoke again. "Well, the show must go on, as they say." He cleared his throat. "Correct me if I am wrong, but I assume your current plan of action is to find the president and make an appeal on behalf of Ms. Spiegel and yourself?"

Charlie scratched the back of his head. "I'm not sure I'd call it a plan, necessarily . . ."

"I thought as much. You cannot. Inspector Javrouche has detention units tactically positioned around the tunnel's perimeter. It's a rather daunting boundary, if I do say so, and I would think it nigh impossible to infiltrate undetected. It is also why I redirected the both of you to this room—if you continued to follow the tunnel walkway, in all probability, you would have been surrounded and apprehended."

Oh, Charlie thought.

"Here." Cartwright produced a key ring with two ordinary-looking silver keys and tossed them underhand to Charlie. "At the end of the passageway behind me you will find a door. Beyond it, the city of New York outside of Javrouche's established boundary. Those keys will give you access to a small apartment, 58 West

Thirty-Sixth Street, the fourth floor. The location is a . . . holdover from an earlier era, but it will keep you safe. You will find further instructions there."

Charlie stared at the keys in his hand, wondering just what exactly he was getting himself into. Even so, he said, "I think we can handle that."

"I have the utmost faith you will." Cartwright once again glanced at his watch. "Regrettably, I fear that time is once more against me. Other urgent matters hang in the balance. The best laid plans, as they say." Cartwright stood, prompting Alice to do the same, and walked the pair to the entrance of the long, underlit passage. "This is where we must part ways, my friends. I sincerely believe you are out of harm's way now, but it would not be the first time I've been dreadfully wrong this rather trying day." He turned to Alice. "And remember, my dear: *All that is gold does not glitter, not all those who wander are lost.*" With his hand drawn across his waist, he bowed slightly. "Be safe, and Godspeed."

Alice's eyes lit up like a child meeting Santa Claus for the first time. "Wait, did you just quote Gandalf?" She spun in Charlie's direction. "He's not actually Gandalf . . . right?"

Despite it all, Charlie couldn't help but laugh. His intuition told him that this was all wrong, that he was walking into a disaster. He rarely ignored such a strong signal, but his options at that point were limited. Maybe that's why he laughed—maybe he knew that the end was around the corner, and so he laughed just because he still could.

"I don't know," Charlie said. "I honestly don't know."

A WALK THROUGH DARKNESS

Alice was no stranger to physical activity—she was a born-and-raised soccer stud—but the stress of the night, the lack of food in her stomach, and the uphill angle of the past half mile had her feeling more than casually woozy. They'd been walking for about twenty minutes, maybe longer, but having left her cell phone in the Jeep, she couldn't say for sure.

The walk itself was uneventful, no bad thing given the chase they'd just been through. The passage was easy enough, the floor smooth with lights strung along the ceiling at regular intervals. The walls were slightly cramped but not close enough to make claustrophobia an issue. Though she'd exchanged a few snatches of conversation with Charlie, he'd spent the majority of their hike silently distracted. Alice would ask him questions, but he didn't seem to notice until she repeated herself. Clearly, the man had a penchant for getting lost in his own head.

"I think I see the exit up ahead," she said, voice raised just above a whisper. She hated how it echoed off the walls, even if she preferred it to the dull resonance created by their footsteps.

"Looks like it," Charlie replied bluntly. He didn't seem to mind having his voice bouncing all over the place.

As the echoes gently faded, the conversation again lapsed back into silence. What made this particular silence nearly unbearable, however, was the question Alice desperately wanted to ask to break it. She suspected good taste dictated it be left unsaid, yet with nothing to distract her, her mind kept wandering back to it. Finally, she cracked.

"Why did you save me?" she blurted out. "And I don't mean just the first time, I mean . . . everything. Why are you doing this?"

In hindsight, it wasn't the most tactful way of asking the question, but the fact remained that she wanted to know. Why go through all the trouble? Why not just leave her be in her room? Honestly—and this wasn't her depression talking—what difference did it make to the world whether she had a pulse or not? Lord knew that the world could use one less deadbeat writer.

She walked on a few more steps before she realized that Charlie had stopped. He stood where he was, both hands in his pockets, just looking at her.

"Isn't it obvious?" he asked.

She gave a shake of her head.

"You needed it."

"That's not what I meant," Alice replied. "What was so special about me that you decided to save me? Or do you save everyone you deal with?"

Charlie hesitated. Not long, but enough for Alice to notice. "No. You're the first one. The only one," he said.

When he made it clear that was all he was going to say, Alice moved a step closer. Maybe she was high on the leftover adrenaline still racing through her veins, but her mind pushed her on, whispered for her to keep pressing. She was in control of this—she'd gotten them through the Cartwright fiasco, hadn't she? In fact, now it was time for Charlie to pay up, and the vig was knowing what it was about her that had inspired this quixotic quest of his.

"Why me, Charlie? Why did you stop me?"

"Like I said, you needed—"

"That's not an answer." Her words were growing bolder with each passing moment. "*Why. Me.*"

He cocked his head slightly, brow furrowed, as she advanced another step, now just in front of him. "You were there and I wanted to save you. Pretty simple."

"And why did you want to save me? What was the reason?" Learning the answer had grown into an obsession, as if she'd become Dr. Frankenstein. There would be no denying her, not anymore. She'd spent the past year convincing herself that there was *nothing* redeeming about Alice Spiegel—that she was a defective piece of humanity, a waste, an annoyance, a net value below zero. But Charlie's intervention had to mean something. It *had* to.

When his response wasn't immediate, she leaned in a little closer, her voice the pattering of light rain on the windowsill. "Please. Just tell me the truth, Charlie."

His gaze lingered on her for what seemed like a long while. The jovial spark in his eyes had run away in the dim lighting of the passageway. In fact, he looked almost sinister, standing there in front of her.

"Fine," he started, but stopped just as quickly, wrestling with himself before ultimately deciding to continue. "Fine. For your assignment, I was given a choice: I could save you or let you play cranium patty-cake. I was so tired of dealing with death that just once I wanted to—*needed* to—see someone get a second chance. You are that second chance."

She stared at him for a long time before finally speaking. "So it didn't have to be me. I just happened to win the Charlie Dawson lottery and, *poof*, here I am."

He seemed very surprised by her response. "I'm not sure I'd put it so cynically . . ."

When he trailed off, Alice had her answer. So that was it, then—being "saved" had nothing to do with her after all. All of it was for Charlie, for some asinine reason that she couldn't give two fucks about. She'd only wanted to hear what made her special. Apparently the answer was nothing.

Alice turned without a word and began marching down the passageway toward the exit.

"Hey," he called out. "Alice, hold up."

But Alice simply steamed ahead. "Fuck you," she answered, a perilous calm wrapped around each word.

"Whoa, hang on. Why are you so upset?" His voice remained composed, but his footfalls were coming quickly now as he tried to catch up to her. "You should be proud of that!" As he pulled up next to her left shoulder, she whirled around on him, eyes blazing.

"Proud? I should be *proud*? Why exactly is that, hmm? Because Charlie Dawson wanted to save me? Poor old Alice, down on her luck, lucky to be saved by some heroic shithead with an ego problem? Lucky to have some, some . . . *meaning* given to her lousy excuse for existence? Whoop-de-fucking-doo! God, just when I was beginning to think that maybe you weren't another self-centered piece of shit, you go ahead and erase all doubt that, yes, you are in fact a self-centered piece of shit."

"Hold on, how does this make me a piece of—"

"Because you saved *me* for *you*, Charlie! My, what an *honor* that is! Am I some medal to you, is that it?" She gave him her patented look of death and truly meant it. "Do you think it feels good knowing that you didn't save me because *I* was worth saving?!"

The tears were hot on her face, the room spinning. Alice hustled toward the exit now, wishing with every fiber of her being that she was outside in the fresh air. Actually, anywhere she could be alone would do. Why did he have to be such an asshole? Why, when she'd just started to—

His hands were firmly on her shoulders before he spun her around. She struggled against his grip, but he held her firm. "Let go of me!" she half yelled, half whimpered.

"Alice!" he said forcefully, trying to make eye contact she struggled to avoid.

"I said, let go!" she shouted, and with a final, massive pull she wrenched herself free.

The way Charlie looked at her then—calm, cool, collected Charlie—made Alice want to hit him with a bus.

"What I said earlier . . . that's not how I meant it," he said quietly.

"No?" was all she managed back. She quickly found that words weren't making sense in her head anymore, and even if they were, she wasn't sure they'd come out of her mouth in anything resembling a coherent sentence.

Charlie let his hands drop to his sides and sighed. Alice was teetering on the edge of a breakdown, a stiff breeze away from plummeting into a very final depression. She held on to herself with a gritty tenacity, the one rational part of her brain still fighting to keep the whole ship afloat.

She could make a run for it—if she hit the ground fast enough, she could probably beat him to the exit. Probably get help before he could catch up. Probably . . . but as her body tensed, ready to bolt, Charlie began speaking, his voice transformed to a gossamer chorus by the echo of the tunnel's walls.

"You have to understand something about me, Alice. If it were physically possible, I would have killed myself years ago. I've never admitted that to anyone, but it's true. I didn't want to be here anymore. My entire life revolved around people dying and I just couldn't stand it. Ironic, I know. I discovered quickly that nobody's happy when they die. I feel like the best I get is someone who accepts it without too much fuss. Seeing that over and over again . . . it eats at you. I've been told more times than I care to count that those feelings would pass, that I'd go numb to it eventually. Two centuries later, and I'm still waiting for that to kick in.

"I had an assignment not too long ago, a kid by the name of Jeremy Bradley. Young kid, rock climber. He was free-climbing in the Badlands when he fell. Broke both of his legs before he tumbled into a tucked-away crevice at the base of the mountain. There was nobody around for miles, and . . . you can probably guess where this is going. I'm not sure what got him first, the infections or the dehydration, but I watched it drag on for days and I couldn't do a goddamn thing. No—*didn't* do a goddamn thing. Do you know what I thought about, standing there for his last moments? I wondered what it would be like for his family and friends, each one of them having to accept that he was dead but never truly knowing, never fully getting closure, always hoping that one day, weeks or months or years down the road, he'd show up, bag in hand, and they'd hug and cry and he'd regale them with how he survived against all the odds. How hard must that be for them? How unfair? I'd had assignments like that before, but that one . . . that one just broke my heart. I almost stayed out in the Badlands and never came back."

He ran his fingers through his hair, briefly turning his gaze back the way they came.

"Then I get your case—special, top secret orders that I don't even get to read until you were about thirty seconds away from oblivion, which is crazy in and of itself. I open the envelope up and read the instructions and I can't believe what they say. Do you know why?"

Alice shook her head.

"Because they gave me a *choice*. And for two hundred and fifty years, that's all I've ever wanted. But here's the kicker: just because I wanted to stop you doesn't mean I could just do it. It had to come from both sides. You give me hope, not because I saved you, but because *you let me* save you. Because you're still letting me, whether you want to admit it or not. Maybe you're right. Maybe I didn't stop you because of who you are. But in some weirdly cyclical way, I think everything that's happened since then has proved how much you deserved to be saved. Fucking hell, Alice . . . you're the girl who lived, and corny as it sounds, maybe you just saved me."

Alice wiped her nose.

"You're right," she said, her voice still quivering a bit. "That was really corny."

Charlie's eyes found hers, and after two heartbeats, he laughed. "I'll admit, it sounded much better in my head."

"I can tell," Alice replied. "And *the girl who lived*? What am I, Harry Potter?"

He looked slightly hurt at that remark. "That's not what I—"

But he never finished, because she interrupted him with a kiss. It wasn't even remotely close to a good one: it was too short, she didn't meet his mouth flush on, his eyes were still open, and his lips were still moving as he tried to speak. Frankly, she didn't care.

There was something special about the way Charlie spoke, something Alice had trouble pinning down. Maybe it wasn't one thing, necessarily, but some combination that when blended together exceeded the sum of its parts. There existed a spellbinding cadence in his words—yes, *spellbinding*, that was the right word, because what was it if not magic?—an understated rhythm that undressed the world, exposed it as nothing more than an illusion. He was the magician in reverse, the man who demonstrated with a flourish that his act was real—it was her pain and suffering, her *reality* that was the cheap trick she'd failed to see through.

His voice enveloped her in a tapestry of woven words while his eyes orchestrated the ebb and flow of his inflections, a conductor flicking the baton in seemingly careless strokes, yet driving a masterful symphony with them. Though doubt and fear and sadness all lingered in the back alleys of her psyche, his voice bore her back in time, back to when she was a child capable of believing in impossible things. And in the dying moments of that first kiss, Alice believed in them anew.

She pulled away. Charlie looked at her, speechless. "You know," he finally said, "you are a very unpredictable girl."

All too quickly, the mesmerizing trance he'd placed her in evaporated, leaving her naked in self-consciousness. Suddenly, she felt more than a little embarrassed by her forwardness.

"Sorry," she said quietly. She once again turned to the exit, now only just ahead. "I just didn't want you to ruin the moment by saying something stupid."

A few steps later, Charlie caught up to her. "What I meant to say," he said, "was thank you for protecting me from my own stupidity."

Alice looked over at him. "Sure," she said, "somebody has to." Then she opened the door at the end of the passageway and they stepped outside, together.

CHARLIE AND ALICE

LOOKING GLASS

When Cartwright had implied that the apartment he was sending them to was old, Charlie had suitably lowered his expectations. At least, he thought he had. Calling 58 West Thirty-Sixth Street a holdover from an earlier era was a generous assessment several orders of magnitude deep. The building didn't stand so much as unwillingly slump between the two newly erected twenty-story hotels on either side of it. The nauseating yellow exterior made it seem like the narrow four-story building was suffering from severe jaundice, while twelve decrepit windows were crammed together on the front face, three windows to a floor. The paint of both the facade and molding was sloughing off in large flakes. Neither adjacent hotel came far enough forward to be flush with the apartment, revealing the previously hidden bleached and discolored brick of the sidewalls.

Yet somehow the room on the fourth floor, though mostly bare and rather spartan, looked and smelled clean. Its layout was that of a large studio, though, in context, closets were considered modest housing arrangements in New York. The only separate room was a bathroom in the far left corner of the rectangular main room. An outdated kitchen stood to their right, two unassuming wooden chairs lazily waiting just in front of what was probably the dining area. Other than a coffee table piled high with old magazines and a new bed in the far right corner, there was no other furniture to speak of.

"Not exactly the Ritz-Carlton," Alice said as she waltzed into the room from behind Charlie, "but it's better than I was expecting ten seconds ago."

"You and me both," he replied. He wandered over to the coffee table and took to riffling through the stack of magazines, looking for possible further instructions, as Cartwright had promised. Alice paced the room, humming indistinctly as she did.

Truth be told, Charlie had been having a hard time talking to Alice ever since her . . . vaguely romantic overture. It had caught him completely by surprise, though strangely enough, he got a sense the person it had surprised the most was she herself. Not that he wasn't flattered by it—quite the opposite, actually. In fact, he couldn't think of the last time he'd been . . . well, kissed.

During his early days as a Ferryman, Charlie spent most of his time quietly pining over his wife. The chance to see her again had driven him into taking Cartwright's offer in the first place, so being forcibly secluded from her while knowing full well she was alive was its own distinct torture. By the time he'd finally been able to let her go—and that was no short spell—his reputation had grown with such cancerous ferocity that all of his coworkers, male and female, treated him with the tulip-tiptoeing caution usually reserved for temperamental dictators. Not that he acted any different than his perfectly normal, charming self, just that he was Charlie Dawson—*the* Charlie Dawson. Apparently fame had a unique way of making pariahs out of its chosen few.

He stole a glance to see Alice standing at the window, her

back to him, weight placed on her left leg, face looking down at the mostly deserted Manhattan street below. The city lights cast her into a nearly perfect silhouette, a lithe shadow pressed against the glass.

She knew nothing of his fame or what his accomplishments meant to humanity at large. Maybe she had an idea now, a general sense of it perhaps, but it was impossible to appreciate without the context a job at the Ferryman Institute provided. She treated him like just a normal guy . . . which, now that he thought about it, was kind of odd. Here she was, the one person who had every right to treat him like a comic book character, instead acting like they'd just had drinks at a bar.

It was . . . kind of nice.

Alice turned around at that exact moment, and despite his best efforts to look natural by flipping through an old *Time* magazine, Charlie knew she'd caught him staring. "Gonna use the ladies' room," she said casually, to which he murmured some unintelligible reply. The door clicked softly behind her.

He shook his head. *Because kidnapping her wasn't enough, let's stare at her like a creep while alone in a small apartment together. Real smooth, Charlie.*

Eager to take his mind off the faux pas, Charlie moved to the kitchenette and spotted the notepad magnetically held to the refrigerator door. A cartoon knight posed heroically in the lower left corner of the stationery, his sword pointed across the paper at a similarly cartoonish dragon, a small puff of flame spurting from its nostrils. The header, written in a blocky, bold font, read, *Fortune favors the Brave!* Paper-clipped to the pad was some cash, a twenty on the top and at least five more bills underneath. However, what had caught his attention was the handwriting scrawled across in a flowing script.

1 AM. 34th and 8th. Time waits for no man.

Though Charlie had never seen Cartwright's handwriting before, the phrasing had all the hallmarks of the man's instructions: purposefully vague and generally unhelpful. At least some things never changed. He pocketed the cash—all one hundred and forty dollars of it—then ripped the top sheet off the pad and stuck it into the breast pocket of his jacket.

The distant blare of a taxi drifted by the window, while in the east, the sky had just begun to brighten. Charlie slumped up against the bathroom wall neighboring the door and let his weight carry his body down to the floor. There he sat, hands in his lap, eyes closed. Then, for the first time that night, he began to earnestly wonder just what the fuck he was doing.

———————

ALICE SLUNK into the bathroom—a toilet, a mirror, and a sink, all clean, praise be to God—and felt an immediate sense of relief. It took her a moment to realize that since Charlie's second unannounced arrival at chez Alice earlier that night (i.e., the time after she plunked him in the noggin with a nine-millimeter slug), this was the first time she'd been alone. That hadn't been her intention—she actually just really had to pee—but it felt good. Refreshing, even (the alone time, not the peeing, though emptying her bladder felt nice, too). Suddenly, she didn't need to be funny or witty or interesting and she could just be *blah*.

Not that she needed to be any of those things when she was with Charlie. Of course she didn't need to be. Why would she?

Alice and Charlie, kissing in a tree. K-I-S-S-I-N-G...

Alice sighed, wondering why her brain had to be such an asshole all the time.

She alternated between feeling exhilarated and deathly morti-fied by that kiss. For the life of her, she couldn't remember what she was thinking when she jumped in for that particular kill. Actually, that probably explained it. No sane person would sloppily kiss their kidnapper (rescuer?) hours after they'd been whisked away, being fed nonsense (confided in?) all the while. To be fair, Alice had been dubious on the whole sanity front from the very beginning. Per-haps this was the evidence she needed to prove she'd been right this whole time, the missing piece she needed in order to write a big fat *I'm insane—QED* on this fucker, turn it in to the proper au-thorities, and wait for them to arrive with the straitjacket.

She turned to leave, but stopped when she caught sight of the pale face of a tired girl looking back at her from across the cracked mirror above the sink. The eyes drew her in, gazing at her with disapproval. Disappointment even. The lower left corner of the mirror was gone, snapped clean off in a neat break. She'd seen that face earlier. Only then she'd had a gun to her head.

She heard Charlie's voice call to her from the outer room. "Looks like we're holing up here for a while."

"Really?" she said, watching the girl in the mirror speak the word.

"If you want to listen to Cartwright's advice, then yes. Meeting at one a.m., Thirty-Fourth and Eighth. At least, I think that's what he means. I'm never entirely sure with him." A pause from behind the wall. "Come to think of it, aren't you tired? I don't have the faintest idea what time it is, but it's definitely late. Or early, I guess."

Alice moved a strand of hair out of the girl's face. She might have been beautiful at some point, that girl, that sad-looking girl. "Insomnia. I don't sleep."

"Fair enough." Another pause. "There a reason for that?"

The girl in the mirror smiled at that. Apparently she found it funny. Why was that? Because he'd asked that question already? No. Because the girl who might have once been pretty should be dead, but she wasn't, and that was funny.

Then the thought hit her again, like a mental double take.

She was alone.

"You don't like talking about yourself much, do you?" Charlie's voice again.

Alice wrenched her gaze from the face in the mirror, only to see a dozen more staring up at her from inside the bowl of the porcelain sink. The broken corner of the mirror must have fallen in, shattering into pieces . . .

. . . some of them very sharp.

"No," the dozen Alices said, "I don't."

She stared at the shard of glass that somehow had found its way into her hand. It wasn't the biggest of the dozen or so lining the sink, but it looked like the sharpest, its tip arriving at a mean symmetrical point. It stared back at her, and she quickly flipped it over to its nonreflective backside.

This was it—the moment that had eluded her ever since Charlie dropped into her life with the subtlety of a construction worker's catcall. Despite the gamut of emotions she'd been put through already, her pervading sense of failure had never left her. Stepped out of the limelight for a bit, perhaps, back into the shadows where it waited, patiently, for a chance to make a dramatic entrance. Then, just as Alice let her guard down, it came forward, announcing itself as Alice's reflection in the looking glass.

"I find it a little unfair that you know so much about me and I don't know anything about you," Charlie said through the wall.

Now, if only she could get Charlie to shut up for two seconds.

"You know a lot about me," she said. "Dead mother, no job, suicidal." She almost laughed at that last one.

"Fine. I don't know anything about you that you've told me. Better?"

Not really, Alice thought. Honestly, why did he even care? Sure, this whole little adventure or whatever you wanted to call it had been fun at times. The chase, now that it was over, was kind of exciting. The whole secret society thing was pretty cool. But it was destined to end. All of it.

That was the problem: after it was over, everything would just go back to the way it had been. Alice was as sure of that as anything she'd ever been in her life. Best-case scenario, she'd end up back in her room, waiting for the little demons of doubt to return to finish the job. It was inevitable, then, and there was no use prolonging the inevitable, was there?

Alice held the makeshift blade to her wrist. *Down the road, not across the highway.* Two quick swipes, boom-boom, and Bob's your uncle. She wasn't entirely sure what that meant, but she'd heard it in a movie once and thought it sounded cool.

"Do you have a boyfriend?"

She stopped. For a brief moment, she looked away from her exposed arm. "What?" she said.

"Girlfriend?"

"No! What does this have to do with anything?"

Alice could almost hear his shrug through the wall. "Just curious. Trying to make conversation and not wonder what's taking you so long in there."

Her heart skipped a beat. He couldn't know what she was doing in here . . . could he? Though Alice didn't see it, focused as she was on talking to the door (even if Charlie was behind the wall), the girl in the mirror lowered her arms to her sides. "What the hell is that supposed to mean?"

"Aside from the obvious?" he asked.

"What," she said, a smooth jet of anger now turning up in her gut, "a girl can't go to the bathroom in peace?"

"They can. I've just never met one that does."

She snorted at that, and if she'd been looking at the mirror, she might have caught the sparkle in her eyes, the contentment on her lips. But as is so often the case in life, she never did, and so the moment was missed. Maybe she would have put down the glass shard in her hand if she had, and who knows how differently things might have turned out?

"I'm taking care of business," she said, then quickly added, "Lady business."

That appeared to do the trick. "Right," he said. "Sorry." Joyful, wondrous silence followed. At least, for a few seconds until he interrupted again. "How long did you date your ex-boyfriend for?"

The question caught her like a sucker punch. She deliberately hadn't talked about Marc with him . . . not that she'd talked about much of anything from her end, to be fair. She hated thinking about her ex, let alone bringing him up, so when Charlie hadn't, she'd hoped that maybe he didn't know anything about that particular situation. So much for that.

If before he'd been slowly dialing up the heat on her anger, now he'd just ratcheted it up to high. Not only was she mad that he *did* know, but she couldn't focus on the task at hand with him stupidly yapping.

"So you *did* know more about me! I knew it!" And to think, she was stuck in an apartment with this guy. Alice was tempted to march back out into the room and stab him a few times just to put him in his place.

After a short pause, Charlie said, "No, just a guess. I've had a couple hundred years' worth of practice at reading people. You pick up a thing or two. Happy to see I've still got it."

That was it—all bets were off. Forget stabbing him. Oh no. She was going to cut him up into little pieces and feed him to a pack of ravenous stray dogs so he'd have to spend several days running through some pit bull's digestive tract until he was very literally turned into a piece of shit. "Listen, you—" she began.

But then his voice was rolling along, not even aware he was interrupting her intended outburst. "If I had to guess, I'd say you two dated around two and a half, maybe three years. Fairly recent breakup, maybe a year or two ago, and you were almost definitely on the receiving end of it. Probably out of left field, too. I think he might have had an exotic name, like Giuseppe or Fernando. You haven't dated anybody since, even if you'd secretly like to, but you're scared you'll never find anyone better than him and will therefore spend the rest of your life wondering what could have been. In fact, you're so scared of that future that you're willing to erase any possibility of it happening by choosing not to play the game at all. Can't lose if you don't play, right?"

Alice stood in the bathroom with her mouth slightly open, completely at a loss for what to do or say. Where the hell did he just pull that out of? Not perfectly accurate but . . . shit. She wondered if he was doing it by accident or if it was all part of some long con that she couldn't see. A section of her mind resented him for the words he'd just loosed, yet bizarrely enough, it was more so because he'd stumbled on a raw splinter of truth.

She would never understand how he did it, but just like that, he'd flicked her wrath dial to off. The anger that she'd been building briefly turned inward before Alice let it flow down, down, down, all the way through her feet and into the ground below her.

"We dated three and a half years . . . and his name was Marc . . ." Alice let the rest—*Other than that, you pretty much nailed it*—go unsaid.

The chunk of mirror felt gross and clumsy in her hands now, like a prince who'd morphed into a frog. The voice in her head that had whispered so seductively for months—the one that promised it would all be over as soon as she pulled the trigger, easy as you like—clamored to be heard now, but she ignored it. Yes, that voice would still be there, she didn't doubt that, and maybe after this was all over, she'd hear those honeyed words again and listen. But for now, Alice wanted to see where this all ended. Charlie had earned that much.

She stared down at her hands, the piece of glass still clutched in the right.

No. Forget Charlie. *She* had earned that much.

Before another thought could enter into her head, she heard the piercing scream from the floor below them.

CHARLIE'S HANDS shot to the ground, ready to propel himself to his feet from his sitting position. A woman's voice, clearly coming from the apartment directly underneath, sounded with such primal, crazed intensity that he almost fell over in surprise. His eyes immediately turned to the door. Sure enough, the bolt was undone.

Not good.

He scrambled over with four long strides, pounced on the lock, slamming it closed. Next order of business: protection. There must be something he could use if they needed it, a knife maybe, or really anything sharp—

"Oohhh, Boris! Booorrrris! Da, daa, daaa, daaaaaaaaa!"

A final loud *thump* followed, then silence.

Charlie leaned his back against the wooden door. For a moment, his mind sat in a state of blank bewilderment. Slowly, he put two and two together—or, in this case, one and one—and burst out laughing. It came in long rolling waves, crashing again and again. For a full minute, try as he might, Charlie couldn't stop. Here he was, thinking that the Institute had finally found them, that their last stand would be in this shitty little apartment in this shitty old building. Instead, they'd just been treated to some rollicking late-night, or perhaps morning glory, action in the sack.

Only after his laughter subsided did Charlie realize what he'd been ready to do. Despite his logical reservations about saving Alice, his heart had staked out its own territory and was more than willing to defend it. And there, it seemed, was his answer. He couldn't possibly know what the right thing to do was. There was no right or wrong choice here, only the choice he'd made, and come what may, he was prepared to fight for it.

He found he was proud of that.

Unfortunately, he was only allowed to bask in the moment for a few seconds before a distinct *crash* echoed from the bathroom. It was the type of sound that almost always earns a follow-up along the lines of *Is everything all right in there?*

"Everything all right in there?" Charlie called as he started walking toward the bathroom. No doubt the noises downstairs had taken Alice by surprise, too. About halfway across the room, however, he swore he heard a muffled yelp from behind the door. "Alice?"

Her response was immediate. "D-don't come in here! Everything's fine!" Her words were one thing. The undercurrent of panic flowing in her voice was another.

"Okay, no problem. I just heard something, wanted to make sure everything was cool." He stopped a step away from the door. A bubbling sense of unease simmered just beneath his skin. *No reason to jump to conclusions.* All the same, Charlie couldn't shake the hunch that something was off here.

"Yup, totally cool. No worries," she said, but the quiver in her voice suggested otherwise.

Should he open the door? He didn't want her to consider him more of a creep than she already did. What if she was on the toilet? He cringed at the thought, knowing full well he'd never live that one down. Still . . .

His hand reached for the knob.

"Charlie?"

He stopped, fingers inches away from the dull brass handle. "Yeah?"

"I need you to promise me something. Quickly."

That earned a raised eyebrow from the Ferryman. "I mean, I don't—"

"Please. Just listen." A spike of desperation punctured the pronouncement. Her voice made it sound like she was holding her collective shit together with duct tape.

"Sure," he said straightaway, "I'm all ears."

He could hear the shaky inhale of breath through the door. "I need you to promise that you won't judge me for what you're about to see. Please."

Now Alice had his full, undivided attention. The feeling of unease had changed into one of inevitable dread. Charlie steeled himself to not react, no matter what happened to be on the other side of the door. "Of course. I promise. No judging."

As he said the last words, the door swung inward, pulling away from his hand before he had the chance to push.

Charlie noticed three things in relatively quick succession. The first was Alice's face. Her bottom lip trembled, and shortly after, the first tear caressed her left cheek. The second thing he noticed was how she was standing. It was a strange pose, her right hand on the doorknob while she stood with her body twisted away from the door. She held her left arm away from her body awkwardly, like she was carrying something she didn't want to touch her clothes. Then she turned her body to face him, and he noticed the third thing.

"Jesus . . . ," he whispered.

A deep gash ran diagonally up her left arm, from the fleshy part of her palm to about two inches above her wrist. She'd positioned her arm palm-up so that the wound pointed toward the ceiling, but the blood was already flowing, dripping in angry streams over the sides of her forearm. Tiny puddles formed on the floor, little lakes of fire scattered among the tiles.

His eyes rose to meet hers. She stared back, eyes wide with an expression equal parts pleading and scared shitless.

"It's not what you think," she said, except with her encroaching sobs it came out, *Ib's nob whab you fink.*

To Charlie's credit, he put his composure back on like a suit of armor. "Shhh . . . ," he said as he shrugged off his jacket. "I know, I know." Thankfully, his mind shut off any conclusions it would otherwise have made and set to work addressing the bleeding issue in front of his face. The location of the cut brought to mind many things, but medically speaking, he'd met the souls of enough suicidal bleed-outs to know that the artery was the main issue at play.

He stepped into the bathroom and gently took her arm, gingerly wiping away the pool of blood sitting on top of it. She winced and whimpered slightly, but otherwise said nothing. Of course there weren't any towels in the room Charlie could use—clearly that was too much to ask for. He made a mental note to have a stern word with Cartwright about that.

"Just hold this against your arm for one second and keep breathing for me, all right?" he said to Alice softly. She absently nodded and pressed the balled-up jacket against the cut. With the jacket out of his hands, Charlie quickly worked his favorite silver tie off, then proceeded to rip his button-down off, Superman-style. Shirt in hand, he tore the left sleeve off and ran it under the sink. After it was suitably damp, he signaled for her to move his jacket. When he dabbed the wound lightly, she recoiled in pain.

"Fuck, that hurts." Her nose was dripping with snot, but she didn't seem to care. "It was an accident, Charlie. I swear."

"I know," he said, eyes only on her arm, "I believe you." He used the rest of his button-down to carefully dry off her arm. This would be the real test.

Charlie had invisibly sat in on enough med-speak to know that a cut along the artery in that area could lead to quick and significant blood loss. However, it wasn't a terribly easy thing to hit, probably by evolutionary design. That being said, the slice in Alice's arm ran on a fierce diagonal—if blood spurted out of the wound now that he'd just cleaned it, it meant the cut could be more than just superficial and things could get bad fast. Otherwise, there was a good chance it would clot on its own.

"Please . . . please don't judge me," she said, and he saw the fresh splash of tears landing farther up her arm. He glanced up at her face, a look of infinite sadness contorting it. "I thought about it, but I wasn't going to. I promise you I wasn't. There was that scream and I had the glass in my hand and I jumped and—" Her sentence devolved into a long groan of pain as she winced at the pressure he was applying.

"Hey, hey, it's all right. It's okay. You're going to be okay."

Or so he hoped.

Moment of truth. Charlie removed the pressure he was applying and peeked at the wound. It was bleeding still, but the tide had already slowed. He breathed an inward sigh of relief. "See? You missed all the important stuff down here. In the grand scheme of things, you made a pretty shallow cut. It's going to hurt like hell, but you're going to be fine. No worries, all right?" Two more wrenching sobs burst out of Alice's chest before she nodded vigorously.

The minutes rolled away in silence, occasionally punctuated with Alice gasping softly in pain. Charlie had taken to wrapping her arm with makeshift bandage strips he'd made from his now torn-up shirt. The final piece was his tie, which he wrapped tightly around the assemblage. All things considered, it didn't look half bad, at least as far as field dressings went.

"How's that feel?" Charlie asked while he rinsed his hands off in the sink. Thankfully, he'd managed to keep the blood off of his white undershirt.

"You were right—hurts like hell," Alice replied, her voice steadying again, "but good overall." She looked at the floor. "Thank you."

He gave her a small smile. "Don't mention it."

They stood in awkward silence again, each no doubt wondering what the other was thinking. Granted, he wasn't entirely sure what to make of her story, but she'd willingly asked for his help. That wasn't nothing.

Alice forced a long breath out, wiping away the streaks of tears from her face. "Jeez. I go years without anybody seeing me cry, and now you've seen me do it twice in as many hours. What is wrong with me?"

"It's not your fault," Charlie said. "Apparently I just have that effect on people. I'm like an onion."

She replied with a loud *hmph*, delicately flexing her wrist as she did. "All this because of those two fucking Russians downstairs."

It was a throwaway remark that initially didn't earn a reply from Charlie, until he let out a long *pfffftttt* that tumbled into solid laughter. Alice looked at him, obviously confused.

"What?" she said, clearly worried that she was missing something.

Charlie shook his head, debating whether he should even point out the pun that clearly had escaped her. Her answering groan suggested that yes, she'd gotten it, but also that he should get a life and stop being an immature man-child.

"Come on," Charlie said, "let's get out of this room. It's stuffy in here."

Alice took his cue, stepping over the blood on her way out. Charlie followed her, taking one last look over his shoulder at the mess before closing the door.

"WHOA!"

The first two steps Alice had taken were fine. So were the third and the fourth. For the fifth, however, the room had mysteriously tilted thirty degrees to the left. She stopped moving, swaying unsteadily in the middle of the floor like a drunk in a hurricane. She was practically falling when she felt Charlie's hands on her shoulders, holding her up.

"Easy does it there, sailor. Looks like you might have lost a bit more blood than I thought." He guided her the few remaining steps and set her down on the bed. Thirty degrees to the left had now swung to fifteen degrees to the right. She sat on the edge of the bed, head swimming, hoping against hope that each passing second would be the second the spinning stopped. The sound of running water played at the edge of her awareness, which eventually made sense when Charlie came back holding a glass of water.

"Here," he said, giving her the cup. Of course, she was already drinking in gulps when he added, "I'm relatively sure it's a clean glass." She stopped chugging long enough to glare at him. After she finished, Alice collapsed backward onto the bed. It was surprisingly comfortable and crisply made, thank the sweet Lord Jesus. The sensation of spinning began to fade bit by bit until, several minutes later, Alice's world had once again reached equilibrium.

Alice wiggled her way onto her elbows in a half-sitting position (though, given her wounded left arm, she leaned heavily on her right) to find Charlie sitting nearby. He'd moved one of the empty chairs closer to the bed but off to the side, so that he wasn't sitting directly across from her. An old magazine was open in his hands.

"Feeling any better?" he asked.

"Yeah," she said, and surprisingly she did. There was a persistent, dull ache in her left arm, but that was to be expected, really. That Russian woman had scared her half to death. *Who the hell screams like that during sex?* she wondered, but to each their own, she supposed. In the ensuing reaction, her arms had whipped around, only she'd been holding her improvised knife too close to her arm and . . . well, the rest was history.

The pain—a searing, biting pain that burned relentlessly in those ensuing seconds—was agonizing. Yet it placed a distant second to the look on Charlie's face when she'd finally opened the door for him. He'd covered it up quickly enough, but Alice would never be able to unsee it. It hit him like a physical blow, a betrayal of everything he stood for, an admission that she didn't give two licks about how hard he was trying to keep one more person out of the morgue.

It was with that in mind that Alice steadied herself for what she was about to say. "Hey . . . so I just want you to know that I appreciate everything you've done for me. I do. I also want you to know that I swear on my mother's grave what happened in there was an accident. I . . ." She hesitated, searching for the best way to describe it. "I seriously considered trying to, you know, make up for my previous failure. But I promise you I decided not to, and silly as it sounds, it's important to me that you understand that."

Charlie studied her for a few moments before closing the magazine and placing his hands behind his head, leaning back in his chair as he did. "I know," he replied. "I believed you the first time. Frankly speaking, you could have done it on purpose—" Alice sat up sharply, but Charlie stopped her before she could interject. "I'm not saying you did; I'm just saying that, either way, it wouldn't have mattered to me. What's important was that you asked for help, mainly because you don't strike me as the type of person who does that often, or at least hasn't recently. Whichever."

She winced at that remark. "There might be some truth to that."

He gave her a flippant smirk back. "Some?"

"Don't get fresh with me, homeboy," Alice said. Her eyes drooped unexpectedly and she stifled a yawn. A wave of exhaustion hit her brain, which in turn floated a vague notion that blood loss had something to do with it. Her body felt heavy and turgid, and before Alice recognized she was doing it, she'd already rolled over into the corner where the bed met the wall. "Wow, I just got— Excuse me. I just got really tired."

"That's good," Charlie replied. "Your body needs the rest. Don't worry, I'll take the first watch, just in case any of our neighbors get frisky again."

She laughed at that, pure and true. Moreover, she felt strangely content lying there. "As long as you tell me a bedtime story first."

Alice heard the sound of Charlie's magazine hitting the floor. "Huh. Well . . . I think I can accommodate that request. At the very least, it's definitely one you've never heard before. It's part of the legend of the Ferryman Council, and it deals with the seven hundred trials of Virgil."

"Virgil?" Alice's interest piqued momentarily before her body continued its shutdown. "As in the guy from Dante's *Inferno*?"

"That's the one. Anyway, this story always puts me to sleep, so hopefully it'll work the same for you." Charlie cleared his throat. "Okay . . . so there's this guy named Charon, who's kind of a jerk, and he's just fought Death to a truce to become the first Ferryman, right? He does his job for years and years, until one day—"

Alice interrupted him. She'd been joking about the whole story-time thing, but now that Charlie had gotten rolling, she had to admit, she was liking it. There was just one thing missing. "You can sit over here, you know."

She couldn't see him, what with her eyes closed, but the pause before his response was telling enough. "What?"

"I said you can sit over here. On the edge of the bed. It'll be easier to tell the story." Her consciousness was fading, so much so that she would never know if she actually said that or if it was a half-remembered dream.

"Oh. Sure." A few seconds passed, then the bed slowly sank behind her. "That work?"

"Mm-hmm," she said. He said something else, but she never knew what it was. She fell into a fitless sleep, devoid of dreams or nightmares. It was the first time Alice had slept peacefully in nearly a year and a half.

DOWNHILL

lice tried not to think it too loudly inside her head—
she didn't even consider saying it out loud lest she
jinx it—but maybe, just maybe, her luck was starting
to change.

The Tick Tock Diner wasn't the classiest eatery to ever grace
New York's five boroughs, but it served edible food and that was
the only criteria Alice cared about at the moment. Nachos, mozzarella sticks, an order of Disco Fries on the way. Yes, things were
totally looking up.

"So, credit where it's due," Charlie said as he took a few measured drinks from his freshly poured coffee. "You solved Cartwright's riddle. Kudos."

That was being slightly generous, not that it would stop Alice
from gloating about it. Alice had awoken only an hour earlier
from her unscheduled nap to find that she had somehow managed
to sleep for eighteen hours. While it wasn't entirely unprecedented
(she'd once stayed awake for thirty-six hours straight during college exams her junior year, then subsequently crashed for a similar
time frame when she made it home), eighteen hours was certainly
at the opposite end of the spectrum as far as her sleep schedule

was concerned these days. She had a sneaking suspicion the frequent spikes of adrenaline from the previous night plus the fair amount of missing red blood cells had played a large part. Alice was more than slightly embarrassed by it, but if it bothered Charlie, he didn't show it.

They'd left Cartwright's apartment around midnight, Charlie carrying his bloody jacket before realizing he should probably ditch it somewhere, the somewhere being a random trashcan on Sixth Avenue. As they made the short walk to Thirty-Fourth and Eighth, they stopped off at a Duane Reade pharmacy to pick up actual bandages and some Neosporin. With their supply run complete, they swung over to the Macy's at Herald Square—the one of Thanksgiving Day Parade fame—which had a convenient public restroom outside. They opted to play it safe; Alice entered first, waited a minute, then unlocked the door for Charlie to follow after. Though Alice was terrified someone might see them sharing the restroom and assume the worst, she still considered the prospect of getting gangrene slightly worse (but only just). Inside, Charlie dutifully cleaned and replaced her makeshift dressings before they were on their way again. When they arrived at their destined intersection, Alice was quick to point out the diner, not because she thought it had anything to do with Cartwright's vague instructions, but because her stomach was openly mutinying in the name of sustenance. It was only after Charlie had followed her point that he realized with a laugh that she had stumbled upon their secret rendezvous point.

Despite her unbelievable hunger begging to be sated, Alice was initially leery of sitting down to eat. A couple of near vehicular homicides made staying in one place seem like a bad idea to her, and she got the impression Charlie felt the same. However, with Cartwright's meeting time imminent, Charlie decided they could do far worse than blending in by ordering some food in the back of the restaurant.

"Ank ew," Alice replied. God, those nachos were good. She wiped a dab of cheese off the corner of her mouth with one finger, then proceeded to lick it clean. The show earned a laugh from Charlie. "What?" she whined defensively. "I'm hungry! You can't make fun of me, I just figured out your crazy friend's little brainteaser. When we're home free, it'll be because of me." Alice shoved another nacho in her face in lieu of an exclamation point.

"Yes, I can see that," he said with a laugh, "and duly noted. Cheers." Charlie briefly offered his mug in a toast before drinking again from his coffee, the cup only momentarily hiding his smirk.

Alice scowled at him, but since it was tough to do that and eat at the same time, her hard look disappeared shortly after another chip found its way to her mouth. You could only be mad at someone for so long when nachos were involved.

"So what exactly are Disco Fries?" Charlie asked.

Ah, the third piece of food she'd ordered. A personal favorite, actually. "Fries. Cheese. Gravy. Amazingness on a plate." She shoved a manageable-sized chip in her mouth and continued. "I used to get them all the time with my ex back in the day. He used to live out by Route 3 in New Jersey when he was in college. There's another Tick Tock Diner out there. On lazy weekend nights, when there weren't parties to go to, we would hit up Blockbuster for a movie, then stop at the Tick Tock on the way home for an order of Disco Fries that we'd split. It was a miracle I didn't outgrow my entire wardrobe that year, now that I think about it. Anyway, some nights, we'd stay at the diner so late just talking that we'd get back to his dorm and fall asleep before we even started the movie. We were regular party animals, let me tell you."

She was surprised at how easily the memory came back, even

if it was in hazy bits and pieces. It was a bittersweet thing, as was the smile on her face that accompanied it.

Charlie set his cup down and looked away before he spoke. "It sounds like it was fun," he said casually. Too casually, Alice thought, but maybe that was just her imagination.

Alice set down the chip she was going to eat and wiped her fingers. An errant strand of hair had fallen in front of her face, which she dutifully brushed behind her ear. "It was," she said. "It was a lot of fun. He was . . ." She stopped herself there by sheer force of will. It was a topic she willfully avoided, mainly because, whenever she mentioned anything related to her ex, small or large, it brought back emotions she didn't much care for dealing with. "He was fun," she said, just to finish her thought.

Charlie took a slurp of coffee, then followed it with, "You miss him."

So much for avoiding the topic. "Was that a question or a statement?" she asked.

"You tell me."

It was a strange feeling to want to confide in someone she'd only just met. In some ways, maybe that's what made it easier— there were no preconceived notions on how she needed to act around that person. It was more than that, though, and she knew it.

She caught a glimpse of the white gauze wrapped around her left wrist. Much more than that.

Somewhere along the way, Alice had begun to entertain the idea that Charlie Dawson actually *was* trying to save her. It seemed completely and utterly beyond belief when he'd first appeared in her room the other night, but now it was starting to seem less crazy. *Actions speak louder than words*, if pithy statements were to be believed, and Alice very much believed that. In fact, Alice realized she wanted someone to trust, who really knew how dark her life had become and didn't judge her for it. Someone whom she didn't need to be strong in front of, who had their own imperfections and faults. Someone she could finally talk to on her own terms, who'd let her be herself.

Alice tapped the edge of the plate with her fingernail, staring intently at the rim. "I hate how he left me—*that* he left me—but I've never met anyone like him, before or since. I've spent the past year and a half alternating between missing him terribly and wishing he'd get hit by a bus. I'm not fond of either of those feelings, but those aren't things you can just change. I mean, I also don't want to be depressed about my life and look how far that's gotten me. You can't rationalize emotions, you know? So yes, I miss him, and I get the feeling I always will."

The waitress chose that moment to reappear with the Disco Fries. "Anything else I can get you two?" she asked as she set the order down next to the nachos and mozzarella sticks. They both declined politely, and she was gone again. Alice wondered briefly if the waitress had noticed her bandages, but she suspected working the late shift at a twenty-four-hour diner in Midtown meant she'd seen far worse. It only dawned on Alice after the waitress left that she'd never ordered Disco Fries without Marc. All of a sudden, she was staring at a plate of gooey, oozing, bitter memories.

"Some people say," Charlie said, picking up their previous string of conversation, "that you never 'get over' someone you truly loved—you just learn to live without them in your life."

Alice absentmindedly slid the plate of fries away from her. "There are also people who say the earth is only six thousand years old and that cavemen battled dinosaurs. What's your point?"

He thought for a moment. "I'm not sure I have one. I just don't want you to think there isn't hope. I've spent too much time in my already too-long life wishing that diving face-first into a canyon would have the same effect on me as it would on you. And then this whole thing happened, and suddenly, I'm kind of glad it didn't."

A harsh laugh jumped out of Alice's mouth without her even realizing it. "No offense, but what could you possibly have to look forward to now?"

Charlie reached across the table and grabbed a fry off the plate. He was slow in bringing it to his mouth, which led to about three or four large drops of gravy plopping onto the table-top, but he eventually got it there. With one big bite, he scarfed it down. After several chews, he appeared, by Alice's estimation, at least mildly impressed. "I'm fine with starting at sharing a plate of Disco Fries with you." And there, on cue, was that stupid grin of his.

At first, Alice didn't know what to say, let alone do. There was nothing to figure out, though—the laughter came a moment later, loudly and naturally. "I swear, you have the corniest lines I've ever heard in my entire life. Straight out of the dork handbook, hon-estly." But, if she were being honest, Alice liked that about him. She took her own fry, and though there was a tang of bitterness as Alice brought it to her lips, once it was past, it almost seemed like she was trying it for the first time.

She was so caught up in the moment that she failed to notice the man in the long trench coat standing next to the table. In fact, it was only after he cleared his throat that either of them did. Star-tled, Alice quickly wiped both sides of her mouth. *This guy must think I'm a slob*, she thought.

"I'm terribly sorry to interrupt," he said politely. His voice was crisp and articulate, but the look on his face—the only thing she could make out thanks to his pulled-down fedora—seemed a bit strange. Eager, maybe? "You don't happen to have the time, do you?" She noticed that both of his hands were firmly tucked in his coat pockets as he spoke, which was more than a little peculiar.

"Sorry," she said, "I just lost my cell phone tonight. You could ask the waitress, though."

"I might just do that," he said. He remained there, smiling, and it was beginning to creep her out. "How is your"—he cleared his throat again—"food?"

It was only then that Alice's mental lightbulb went off. She knew what was going on here: she was being hit on! Alice was no stranger to that particular phenomenon—she was an attractive girl in her own right, thank you very much—just that . . . well, maybe she was a touch out of practice. Even so, flattered or not, she wasn't in any particular mood to humor the guy. Whoever he was, he made Charlie seem normal and well put together by comparison.

"Good," she replied, hoping that would end it. She shot a glance at Charlie, hoping he might be able to table the proceedings. He never saw the look she gave him, however, because his entire focus was dedicated to the man standing at their booth. She was about to look back toward the man when Charlie's eyes shot open, practically bulging out of his head. He made to stand, but was stopped midway when the mystery man planted his left hand on Charlie's shoulder and pushed him back down.

"Now, now, Mssr. Dawson. Your food just arrived. Please, sit. Eat. There's no rush. In fact, I'd recommend you enjoy what little time you have left. And just to be sure that we keep our discussion civil . . ."

The man lifted his right hand slightly out of his pocket, revealing the butt of a pistol. When he was sure they'd both seen it, he pressed the barrel against the front of the jacket, making it rather clear that the barrel was pointed toward Alice.

"Civil, yes?" the man said.

Charlie reluctantly complied, but not before giving the man a look that transcended a *death stare* by several hundred megatons. She'd only seen Charlie angry once before—for a brief moment after the solicitor had called, after he mistakenly thought she'd hung up on Cartwright—and it was only a glimpse, at that. But the look in his eyes now—whole cities burned in that reflection.

"Javrouche, you son of a bitch," he growled.

That was when Alice finally put two and two together. Javrouche. The bad guy. They'd been caught. To put it poetically: *Game over, man. Game over.* She stared across the table, desperately holding back tears, refusing to cry for a third time. This was bad—she knew it, and she could tell beneath Charlie's unhidden contempt that he did, too.

"There's no need to be a sore loser, Mssr. Dawson. You tried, you failed. The world will continue to turn tomorrow, I assure you. Now then, would you be so kind as to bring me over that chair? Slowly, if you please." Charlie rigidly stood up, then grabbed a chair from the empty table beside them and placed it at the middle of their booth. "Good. Now sit. Slide over as close to the wall as you possibly can. There's a good man," he said as Charlie complied. "Excellent. See, Mssr. Dawson, following the rules isn't quite so hard, is it? Maybe you *can* teach an old dog new tricks."

"How the hell did you find us?"

"How, indeed . . . ," Javrouche said. He reached into his jacket pocket, the one not stuffed with a handgun, then flicked something into the air. It was small, about the rough dimensions of a typical American dime. It hit the table was an understated *clink*.

"A simple and very small tracking device. Fortunately, one of my officers was able to affix it to your jacket sleeve before you apparently rolled away to freedom late last night. We noticed your jacket stopped moving not too long ago. Found it in a garbage can, which I thought was ironically appropriate. And now, here I am. I can only assume you missed me terribly."

Alice could practically hear Charlie's teeth grinding against each other from across the table. "Fuck you, you little rat bastard."

"Careful now, monsieur. You should know better than to upset a man with a twitchy trigger finger." Javrouche adjusted his hat. "Let's be honest with each other. I'd advise against calling my bluff. We both know I have no qualms about pulling this trigger."

Alice didn't much like the sound of that.

Charlie's eyes remained lit with rage, but an undercurrent of desperation swirled in them now. "What do you want from me, Inspector?" he asked quietly. "I'll do whatever it is, but she has no part in this. All right? Just let her walk."

"It's a bit late for bargaining, don't you think, Mssr. Dawson? Besides, you're making a very poor assumption about what I want . . ." He leaned in close, his voice now a mere whisper. "I want justice, Mssr. Dawson," he breathed slowly. "You've already cost me my son. I won't let you take the Institute from me as well."

Alice's focus darted between Charlie and the man he referred to as Inspector. What did that mean? Was Charlie hiding something? Trying to follow their conversation was hard enough as it was. Trying to do it knowing she could be riddled with bullets at any moment made it exponentially more difficult.

The Ferryman bristled. "That wasn't my fault. What you're talking about—this, all of this—isn't justice. It's revenge for a crime I never committed."

"The difference here, Mssr. Dawson, is perspective. Benedict Arnold—hero or traitor? Depends on what side of the Atlantic you hail from. Charles Dawson—hero or traitor?" He cocked his head slightly, just enough so that Alice could make out the embers in his eyes. "Easy to see where I stand on that issue, isn't it?"

Charlie's eyes went cold as he stared back. Even Alice found herself frightened at how hardened they looked. That calm, easygoing nature of Charlie's seemed a distant memory now.

"I was given a choice. I haven't done anything wrong."

A callous simper danced across Javrouche's face. "And yet you've done an awful lot of running for an innocent man."

Alice's eyes studied Charlie, watched him scowl. He glanced at her, his eyes sizing her up, wondering perhaps what words to use in front of her. "You would've killed her if I didn't."

Javrouche paused, then slowly turned to Alice. His expression had gone blank. He, too, appeared to be sizing her up.

"Would have?" he said. His gaze wandered back over to Charlie. "I still might."

Alice really, *really* didn't like the sound of that.

"Here's what I don't understand, Mssr. Dawson," Javrouche said, tilting back his chair ever so slightly as he spoke. "You're a clever man. Personal feelings aside, even I will grant you that. You know the ramifications of what you're doing. Yet you're risking the exposure of the Ferryman Institute and all the catastrophic consequences that come with it for what? A scrawny girl with life expectancy issues?"

When Charlie offered no immediate reply, Javrouche turned to Alice. Despite the twist that tugged at the corner of his lips, his eyes burned at an intensity that caused her to shrink away. The words left his mouth at a volume just above a whisper. "Did you know that, Mlle. Spiegel? If word gets out that Ferrymen exist, humanity might very well cease to be. All because you're alive. Amazing, isn't it? The extinction of the human race because your heart beats on, ba-dump, ba-dump—" His voice rose a bit higher. "Because your lungs continue to pump, in and out, in and out—" Higher still. "Because the synapses in your brain are still firing, still filling your mind with inane thoughts—" His words came out with assured confidence now, spoken like an expert salesman explaining the virtues of his mag-*nificent* new vacuum. "Because you continue to *be*, Mlle. Spiegel, because you lived, because of you—"

With a massive *bang*, Charlie's fist crashed into the table. He loomed over the booth, towering over the seated Inspector. Molten fury flowed through his expression, his entire body trembling with volcanic rage. Alice looked on, a party of tears knocking at the door behind her eyes, yet she held them back. An attempt to fully comprehend everything failed, but the vague nugget she managed to absorb—that she might be the catalyst for the end of the world—hit her hard and sharp.

"Not another word, Javrouche. I stopped her. The potential repercussions of that rest on me. But so much as *hint* to Alice again that this is in any way her fault and I will tear you limb from limb and enjoy every fucking second of it."

The entire diner had turned to focus on him, to stare at the crazy man standing at his table. Javrouche, however, simply chuckled in amusement.

"Sit down, Mssr. Dawson," he said calmly. "You're making a scene." The barrel of the gun pushed slightly harder against his jacket's pocket. Charlie obliged, but the motion was drawn out. His eyes never ventured from the Inspector's face.

The diner door suddenly swung open and Alice watched several men walk in, each wearing body armor.

Javrouche pulled the hat off his head and set it on the table. "Perfect timing. I'm glad our discussion was engrossing enough to hold your attention while I waited for the cavalry to arrive." One of the newly arrived officers walked up to Charlie and produced a pair of handcuffs. "On with the handcuffs, Mssr. Dawson. Cooperate and I see no reason for me to use this little toy of mine."

It took Alice a moment to realize he was talking about her. *He's offering me safety!* she realized, and the part of her brain suddenly interested in self-preservation jumped at the chance. But Alice knew it was a lie. He would renege on his deal the first chance he got. Everyone knew it.

Except Alice also knew Charlie wouldn't be able to pass it up.

Alice looked over at the Ferryman and shook her head. "Don't," she whispered. The word had barely left her mouth when she found herself staring down Javrouche's gun.

"Ah-ah," Javrouche said. "No help from the audience." With the gun still leveled at her face, Javrouche turned to the few people left in the diner and spoke clearly, his voice radiating authority. "It's all right, everyone. We have the situation perfectly under control. However, for your own safety, we suggest that you calmly exit the premises."

Alice vainly hoped that perhaps someone would stand up to Javrouche—question him at the very least—but, not surprisingly, once the gun was drawn, no one needed to be told twice. *Cowards,* Alice thought as she glared at the evacuees.

"And now we have the restaurant to ourselves. How romantic," Javrouche said. "Now then, the cuffs, please, Mssr. Dawson."

"Charl—" Alice was immediately interrupted by what sounded like a small cough followed by the blistering *crack* of wood splitting. Splinters flew into her face, foam padding from the seat cushion exploding around her like entrails. She was too shocked to even scream, her voice a tiny pocket of air trapped in her throat. A small plume of smoke snaked out of the silencer on Javrouche's gun.

"I warned you once already, Mlle. Spiegel. Twice is my absolute limit."

Alice opened her mouth to speak again, but was interrupted by Charlie. "I'll put on the goddamn cuffs, all right?!" he yelled as loudly as he could, then looked directly at her. His eyes were an unreadable mix of emotions, but his words that followed were clear enough. "Sit there and stay put. I mean that." He slid out of the booth and offered his hands to the man in the body armor. The man grabbed Charlie's right arm fiercely and pulled it behind the Ferryman's back before slamming the cuffs on tightly.

"An excellent decision. Gentlemen, please escort Mssr. Dawson to the exit vehicle." The armored men hauled Charlie up and began marching him to the front of the room.

It was painful watching them lead Charlie away—that was what struck Alice the most. She could feel the tears welling up in the corners of her eyes. *Don't give them the satisfaction*, she thought.

Sure, things the past two days hadn't always been great. It started with her almost killing herself, then moved on to shooting a man in the head, and finally ended with her being whisked away by a stranger to inadvertently become a fugitive from a clandestine organization trying to murder her. There were a couple near-death experiences mixed in there, which mostly involved driving really fast while dodging big cars. There was that kiss, too—a kiss she was no longer embarrassed by, particularly now that she and Charlie had reached the end of their road together. Heck, she'd even managed to eat some of her nachos before they were covered by particleboard debris and seat guts. Everything had seemed so positive just a few short moments ago. Why was life so cruel to her?

Alice caught herself before she slid down what she knew

would be an unproductive train of thought. There had to be something she could do, *anything*, but she watched them lead Charlie away, step by step, and still she had nothing.

Well, there was one thing . . .

"I hope you all get penis rot and your dicks fall off while you're fucking your mothers in the ass!" she yelled after them. The opportunity to tell one person, let alone a group, that you hoped their respective dicks fell off didn't often present itself, so chalk that one up in the win column. Sure, it wasn't much, but it made her feel slightly better. One officer stopped at the door and began to turn around when Javrouche gave him a firm push through the door and put a quick end to that.

The Inspector himself was halfway through when he stopped. He turned to her, his face pensive.

"I hate to be the bearer of bad news, Mlle. Spiegel, but this is the part where I tell you I was lying. I never had any intention of letting you live. You know too many things and are too large a liability to be left to your own devices. I'm woefully sorry that fate has dealt you such an unfortunate hand. Please give my regards to whatever Ferryman guides you to the afterlife."

Javrouche pointed the gun at her. "Au revoir, mademoiselle."

Time stood still. In other circumstances, Alice would have found Javrouche's completely expected betrayal rather hilarious, but unfortunately, like her life, the list of other circumstances she would experience had been cut short.

She closed her eyes and waited for the end. Perhaps it was fitting that the taste of Disco Fries lingering on her tongue would be the last thing she remembered.

So be it, she thought. And there it was—the final thought she'd been looking for ever since she started on this crazy adventure. Succinct, poignant . . . that would do. That would do nicely.

She smiled.

Except, instead of nothingness, she heard three noises in such quick succession that they were nearly superimposed on one another: *Gwuagh!—p-tink!—THUMF!* When her brain had a moment to sort out that auditory puzzle, it concluded that it kind of sounded like a man shouting in surprise, a silenced pistol going off, and the bullet from said pistol crashing into a wall.

Her eyes popped open.

It took her a moment to realize that two men—Charlie and the Inspector—were now tussling on the ground. As she began to piece things together (in her defense, her brain had been busy peacefully accepting its impending demise), Charlie regained his feet—how he managed that with his hands cuffed behind his back, she didn't know, but there it was. The other officers seemed caught in a state of shock, completely taken aback by Charlie's sheer audacity. Javrouche was lying flat on his back, gun now pointed menacingly at the ceiling like a hit man turtle flipped on his shell. Charlie must have barged into him somehow, which meant he'd evidently saved her life—again. Man, what was with this guy? Was there any situation he couldn't get out of? He looked pretty dreamy right then, running toward her with his hands completely locked behind his back, his eyes desperate but still calm, his lips opening in—

"*Run!*" he screamed as he scrambled toward her.

It snapped Alice out of her reverie, and she quickly came to terms with the fact that she was, in fact, very much still alive, though, if she didn't move fast enough, not for much longer.

She got to her feet, cut in front of the Ferryman, and burst through an *Employees Only* door at the back of the dining room. The hallway split in two directions. Straight ahead looked to be a series of small offices, while an entrance to the kitchen sat a few feet to their left.

"Go left!" Charlie yelled from over her shoulder. A dreadful crash went through the air as Charlie kicked over tables and chairs, making an impromptu barricade against the door they'd just clambered through.

The voice of Javrouche bellowing instructions rolled like thunder in the distance. Alice darted quickly to her left.

"What now?" she yelled as they suddenly found themselves in the kitchen. It was modestly sized, or so Alice imagined, given the premium space went for in New York. The cooks' reactions to her and Charlie's unannounced entrance were a mixed bag: some were shocked, others angry, a handful way too busy frying potatoes to give a crap. Apparently, just like in the movies, no good diner kitchen was complete without the obligatory cook who saw a pair of strangers running through his kitchen and shrugged.

"You need to cut off my hands!" Charlie called from behind her. He stumbled momentarily after he bumped into one of the more visibly upset cooks, but he managed to keep his feet.

Alice stopped midstride. "I need to *what*?"

"I need to get these cuffs off and that's the quickest way to do it." At her look of extreme shock, he continued with waning patience. "They'll grow back, you know that. Come on—we're wasting time. Grab that knife and close your eyes if you have to."

This wasn't quite the escape Alice had envisioned. The cooks were now chattering ceaselessly, mostly in Spanish, as Alice eyed the cleaver that just so happened to be sitting right in front of her. Even though she knew Charlie was telling the truth, the simple thought of actually chopping off someone's hands, immortal or not, made her gag.

Charlie, meanwhile, had already turned around and placed his arms on one of the prep tables as straight as he could. *Oh man . . . this is totally going to suck*, she thought.

She wrapped her fingers around the heavy blade and lifted it up just as one of the cooks—apparently the most brazen of the bunch—approached her with a look she didn't quite care for. He rattled off something she didn't catch, but his body language was pretty universal. Alice translated it to something like, *Tell me what the fuck is going on here before shit gets real.*

For Alice, the proverbial shit was already the genuine article, so she honestly couldn't care less about explaining the situation. However, she wanted him off her back, and yesterday. It occurred to her then that she might be able to kill two birds with one stone. She inhaled sharply, held her breath, then brought the thick knife down twice in quick succession just below Charlie's wrists. Two loud *THWHACK*s silenced the room as the sharpened blade separated Charlie's hands from his arms, cuffs and all, with an easy grace. Without stopping, Alice whirled around with the knife still gripped tightly in her fingers, eyes blazing. She just so happened to find herself pointing it at the outspoken cook who'd been—or at least had seemed to be—threatening her and who now—again, seemingly—appeared to be shitting a brick. Like riding a bike, stilted Spanish she'd picked up from playing against the more culturally diverse soccer teams of Central Jersey combined with several years of half-remembered high-school classes into one fantastic outburst.

"*¡Cállate! ¡Fuera ahora, estúpido mexicano, o voy a cortar tu pene!*"

Much like the diner patrons earlier, the chef and his amigos didn't need to be told twice. Everyone bolted for what she assumed was the back door with the realization that *la gringa* was clearly *loca*. The outspoken chef, whose unmentionables she'd just threatened to chop off, turned as he reached the back of the kitchen and gave her a menacing but almost tired glare.

"*¡Soy dominicano, puta!*" And with that, he was gone.

"I had no idea you were so racist," Charlie said as he surveyed his new stumps. Already, they seemed to be reextending themselves back into hands. "He was obviously Dominican."

Alice winced. "You speak Spanish?"

"I've picked up a few languages over the years. Comes with the territory."

She lined up a snide retort, but wasn't given the chance to use it. The noise in the kitchen suddenly escalated as a group of Ferryman officers burst in. With a small yelp, Alice bolted toward the back. She was getting nervous—the adrenaline was pumping, and the few undigested bits of garbage food she had managed to stuff down her face were roiling in angry protest. There was no time to be sick, though—not now. They needed to escape, to find Cartwright, to get this whole thing cleared up.

The past few minutes had given Alice a very good idea of what was waiting for her if she was caught—it rhymed with *breath*, which, coincidentally enough, she was running out of. A hallway cut sharply to the right at the back of the kitchen, the same direction the cooks had run, and she prayed to whatever god would listen that there was an exit at the end of it.

"I'm getting rather tired of chasing you, Mssr. Dawson," came Javrouche's voice, pushing through the room like a foreboding wind. A cacophony of pots and pans crashing into various things enveloped the room.

Alice followed the hall to the right and was buoyed by the sight of an unremarkable brown door with a rusty-looking bar handle. *Please don't be locked, please lead outside, and please, for the love of God, be easy to open.*

She finished her quick prayer to the Saint of Door Opening (she had no idea if that was a thing, but decided "Saint Jeremiah the Opener" sounded plausible enough) and, without slowing down, slammed her body into it. Her right arm went numb with the impact, but it swung open easily enough (*Praise be to you, Saint Jeremiah*) and she found herself stumbling out into a small alleyway. Off to her left, a dilapidated chain-link fence leaned forward, while to her right, the sound of Eighth Avenue traffic—and hopefully escape—played endlessly on a loop. It was the easiest decision she'd had to make in a while.

"Go!" Charlie yelled. "I'm right behind you!"

Though she wanted to shout something snappy back at Charlie, Alice found herself lacking the necessary oxygen required for sarcasm. She winced slightly from smashing into the door, only just realizing that she still held the knife from the kitchen in her right hand. Given the previous night's accident, probably not the smartest thing she'd ever done.

They burst out onto the sidewalk, Eighth Avenue straight ahead. Alice didn't exactly have directions on what to do at this point, so she turned to her left to head uptown, away from the fateful diner. She'd only taken two steps when she saw them—a group of Ferryman officers, four or five strong, heading toward them. One about-face later and she was heading in the opposite direction, only to see a trio barreling out of the Tick Tock. She froze.

"There!"

Alice took a peek over to her right, only to immediately regret it. Three more officers, with Javrouche keeping pace behind, his gun in hand, were following in their footsteps. She kept her eyes focused on the Inspector as she cut to her left, her brain telling her she needed to not have that godforsaken gun pointed at her again. She needed to get away. She needed to escape.

Alice never saw the taxi coming.

By the time she realized that she was standing in the middle of a car lane, the taxi was already bearing down on her. Its horn blared in protest, its tires squealing in horror as the brakes clamped down in an effort to stop on a dime. This cab was in rough shape, however, and its brakes probably couldn't have stopped on a runway, let alone a dime. She caught a glimpse of the driver, but it was hard to tell what he really looked like the way he was screaming from behind his windshield. Alice realized quickly that it was too late. She'd practically jumped out in front of it, and like the notorious deer in the headlights, she just stood there, staring at the lit-up words *OFF DUTY*.

A pair of hands suddenly pushed her farther into Eighth Avenue, her body tumbling through the air both from the force and the sheer unexpectedness of it. Behind her, she could hear the cab slam into something with a muted *crunch*, followed by a heavy *thud*. Several loud snaps and pops scattered out into the night air, almost the same sound that wet logs make when placed in a fire.

Next thing Alice knew, she was hitting pavement. She could feel her clothes and skin ripping and tearing as she skidded along the street. Her right shoulder, which bore most of the initial impact, seared with an ungodly pain before her head bounced off the ground.

Hard.

For an instant, a burst of colors dazzled her, dancing across her eyes. She lay there for a moment, wondering what the hell had just happened. Then, some unconscious function of her body implored her to get up. In a daze, she staggered to her feet. Her mind felt wrapped in cotton, most of it seemingly lost to the reaches of shock. The only thought that drove her on was that of escaping, a notion that felt embedded into her psyche now at a subconscious level.

Though she'd made it to a standing position, her legs wobbled as if she were caught in the middle of an earthquake. The cab-driver jumped out of the car with his hands on his head, bewildered by the scene in front of him, but she ignored him. She barely registered Charlie's crumpled body at first, splayed out in front of the cab though it was. He was saying something to her—what was it? She couldn't make it out. Nothing audible seemed to be registering properly, actually. He was telling her something through gritted teeth. Alice frowned. She wanted to see him smile again.

The cabbie was looking at her now, talking quickly based on how his mouth was moving, but she couldn't make out his words, either. He seemed concerned about something, but all she could focus on was a long streak of gray in his bushy beard. Behind the taxi driver, on the side of Eighth Avenue opposite the diner, a man was running toward them. He looked familiar—where had she seen that man before?

That wasn't important. She needed to focus. What was she supposed to be doing again?

Escaping.

Yes, that was it. Charlie was crawling toward her now, but wasn't getting anywhere very fast, what with his left arm and leg looking like two snakes slithering next to him. At a conservative guess, they must have been broken in six or seven places. Good thing he didn't feel pain or anything. Alice watched his lips carefully. It looked like he was saying the word *go*, over and over again. Well, duh—she knew that, but she couldn't go without him. They were in this together, and they were going to escape together, too. They just needed to cross the street, that's all. To get away from the men chasing them. Where were those guys anyway? She turned and looked back toward the diner . . .

. . . and there was Javrouche. Pistol in hand, he grabbed Charlie underneath his arms. The Inspector was shouting something, and suddenly the pistol was pointed at Alice. She could see right down the long barrel of the silencer, almost as if it were an extension of his outstretched arm. Even so, Javrouche's attention was on Charlie, whom he continuously tried to lift up, but couldn't. Seeing this, two officers were running over to assist the Inspector.

Except Charlie acted first.

With the help of Javrouche's partial lift, he was able to spring off with his good leg in a pseudo dive. As he stretched out in midair, he swung something metallic-looking in a long but improbably quick arc. Despite the speed at which things were happening, Alice determined it was her cleaver from earlier. It must have popped out of her hand when she'd been pushed away from the taxi.

Just after the glinting flash of the knife, Javrouche's pistol was falling. Well, actually, Javrouche's hand still gripping the pistol was falling, most likely because Charlie had just cut it off. The Ferryman's dive didn't take him very far, but he twisted his body so that he would land on his left shoulder. This opened up a path for his knife to find its way almost completely through Javrouche's right knee. With the sudden loss of support from his right leg, the Inspector crumpled wordlessly to the ground.

Alice could only watch in awe as Charlie scampered along the ground to Javrouche's now free gun. He didn't have time to remove the Inspector's severed hand from the pistol, so instead, he rolled over on his back and depressed Javrouche's finger. Two muffled gunshots fired in turn. With the oncoming men less than ten feet away, Charlie had aimed for their heads and, sure enough, the two officers tumbled to the ground, much like Charlie had in her bedroom.

The officers who were waiting along the sidewalk began making their way forward, but cautiously. Alice took a step toward Charlie and nearly stumbled, but managed to hold steady. He, too, was finding his own feet. His leg had apparently healed enough that he could stand on it, even if she could still see it mending before her very eyes. He stood for a moment with his back to her, gun pointed menacingly at the targets in front of him, switching his aim every second or so. Then he turned to her.

His expression could only be described as animalistic. Spittle flew from his lips while his eyes, round as she had ever seen them, tried to lock on to her own but vibrated with a frantic energy. He was screaming at her, she realized. It was easy enough to read his lips: *Get out of here!* he was yelling, mixing in a few *Run!*s for good measure. The moment only seemed to last an instant before he turned around again. In the nick of time, too—a Ferryman officer was charging Charlie's momentary blind spot, but he dropped the man with another well-placed shot to the skull.

Charlie began shouting at the men in front of him in a rabid frenzy unlike almost anything Alice had ever seen. Who was this guy, and what had he done with Charlie? This couldn't be the same person. This man . . . scared her. Didn't he understand that they needed to leave together? Wasn't that the whole point? Now that they had the gun in their possession, it wouldn't be hard to run again. It took most of the danger out, anyway. She had a few cuts and bruises, sure, but she'd be able to move, and Charlie was almost completely healed again. They were running out of time, though—Javrouche was rising up like a wounded viper while the two officers Charlie had shot moments earlier were also beginning to stir.

She needed to get him to stop, needed to get his attention. He was shuffling backward, drawing closer to her. He changed the target of the gun at a blistering pace, shifting his focus almost neurotically, the quintessential cornered animal. She took a step forward and grabbed his shoulder. Now was their last chance. They needed to run and—

Charlie wheeled around with uncanny speed, the gun pointed at her below her right shoulder.

P-tink!

A small flash jumped from the end of the silenced pistol, and immediately, Alice felt her body spasm. The world seemed to stop moving. She went to take a step back but found her feet glued to the ground. A small, distant pain in her chest floated to her mind. She put her hand to where it hurt. A small hole perforated her shirt somewhere between her right breast and shoulder. When she put her fingers to it, they came back stained red. With blood. Her blood.

Oh, she thought. *That's a problem.*

The pistol fell from Charlie's hand. He slowly began to reach out for her, but a group of officers seized the moment, three of them tackling him. Not that they needed to—Charlie had gone full rag doll. Alice watched as Javrouche's men loaded Charlie into a van parked in front of the Tick Tock Diner, his eyes staring into hers the whole time. Her vision started to tunnel before her legs gave out from under her. Despite falling heavily to her knees, she felt no pain. With Charlie successfully inside the van, Javrouche took one final, pitying look at her. He moved on, slamming the door closed. Slowly, slowly, her vision continued to fade. The rest of her body hit the ground. Alice felt so incredibly tired. All she wanted was to sleep . . .

A man. There was a man standing over her. It was the man

who'd been running toward her before. He looked like Cartwright, but he looked so forlorn, so upset. He smiled at her. She tried to return the gesture, but it was hard. She felt so weak. He was saying something now. She wondered what it was. She couldn't hear the words, and now the sounds of the world seemed so very far away. Slowly, slowly, she closed her eyes and her world became nothingness. There was no light, no pain, no sound.

Just nothing.

HANDLING THE TRUTH

How many hours had it been? Charlie didn't know. He wanted to guess somewhere in the ballpark of twenty, but it could've been an eternity, given how long it felt. He found it slightly amusing that, as far as the human condition was concerned, being happy or in love or experiencing whatever other sappy emotions there were made hours fly by in minutes, while his current emotional condition stretched minutes into days.

Charlie opened his eyes, though he might as well have kept them closed for all the difference it made. The cell was perfectly dark and, save for his pathetic self, completely empty. At one point, he thought he could faintly make out the outline of his hand held two inches from his face, but as he flexed his fingers, he realized it was all in his head. He leaned up against what he assumed was the wall—his body merely stopped, with no tactile stimulation to tell him why.

The Institute called it Purgatory. It was a uniquely Ferryman punishment, the cells having been specially crafted—some said with the same magic that had created the Ferryman Keys—to be devoid of any and all external stimulation. A prisoner in Purgatory was essentially left to rot.

Except the body of a Ferryman prisoner didn't waste away. Just their mind did.

Most of what anybody knew about Purgatory was hearsay. It was an extreme punishment even by Javrouche's standards, which, if nothing else, said something about its efficacy. However, it remained a legal punishment on the books, just one spoken of in hushed voices. Stories circulated about infamous Ferrymen who'd been sentenced to stints in Purgatory—men and women who'd eventually lost their sanity after only a decade, or a year, or a month, or even a day. Charlie suddenly found himself with a much better frame of reference for those stories. Even knowing that he would be taken out of this cell soon for his trial, he could feel the anxiety building in his chest. He'd gone in thinking most of those stories were nonsense. Now he wasn't so sure.

What made Purgatory so frighteningly potent was its ability to turn a mind against itself. Since his incarceration, Charlie had been avoiding a particular thought. But as the minutes in pure darkness ticked away, he found it harder and harder to escape from it. The thought wormed its way into his head, a parasite hellbent on lodging itself as deeply into his mind as it could. And then, as the parasite took hold, Charlie realized there was nothing more he could do to stop it.

Alice Spiegel Alice Spiegel Alice Spiegel Alice Spiegel . . .

In his head, her name echoed endlessly. Before his eyes—open or closed—it floated, always in view. His lips reminded him what hers had felt like. Her laugh played in his ears.

They'd formed a connection, the two of them. Charlie saw something tremendously admirable in the way that, at her lowest moment, when she was wagering that whatever existed beyond the mortal world was better than anything life could offer her on earth, she took a chance on him. And in that fleeting chance, Charlie had found somebody with whom he felt so comfortable, so at ease, that frankly he didn't know what to make of it. There was only one person in the world who'd captured his attention so thoroughly, and he'd married her. The fact that Elizabeth and Alice seemed to share so many quirks wasn't lost on the Ferryman.

When Charlie and Alice had exited the passageway underneath the Lincoln Tunnel, he had a profound realization: the answer he'd given her about why he'd saved her was wrong. Maybe initially it was right—it was tough to think clearly walking in that cramped tunnel—but since then, his answer had grown up. Matured. Or, perhaps, come to embody something closer to the truth that Charlie hadn't been able to see.

What he really wanted for her now was to live. For her to fulfill the potential he saw in her. He wanted her to be happy, to have a chance to look back on her life and laugh at the impossibly low lows of it. And frankly, he wanted to be a part of that. He wanted to learn more about her. Laugh some more at lousy jokes. Just *be* together. She would have called that cheesy and corny, probably rubbed it in his face mercilessly, but right then and there he would have given anything in the world for that, no questions asked.

But that chance was gone now, shot and killed as it were by a bullet he'd fired.

A loud *clank* echoed through the room. Blades of light began streaming in, temporarily blinding Charlie.

"Rise and shine, Mssr. Dawson."

Indistinct shapes picked him up roughly by the arms and carried him out of his cell. Charlie didn't feel much like walking, so he let them drag him along.

"I have to ask, Mssr. Dawson," came Javrouche's voice from

behind him, "was your taste of Purgatory that awful, or is there something else weighing on your mind? Something to do with killing that girl you were trying so desperately to protect, perhaps?" The Inspector's rhythmic footsteps were unmistakable as he marched at the rear of their group.

"Fuck off," Charlie muttered, mostly to himself.

"Sorry, what was that? I couldn't hear you." Javrouche moved in front and stuck his ear in Charlie's face.

Charlie stared at the ear in front of him, then lunged forward and chomped down, ripping his head sideways. He felt the mangled piece of flesh in his mouth, and quickly spit it out.

"I said, *Fuck off.* Did you hear that?" Charlie said flatly.

Javrouche responded by punching him in the face. Not that it mattered—Charlie didn't feel it and the nub that was Javrouche's left ear was already beginning to re-form. Still, he'd goaded Javrouche into losing his cool and that was a small moral victory. The Inspector strode off down the hall, the two guards dragging Charlie along as they followed.

After several minutes of lugging Charlie around like a sack of potatoes, the group arrived at a large set of oaken double doors. The glossy brown sheen from the finely paneled exterior radiated in the obnoxiously blank hallway they'd just meandered through.

Javrouche stood in front of the doors, his hands resting eagerly on each of the handles. His anger had apparently already worn off. "Shall we?" he asked over his shoulder, eyes glittering with excitement.

The doors swung open as Javrouche pushed, and Charlie was pulled into the light of the Ferryman Institute's High Court.

The room itself wasn't overly large, though it was well lit and very formal. The entrance stood directly opposite the Judicator's bench at the opposite end of the room. From what Charlie understood, individuals uninvolved in the case weren't permitted to attend the hearing, so there was little need for a big space. A few long wooden benches lined each side of the room, separated down the middle by a main aisle inlaid with polished marble. A small stand sat in front of the Judicator, where the accused stood for the duration of the trial. Two antique oaken tables were placed to each side of the stand for a prosecutor and defense counsel, respectively.

Behind the Judicator's bench sat a middle-aged man dressed in a long, flowing black robe. A hood adorned the back but was presently laid down. His hair was a light, hazy brown, shot through with streaks of gray near his ears. An ornate gold placard situated in front of him read, *The Honorable Judicator Joshua A. Dales*.

Javrouche took a position behind the leftmost table, whereas Charlie was deposited behind the stand in the middle of the floor. With that complete, the two guards who'd carried him in claimed spots below Judicator Dales and snapped to with military precision.

The Judicator took a quick survey of the room, his eyes lingering on Charlie with a hint of curiosity, before he rang a delicate handbell with his right hand. It was a tradition, no doubt, but Charlie found it pretentious and annoying. Then again, he probably wasn't going to like much of anything that happened in the immediate future.

"I believe it is time we bring this session to order," the Judicator said with an earnest casualness that Charlie found curious in his own right. "Inspector Javrouche. Please recite the charges that are being brought against the accused today."

"If it may please the Judicator." The Inspector rose from his seat, stealing a glance at Charlie as he did. "Before the honor of the Ferryman Institute, I present today Charles Ronald Dawson. I hereby formally charge the accused, henceforth the defendant, with the following crimes: One. The deliberate removal of a Ferryman Key during the course of an assignment. Two. Failure to comply with the Ferryman Institute's law stating that no information relevant to the Institute or Institute affairs shall be revealed to non-Institute personnel. Three . . ."

Charlie's mind wandered as Javrouche continued to list the litany of charges. It didn't matter what they were, as Charlie already knew what the Inspector was angling for: Purgatory, and a long time in it. He was sure that Javrouche had deliberately stuck him in that cell before the trial just to tease Charlie with a little taste. To Javrouche, Charlie was a threat to the Institute, a rogue agent desperately in need of permanent confinement.

Maybe the Inspector was right.

In a way, Charlie hoped Purgatory was on Javrouche's mind—it was the only fitting outcome for his failure. He could picture it in his head already. The absence of light in the cell would create the perfect canvas for Charlie's mind to replay him shooting Alice, over, and over, and over again.

". . . finally, one count of resisting arrest. These are the charges we bring against the defendant today."

Dales fingered the inside of one his robe's sleeves. "That is quite the list, Inspector. Given the charges you have brought before me, what sentence do you, in representation of the Institute that you are contracted to serve, seek today?"

Charlie placed a mental bet on Purgatory for two hundred fifty years, with first check—the first time anyone was allowed to open up his cell and see how much of his brain had leaked out his ears—at twenty-five years.

"If it may please the Judicator," Javrouche began, "Mr. Dawson is a terrorist and traitor to the Institute. The prosecution has concrete evidence for nearly all its charges and aims to prove the rest beyond a reasonable doubt. Given the serious nature of these accusations, we, the Ferryman Institute, are seeking maximum punishment. I am asking of this court a sentence of five hundred years in Purgatory, with first check being set at fifty years."

Charlie couldn't help but laugh. Leave it to Javrouche to double the numbers, the crazy bastard. Even so, it didn't change the plan Charlie had concocted in his cell.

However, apparently his sudden reaction had not gone unnoticed. Judicator Dales nonchalantly turned his attention to the stand.

"Mr. Dawson?" he asked politely.

Charlie looked up. "Mmm?"

"Are you aware, Mr. Dawson, that some dreadfully serious accusations are being leveled against you right now?"

"Fully aware, Your Honor."

The Judicator's expression turned stern. "Are the proceedings too boring for your liking, then?"

"No, Your Honor, and I apologize for giving that impression," Charlie said calmly. "I'm just waiting for the part where you ask me if I'm guilty or not so I can save everyone here some time and trouble."

The Judicator straightened in his seat. The words out of Charlie's mouth, on their own, seemed flippant and rebellious, but Charlie could hear the deep sense of earnestness in his own voice just as well as anyone else in the room. Maybe that was what made him such a damned good Ferryman—he spoke, and people believed. He wished he'd figured that out earlier, instead of moments before he was locked away for half a millennia.

"Well," the Judicator began carefully, "given that you are aware of the charges being brought against you, I suppose we can move things along." He cleared his throat. "In front of this noble office, with your honor foremost in your mind, do you, Charles Ronald Dawson, Ferryman Number 72514, confirm or deny the charges brought against you today?"

Javrouche gathered a report in front of him, the quiet ruffling of his papers the only noise in the room. Charlie noticed that the Inspector's body was tense, already preparing to stand in objection. Charlie almost smiled. If only Javrouche knew. He dragged the silence out, waited 'til it was pregnant, then straining, then practically bursting. When he knew Dales was a second away from repeating the question, he spoke.

"I confirm them," he said loudly. "All of them. I am guilty on all charges, wholly and completely."

If the hush that had prevailed before Charlie's reply was born out of tension, the resulting one was born from utter disbelief. Javrouche was frozen, half standing, his body hovering in the air above his seat, objecting to a statement that never arrived.

Judicator Dales seemed just as surprised. "You're . . . guilty?" he said, more question than affirmation.

"Yes." Charlie answered clearly, without hesitation.

"You don't want to refute any of the charges brought against you?"

"No."

Dales momentarily leaned back in his seat. "None of them?"

"None of them, sir." As Charlie spoke, he watched out of the corner of his eye as Javrouche slowly lowered himself back into his seat.

A thoughtful frown worked its way across the Judicator's face. "Inspector," he began slowly, "am I correct in saying that no plea bargain was reached prior to the beginning of this session?"

Being spoken to seemed to revive Javrouche. He, too, cleared his throat. "You are correct, Sir Judicator. The Office of Ferryman Affairs refused to entertain bargains of any kind based on the strength of its case."

Dales's gaze slowly walked back across the room to Charlie. He was tempted to start cackling like a lunatic, but the last thing he wanted was to have the Judicator stop taking him seriously. Appearing to be in a completely lucid and rational state was all very important to the plan.

"Mr. Dawson," the Judicator began. He leaned forward, both of his forearms resting on the oaken surface in front of him. "Forgive me for saying this, but never has there been a Ferryman who's stood before me, or any other Judicator for that matter, and willingly taken such an extreme punishment without so much as a hint of a defense. The punishment you've just accepted is unprecedented. It makes me wonder if there's something here I'm just not seeing. Now, I am well aware of your Ferryman record and would like to think the high esteem your colleagues hold you in isn't completely unwarranted. With that said, surely at the very least you can explain everything that's happened in your own words?"

Almost as soon as the last words were out of Judicator Dales's mouth, Javrouche was standing to argue. "Judicator, I object completely. You cannot show any favor to the accused. If the defendant—"

But Charlie had decided well before he'd entered the room that if these were to be his last actions as a Ferryman, then it would be his show, not Javrouche's.

"No," Charlie said with such authority that his voice easily rose over Javrouche's, interrupting the Inspector's protests, "I refuse."

If anything, Charlie was pleased to note that his actions— which he'd designed to be as shocking as possible—were having their intended effect. Both the Judicator and Inspector looked taken aback.

What caught Charlie by surprise, however, was how quickly Dales recomposed himself. "I must admit, Mr. Dawson," he finally said, "you've put me in quite the predicament. While the evidence certainly has its merits, I feel as if there are explanations here that you're not providing. In that sense, I believe the charges to be grossly inappropriate and yet you've already accepted them. Why?"

This, however, Charlie had not accounted for. Dales was proving to be quite obstinate about judging him guilty and just being done with it. "Why what?" Charlie asked.

"Why are you accepting the charges?"

Javrouche tried to interrupt again—"Judicator, Your Honor"— but once again, Charlie's voice trumped the Inspector's.

"Because I killed an innocent woman today," he said, firm and loud. He hadn't necessarily thought that response through, but he felt the need to dictate the course of proceedings.

The small collection of people in the room once again fell into silence. Even one of the stone-faced guards raised an eyebrow at Charlie's reply. Both Javrouche and the Judicator stared at him. They exchanged a glance, which spurred Dales into checking the documents in front of him.

"Mr. Dawson, nowhere in this report does it mention you killing anyone . . ."

A stark vision of Alice bringing her hand away from her chest appeared before Charlie's eyes, and that, it seemed, was enough. His carefully constructed plan dissolved into nothing and his demeanor with it. Before he could even consider what he was doing, the words were pouring out. "Allow me to enlighten you then, Josh. Can I call you Josh? Great. Let me set the stage for you. For once during this godforsaken job, I was given a choice. At this point, I don't even know if it was real or if somebody was just fucking with me—who the hell knows—but I *believe* I was given a choice. It read, *Be a Ferryman or save the girl.* I chose to save the girl, and given that choice to make a million times, I would make the same one every time.

"This particular girl's name was Alice Spiegel. According to the assignment sheet I was provided, she was about to commit suicide. She didn't. You know just as well as I do that shit like that doesn't happen. Now, you could make a good case that she didn't because of me, and I wouldn't argue with you. That's not the catch, though. The catch is what happened after I left, because even after I disappeared from her life, she *still* didn't kill herself. That would have been the opportune moment, right? No one around, box full of bullets, handgun ready for round two. Simple, easy as you like. But she didn't. Then I eventually made a second contact with her—a point I'm sure the Inspector has *exhaustively* elaborated on in his riveting report sitting in front of you—and she decided to take a chance on something that must have seemed so ridiculous that anybody else would've pissed themselves laughing. Being chased by immortal people who guide you to the afterlife? What normal human being would honestly believe that?

"She did. She took that chance because it meant that maybe she was wrong, that maybe her life wasn't predetermined bullshit that meant *nothing*, and maybe, just maybe, there still existed this unfound capacity for something new, something *unbelievable*. 'Cause that's what she needed. She didn't ignore the new evidence in front of her—she *embraced* it.

"And what did that get her? A gunshot to the chest from yours truly. All the feelings I'd had pent up, and I just lost it. She grabbed me, and before I knew it, I'd squeezed the trigger, and . . .

I am no hypocrite, Judicator. I can't look at another soul again and talk to them about moving on to a better life. I can't. I'm done."

Dales didn't reply initially. He hesitated, clearly running Charlie's words against some unknown compendium he had stored in his brain. "We . . . do have counseling for this sort of thing, Mr. Dawson. It would be easy to get you help."

"I promise you I will do something illegal the first chance I get, and we'll just be here again under worse circumstances. I will make it heinous, too, so that these words will rest on your conscience. Like I said, I'm done, Josh. It's over. I am responsible for the death of an innocent girl whose biggest mistake was rising above the biggest mistake she never made."

Charlie would have loved a seat right then and there, just to have something to drop into, but unfortunately he had to settle for standing where he was. Strange, he thought, that he and Javrouche would be rooting for the same outcome now. They wouldn't need to strain themselves rooting too hard, however—Charlie knew he'd won. He'd tied Dales's hands so tight there'd be nothing he could do. The evidence would have to be treated as incontrovertible and therefore carry with it at least two hundred and fifty years in Purgatory, which was Charlie's original estimate.

There was nothing left but the sentencing.

The Honorable Judicator Joshua Dales looked down at Charlie, hands folded in front of his face. Behind his eyes, pity shifted in tiny grains, stuck falling to the bottom of the hourglass. "Very well, Mr. Dawson—you have your five hundred years of Purgatory. However, I'm setting the first check at one year." Javrouche began to object, but Dales quickly hushed him. "I follow the letter of the law, Inspector, but something about this case doesn't strike me as quite right." He rang the delicate handbell that signaled the end of the session. "I only pray that one year is kind to you, Mr. Dawson."

It was done. No more lives to ruin, no more false hope to give. It would just be him, alone with his thoughts, and he was already well acquainted with how vicious they could be.

The two men standing beneath the Judicator's bench came forward as Javrouche quickly approached the bench, no doubt to quibble over the first check. *Let him*, Charlie thought, and a vicious, masochistic part of the Ferryman hoped the Inspector succeeded.

The men led him toward the courtroom's exit off to the right of the room, the white hallway beyond beckoning. Having barely survived less than a day in Purgatory, Charlie was sure he'd be a broken man sooner rather than later. For all his upcoming misery, he took one last look around the room. It would be the last bit of . . . well, anything, really, he'd see for, at the very least, a year. It wasn't much, but it was something. Satisfied, Charlie turned to the exit, ready to be led away.

Then a voice rolled in from the back of the courtroom.

"Excuse me? Am I too late for the trial?" came a distinctly British accent. "I'm afraid I heard most of it through the set of doors, but most regrettably, they were locked until moments ago."

Charlie's mind went blank. Slowly approaching the Judicator's bench was none other than William Henry Taylor Cartwright IV.

The guards holding Charlie quickly released their grips in unison and moved toward Cartwright, but Dales was already holding up his hand to stop them. "No need for that. I know this man," he said. Turning his attention to Cartwright, he said, "If you've been listening, then you should know that I've already reached my verdict. An appeal will have to be filed through the appropriate channels if you'd like to object."

But Cartwright ignored the Judicator's remarks and continued walking forward until he was standing behind the table reserved for the defendant's counsel. Once there, he bowed politely.

"Before I say anything else, please allow me to sincerely apologize for my tardiness, Honorable Judicator Dales. I arrived as quickly as time would allow given the circumstances, and they are a most unbelievable, unusual set of circumstances, I can assure you." Cartwright stood casually behind the table, hands folded neatly behind his back, a quiet air of self-assurance asserting itself in his posture. "While I understand you have already rendered a verdict, Sir Judicator, I believe under Provision W36D13L0, a defendant who has been deliberately misled may demand an immediate retrial. To that point, I believe there are very important elements to this case that need to be clarified in an effort to exonerate my dear friend Mr. Charles Dawson.

"First and foremost, I simply must correct a rather egregiously erroneous statement made by the defendant, one which I think has grounded his stubbornness and therefore falls within the boundaries of the aforementioned provision. He had stated, rather categorically, that he was responsible for the death of one Ms. Alice Spiegel. I am afraid that is simply untrue."

Cartwright, the sly grin deepening underneath his twirled dark mustache, shot a quick sidelong glance at Charlie. "In fact, I daresay it is impossible, for the sheer fact that my new acquaintance Ms. Spiegel is very much not dead. She is alive and mostly well, undoubtedly due to some rather excellent medical attention. I would present her as evidence to this venerated court to confirm as such; however, I'm afraid she isn't in any condition to be prancing about quite yet, so I regret that my word must do." Cartwright cocked his head. "I am aware of the paperwork involved in convening a retrial, Honorable Judicator Dales. Perhaps then, in light of the new evidence, you might consider hanging your verdict—

something, as I'm sure you're aware, you are quite within your right to do—and resume the trial?"

Charlie realized his mouth was hanging open. He couldn't believe what he was hearing. Apparently, he wasn't alone there—Javrouche looked like he'd just been punched in the stomach.

Dales considered Cartwright's statements. He sighed dramatically. "You've made a rather compelling argument, though I can't say I'm surprised to hear as much coming from you. Very well. Let the record show that the court has hereby decided to resume the trial of Mr. Charles Dawson in light of new evidence to the case."

Javrouche looked between Cartwright and the Judicator sitting above him. "What—"

But then Cartwright was continuing again. "I sincerely thank you, Sir Judicator. Now, in addition to the information about Ms. Spiegel, I would also like to corroborate Mr. Dawson's claims about the unusual nature of Ms. Spiegel's case. I'd like to admit this letter, signed by the acting president of the Institute, as evidence, which states that the defendant was in fact given the choice he described moments ago. That choice, however, was classified under the highest level of secrecy available to the president, which is why its record doesn't exist."

The Inspector's voice cut through the air like a rusted knife, his eyes darting back and forth like an overeager dog. "Excuse me, Sir Judicator, for interrupting, but would anyone care to explain to me why this man isn't being promptly escorted from these chambers?"

Cartwright leaned forward and looked across at his counterpart. "My sincerest apologies," he said politely. "My dear friend Charles was being judged without counsel. Under the articles of the Ferryman Institute Fair Trial Act, I am merely providing that. This wouldn't be my first time in such an environment, if I do say so."

"You're missing my point." Javrouche waved impatiently. "I want to know who *you* are, exactly."

Before Dales could speak, Cartwright was talking again. "My word, how rude of me. Please allow me to introduce myself. I go by William Henry Taylor Cartwright the Fourth. It is a pleasure to finally make your acquaintance, Inspector."

The recognition of the name slowly appeared on Javrouche's face. "Cartwright? But that's impossible . . . ," he said. The Inspector's eyes narrowed perceptibly, as if he sensed he'd been placed in a trap but couldn't quite figure out what would set it off.

"Really?" Cartwright said. "I find that rather remarkable given that I'm presently standing directly in front of you."

Javrouche gave a derisive sneer. The formality he'd maintained throughout the trial was beginning to wear thin. "Allow me to re-phrase. My office has been very interested in a person going by that name. In fact, I have a few questions for him." Then he turned to the Judicator. "Honorable Judicator, I humbly request your per-mission to arrest this man."

Dales went to interject again, but Charlie noticed he stopped when Cartwright gave him a look. Instead, Cartwright replied. "Allow me to explain," he said. His cadence had changed to that of a man who was suddenly done with witticisms. "Cartwright is not my given name. However, you would have known that had you not invoked a Ferryman Affairs Privacy Consultation Override with-out the Institute's consent."

"I acted well within the scope of my position," the Inspector countered.

"After being repeatedly ordered over the course of several years to leave Mr. Dawson alone? I think not."

At this point, Charlie felt as if he might as well have been lying in the fetal position sucking his thumb for all the good he was having on the conversation.

Javrouche straightened his posture, eyes still focused on Cartwright. "And let that man wander around, doing as he pleases, breaking cardinal rule after cardinal rule? Do you expect me to sit and watch as he brings about the end of the world? You've come here preaching, but what is more dangerous than a man who threatens to reveal our organization to the world, monsieur?"

Cartwright's voice cracked back in rebuttal. "A man who uses that as an excuse to abuse his authority! You've received multiple orders from the highest echelons of this organization to cease all interactions with Mr. Dawson, and yet you've thoroughly ignored them all. I doubt not the love you have for this institution, Inspector, but don't insult me by insisting this case is being pursued purely in the interest of its protection. If you cannot see the personal grudge in all this, you have blinded yourself to it." Charlie had never heard Cartwright raise his voice, let alone speak with such a harsh tone. "While I'm on the topic of abuse of authority, Inspector . . . would you care to explain the mysterious warehouse where you conduct your 'advanced' interrogations?"

"I don't see what relevance that has to the matter at hand," Javrouche replied.

"You don't, Inspector? I find that peculiar. Perhaps Mr. Dupine and Ms. Johnson would find it peculiar as well? After all, you only left them dangling over a vat of hydrofluoric acid."

He did what? Hydrofluoric acid? Charlie had never even heard of that.

Javrouche stared at Cartwright in apparent disbelief. "Where did you hear that?" He looked too shocked to be angry. "Who the hell are you? Really."

Cartwright went to speak, but this time Dales interrupted him. "I believe under the Ferryman Bylaws I am required to perform this part, Mr. . . . Cartwright, was it?" Though Cartwright looked eager to argue the point, he instead sighed in resignation and merely nodded.

Dales said: "Inspector Javrouche. What do you know of the Ferryman Council?"

"Again, I don't see what that has to do with this case whatsoever," he replied. As per the question, Charlie had to admit he was wondering the same thing.

"You will momentarily," Dales said. "Now then, my question, please."

Javrouche looked at Cartwright, then Dales, then finally Charlie, where his eyes seemed to linger just a bit longer. When he began to speak, his gaze still bore down on the Ferryman. "I don't know anything about the Ferryman Council. They're a made-up story that gets repeated to new Ferrymen to give context to their new lives."

Dales grimly shook his head. "You are incorrect about one salient point."

The Inspector sighed. "Of course I am. And what part would that be, exactly?"

The Judicator leaned forward, clasping his hands together. "The part where you called it a made-up story."

It was tough to say, really, given that he couldn't see himself, but Charlie had a sense that he looked just as dumbfounded as Javrouche right then. However, the Inspector recovered quickly.

"And what of it?" Javrouche asked, his voice dipping into indignation. "What does the Ferryman Council have to do with this case? Mssr. Dawson has already admitted his guilt. There is nothing left to discuss."

Dales turned to Cartwright with a pensive brow. "Would I be correct in assuming that Mr. Dawson is directly under your supervision?" he asked.

"You would be," Cartwright replied.

The Judicator turned his attention back to Javrouche. "The arrival of Mr. Cartwright has cast this case in a new light. Inspector, I regret to inform you that you should have both announced your invocation of a Privacy Consultation Override and followed it up with the president's office. That would have saved us all some grief tonight."

"I don't understand—" Javrouche began, but Dales stopped him.

"Nor should you. I'll explain. Had your plans to initiate a PCO been known, you would have received strict orders from the president of the Institute to stop them at once. The reason is that Mr. Dawson has been placed under direct supervision of the Ferryman Council. That is unbeknownst to you and even to him, or so I assume. Once such an action takes place, it is the Council's responsibility to discipline him for misconduct. Furthermore, that is why PCOs must be cleared first. That is also why you've already received several official requests on behalf of the president not to pursue Mr. Dawson. Now—regarding the existence of one William Henry Taylor Cartwright—I can say—"

"The Fourth," interrupted Cartwright. He smiled courteously. Dales rolled his eyes.

"William Henry Taylor Cartwright the *Fourth*—I can say that you won't find him in the Institute records. The reason being that he doesn't officially exist. The man standing in front of me is, in fact, one of the original founders of the Institute, whom I met upon being sworn in as a Judicator, and whose identity I am sworn to protect. This man's true name is Virgil."

Charlie looked at the man standing to his left. Virgil. As in one of the cofounders of the Institute. The mythical Ferryman who was immortalized in Dante's *Inferno* and superseded in importance only by the first Ferryman, Charon. Cartwright—the man who spent an inordinate amount of time sipping tea and whipping elegantly sarcastic remarks in Charlie's direction—was *the* Virgil.

What the fucking fuck was going on here?

"Well," Cartwright—now Virgil—said sheepishly, "technically Vergilius, but Latin endings seem so out of fashion these days. Virgil works rather nicely, I think. Wouldn't you agree?"

I DREAMED A DREAM

This couldn't be happening. It was impossible. Alice surveyed the room. Sure, the stark white walls, ceiling, and floor were unusual, as were the white blanket and sheets that rested on top of her. But those were all plausible things that followed logic—someone found her and put her there. Even though the interior design was monochromatic to the point of strangeness, that set of circumstances made sense.

The fact that her late mother was sitting at the edge of the bed, looking healthy and spry, did not.

White room filled with lots of white things: sense.

Dead mother no loner dead: no sense.

Which led Alice to her next conclusion. "Holy shit," she said as her mother tenderly stroked her hair, "I'm dead, aren't I?"

Her mother shushed her gently. "Don't be silly. You're just dreaming, sweetheart."

Alice looked up at her mom. Actually, that made a little bit more sense, even if it wasn't quite as satisfactory. "So am I having one of those Harry Potter moments where you tell me you've been in my heart this whole time and this dream is really just a way for us to reconnect? That would be *so* awesome."

Her mother smoothed out the sheets with her hand. "I didn't think it could be possible for a child to read too much—especially with your generation—but I'm beginning to wonder about that."

Alice frowned. "You always said I watched too much TV."

"You did," her mother said as she brushed an errant strand of hair out of Alice's face. "But you always had a very addictive personality. You did too much of *everything* that interested you at one point or another. God, remember your Lisa Frank stage? You must have had fifteen binders filled with stickers of pink unicorns and purple dolphins."

Alice's heart seemed to jump forward a beat as the nostalgia took hold. "And Friendly's Cone Head sundaes."

Her mother laughed. "Grilled cheese sandwiches and Cone Head sundaes, every single time."

"Why didn't you ever make me try something new? I got the same thing at Friendly's for like twelve years."

Mrs. Spiegel shrugged. "It made you happy. Your sisters never took to that place like you did, so it was kind of fun to have our own little thing. Besides, it's not like we ate there all that often, especially as you got older."

Alice propped herself up on the crisp white pillows behind her. As she sat up, she had a chance to really comprehend the space she was in for the first time. It was definitely disorienting being in a place that was so . . . blank. Alice didn't often remember her dreams, but even so, she felt sure she'd never had an experience quite like this. It was like her brain forgot to load the color when it booted up into dream mode.

Her mother, on the other hand, was a painfully familiar sight. A few wrinkles were scattered across her baby face, the one that had always made her appear ten years younger than her driver's license said. She was petite, yet somehow always managed to fill a room with her personality, one of the many things Alice admired about her.

"So it seems like you've had an interesting couple of days," her mother said casually. Alice gave her a raised eyebrow in return. As if sensing the question behind the expression, her mom continued, "This is your dream, remember? I know everything that's happened."

"Right . . . ," Alice said, nodding slowly. She stopped, trying to recall everything that had happened thus far. Some of the details were a little hazy, but she felt like she got most of it. "It's definitely been a trip."

Alice's mother stroked her daughter's hair. "You were going to kill yourself."

That was one of the few things Alice had no trouble remembering. She wasn't necessarily ashamed about her suicide attempt; she just felt that there was something inherently weird about talking about it with her dead mother.

"Thank you for the blunt recap," Alice replied with a huff.

"Again, your dream."

Alice straightened up in the bed some more and tried to kick the sheets off, but after four kicks they were still covering her legs. "Yeah, well," she said as the blankets kept getting more tangled around her feet, "that doesn't mean I get to control what happens." Finally, she just tried to pry her lower half free with her left hand, but somehow the sheet was twisted around her left leg, so she needed to roll over first. "See? Like this shit! I mean, stuff. Like this stuff. And to top it all off, you're here—my mother, who I've been missing terribly since the day she passed away, is right here, right next to me, finally, and yet emotionally I don't feel anything . . . I don't know, what's the right word? Special? It's like you never even left. I guess because I'm dreaming this, it all just seems normal, which, frankly, isn't fair. On top of that, I know the moment I wake up, I'll realize it was all a dream, and I'll be so sad that I just never want to get up and out of whatever ditch I'll inevitably find myself lying in."

With a yell of frustration, she gave up trying to get the sheets off of her and flopped back onto the bed. "It's like, this whole thing has been so surreal. So . . ."

"Hollywood?" her mother offered.

"If you say something about it being my dream again—"

"Alice, you've dreamed about making it in Hollywood since you were four." Her mother lay down on the bed next to her, just like she used to do when Alice was growing up. "Lighten up a little. You're alive!"

"Funny, people keep telling me that like it's a good thing."

"It is!"

Alice sat bolt upright. This was not a discussion she wanted to have right now, and yet something in her mother's tone flipped a switch in Alice's head. "God, why does everybody keep saying that?! It's a good thing according to who, exactly? You? Charlie? Neither of you have any idea what it's like to be me. I'm single, I don't have a job, I don't have any close friends, I can't go back to school because what's the point, I can't make any money as a writer, I'll never find a guy who is even half as perfect as Marc, and even if I did, why would he date me, my mom—the one person I most aspired to be in life—is dead, and the one time I finally work up the courage to put an end to all of it, some guy shows up *literally* out of thin air and puts the kibosh on that. My life is nothing but one big exercise in pretending that everything is just *fucking grand* while on the inside I'm miserable. So no, Mom, I don't see it as a good thing."

Her mother sat up slowly next to her. She looked somehow

angelic framed by the white walls behind her. She edged closer to Alice before placing her hand on top of Alice's own. Just like that, Alice found herself looking deep into her mother's hazel eyes. "You need to wake up now, Alice," she said slowly.

That was not the reply Alice had been expecting. More to the point, it wasn't the one she wanted. "Wait . . . that's it? We just started talking, and . . . you can't just leave now."

Her mother flashed a sad smile. "Not my choice."

"Well, if it's my dream like you keep saying it is, then it should be my choice, and I say you're not going anywhere."

Her mother stood up, and though Alice tried to follow suit, she found herself too tangled in blankets to accomplish the task. "I'm sorry, Alice," her mother said with an air of finality, "but it doesn't work that way."

"But you can't leave," Alice said. "You have to fix me!"

"There's nothing to fix," her mom said, and she started to walk away.

"So you're just going to leave your suicidal daughter like this, right after she's been kidnapped by some strange man after she planned to put a bullet through her head? I just want to make sure I'm understanding all of the nuances of this situation correctly."

Her mother stopped and then turned, tucking a fallen strand of her own hair behind her ear as she did. She suddenly seemed as if she bore the weight of the world on her shoulders, and yet, in typical fashion, still gave the impression she could take another solar system's worth. "That's actually exactly why I think she'll be okay . . . because a strange but compassionate man showed up and somehow managed to get through to her when it seemed like no one else could. Even if she doesn't want to admit that to her own mother."

The stinging anger Alice had felt moments ago dissipated

slightly. That also wasn't the reply she had been expecting. She was beginning to wonder if she was very bad at predicting what people were going to say or if the people she associated with just generally said crazy shit.

"I feel like everybody is talking to me in riddles tonight," Alice said, rubbing her temples. "I swear, it gets old really, really quickly."

"How about I put it this way," her mother said as she moved back next to the white bed again. "Do you normally kiss men after they've kidnapped you?"

So that's where this is going. Alice sighed and flopped back down. "Tough to say. I am one for one in that category, so statistically the answer is yes, one hundred percent of the men who have kidnapped me, I have kissed. Maybe I get aroused by kidnappers."

Her mother chuckled. "I would say I'm encouraged you feel comfortable sharing that with me, but honestly there are certain things I can live without knowing."

Alice turned to face her mother. "Being dead, you technically did. Live without knowing it, I mean."

"Hey!" Her mom slapped her playfully. "You know what I meant!"

Now it was Alice's turn to shrug. "The fact of the matter is that you're ignoring what I said earlier about my life."

"I am, only because I don't really believe that's how you truly feel anymore."

Alice rolled over so she was looking across at the white wall opposite her mother. "So you think I'm lying."

"Of course not," her mother said earnestly. "I would bet anything in the world that's exactly how you feel right at this very moment. But I don't think it's going to stay that way, and I'd bet part of you thinks that, too."

"Yeah, well, apparently that part of Alice is either currently malfunctioning or doesn't bother showing up in dreams. Take your pick."

"As long as she's there, that's all that matters." Her mother squeezed Alice's arm. "I miss you guys so much."

Alice rolled back over and sat up. Her hands fell into her lap, and she found herself staring at them. She wanted so badly just to look at her mom again, but couldn't. Was that because it was part of the dream that was out of her control or because she had an unshakable feeling this would be the last time she'd ever have a moment like this?

"I miss you, too, Mom. More than you could ever know. I just want to know what to do."

"You already do. Here's a hint: it rhymes with *barley*. Go find him." Alice then felt her mother's lips pressed against her forehead, and it seemed so annoyingly, heartbreakingly real. "You've been in Wonderland for too long, my precious little Alice. You need to wake up now. And just so you know, I will always be in your heart for as long as you need me. I love you so very, very much."

ALICE AWOKE with the words *I love you, too* poised daintily on the edge of her lips.

She was arrayed in a mess of blankets in a white room, which initially caused her no shortage of confusion. However, she eventually noticed that the walls were not as perfectly blank as in her dream, and now other colors floated about the room. Her bed was composed of dark gray sheets and a yellow blanket, which was garish, to say the least, but comforting in the sense that at least it wasn't white. There was also the young man sitting casually in a chair across from her on the other side of the bed who was—

Alice yelped in surprise as she realized she wasn't alone, pulling the sheets up instinctively toward her face. In response, the man held up his left hand in what Alice assumed was a placating gesture. With his other hand, he slipped something that glinted in the light into his pants pocket, and though it seemed vaguely related to something she'd seen earlier that night, she couldn't quite remember what.

Before her mind could travel further down that path, he was speaking to her.

"I see you are awake now," he said with a noticeable but not overbearing Russian accent.

Alice had so many questions that she wanted to ask—who, what, where, why, when, how, rinse and repeat—but with her brain still not completely recovered from her dream, the best she could do was a stilted and delayed "Am I?"

The man laughed quietly before standing up. He walked over to a small nightstand on his side of the bed and took a glass of water from atop it. With a slow and deliberate motion, he offered it to her. "I have a feeling that your questions may be outweighed by your thirst, no?"

After he spoke, Alice became acutely aware of her mouth, namely that it felt like someone had poured the Sahara down it while she'd been out. She accepted the glass and began drinking in such satisfied gulps that water began to dribble down her chin.

"Easy, easy!" the man said with a small laugh. "I have plenty more, but you're still recovering. It's best if you sip slow."

Alice exhaled and looked at the almost empty glass she now held in her hands. "Noted," she said absentmindedly. There was a dull pain coming back to her, down by her shoulder. As she moved to examine the area it was coming from, she noticed that her clothes were gone. In place of her white T-shirt and jeans she found what she could only describe as a loose-fitting hospital shirt and a pair of baggy pants made of the same material. Her mind was trying to puzzle together what exactly had happened, but she felt like she was in a deep fog. A pang of regret washed over her as memories of her mother came back, and it was all she could do to keep from tearing up. She sipped some more water from her glass instead.

"My name is Begemot. Cartwright asked that I stay with you in case you woke up. As is usual, his instinct turned out to be correct. Don't worry—you're safe here. There will be no more running away now, I promise."

Alice looked over at him. His eyes seemed sharp, even if they were partially obscured by his drooping eyelids. Both his words and demeanor felt refreshingly calm.

"How did I get here? And where is *here*, exactly? And where's Charlie?" Alice asked.

"I see your injuries haven't dented your curiosity much," Begemot said. "Cartwright brought you here with some help, the here being the Ferryman Institute. We may have bent a rule or two in the process, but you needn't concern yourself with that. You were in need of immediate care and, unfortunately, a conventional place of treatment might not have been fast enough. I hope you don't mind our modest accommodations. I will admit, they don't often see much use."

Alice surveyed the room again. "Well, your blankets and sheets are ugly as shit, but I'm not dead, so you're doing okay in my book."

A small grin perked up on his face. "I'll pass that on to my superiors."

Alice felt strange. Part of her wanted to curl up into a ball and just lie there, a not unfamiliar feeling for her of late. But the other part fixated on Charlie. Where was he? Why wasn't he here? Was he all right? Her thoughts were scattered and fuzzy, like her brain was trying to run underwater. She felt drunk and slow and mentally clumsy.

What should I do?

And suddenly, like the proverbial lighthouse shining through the night, the answer was there. She didn't know why, or how, or any of those silly little details she'd undoubtedly go back and try to figure out after the fact. She just *knew*.

"You never answered my question about Charlie," she said. She was attempting to be casual, but there was no mistaking the hint of anxiety in her voice.

Begemot's placid gaze acquired an offhanded smirk, and he slumped back against his chair. "It was a question I was trying to avoid, but I can see that's not going to happen. Cartwright went to him. That's all I know."

That seemed like a lie, but Alice was in no position to call him out on it. She forged ahead. "I need to see him," she said matter-of-factly.

He smiled again, but it was different this time. A ruse, and Alice saw right through it. "I'm afraid I—"

"You seem like a really nice guy," she said, interrupting him, "and I'm extremely grateful for everything you and Cartwright and whoever else have done for me, but I don't think you understand. I *need* to see Charlie. I'm sorry, and I know this kind of makes me a horrible person after all you've done for me, but I won't take no for an answer."

If her admittedly levelheaded demand (levelheaded in spoken tone, anyway—asking to see the guy who'd just shot and nearly killed you was, from a logical standpoint, less "levelheaded" and more "certifiably insane") bothered him in any way, it certainly didn't show. He considered her statement, completely unfazed, before pointing at her shoulder. "We just got you patched up. It's not a good idea for you to be up and about. Rest is my advice."

"Listen," Alice began, but already her brain was elsewhere. All she could think about was getting up and moving. It was just a feeling, a *strong* feeling, that she needed to get out of there. She tossed aside the covers, and to her relief, they didn't pose the tangled threat that the ones in her dream had.

Her feet felt the cool tiled floor, and slowly Alice pushed herself up. She wobbled a bit as she straightened out, then had to fight off the light-headed vertigo that accompanied it. When she achieved relative stability, she looked over her shoulder at Begemot. "Have you ever felt like you just instinctually know something that you have no business knowing?" she asked as she began to make her way gingerly around the bed.

Begemot seemed poised to stand up, but the question kept him in his seat. "Maybe," he finally offered.

"Well," Alice said with one passing shuffle step at a time, "that just happened to me. For whatever reason, I just know I need to go find Charlie. I understand that I'm supposed to wait here and hope for the best, but I can't do that. Not that this is going to mean anything to you, but I recently learned from some crazy, bullet-stopping dork—and I mean that in the nicest way possible—that sometimes you have to trust yourself and do what you believe is the right thing even if the world tells you otherwise. I've spent too much of my recent life being willfully blind to the choices I was making because I'd convinced myself that they didn't even exist. Like I didn't have any control over my life, you know? Now I'm choosing. Please. Help me find him."

The man regarded her carefully, perhaps trying to figure out if she was bluffing. The look on his face had shifted into one of calculation. Alice got the sense that, behind his indifferent exterior, he was weighing everything with his full attention. Finally, he stood up.

"I would almost say that this strikes me as somewhat ungrateful. We've already put ourselves at considerable risk for you, and now you want me to do so again without understanding the circumstances." It was a statement, not a question. "I don't like that."

Alice made to interject, but he spoke over her. "However, your friend Mr. Dawson has made a career out of trusting his intuition, and I've yet to see it steer him wrong. Perhaps the same could be said of Cartwright as well. I don't believe in coincidences, Ms. . . ." He trailed off there, just then realizing he wasn't actually acquainted with Alice.

"Spiegel," she said quickly.

"Ms. Spiegel, yes, I remember now. I will admit, what you're asking me to do is . . . well, let us call a spade a spade—it is potentially worse than career-ending. Should things go as poorly as I imagine they possibly could, we may both find ourselves traveling to the afterlife tonight." He reached next to the nightstand, where an old gray hospital cane was propped. Begemot passed it to Alice across the bed. "Let's hope some of Mr. Dawson's divine intuition has rubbed off on you."

An awful feeling of shame crept in from all sides as Alice clutched the cane in front of her. Her haste to find Charlie was a strong wind at her back, but it didn't assuage her feelings of guilt. This man had helped save her life. Even if she was still somewhat on the fence about whether that was a good thing or not, somewhere along the way she'd regained enough perspective (temporarily, at least) to realize what an amazing thing that was. Now, on top of everything he'd already done—which sounded like a lot—she was asking him to put everything on the line, again, for her.

"I'm sorry," she said. "I didn't realize that's what I was asking for. Why exactly is it so dangerous?"

Begemot was standing in the doorway now, his hand on the knob. With a daring smirk, he looked back at her over his shoulder. "Because you're about to become the first human to spy on the Ferryman Council."

"That does sound mildly terrifying." Alice took the cane in her left hand. "I'm in."

CHARLIE

THE FERRYMAN COUNCIL

S o let me get this straight," Charlie began, but he was derailed by his efforts to match Cartwright's—or rather, Virgil's—pace. Though Cartwright was more of the strolling type who seemed to take pains to meander, Virgil strode with a purpose Charlie found slightly disconcerting.

"Go on," Cartwright said with his traditional unperturbed attitude.

"Alice is alive?" Charlie asked as he caught up.

"Very much so."

"And I'm not being sent to Purgatory?"

Cartwright looked over at him with a sly smile. "Not yet."

"And you're one of the original founders of the Institute acting as some run-of-the-mill late-Victorian British gentleman Ferryman mentor?"

Cartwright waved his hand dismissively. "I would argue strongly against your use of the word *acting* as I *am* your mentor, in the truest sense of the word. My position at this Institute has no bearing on that, nor do I act any differently with or without my given name."

"Speaking of, as a born Roman, why are you so . . . British?" An odd question, but Charlie didn't know how else to frame it.

"Tea," Cartwright replied. "And Shakespeare, I suppose, who inaugurated the rise of England as a literary and cultural powerhouse, a rise in which I was more than happy to immerse myself. It was so very similar to Rome back in its heyday, flaws and all, that I'd finally felt home for the first time in centuries. But mostly tea. You simply cannot fully appreciate its ambrosial qualities without first being a subject of the queen."

"What about the Ferryman Council stories? Is there any truth to them? Did you actually say those things?" Charlie asked. He felt disturbingly similar to a small child with all the questions he was slinging.

"They are mostly true," Cartwright said. "Some parts have been embellished."

Charlie finally managed to match Cartwright's stride. "An example being . . . ?" When Cartwright said nothing, Charlie continued. "Right, so back to my first question."

"I sincerely hope this isn't tumbling into an infinite loop of inquiry," Cartwright remarked.

Charlie ignored him. "How do you know Alice is alive? Javrouche told me I'd . . . she was dead."

They were approaching the end of a long hallway, not dissimilar to the one that connected Charlie's office to the control room, except it seemed older, somehow. He also hadn't seen anybody wandering around since they'd left the courtroom, and Cartwright was regularly unlocking doors Charlie hadn't even known existed.

"Because I arrived shortly after you were unceremoniously apprehended and had her brought here. She'd lost a considerable amount of blood, but she stabilized some hours ago. I have it on rather good authority that she'll make a full recovery."

Charlie didn't quite know what to say. It was like being one of the twelve disciples, thinking that this groovy guy you've been following around for a while has finally kicked the bucket, only for him to walk in the door a couple days later. Alice was alive. There existed in Charlie a crushing, shame-fueled guilt that made him wonder if he'd ever be able to show himself in front of her again. He'd almost killed her, after all, which was generally considered a bad way to endear yourself to someone. However, the fact it was even an option again was nearly beyond belief.

"Surprised?" Cartwright asked, apparently bemused.

Charlie shrugged. "You could say that, yes."

"Well," Cartwright replied as he opened one final door, "I would wager the first of many tonight."

Charlie was inclined to believe him.

Beyond was a dimly lit spiral staircase. The steps were narrow, cut from stone, giving way to uneven landings from one to the next. If ever there was a place where Hamlet would have met his father's ghost, this was it.

"Not much for Ikea upgrades, I take it?" Charlie said. With the weight of Alice at least partially off his mind, he felt his sarcasm returning to its normal dry sensibility.

"I would advise against judging too quickly," Cartwright replied.

The pair began climbing the winding staircase in silence. With each step, the walls seemed to press a bit closer. Small yellow lights were embedded in the floor every five stairs or so, but the light they gave off was paltry and often flickering. There were no windows to speak of. They marched upward at a steady pace, climbing well over a hundred stairs before Charlie lost count.

Just when Charlie was about to break the silence, they arrived at a large stone landing that eventually gave way to an ornate, solid-wood door. Without much fuss, Cartwright fit his Ferryman Key into the small, intricate lock just below the doorknob.

"Welcome," he said as the door swung open, "to the chambers of the Ferryman Council."

The room Charlie was ushered into might as well have been a spaceship cockpit compared to the staircase he'd just climbed. A strong but somewhat muted light shone down onto a luxurious table in the middle of the floor. The table seemed to be a perfectly cut, smooth circle of glass, polished to an incredible sheen. The room itself was circular as well, Charlie noticed, with glowing computer monitors lining the walls. Their screens continually changed from one instant to the next—some displayed rapidly changing pictures, like a slideshow gone haywire, while others seemed to be showing near-continuous streams of text. Charlie wondered for a brief moment whether the lines on the screens corresponded to people, each line one more soul on its way to the afterlife. The thought was both awe inducing and utterly horrifying.

"Pretty amazing, isn't it?"

The booming baritone voice brought Charlie's attention back to the table, which he only then realized was occupied. Just beyond the circle of light sat a cadre of figures, each one obscured by shadows. A dark hand reached out and tapped the table's surface. To Charlie's great astonishment, a holographic keyboard with several corresponding buttons next to it appeared, the keys vaguely orange and transparent. The hand then touched a translucent button on the side of the floating keyboard, causing the pressed key to momentarily flash.

The light above the table suddenly grew in intensity, revealing seven sitting figures: five male, two female. To call them a diverse group didn't quite do the ensemble justice.

The man immediately to Charlie's left possessed a rich olive complexion with very dark hair, which was a sight to behold in its own right. The sides were cropped neatly except for two large spikes of hair that jutted up above his ears. The top and front of his hairstyle—if you wanted to call it that—protruded several inches past his face in a sort of outlandish pompadour. Combined with a somewhat fierce expression, he vaguely reminded Charlie of an exotic wolf.

In complete contrast was the beautiful, golden-haired woman sitting clockwise from him. She was remarkably pale, like a porcelain doll, yet still perfectly vibrant. Her hair fell easily to the small of her back, gentle waves whispering throughout it. Wrapped around her neck was a brilliant necklace, its band ornate and delicate, while the massive red stone that hung from it seemed to burn with an inner flame.

And so it went around the table: a proud-looking man with a military posture; a rich, ebony-skinned man with an exuberant grin; a raven-haired woman with glowering eyes; a man with distinctly bronze skin who gave off an air of disinterest; and a hooded man hidden underneath a plain brown cloak.

The man sitting directly across from Charlie—the one with the sable skin—now addressed him. Charlie realized quickly from his baritone voice that he was the one who'd spoken earlier.

"Charles Ronald Dawson," the man said, enunciating each part of Charlie's name. He initially said nothing after that, instead nodding his head gently as if he were continuously reaffirming Charlie's existence, then said, "I sincerely apologize for the circumstances you've had to deal with of late. Let me be the first to tell you that we never intended for things to turn out this way." He paused again for a brief moment, realizing he'd forgotten something. "But where are my manners? Please, sit," he said, gesturing to two empty chairs.

Charlie considered it. For whatever reason, an animal instinct told him sitting there was dangerous. "I appreciate it," he said, "but I think I'll stand."

The man's expression never changed, but he slowly leaned forward. "Sit, Charlie," he said in no uncertain terms.

Charlie sat. Cartwright took the chair next to him. With the pair now seated, the man continued.

"Before I go any further, I suppose some introductions are in order. My name is Charon. I am the original Ferryman, and this is my Institute. The men and women you see before you are undoubtedly the best of the best. The . . . legendary ones, if you will, and names I'm sure you've heard before." Charon started by pointing at the man with the olive skin and ridiculous hair, then went around the circle, indicating names as he went. "Anubis. Freya. Michael. Morrigan. Sraosha. And Azrael. The first one I recruited, however—the man who helped found this wonderful organization—is sitting next to you, though I believe you've already picked up on that."

Charlie took a peek over at Cartwright, who for once seemed almost unsure of what to do. He just sat there, staring off into space, failing to even acknowledge Charlie's gaze.

"Hi," Charlie said. "You, uh, have a very nice room." A variation on that line had worked with Alice. Actually, she'd shot him in the head after that. Charlie hadn't quite thought that one through.

"Thank you. Are you comfortable? We have quite a bit to discuss, so please, tell me if you're not."

Charlie swept his eyes across the table, trying to judge facial expressions. He couldn't glean a single read from anyone. An old poker proverb came to mind: *If you can't spot the sucker at the table, it's you.*

"I'm great. Thank you," Charlie said. He couldn't believe this was all happening. *Actually* happening.

"Fantastic. Has Virgil mentioned why you're here?" When Charlie shook his head, Charon said, "Because you've assembled quite the eventful service record, Charlie, and we thought it high time we all sit down and have a chat. So, then—let's talk about you.

"Two hundred fifty years ago, Virgil discovered you. Being in the Council doesn't preclude us from engaging in Ferryman activities, but we do it with discretion. Regardless, one thing we do not do is recruit new Ferrymen. Though it's not a formal prohibition, we leave that duty exclusively to the president. However, when Virgil returned with you in tow, he insisted there was something special about you. In fact, he was so sure about it that he voluntarily wagered his position on this Council to prove it. Thankfully, we don't have to discuss what would have happened should he have been wrong. Your record speaks for itself. You've been the longest-serving, most successful Ferryman this institution has seen in over a millennia. Needless to say, Virgil's decision was vindicated quite spectacularly."

Charon paused. He tapped a gentle rhythm out on the table's surface, and said nothing for several seconds. Finally, he looked directly at Charlie. "However, about fifty years ago, Virgil came to us rather concerned. He was becoming increasingly convinced that, despite your aptitude for being a Ferryman, you hadn't acclimated to the, shall I say, *mental rigors* demanded by the position. There was some suspicion on his part that your condition had been deteriorating for several decades already, if not longer. He was particularly worried the constant death involved was getting to you . . . only you happened to be incredibly adept at hiding it. That time

frame coincides with a noticeable uptick in your nonresponsive-
ness to emergency assignments, as well as an increase in your decisions to leave the Institute's campus unannounced, so we never
ruled it out. What do you say to that, Charlie?"

The question caught him a bit off guard. He hadn't imagined
he was here to do a lot of talking, and on top of that, his mind was
still frazzled from the events unfolding around him. Everything
was happening so fast. Not even an hour ago, he'd been on the
verge of a horrifying incarceration.

Charlie looked around the room. He knew the answer to that
question but wasn't sure he wanted to be saying it in front of these
people. Instead, he leaned back in his chair, opted for a shrug, and
weakly said, "I don't know."

The rest of the Council seemed to finally come to life. Looks
were exchanged among themselves, though Cartwright maintained his stoic nonchalance. Charon, for his part, raised an eyebrow. "I see." His finger once again resumed tapping on the table,
his eyes suggesting he was deep in thought. Charlie waited patiently in silence. After what seemed like an inordinate amount of
time, Charon touched a button on his holographic keyboard, then
refolded his hands.

"Styx, open video marked *Dawson E7*," Charon said to no one
in particular. A soft chime echoed in response, seemingly out of
thin air. Suddenly, a small rectangular video appeared on the table
in front of Charlie as well as at every other station. Before the
video could start playing, however, the military-looking man to
Charon's right—Michael, if Charlie's memory served—balked.

"You can't be serious!" he barked, searching the faces of his
colleagues around the table. "We can't show him this!"

"Though it pains me to say it, and though I would argue
with his word choice, I agree with the spirit of Michael's objec-

tion." Charlie looked over at Cartwright, surprised to see him speaking.

Charon looked at both objectors yet stayed silent—a trait Charlie was noticing as a recurring theme with the man. "I disagree," he finally said. "Given everything that's happened, I believe he's owed this. And Virgil, I imagine your objection is more personal than anything else. As such, your objections are noted but overruled. Styx, play video." Another soft chime, and the image began to move.

It appeared to be a recording of a meeting, and as the video continued, it became increasingly obvious it was a meeting of the Ferryman Council. All eight of the Council members were there, plus a lone, empty chair positioned directly below the camera. Cartwright was standing up with both his hands on the table. His mouth was moving, but there was no sound coming out of it. As if hearing Charlie's thought, Charon said, "Styx, increase volume." The chime again, and then Charlie could hear every word. He watched with rapt attention as the scene unfolded before his eyes.

———

". . . ARE NOT ROBOTS! They are not our *tools*! Why is this so hard to understand?" Cartwright backed away from the table, pacing between his chair and the open layout of the room behind it.

"Virgil," Charon said flatly, "you need to calm down."

Michael spoke up just as the last syllable left Charon's mouth. His voice was relaxed, but somber. "Perhaps not tools, but you're failing to recall that we exist solely to serve the mission. Where would humanity be without us? How many souls would be wandering the earth if not for our guidance? We have the data. You've seen it. We know how vital it is to keep the souls of the dead away from those of the living. Think of how destructive a single poltergeist can be to a community. If not for Ferrymen, that number could be exponentially higher. The human race could very well cease to exist if not for the Institute."

Cartwright stormed back to the table. "And what does that have to do with Charles?" His eyes darted around the circle. "Hmmm?"

The woman with the pale skin and the long blond hair, Freya, spoke up. Her voice was flavored with a slight Scandinavian accent. "I believe what Michael is trying to say is that we can't sacrifice the needs of the many for the sake of the few. Not that I doubt your assessment, Virgil, but aside from your claims, there is no other evidence to support your position."

With a cry of exasperation, Cartwright threw his hands into the air. "Can you not hear yourselves speak! No evidence? What of his continued disappearances to avoid emergency duty? Or his transfer requests? Over six thousand requests to be allowed to retire, all rejected. How about my numerous reports of his blatant and repeated attempts at suicide? He's presently lying, alone, in the desert, and has been for nearly a *week*! Do you think he's out there working on his *bloody* tan? What should I say to him when I go meet him? *Chin up, old sport*? I shudder to even think how much I'm betraying his confidence by telling you all this, but you refuse to listen! What do I gain by fabricating this story? Please, enlighten me."

Sraosha interjected. "Regardless, he's the best Ferryman we have. You've seen the numbers, Virgil. Ferryman performance has been down year after year after year. Our percentage of successful crossings has decreased by nearly five percent in the past century alone. Human skepticism continues to rise. It's little wonder Death is starting to invest in rival organizations. We've lost nearly thirty-five percent of the soldier demographic to the Sisters of Valhalla. I'm not condoning our behavior, but surely you can at least acknowledge there's a certain pragmatism to all this. Dawson is the only thing keeping us from a free fall."

"Your point?" Cartwright asked.

The remark set Michael into a fit of scoffing. "To even say that shows you're too close to this. You can't view this objectively anymore and you haven't been able to for some time. We can't afford to lose him. It's that simple. You know it as well as any of us here. He's too valuable an asset, and we need to make use of his expertise for as long as we can. If that's for less time than any of us would like, then so be it. If our performance doesn't improve, we could be looking at losing seats on this Council. Just as Death giveth, Death taketh away. Or have you conveniently forgotten that, cofounder?" The last word he carved out of spite.

"Damn your bloody seat straight to hell!" Cartwright yelled, his voice rising in a righteous crescendo. "If that's what it means, then take mine and be done with it! Is that all you care about? Forget our performance numbers, forget Death, forget this godforsaken Council—Charles is my friend and we're killing him!" He slammed his hands on the table in indignant fury.

"Enough, Virgil!" Charon's voice roared back in equal measure. Everyone at the table went silent, including Cartwright, who was standing just off to the side. He stopped his pacing, but glared across at his fellow Council member. "That is enough." Charon exhaled sharply, then picked up a dossier that was sitting in front of him. He paged through it lazily, making it perfectly clear his attention wasn't on the documents in front of him. He tossed it back on the table. "Freya brings up a valid point. If his mental state is deteriorating like you say it is, why hasn't he shared it with anyone? Why not his team? Why not you? Why hasn't he sought help?"

Cartwright circled the table, fingers pinching the bridge of his nose. "Because," he began wearily, "that's exactly the type of person he is. He's too proud to say anything, too aware of how people look up to him. And I would argue his transfer requests *are* a cry for help. Yes, yes, I know what the rules are," he said, waving off Michael. "I understand they are to be treated as anonymous. But not a *single* failed case in two hundred and fifty years. Good heavens, Charon . . . you've heard how reverently other Ferrymen speak of him. They adore him. It's just not in his capacity to openly betray that. Think of his misstep with Javrouche's son years ago—it nearly killed him. Why do you think he's almost completely removed himself from doing emergency cases? The man is simply incapable of saying no and it's eating him alive."

Anubis turned to face Cartwright. "How sure of this are you?" he asked.

Cartwright sighed. "I would stake everything on it." He paused, letting the gravity of the statement fill the room before continuing. "If we don't do something, we're going to lose him. Though I feel sick even saying this, I have a firm belief that, should this continue, he is going to make a grave mistake, unintentionally or otherwise. I am as sure about that as I was sure that he would become one of the Institute's greatest assets, and my wager is the same now as it was then."

Looks were exchanged around the room as Cartwright took his seat, though he still seemed far from calm. The woman with the dark black hair next to Charon, Morrigan, spoke. "Well, I for one am not about to question your judgment. You've been right about him so far. What do you propose?"

Cartwright looked around the table. "With that in mind, I suggest he be allowed to transfer out of the Institute."

There was a collective surprise from the other members of the Council, but most quickly moved on to disagreement. Charon eventually summed up the feelings succinctly: "I'm sorry, but that's unacceptable. There has to be an alternative."

Cartwright was about to speak when an off-screen voice interrupted. "I may be able to help with that."

All the heads at the table looked in the direction of the female voice, which was clearly coming from an off-screen source.

"Madam President. How nice of you to join us," Charon said. "I was beginning to worry."

"Duty called," replied the president. "Now, about that plan. I have an idea I'd like to present to you. While I understand that transferring him out seems ludicrous now, what if we had a way to first test Virgil's hypothesis . . ."

CHARLIE LOOKED UP from the video in such shock that he didn't even realize it had ended. "Wait," he said, his brain reworking through the conclusion it'd just drawn. "I know that voice." He was staring at Cartwright, who, for the first time since they'd sat down, returned the favor. Though he seemed extraordinarily tired, a small grin tugged at the corner of his mouth. Charlie barely even noticed. His brain was already taxed trying to comprehend his situation—the Council, Charon, the questions, this video—but now . . .

Tapping heels announced themselves on the hard floor of the Council's chambers. It was a march Charlie had heard countless times before. Yet it was the voice that gave it away, well and truly.

Charlie turned slowly, almost carefully, to see the approaching form of Melissa Johnson.

She smiled. "Hi, Charlie."

THE TRUMAN SHOW

rom over his shoulder, Charlie could hear Cartwright chuckling softly. "Your timing, Madam President, is, unsurprisingly, perfect."

She inclined her head briefly in his direction. "I see everyone's here, including our guest of honor." She stopped several feet in front of Charlie, folding her hands together. If there was anything different about the Melissa standing in front of him from the one he'd worked with for several years, it wasn't obviously apparent. Her outfit—skirt, blouse, heels—matched her usual attire, while the bag she had slung over her shoulder was one Charlie had seen before.

Charon spoke up then, and even without looking, Charlie could very much tell he found a nugget of humor in the reveal. "Charlie, please allow me to introduce you to the president of the Ferryman Institute."

Charlie let out a quick, unceremonious laugh. "We're acquainted," he said flatly. Melissa kept silent, though he thought there was a hint of apology in her eyes.

Charlie looked at her, his eyes inspecting her from head to toe, searching for something unique about this woman relative to the one he'd gotten to know over the past several years. Try as he might, he continued to arrive at the same conclusion: the president of the Institute was his team manager. The same team manager he'd fought with, laughed with, dropped his towel in front of—

Wonderful, he thought. *The president of the Institute has seen my penis.* This was getting better by the second.

"Before I say anything else, I just want to say, please, Charlie—don't take this personally," she said before continuing her walk over. As she approached, a young woman entered from a different door—apparently there were hidden ones all over the room—than Cartwright and Charlie had. She was carrying an extra chair, which she placed next to Charon. Melissa whispered something to her that Charlie didn't catch, to which the girl dutifully nodded and walked out. Melissa took the new seat.

Charlie looked across at her. "I'm sorry if this is a somewhat tacky question to ask the president of this Institute in front of the legendary Ferryman Council," he began, "but what in the holy hell is going on here?"

Melissa pulled out a folder from her bag and opened it on the table. "I figured you might have some questions," she said. The young woman returned with a glass of water and placed it on the table in front of the president. Melissa quietly thanked her and took a long drink before setting it back down.

"If by *some* you mean several hundred, then yes, I have some questions," Charlie replied.

"I'm glad to see your recent adventures haven't put much of a dent in your sense of humor," Melissa said. "All right, fire away."

The truth of it was that Charlie didn't even know where to start. So, he went with the first question that popped into his head: "I thought you were my manager?"

"I was and still am, in fact. I've been serving in both capacities for several years."

"Is that even possible?" Charlie asked.

"Sometimes it pays to be a good multitasker. I know it seems slightly disingenuous now, but I promise you that I have acted in my full ability as your manager. The résumé that I gave you when I applied to the position was completely accurate, aside from leaving *President* off of it, obviously. If I'm perfectly honest, yes, there were times you drove me crazy, but I was and am proud to manage our team. Cross my heart."

Charlie sat back in his chair. "But why? You're the president. Why take the position as my manager?"

Melissa paused for a moment, lips pursed. Then she said, "Because of you, actually. Virgil was becoming increasingly concerned about your change in behavior. He was able to keep tabs on you outside of the Institute, but he had no way of seeing how you were behaving during assignments. After listening to that for a year, I decided to do something about it. Management of all Ferrymen falls under the jurisdiction of the president, so it's not like it was a totally outrageous thing to do."

"Just mostly outrageous," Michael chimed in.

The remark earned a shrug from Melissa. "You'd become something of a legend in your own right. I'd interviewed a few of your former managers and they all hit on the same thing: great guy, amazing Ferryman, but distant and kind of worrying to be around. So, I decided to see for myself what you were really like. Besides, it was my first big act as president. I mean, I've only been at this a year longer than I've been your manager, so there you go."

Charlie wasn't really sure he was processing any of what was being said. It was more like he was just storing the information in his brain so he could go through it another time when his cognitive functionality wasn't doing the mental equivalent of weeping in the corner.

"And the Presidential Assignment I was given . . . ?" he asked.

"Yes, it was actually a Presidential Assignment," she said. "The story I told surrounding it was a bit made-up, though I do have somebody working for me named Gabriel. The assignment was actually the culmination of the video you were just watching."

"Allow me to cut in here." Without missing a beat, Charon was speaking. "Though President Johnson wasn't able to provide any substantial evidence to corroborate Virgil's conjectures about you, she did feel strongly enough about it from a circumstantial standpoint to support his hypothesis that we were losing you. Other members of this Council, however, weren't as readily accepting of that conclusion. I won't mince words with you, Charlie—your importance to this organization can't be understated. You've seen the video. You're a hot topic around this table. That being the case, it would have been . . . imprudent, on our part, to squander such an asset if we didn't need to. We needed to be sure about you."

Melissa took over the conversation again. "So, we proposed a litmus test, of sorts, to see how you would react in a situation that called for an instinctive response."

The words from the letter resurfaced, and for a brief moment, it was like Charlie was standing in Alice's room all over again. "In other words, *Be a Ferryman or save the girl*," he said.

"That's exactly right," Melissa replied.

"But why that choice?" Charlie asked.

"That was my doing." Cartwright still looked drawn and more than a little haggard, but there was a familiar twinkle in his eye. "We created an artificially short time frame so as to force you into a reaction, and we opted for a very polarizing choice. You'd been perfect as a Ferryman for two hundred and fifty years, Charles. Why would you throw that away? If all you cared about was the job and nothing more, the logical answer that followed was you wouldn't. That's what I wanted to demonstrate—that you weren't just some automaton programmed to successfully complete Ferryman cases. You had other thoughts, other goals you wanted to achieve, other dreams that you would pursue even in the face of harrowing consequences. And I was convinced all you needed was a choice."

That moment in Alice's room washed back over Charlie, and his mind relived the decision he'd made. The next question then was easy enough. "If that assignment was all part of your plan, why send Javrouche after me?"

Melissa flipped through the papers sitting in front of her, shaking her head. "We didn't," she said. "You were meant to make your choice and then report back here, where we would have this very same meeting. Even though he had never gone so far as to formally charge you in the past, Javrouche had been warned on numerous occasions to cease and desist all actions against you. He didn't, obviously, and eventually invoked a PCO without informing anyone. It was his way of skirting what he believed to be an unfair bureaucracy protecting you. I had the authorization to stop it, but if you remember, I was, uh, incapacitated, let's say, by one of those godforsaken capture rifles before I had the chance." She involuntarily shuddered at the thought. "Ugh. That was painful. Anyway, the Council is unfortunately not allowed to directly interfere with the Institute per the bylaws outlined in our original charter. Only the president can affect the day-to-day operations of the Institute. Gives the system a nice set of checks and balances. With me incapacitated, they were helpless to do anything. They are a secret, after all. After that, Dirkley and I were taken in to be interrogated, at which point it was pretty much impossible for me to do anything. By the time Virgil's second-in-command, Mr. Begemot Koroviev, was able to get us free, even a presidential order wasn't enough to get Javrouche to stand down."

"Wait," Charlie said. "Koroviev is Javrouche's second-in-command, not Virgil's." He blinked. "Please tell me Koroviev is Javrouche's second-in-command."

"He is," Melissa said. "He's both, actually. Are you familiar with the term *double agent*?"

Charlie cradled his head in his hands. "Jesus, Mary, and . . . Can you guys stop screwing with my head for like two seconds?" He lifted his head up and inhaled. "So Koroviev is a double agent. That is . . . You know, I don't even know what to think about that right now. Let's move on. If you knew Javrouche was trying to come after me," Charlie asked, "why keep him as the head of Ferryman Affairs? Judicator Dales seemed to think I was under your care, or something like that."

This time, Michael leaned forward and addressed him. "Simple: Javrouche was remarkably effective in his position, something I'm sure you can relate to, Mr. Dawson. As your manager mentioned, until now, he hadn't formally come after you, merely pushed back. He was warned off of you, and we believed him to be a professional enough individual to continue respecting that. We were aware you two had history, but up until this recent madness, we had little reason to believe he'd act so recklessly."

"By the time we got word from Koroviev that Javrouche was issuing a PCO," Melissa added, "he'd already confronted you and incapacitated me. Whether he intended it or not, his timing was perfect."

Charlie briefly wondered what would have happened if Dirkley hadn't pushed him through Alice's door. How differently would this all have played out? Would this have been sorted out sooner with less drama? Would Javrouche have made good on his promise to end Alice's life? The near misses and secret machinations made his head hurt.

He scratched the back of his head. "I have to admit . . . there's one thing I particularly don't understand." His eyes swept the table, noting that everyone was staring back at him. "Why all the secrecy? I just don't see the upside of keeping yourselves hidden." And truthfully, he didn't. If he hadn't been feeling quite so overwhelmed at the moment, Charlie suspected he'd be more than a little aggrieved by the Council's clandestine agenda.

"Ah, yes. I had a feeling we'd come to this one," Charon said slowly. "Let me ask you something, Charlie. If you were average Joe Ferryman, would you rather believe that the Ferryman Institute ran itself by some naturally occurring magic, or that a group of eight men and women, along with the president, controlled it and by extension the fate of humanity?"

"I'll be honest," Charlie replied, "I don't know what average Joe Ferryman would say. However, I do know that not-so-average Ferryman Charlie Dawson would have loved to know he was getting jerked around for two and a half centuries."

Maybe Charlie wasn't feeling quite as overwhelmed as he thought.

"You misunderstand, Mr. Dawson." Freya this time. "There was no *jerking around*, as you put it. You agreed to serve the Institute, and so we put your talents to use. No more, no less. No one expected you to be the savant you turned out to be, perhaps save Virgil. Whether you believe it or not, you've been an invaluable asset to us. Yet, if you knew of our existence, would you still have served like you have, or would you have rebelled when you held a conflicting position?"

Though he was tempted to be contrarian, Charlie bit his

tongue. It was a losing battle—she was right, and he didn't have the heart or composure to argue a side he didn't truly support.

Charon's baritone voice spoke again. "It seems you understand Freya's point. Now, imagine that dilemma but on an Institute-wide scale. If a fraction of the Ferryman Institute population disagreed with a decision of ours, the resulting waves of malcontent could be devastating. Apocalyptic, even. I can sympathize with your frustration at our secrecy, but understand that it's a necessary evil."

Charlie gazed across the table, looking directly at Charon as he spoke. "I don't think you give your employees enough credit," he said.

The original Ferryman appeared entertained by the response, but his eyes sharpened subtly. "And I don't think you've been around long enough to make that assessment."

There was a certain madness to being told all of this, and Charlie knew it. All the reasoning, the intrigue, the justifications, the shadow games being played out on a stage no one in the Institute even knew existed. It was like living for decades in a place only to find that it was a set, a bunch of props cobbled together that he was only now seeing behind for the first time. And Charlie . . . he was the unknowing star of the show.

They sat in silence for a while—how long, Charlie couldn't say—before he asked the last question he had.

"So," he said casually, "what now?"

He knew they were clever enough to read between the lines. He'd taken their test; whether he'd passed it or not—if that was even a thing—was an entirely different story. Now it was time for him to know what that meant.

All eyes turned to the man and woman sitting across the table from Charlie—in some ways, arguably the two most powerful people that no one even knew existed.

Melissa was about to speak when Charon interrupted her: "Charlie, we'd like for you to join the Ferryman Council."

That wasn't something he'd even remotely been expecting to hear. Then again, none of this had been.

"Sorry . . . ?" he said, nearly choking on the word.

Cartwright and Melissa looked just as dumbfounded. "Charon, what are you—" Melissa began, but the head of the Council continued on.

"You've been a vital resource to this Institute. One of the best Ferrymen we've ever seen. Being able to triumph after your assignment went into completely uncharted territory is just proof that you belong here. That you should be one of us. I believe Death would fully support adding another seat to our table—but only if it's for you. Look at the people around you, Charlie. Only eight have ever served on this Council. In the entirety of human history, only *eight* people. Imagine that. Abilities that even a Ferryman would blush at. It's the closest man could ever hope to being a god."

Suddenly, Cartwright was standing up, eyes blazing. "What is the meaning of this?!" he demanded.

"Sit down, Virgil," Charon shot back, his voice starting to rise.

Cartwright stood his ground. "We had an agreement!"

Charon stared him down, glaring at him. "He's demonstrated a level of talent that is on par if not greater than what members of this Council currently possess. You have to be able to see this, Virgil. Transferring him out is completely off the table."

A smattering of responses floated around the table, but the woman known as Morrigan spoke up. "I'm sorry, Charon, but the agreement was binding. He is allowed to transfer out if he so chooses. Whether it is agreeable to you or not now has no bearing. No one will stand with you on this."

Anubis folded his arms across his chest. "She's right. If we can't abide by our agreements, we will lose our order. Like it or not, this decision isn't yours to make."

The ebony-skinned man looked poised to continue arguing when Freya placed her hand on his. Charon looked over at her, and she gently shook her head. With a sigh, Charon withdrew, his posture noticeably shrinking as he sank back into his chair.

"I know a futile argument when I see one. So it is. However, while I won't force the issue, I only ask that my offer be allowed to stand."

Charlie was beginning to get the feeling that he was completely over his head in this discussion. Still, he had questions, and it wasn't like he could find himself in a much worse predicament. "Excuse me," he interjected, "just to make sure I've got this right: I can become a pseudo god or die? Those are my only two choices?"

Freya tossed her hair back with effortless grace. "Transferring out isn't technically death, but for simplicity's sake . . . Yes, you die."

Charlie let his body slump down into his chair. So, those were his options: become a demigod or die. He laughed, only because, in one of life's bizarre twists, it was a laughably easy decision. He'd only dreamed about it for years. Yet for a moment, his mind turned to Alice. It seemed that whichever he chose—Council or death—their time together had come to an end. What right did he have to see her, anyway? He couldn't imagine a scenario where she would want anything to do with him. What was done was done. It was about time he got to ride off into the sunset and disappear for good. Alice would be just fine without him. Hell, it was probably for the best.

He raised his eyes to the group. "If those are my options, then I'd like to transfer out."

Several members of the Council dropped their heads or shook them lightly in disappointment. Charlie felt slightly bad about that, but it was his decision to make. He wasn't about to let them shame him into confirming his immortality for effectively forever.

Then he turned to Cartwright. Despite the look of misery carved into the man's face, he still managed a smile for Charlie. "It appears, my old friend, that your just reward has finally arrived. I can think of no man who deserves that more than you."

The moment was too bittersweet for Charlie to react. If there'd been one constant source of happiness in Charlie's life, it had been Cartwright. The man had been there from the beginning—had guided him, taught him about the Institute, and, most importantly, been a friend in the truest sense of the word. It was impossible for Charlie to escape the feeling that Cartwright would miss him (the feeling was mutual), but there was something indescribably heroic about a man who would sacrifice his own happiness for the sake of a dear friend.

"Thanks," Charlie said. His voice cracked ever so slightly. "For everything. I'm sorry I ever doubted you. I mean that. Maybe if I hadn't been so stubborn, things would have turned out differently."

Cartwright shook his head definitively. "To ask for more out of your friendship would be nothing short of greedy. I am a blessed man to have been given the privilege of your companionship as it was. Never forget that."

Across the table, Melissa withdrew a gold key from her bag and set it on the table. Charlie knew without asking whose it was. The familiar lines of the word PORTHMEUS gleamed underneath the light. "I had it tracked down before I arrived," she said. "Figured you might be wanting it for a situation like this."

Charlie gave a halfhearted smirk, but there was little warmth in it. He found it strange that he felt so sad. "You were always the one who kept me organized," he said.

"Are you sure about this, Charlie?" Charon asked. "You're passing up an opportunity that—"

"I'm sure," he said. "While I'm beyond flattered by your offer, I'm not the man you want. Trust me. I have no business shaping mankind's future. I couldn't even shape my own." He surveyed the room one last time, then exhaled a long, deep sigh. "Let's just get this over with."

This was it. This was the end. Having waited two hundred and fifty years, he'd always thought the event would seem more momentous, but now that it had arrived, it felt strangely . . . hollow. As if something was missing.

Melissa pulled out a sheet of paper from the folder in front of her. "It's settled, then. The Council will serve as the required witnesses. This is binding and cannot be undone." She looked at Charlie. "Are you ready?"

He nodded.

Melissa cleared her throat. "By the power vested in me by this Institute, I hereby acknowledge the termination of Ferryman Number 72514, Charles Ronald Dawson, effective immediately. May he find peace and—"

But Melissa never finished the invocation. A set of auxiliary doors across the room burst open, and in limped one Alice Spiegel and a completely embarrassed Begemot Koroviev.

"Jesus H. Christ, Charlie, you were actually about to go through with it! God, I knew you were an idiot, but I didn't think you were *that* much of one." She hobbled in with the aid of a cane, clearly in a bit of pain. Koroviev reluctantly followed, looking unusually helpless. She surveyed the room casually before opting to stop in the middle of the floor. She waved her cane at the Ferryman Council with a lack of anything bordering politeness. "Howdy, gang. I'm Alice Spiegel, apparent subject of your messed-up little assignment. Pleasure all around, really. I think I'm supposed to say thank you for sending that weirdo over there to rescue me, but I'm a little annoyed that you were about to kill him, so try not to hold it against me when I don't."

If anyone said anything as Charlie stood up, he didn't hear them. If they tried to stop him as he ran toward her, he didn't notice. If all of existence had exploded in that very instant, he would have reassembled the particles of the universe atom by atom until he'd reconstructed this moment, because, as it turned out, *this* was the moment he'd waited two hundred and fifty years for.

He just hadn't realized it until then.

As Alice went to speak, Charlie took her in his arms and kissed her. Really, really kissed her. The kind of kiss that invited no awkwardness or envy from those who happened to bear witness to it. The pull it exerted on those nearby was impossible to escape, and in that all-too-fleeting moment, there was only the kiss and nothing more. They burned with the singular intensity of those who had lost but found anew, who had walked to the very edge of the world and come to realize that, should they just turn around, the last step that would end it all suddenly became the first step of a new beginning.

In short, it was everything their first kiss wasn't.

When they finally pulled away from each other, neither one spoke. They simply looked at each other with eyes devoid of judgment. Then, slowly, gently, Alice wrapped her good arm around Charlie's neck and pulled herself close. She began to speak, her voice small and delicate, almost as if the bravado she'd barged in with had never been at all.

"You know, you've done a few stupid things since we've known each other. And I'm not sure it's even right for me to say this. Your life is your own, you know, and it's not like we've known each other for that long. But if you'd left just now, that would have been the dumbest, most hurtful thing you could have possibly done to me." He could feel her squeeze him just a little tighter, hear the small sniffle that she tried to block out by pressing her face deeper into his chest. "I don't know how you could possibly think it'd be all right to leave, forever, after what we've been through, without saying good-bye."

An indescribable pang of guilt hit Charlie like a wave of frigid water. He knew she was right. He'd tried to justify his quick departure as being the bigger man, letting her go on with her life, but he saw it now for what it was: cowardice. He'd been trying to escape her, trying to run from her given what he'd done.

Except it was more than just that. It was such an alien concept to him, something he hadn't dealt with in years—something so devastatingly human it just hadn't occurred to him: the idea that she might reject him. As the realization took shape in his mind and presented itself to him, he knew it to be true. For hundreds of years, he simply hadn't had to deal with that aspect of the human condition—so long that he couldn't see it for what it was. His own words suddenly came flooding back:

In fact, you're so scared of that future that you're willing to erase any possibility of it happening by choosing not to play the game at all. Can't lose if you don't play, right?

There are few ways to feel like more of an asshole than to be reprimanded by your own advice. So it was.

"I know," he said. "I'm sorry. About everything. I just thought you'd never forgive me. I shot you, Alice. I had the gun and when you grabbed me—"

She raised her head up quickly and shushed him. "Stop," she said. "Please. I know already, and I forgive you." Then she kissed him sweetly on the forehead. "We're even now, though, okay? You've shot me once, I've shot you once, so how about we stop shooting each other for a little while? Deal?"

Being well and truly at a loss for words at this point, Charlie simply wrapped his arms around her and, as delicately as he could, just held her. "Sure," he said. "I think I can manage that."

Though it felt to Charlie as if the two of them were the only people in the room, it became clear a few seconds later they weren't. "Care to explain, Begemot?" came Charon's voice.

Before Koroviev could respond, Alice was already answering for him. She spoke defiantly, even as she wiped at her eyes. "Excuse me? Yeah, hi, me again. For the record, it was totally my fault. I made him do it. I told him I needed to see Charlie, urgently, that I knew something bad was going to happen. I mean, it turns out I was right, but still, I know what he did was against policy or whatever."

Charon's words were ice. "That doesn't excuse this transgression."

"Except," Melissa said, "he saved Dirkley Dupine and the president of the Institute, that being me; tracked Javrouche as our eyes and ears; and most likely saved Ms. Spiegel's life by informing Virgil about Javrouche's impending arrest of Charlie. I think that should count for something."

Charon merely sighed and shook his head. He, too, was looking increasingly helpless. "A matter of discussion for another time."

Alice looked up at Charlie, still in his arms. "Who's Virgil?" she asked with a raised eyebrow.

He gave her good shoulder a gentle squeeze. "Long story," he said. "Nice outfit, by the way."

"Thanks," she said, looking down at her ensemble, "they were out of pink." She patted him on the chest before taking a step back and clearing her throat. "So, what happens now?"

Charlie honestly hadn't thought that far ahead and wasn't sure he wanted to. "I might be able to delay things for a while, possibly until you've recovered. Buy a little bit of time. Other than that, my options are pretty limited."

Alice smiled weakly. "I heard through the door. Doesn't sound like you really have much to work with."

He shrugged. "It is what it is." He was stalling, truth be told. It just felt like the moment he stopped talking to Alice, it would all be over. He'd have to go through with his choice and disappear into the afterlife beyond or, worse yet, consign himself to immortality. Suddenly, standing with Alice next to him, neither option seemed very appealing. The chance to leave—the option he'd always wanted—was finally on the table, and yet this girl standing in front of him made him reluctant to even consider it.

It seemed the moment was just about ready to slip away when Melissa jumped to her feet and turned to face the man whose team she'd managed for years. She'd been watching him and Alice, but Charlie realized only now that her eyes were slightly damp.

"There's another option. A better option," she said. She spoke with the same fervor of a preacher visited by God in the night. Melissa looked between Charlie and Alice, weighing something against the two of them. "I have a proposition. I want to offer you my position as president of the Institute."

At this point, Charlie wasn't even surprised anymore. The way things were going, he fully expected to be asked to take over as King of the Universe before the day was over. What was surprising, however, was Cartwright's immediate and visceral reaction to her offer.

"Madam President, you can't be serious!" Charlie couldn't remember a time when he'd seen Cartwright this upset in person.

"No more, and that's an order," she whipped back, though the tone lacked anything harsh in it. "This is my decision and mine alone, Virgil. Not another word." Cartwright almost visibly held his tongue.

She turned toward Charlie again, picking up her folder as she did. "So, the presidency. It can be a real pain in the ass, and the hours can be long, particularly when you have Ferrymen who regularly disappear on you, hint hint. It's rewarding, though, and you get to focus more on the people at this place than the morbid stuff you're used to dealing with. It's not a perfect trade, but it's a step in the right direction. However, there's one perk that comes with the job that I think you'll find particularly interesting. You see, Charlie, the Institute has this rule . . ."

As she spoke, she opened the folder and placed one of the edges in her palm.

". . . that while the president runs the Institute, they must be a mortal. The presidency brings with it a lot of power in its own right, so it'd be too dangerous to put that in the hands of a person who doesn't die. Again, checks and balances and what have you."

Charlie flinched as Melissa ran the folder savagely across her palm. She grimaced as the thick edge dug into the fleshy part of her hand.

"What that means, though, is that I can offer you something no one else can."

With her hand clenched in a tight fist, she held it over her glass of water. Just when Charlie was about to ask her what she was doing, he saw it. Dripping down from inside her hand, the color of pure crimson, was blood. A large drop hung daringly above the glass until, finally, it fell into the water with a tiny splash. The blood diffused throughout the liquid, spreading out among the water like sanguine smoke. Stunned, Charlie looked up from the glass to find Melissa's eyes, glimmering with a kind of shimmer reserved for the mad geniuses of the world, locked on his own.

"I can offer you your humanity back." A grin commandeered her lips, which only made her expression seem more frenetic. "So, what do you say?"

HOPE

Alice didn't really have any idea what was going on, but the word *humanity* had been used and suddenly the whole room seemed like it was going to collectively lose its shit. It didn't take a rocket scientist to realize that, one, nobody there had quite expected to be talking about this and, two, there was something else going on, something no one was addressing.

Apparently, Alice wasn't the only one with that feeling, either.

"Madam President, surely this merits some discussion," the woman with the blond hair said.

"I agree," a man buried underneath a hood added, followed by the rest of the gathering more or less voicing the same opinion.

Melissa, however, didn't seem too bothered by what they thought. She continued pulling files from the bag she'd brought with her. "As I told Virgil, this is my call."

"Except the Council is to determine your successor," a dark-skinned man replied. "You should be well aware of that. We picked you, after all. This isn't your choice to make."

"The other option is you lose Charlie for good," Melissa countered. "Given every conversation we've had about him, including the one we literally just had a few minutes ago, do any of you really object?" She shook her head. "Not for nothing, but I'm making some pretty awesome lemonade over here with the lemons we've been dealt."

Alice didn't really know who this Melissa character was, but she approved of her spunk.

"Whether or not we object is beside the point." The other woman, the one with dark hair, this time. "You're overstepping your bounds here, Madam President."

Melissa took a long look at the people circled around the table, then sighed. "I apologize if I'm coming off as a bit flippant. I don't mean to be. However, this whole entire mess is my fault, and this feels like an opportunity to make amends. Besides, technically I *can* appoint my own successor. It's just whether or not you decide to oppose my decision that matters."

Alice leaned in close to Charlie's ear. "Based on how you made it sound, I thought your job would be a lot more blood and thunder and a lot less . . . I don't know, C-SPAN-y," she whispered.

"It usually is. If it makes you feel any better, I have no idea what's really going on here, either," he whispered back.

"Oh. Fair enough," Alice said. She thought for a moment. "Why would that make me feel better and not, you know, mildly concerned?"

Charlie thought about that. "That's a good question," he said. He never provided an answer.

When Alice let her attention rejoin the conversation, Cartwright was speaking. "As long as there is an acting president, we cannot directly influence Institute matters. That fact is unavoidable. Our only recourse to overturning a presidential decision, then, is a unanimous vote opposing it. Much as it pains me to do so, if this is what our president has decided as her course, then I will support her in it. I shall not vote against her."

A man sitting across from Cartwright rolled his eyes at the remark. "Of course you won't. When this is all over, I'd like to open an examination into your own actions."

"I await it with bated breath," Cartwright replied.

"Enough. Regardless of the circumstances, with Virgil's vote, the president's decision stands," said the dark-skinned man. "You have our consent, Ms. Johnson, begrudging though it may be."

Melissa gave a short bow. "Thank you, Charon. I assure you I'm acting with the Institute's best interest at heart."

"Let us hope," he replied.

As the immediate conversation seemed to die down, Charlie took a step forward. "Can I interrupt for just a second?" he asked.

"The floor is all yours," said Melissa, who at that point had returned to sifting through folders in her bag.

"Great," Charlie said. The lack of enthusiasm in his voice suggested he meant otherwise. "So, the president—that being you—isn't immortal?"

"Correct," Melissa said. "Remember: checks and balances."

"Sure, I get that. But shouldn't you have bodyguards or something? Aren't you worried about . . . well, I don't know how to put this any other way, dying?"

The dark-skinned man spoke next. "The primary reason both the president's identity and mortality are kept secret is for their protection. As for death, every mortal dies eventually. The president is no exception. When their time comes, we choose a new president and move on."

"I can't help but feel like there's a catch here," Charlie said matter-of-factly. He looked around the room, searching for affir-mation, but when there was none to be had, it only deepened his suspicion. "Right, then. What's the catch?"

Melissa was now carefully laying out sheets of paper, signing them in spots before placing them into orderly rows. "No catch," she said, answering quickly without even looking up. "If you be-come president, you still obviously can't live a normal life, per se, but it's much closer to the real thing." There was an eerie silence that followed her words, and for her part, it seemed like Melissa was trying to look as busy as possible signing papers.

"Mel," Charlie said. When she didn't look up, he raised his voice, speaking firmly and with conviction. "Mel!" That did the trick. "What's really going on here?"

"You're becoming president of the Ferryman Institute," she re-plied, as if they were going to get ice cream. Without missing a beat, she was back to doing paperwork.

Alice eyed her carefully. The expression on her face seemed completely neutral . . . almost too neutral. Was that even possible? Was she reading too much into this? *That* was definitely possible, but something about this just didn't seem right. Not that she wasn't rooting for this to happen, even if she felt slightly guilty that it was a somewhat selfish motivation. It was just that, if Char-lie became president, he'd be just an ordinary guy again . . .

Her thoughts trailed off as she surveyed the room. The Coun-cil members were either talking quietly among themselves or keeping busy with what seemed to be computers built into the surface of the table they sat around. As her gaze shifted, no one seemed willing to meet it. She caught Koroviev's eye and raised her eyebrow. He responded with a shrug. Alice moved on to Cart-wright, or Virgil, or the Artist formerly known as Cartwright, or whatever it was he was going by these days. Their eyes met briefly, but he immediately looked away. For some reason, that struck her as odd. She let her focus linger there, and after a moment or two, he looked back again. He seemed tormented by something and her eyes were only making it worse, almost as if they'd assumed the same power as the beating of the telltale heart. Sure enough, after a few seconds, Cartwright practically jumped out of his chair.

"Madam President, I apologize, but you can't do this without telling Charles the whole truth. He has a right to know."

Charlie looked back at him in confusion, and Melissa's expression turned sour. A few of the other Council members looked over, apparently trying to appear uninterested when Alice guessed they were anything but.

"Virgil," Melissa began slowly, like she was trying to put together the words one at a time as they came to her, "I gave you an order—"

"That I have disobeyed willingly, for which I apologize from the depths of my heart. But Madam President—nay, Melissa—I think your current plan is a recipe for more harm than good, and I simply cannot sit idly by and watch it happen. You are the president, yes, but you are a friend first." He exhaled loudly, perhaps physically letting out what he'd been keeping bottled in his chest. "Please, tell him. He deserves to know." And with that, he reclaimed his seat.

Melissa's eyes fixed themselves on the table she currently stood above. She lightly tapped the pen she'd been using against the glass surface, *tap taptap tap*, in no particular rhythm.

"I wouldn't call it a catch," she said, raising her face to look at Charlie, "but there is something you should be aware of. Before I tell you, I want to reemphasize that this is a decision I'm making willingly, by myself, without any external pressure." She finally stopped tapping her pen and sighed. "When a president voluntarily resigns and signs over the position . . . that person must then transfer out."

The words filled the room, ghosts that haunted the silence that followed. Alice didn't realize what that meant at first, but slowly, as she remembered the conversation she and Begemot had been eavesdropping on, it occurred to her: this woman was quite literally going to die for Charlie.

Holy shit.

But Charlie never flinched. He stared right at her, unmoving. "You're killing yourself. For me."

Melissa stood and began walking around the table to where Charlie was standing. "In a way I am, yes. Tempting as it is, I'm not going to blow smoke up your ass and tell you I'm not. It's also incredibly scary, finally facing your own mortality. I always believed I'd be ready for this, and truth is, now that it's here, I don't feel quite as sure as I thought I would. But here's the thing, Charlie. We're all going to die. Even for these guys here"—she motioned to the circle of Council members, all listening now—"it's going to happen eventually. The universe will end at some point, or the human race will drive itself into extinction. Who knows. But I've been here for a while. I've gotten to see how you operate up close. And frankly, I look at the two of you and I *want* to give this to you. Am I afraid of what's waiting for me on the other side? Abso-fucking-lutely. But I'm much more afraid that if I don't do this now, I'll regret it for however many years I've got left."

Mere feet away from him now, she held out both her hands. In one, a single sheet of paper and a pen; in the other, a golden key with a note attached to its handle. "You've always been a bit of a mystery to me, you know that? It seems like you've always held so much back. It's like you can't let anyone else bear the weight but you. You're still human, though, Charlie. Don't force yourself to be a martyr. You're a good man. Let me do this for you."

Melissa and Charlie stared at each other, neither one willing to be the first to look away.

With an unexpected swipe, Charlie snatched the sheet of paper, signed it, and slammed the pen on the table. His mouth was clenched tight as he glared at Melissa. Then he wrapped her tightly in his arms in a strong bear hug.

"Goddamn you," he whispered, loud enough for the room to hear, though Alice was sure he didn't care one iota who heard him. "Just . . . fuck."

Melissa lightly pushed him back so he was at arm's length. Her lips curled in one of the gentlest smiles Alice had ever seen, as if Melissa's benevolent act were manifesting itself on her lips. Alice could practically feel her heart melting in gobs inside her rib cage.

"Don't be afraid about what's going to happen, Charlie," Melissa said. "You and Alice weren't listed. Be brave."

The moment she finished speaking, the gunshot rang out.

Alice screamed reflexively at the sound, not knowing where it had come from. Melissa's body spun around, ending in a crumpled heap on the floor. Charlie's eyes went wide, unable to comprehend what had just happened. But even before the crisply enunciated voice spoke and confirmed her worst fears, Alice knew.

"My apologies for interrupting, but I'm afraid I have some unfinished business that needs attending to."

Alice turned slowly to see Inspector Javrouche marching into the room with a measured *tip-tap* across the hard floor. Both the pistol in his hand and the hard, thin line on his face were drawn and leveled at Charlie. With his other hand, he'd propped a long, futuristic-looking rifle against his shoulder.

"What an eventful day today has been. To think—on the very day I learn of the Ferryman Council's existence, I get to meet them. Will wonders never cease. So, my first question: How long does it take for Mssr. Dawson's new mortality to take effect?" Another gunshot, but this one was followed by a short, guttural scream of pain from Charlie. Alice watched in compounding horror as he fell to the ground, clutching his leg.

"I suppose that answers that," Javrouche said. "I have to ask—how does it feel to be human again, Mssr. Dawson?"

There was a blur of motion off to Alice's side, and it took her a moment to make out the form of Begemot rushing toward Javrouche. As he closed in on the Inspector, she prayed that he would make it in time. But Javrouche saw him coming. Alice watched in bewilderment as the Inspector swiftly stuck the pistol into his belt, then, in the same motion, aimed the rifle at the onrushing Koroviev and fired. With barely two steps of distance to close, Koroviev's body abruptly seized up in a massive spasm. His forward momentum carried him past Javrouche in a series of dramatic tumbles until his body eventually settled to the ground in a fit of convulsions.

"Greetings, Koroviev. I was actually about to thank you for leading me to this tucked-away little cubbyhole. You were easy enough marks to follow, especially given Mlle. Spiegel's rather pronounced limp." Javrouche continued to move toward the Council's table. "And what a reward it was, to be able to listen in on a conversation like that. Who knew the Institute had set so many furtive plans in motion?"

Alice instinctively backed away, trying to stay close to Charlie but at the same time trying to get as far away from Javrouche as she could. At the head of the table, Charon rose to his feet in a majestic but incandescent rage.

"What is the meaning of this, Inspector?!" he bellowed, his eyes wide but his eyebrows drawn into lines of fury.

"Bonjour, Mssr. Charon. It is an honor." Javrouche stopped his march several feet from the table's edge. His gaze shifted from face to face, each expression twisted into some form of anger or shock. "As well to the rest of you, Council members."

"What you are doing is an *outrage*," snarled the blond-haired woman. Other members took to their feet. Not a single pair of eyes focused anywhere but on Javrouche.

"I can't help but agree—Mme. Freya, I assume? Horrifying, isn't it, that ensuring the safety and protection of the Ferryman Institute has come down to me."

Alice glanced down at Charlie, who was rolling over onto his knees. A small streak of blood traced where he'd dragged his leg across the floor.

"What do you know of saving the Institute?" Cartwright asked.

"By the shape of things, I'd say a considerable amount more than you, Mssr. Virgil. Or is it Mssr. Cartwright?" He allowed himself a quick smirk before it melted away. "This Institute means everything to me, and I will not let it fall apart willingly. Fortunately, it appears that fate hasn't abandoned me just yet."

"You're making a mistake, Javrouche. There's no need for this." It was the strange-looking man standing next to Freya who'd said that.

"There *was* no need—I was happy enough to leave unnoticed after I'd heard Mssr. Dawson agree to transfer out. Except that never happened, and instead your Council essentially said, 'Thank you for nearly exposing our Institute to the world, Mssr. Dawson. Here is the *most powerful position we have*.' I couldn't stand idly by after that, messieurs and mesdames. In time, when you look back on this moment, you'll see the truth in that."

"I could not possibly disagree with you more, Inspector," Cartwright said as he steadily circled the table.

"Is that right?" The Inspector responded by retrieving the pistol from his belt and pointing it at Charlie's head. "You're more than welcome to stop me, then. Any of you."

Acting on what appeared to be pure reflex, Cartwright jumped forward, his hand extending as he tried to grab the pistol gripped in Javrouche's hand. However, just as the tips of Cartwright's fingers would have made contact with the weapon, they suddenly disintegrated into a thousand orange and black particles, bursting into the air in wispy strands. As his momentum carried him forward, Cartwright's fingers continued to split apart, until they'd completely dispersed into a cloud of specks. It was as if an invisible sieve surrounded Javrouche's gun, and Cartwright was pushing his hand farther and farther into it—like pushing cheese across a grater, only one so fine that it didn't shred cheese so much as turn it into granules akin to grains of sand. The particles that had once composed Cartwright's hand floated in the air nearby as if they were embers being blown around a campfire on a breezy night.

By the time Cartwright was able to stop, he'd lost everything at and above his wrist. He pulled his arm back from Javrouche immediately, and as he did, the particles followed, each one darting back into the place it had originally been. In no more than a second, Cartwright's arm was whole again, hand and fingers back where they belonged. Cartwright clenched his teeth in seething anger, eyes smoldering, but he moved back several feet from where Javrouche stood. The Inspector saw it all, and a daring grin broke out across his face.

"Except you physically can't, can you?" Javrouche said. "*As long as there is an acting president, we cannot directly influence Institute matters*, or something to that effect, no? I had no idea you meant it so literally. I take it that was the same reason nothing could be done while Mme. Johnson was in my care. Here you are, bound by your own ridiculous machinations. The irony is almost too much."

Alice almost didn't recognize the voice that responded. It was Cartwright's, but distinctly hushed, a subtle quiver embedded in it. Each word he spoke seemed to carry with it an assurance of abundant wrath. "I swear to you . . . you will be judged for this, good sir."

Javrouche advanced several steps closer to Alice, gun still drawn. "Judge to your heart's content. I follow the law, Mssr. Virgil. I don't fear justice."

The gun remained pointed at Charlie as he pulled himself up to his feet. A small hole perforated his right leg about midthigh, the pant leg that surrounded it quickly turning red. However, Javrouche then began to methodically turn until the business end of the pistol was pointing squarely at Alice's forehead. Frankly speaking, she would have preferred it pointing just about anywhere else.

"Let's talk, Mssr. Dawson. I have some requests."

Alice didn't know what to do. Really, what could she do? If she moved, she'd probably be shot. If she didn't move, she'd probably be shot. Stuck between a rock and a hard place or, in this particular case, a head shot and a dead place. She stood there, trying not to look as petrified as she felt.

"I'm listening," Charlie said.

"I figured you would be." Javrouche indicated the Council with a flick of his head. "Instruct them that this is between us. They are to all move away from their table; then there is to be no speaking, no moving, no interruptions of any kind on their part. Breaking that will end this conversation abruptly with a *bang*, if you catch my drift."

Charlie looked over at the Council, spent a moment studying their faces, before returning to Javrouche. "They heard you," he replied.

The Inspector shook his head. "It has to come from you. A president's orders, as they say." Since his arrival, Javrouche had remained eerily even-tempered, a trait Alice couldn't help but think made him even more dangerous. However, she caught the rather obvious note of disgust in his last remark.

"Charles—" Cartwright began, but he was stopped by Charlie's raised hand.

"Do as he says. That's an order."

It was impossible to decipher the expression on Cartwright's face then—hurt, ashamed, furious . . . There were shards of each there, distinct pieces that shifted in the light. He bit his trembling lower lip as if to steady it, and said nothing. Alice didn't think he needed to—she understood how he felt perfectly. Per their instructions, the Council members moved away from the desk, standing several feet away now in one irate-looking pack.

"Congratulations on your first official act as president, Mssr. Dawson," Javrouche said. "I'd say your tenure is off to a wonderful start."

Charlie's face remained neutral. "Alice has nothing to do with this, Javrouche. I'll cooperate, but only if you leave her out of it."

"Unfortunately, I disagree, Mssr. Dawson—Mlle. Spiegel has quite a bit to do with this. She also makes an excellent bargaining chip." Javrouche carefully set the long rifle against the Council's table, his focus alternating between Charlie and the sights of his pistol. Alice tried to subtly step out of his aim, but the Inspector kept the gun trained on her. She was really beginning to hate how good he was at that.

"Next order of business," the Inspector continued. "I want you to relinquish your position and appoint me as president."

Charlie let out a bark of laughter, but cut it short when he realized Javrouche wasn't joking. "You can't be serious. The Council will overrule that decision immediately."

"That's certainly one possibility. However, I see it this way—if they unanimously object to your decision, I'll kill Mlle. Spiegel, shoot you in your other leg, and be on my way. With you still alive as president, the Council can't act to stop me, nor would you be in any physical shape to. By the time you move against me, I'll have already made an announcement to the Ferryman Institute detailing *all* of this—all the deceit, the schemes, the plotting. Your first day as president, and you'll be contending with a civil war."

Javrouche moved a step closer to Alice. "So can you really assume then, monsieur, that everyone will object to my presidency? As Mssr. Virgil said, all eight Council members must oppose your decision for the objection to stick. All it takes is one sympathetic voice—one Council member with a bit of foresight—to see how I could raise the Institute to new heights . . . or one who sees the ramifications of my plan and simply won't take that risk."

It was clear from the look on Charlie's face that the Inspector's argument had struck home. He stared at the Council members, eyes searching their faces for any hint of a suggestion. Alice, however, couldn't see any way he could play this hand without losing.

"So, Mssr. *President*," the Inspector said, "what'll it be?"

Charlie's gaze returned to Javrouche. "So this is your version of justice, huh? Running around, shooting people left and right, threatening everyone? This is how you right all my wrongs?"

But Javrouche only sighed. "Come off it, Mssr. Dawson. I'm no idiot. Stop stalling. The presidency or the girl. Time is running out. Choose before I choose for you."

Alice's eyes shifted over to Charlie, who she just now noticed wasn't even looking at her or the Inspector. He seemed to be looking down at his right hand on the table, which he was using to support himself. There was something in his expression, though, something odd . . .

Suddenly, Charlie started to laugh. It was a quiet sort of chuckling, the type that often comes with a slow and steady head shake, as this one did. Alice went from confused to scared. Javrouche, however, was not amused.

"What's so funny?" His eyes burned holes in Charlie, but the Ferryman continued laughing to himself. With a *click*, Javrouche pulled the hammer back on the pistol and thrust it in Alice's direction. His voice boomed as he finally appeared to lose the tenuous hold he'd still had on his sanity. *"I asked you what is so goddamn funny?!"*

With three long but quick strides, he wrapped his left arm around Alice (who shrieked wildly in response and no, she wasn't proud of it, thanks for asking) and pressed the barrel into her temple. "So help me, I will paint the floor with her brain matter! *Answer me!"*

Charlie finally looked up from the table, and Alice was stunned to see tears rolling down his face. "Go ahead," he said nonchalantly. "Pull the trigger." He punctuated the last words with a sniffle, but his expression was steel resolve.

It wasn't the answer Javrouche had been expecting. Even more so, it wasn't the one Alice had been, either. What did he just say? It couldn't have been what she thought he'd said, which was *Pull the trigger*, because if that was supposed to save Alice's life, she was having a hard time figuring out how. Unless . . . he'd chosen securing the presidency over saving her? Rationally, it made sense—the good of the many over the needs of the few. Was that why he was crying? But—oh God, no—he wouldn't . . . would he? She felt a wail of despair welling up inside her as tears of her own began to rush down her cheeks.

Jesus, how many times could she almost get killed with these people? All right, so she had made the mistake of wanting to die not so long ago, but she knew better now. *I get it already!* she thought. *Whoever you are out there, you win. I don't want to die anymore, okay? I haven't for a while. I'm sorry. Please, just get us both out of here alive!*

"Charlie—!" Alice started, but cried out in pain as Javrouche ground the gun harder into her temple. She wouldn't have been surprised if the barrel had broken her skin. Her breath came in short drags, his arm an anaconda wrapping tightly around her neck.

"You think I won't do it?" Javrouche asked, the calmness in his voice a stark contrast to the frenetic style of his actions. "Is that what you think? Do you take this for a bluff, Mssr. Dawson?" He twisted the gun, eliciting another shot of pain from the side of Alice's head to her mouth.

However, Charlie seemed completely unfazed by the entire situation. He took a hobbling step forward, then another one, then another. "I don't care what you do, Javrouche. I never have. Honestly, right now, I just feel sorry for you. You haven't tried to be a bad guy. Shit, I'm not even sure I think you are one. You're just someone trying to do his job to the best of his ability, and if nothing else, I can respect that. In fact, it took me until now, but I think I've finally figured it out. You're as much a victim of this place as I am. The other side of my coin, if you will."

Javrouche scowled. "Don't insult me."

"We are, though, aren't we? I've been wanting to leave this place for years, Inspector. Did you know that? But they never let me, and so I had to keep going. Had to keep moving souls on.

Had to keep watching people die. And all the while, the only thing I could do to stop myself from completely breaking down was run away." He hesitated there, apparently unconcerned by Alice's precarious position. "If all those years ago, I'd have known that assignment was your son, I would have taken it in a heartbeat. I didn't, though. I only found out a few days later. Sometimes I think about it and tell myself I was so worn down, I wouldn't have been able to save him anyway. In the cold light of day, I think that's me just trying to cope. Your son's case . . . I know I've said this before, but I want you to know—really know—that I truly regret not taking your son's case to this day. People say I've never failed a case, but I know better. But even though I regret it, I've stopped blaming myself for it. I'm no Council member, no god. I'm only me. Just an ordinary guy in an expensive-looking suit who happens to be good at talking to dead people. And maybe one live one. But that's all I am."

The vise grip on Alice's neck loosened marginally as Javrouche's sneer finally disappeared. "Do you know what I think, Mssr. Dawson? I think this is bigger than that. This is our destiny, you and I, and there's nothing we can do to stop it. You will destroy this Institute, or I will save it. Either-or."

Charlie turned to Alice, her nose sniffling something fierce, her eyes burning and her head aching from the cold iron being forced into her skull. His look was solemn then, before he turned his attention back to Javrouche.

"There is no such thing as fate or destiny. *The man who searches longest for the strings of fate often finds them, while the man who seeks them not knows himself to be free.* I finally get that now. What happens next is what you decide to do, nothing more." Charlie exhaled. "Your call, Claude. Go ahead and pull the trigger. I promise I'll ask them for leniency when this is all over."

For the most fleeting of moments, the Inspector seemed to lose all of his energy. Alice could understand the feeling—she had quickly grown to hate when Charlie pulled that shit, too. It would be nice if she could understand what he was talking about before she had her brains blown out.

But then Javrouche snapped back to himself, squeezing Alice's neck viciously with his left arm, wrenching her head closer. "Suit yourself. Using Mlle. Spiegel as my volunteer, please allow me to demonstrate what it feels like to watch something you love slip away."

A thick line of pain ran straight through Alice's skull, the sirens in her brain blaring in alarm. She tried to cry out, but she couldn't breathe now, the anguish catching in her throat as it pulled closed. Her hands shot to Javrouche's arm, tugging wildly in an attempt to loosen the iron grip on her neck, but it was no use. *This is it*, she thought. *My luck has finally run out. Really, honest-to-God run out.* She struggled to look up, trying to get one last glimpse of Charlie. She succeeded, but his eyes were locked on Javrouche. A pang of a million different emotions flooded her system.

So be it, she mused.

Those words again, still just as fitting. This time, however, she refused to close her eyes. She would give herself every last second she had left. That's how she wanted it.

Click.

Alice could feel Javrouche stop moving.

Click click.

"No . . . ," he breathed.

Click click click click click . . .

The gun was empty.

And that's when Charlie punched the Inspector square in the throat.

Alice immediately felt the pressure on her neck loosen as the force knocked the Inspector off balance, allowing a pinhole of air to weasel its way into her lungs. It was now or never—Alice gathered what strength she had and pushed upward with both hands against Javrouche's arm while simultaneously ducking. To her unbridled relief, she slipped out from his grasp. She followed it up with her best action-hero impression by diving for the nearest chair and hiding behind it, coughing all the while—so, all in all, a pretty lousy one.

Charlie followed up his first effort with another haymaker, this time from the left side. Javrouche seemed to have been caught completely off guard by the first punch and therefore was blindsided by the second. Charlie's knuckles connected cleanly with the Inspector's jaw, distorting the man's face into an odd contortion. With his balance already off, the second hit sent the Inspector to his knees.

As Alice began piecing together a picture of her surroundings in her head, she caught sight of the Council. Some of them stood looking on, either completely captivated or just mildly interested. Cartwright and the dark-haired woman had used the commotion to sneak over to Melissa's prone figure. Charon, meanwhile, had darted back to the Council's table. His eyes never left the fighting pair, but his fingers worked furiously over the desk's surface.

It was then that she noticed the rifle leaning against the table. Charon glanced in her direction, and for a moment, they made eye contact. Without a word between them, he slowly nodded.

The Inspector halfheartedly tried to push himself up, but Charlie lashed out with a standing kick that landed just behind Javrouche's right ear, knocking him and his pistol down.

"Fuck, that hurt!" Charlie yelled as he clutched his bleeding leg. "I totally forgot about my leg. Fucking hell!"

The doubled-over Ferryman never saw Javrouche coming.

The Inspector charged shoulder first, connecting with Charlie like an irate battering ram. The two tumbled to the ground in a heap, bouncing and rolling along the floor. As their momentum ran out, the two men grappled, each struggling to get a solid grasp. As time passed, however, it was clear that the Inspector's lack of both pain and fatigue was swinging the pendulum in his favor.

"Do you remember making a joke about using me as your piñata, Mssr. Dawson? I'd love to hear it again."

He snuck in a left jab that pummeled Charlie right in the nose. The Inspector used that moment to square up, pinning Charlie beneath him with his legs and opening up the chance for him to use both of his hands. Even without his various supernatural abilities, his position gave him the clear advantage.

Alice, however, hadn't been idle.

"Hey, asshole!" she called.

Javrouche feinted with his left hand, then cut across Charlie's nose again with his right. Even Alice heard the vague crunch his fist made when it plowed into the cartilage there. Only after the punch connected did Javrouche glance over, expecting nothing but instead getting a full view of Alice aiming the capture rifle straight into his left eye. He froze.

Alice readjusted her grip on it. She'd never fired a gun this large before. Even after a considerable amount of time spent at the range, she hadn't the faintest idea what kind of kick to expect. As she pressed the butt harder into her shoulder, she said a quick prayer that Javrouche didn't notice her wincing.

"Must be difficult pressing that into your injured shoulder, Mlle. Spiegel."

So much for that. *Well, fake it 'til you make it.* This was only going to work once—if that—and she had to make it count.

"It could hurt ten times as bad and I'd still be able to make this shot," she said. It was a bluff: the distance was short, maybe ten to fifteen feet, but the rifle felt unwieldy even propped against her shoulder—not to mention she wasn't entirely confident the gun had any ammo left to dispense.

The Inspector seemed to consider her statement. "It's out of rounds, you know."

Jesus, what was with these people seeming to always know exactly what she was thinking? Was her poker face really that bad? Maybe that's why Marc always refused to take her to Atlantic City. Alice forced a Cheshire grin to spread out greedily across her face. "Nice try. I almost believed you for a second there," she said, and repositioned the gun, lining up her shot.

Despite her bravado, Alice's arms were getting tired and it was taking everything she had to keep them from shaking. Should she take the shot? What if Javrouche was right and the gun turned out to be empty? The only thing keeping him occupied appeared to be the threat of a loaded weapon. Or what if she missed? She had no idea how long it would take for the rifle to cycle, or if there even was another round to cycle, and anything longer than a second was probably too much.

Alice took a deep breath, trying to calm her nerves and focus on the sight at the end of the rifle. It dipped and weaved like a moored boat floating on rough seas. Her finger felt for the trigger, sliding its way across the guard, inching toward the little metal hook that made all the magic happen. Exhale. Inhale. Hold. Javrouche's body began to tense up, rising discreetly, standing.

Now or never. Her finger felt the resistance on the trigger as she slowly started to squeeze.

Before she could fire, Charlie pistol-whipped the Inspector right across the face.

The sandalwood-gripped steel shattered the Inspector's jaw, snapping the mandible like a dry wishbone as he fell to the floor. Charlie quickly struggled to a sitting position, a vibrant stem of blood blooming from his very broken nose. When he'd gotten ahold of the Inspector's other gun, she couldn't say, but she certainly wasn't going to complain about it.

"Alice!" Charlie barked. However, his follow-up to that (Alice's mind instantly assumed B movie fluff, something like *Shoot the bastard!* or *Avenge me!* or *Get to the chopper!*) was turned into a muffled grunt by Javrouche's foot. The Inspector had rather cannily used his momentum to tuck into a tight spin, wheeling around his back leg with a vicious strength that caught the Ferryman right in the head.

Javrouche wasted no time getting to his feet, Charlie sprawled out before him like a red carpet. If before Alice had had a suspicion that the Inspector was being cautious because of the rifle, his eyes clearly stated that was no longer the case. He worked his jaw methodically, a proud prizefighter awaiting the bell to signal the final round. Or maybe it was just repairing itself. Alice couldn't really tell with these weirdos.

Focus, she thought, reminding herself just where she was. She inhaled again, propping the rifle up, but the end of the barrel traced a stumbling path in the air, a drunken bumblebee trying to find its way home. There was a vague commotion behind her, but she ignored it.

Javrouche, however, did not.

With a look composed of equal parts disdain and resignation, the Inspector bolted for the door Alice and Begemot had entered from, taking off at a rather impressive pace. Alice straightened in surprise for a moment before instinct took back over, her body naturally tracking him from behind the sight as he sprinted across the room. Her finger slipped back in front of the trigger, teasing it, waiting. Javrouche reached the door and turned.

The adrenaline pulsed to the very tips of her fingers, then seemed to evaporate, a surreal sense of calm taking control in its absence. The helter-skelter pattern of her rifle ceased, giving way to a compact figure eight. She closed her left eye and watched as the world quietly drew to a standstill. She stared into the face of the man who had tried to kill her several times over. Her index finger twitched over the trigger.

Now, her brain shouted. *Now!*

She couldn't do it.

Time resumed its normal flow, and two men rushed past her, chasing after the fleeing Inspector. "That's your man!" Charon shouted after them. "I want him brought *down!*" Alice stayed standing, letting the rifle down slowly. Then, without consciously realizing it, she quietly sat on the floor.

Moments ago, she'd had every intention of shooting Javrouche. On evidence, the bastard deserved it. And yet she saw the look on his face—the last one before he made his final escape, for what must have been only an instant in the real world—and recognized it immediately.

It was the same awful, pathetic look she had seen staring back at her in the mirror of Cartwright's apartment seconds after she'd accidentally slit her wrist.

Translated, it read: *My God, what have I done?*

Once she saw that look, she knew, for good or ill, that she wouldn't be able to pull the trigger. She had discovered a small piece of herself reflected in Javrouche's expression, and suddenly, Alice had found herself pitying him. Maybe they weren't as different as she'd believed—two wayward souls who, in their own time, had seen the error of their ways. Maybe there was hope for him yet, like there had been for her. If ever there was a person who'd come to believe in redemption, it was Alice. And so, with her mind unable to decide which choice was the right one, she'd let the Inspector go. She simply couldn't bring herself to judge him.

With Javrouche gone, a few of the remaining huddled Council members hurried to their desks, typing feverishly. They spoke in hushed tones to each other, and though Alice couldn't quite make out the words, their sense of urgency was obvious. Freya joined Cartwright and the other woman next to Melissa, the two wearing notably grim expressions as they crouched over her. Alice made a note of it, her brain taking stock in a way that made her feel like she wasn't even there. Just a casual observer, watching it all on TV from somewhere far away, wondering when the next commercial was so she could go pee.

"Don't bother," Charlie said to Cartwright as his small group tried to revive Melissa. He'd gotten himself standing again but certainly looked worse for wear. A messy blotch of blood was smeared across the lower half of his face, a *welcome back to mortality* gift from his swollen and slightly crooked nose. When Cartwright turned, his expression one of plain anger at Charlie's words, the Ferryman flipped him a key with a note attached.

"It says I'm to be her Ferryman when she dies. She's still alive, but she's only got another hour if the ETD is anything to go by. I would just do your best to make her comfortable." He shook his head dismally. "She walked into the room knowing she was going to die. She kept it a secret from us the whole damn time. With giving me the presidency, with everything . . ." His voice trailed off.

As Charlie moved gingerly over to Alice, Cartwright read the note. His expression changed before her eyes, his jaw slightly agape. "Good heavens. I had no idea . . . ," he whispered.

"That makes at least two of us." Charlie pointed in the direction that the Inspector had fled toward. "Who were those guys chasing after Javrouche?"

"They would be Charon's retinue," Freya replied. Though she was speaking to Charlie, Freya's eyes remained fixed on Melissa as she gently stroked the injured woman's hair. "We all have an Institute member or two at our disposal. For example, Koroviev has been working with Virgil for quite some time. It's a . . . convenient way for us to circumvent the issue of directly interfering with the Institute's affairs. Unfortunately, they're not always free and available when we need them—they have positions of their own to hold. Luckily for us, it seems Charon was able to get in touch with his during your scuffle."

Charlie put his fingers to his nose, but instantly recoiled in pain from the contact. "I'm getting the sense that there are a lot of things I still don't know the truth about around here."

"Perhaps," Cartwright replied. "Whilst we're on the topic of the truth behind matters, however did you know that Javrouche's gun was empty?"

"I've been wondering the same thing myself," the dark-haired woman added. "With all due respect, that seemed like quite the gamble." She removed her hand from Melissa's right shoulder, and Alice could see quite clearly that it was covered in blood.

"I didn't. It was only a theory. It only occurred to me after reading Melissa's note, which I didn't see until she'd been shot and my hand happened to land on the key. Right before she was shot, she told me that we weren't listed—me and Alice—and to be brave. It didn't make any sense to me at the time, but after reading the note, it felt like that's what she was driving at. If Javrouche was going to kill Alice, there would be another Ferryman here, or at the least, we would know about it on some level. So I started thinking, what if his pistol was the same gun from back at the Tick Tock Diner? If it hadn't been reloaded since then, that meant six rounds had already been fired. Just now, Melissa was seven and I was eight. I don't know much about guns, but that's an old-looking one. I thought eight shots might be the most it could hold."

He'd arrived in front of Alice now and offered her his hand. She gazed up at him. "So," she said benignly, "you decided that when I had the barrel of a gun against my head was the ideal time to play Dirty Harry?"

He shrugged. "Do you want me to ask you if you feel lucky?"

"No," she said as he helped her to her feet. "The answer to both questions is no."

"Really?" he asked. "I'm having a hard time thinking of another person who's gotten out of so many tight situations in such a small window of time."

"Ha-ha—you're not funny."

Without warning, Charlie's eyes rolled to the back of his head. His body lurched forward, collapsing in a heap.

"*Charlie!*" she screamed as she threw herself on the floor next to him. She put her fingers to his neck. There was a pulse, but it felt weak. Someone else was soon kneeling across from her, and she was relieved to see it was Cartwright.

"I–I don't know what happened," she stammered. "We were talking, he seemed fine, and . . . and . . ."

She felt his hand on her arm, and he shushed her. "It's all right, my dear, it's all right. His body is in a weakened state—it's simply not used to being mortal. Excess levels of fatigue are normal after such a process. I'm sure that, in concert with his loss of blood, just proved to be a little too much for him."

As if to confirm Cartwright's point, no sooner had he finished speaking than Charlie began to softly whimper. The two looked down to see him crying quietly to himself.

"Oh my God, Charlie." She squeezed his hand. "We're getting help for you right now. How badly does it hurt?"

Charlie draped his arm over his eyes so they couldn't see his face. His quiet whimpers moved on to a rolling sob. After a few false starts, he finally managed to speak. "It's not that," he said, voice hitching. "It's just been so long since I've felt anything . . . the pain . . . just feels so damn good. And that's just such a stupid, shitty thing to say, but fuck me, I missed it so much."

And that was when he completely lost it.

Alice was momentarily taken aback. There was something about watching a grown man weep uncontrollably that she found inescapably heart-wrenching. However, she didn't have the faintest idea what to do. How the heck was she supposed to comfort someone who'd lived the life Charlie Dawson had? With a look of mild panic on her face, she turned to Cartwright, only to find him looking thoroughly amused. He patted her arm twice, then stood up.

"*Omnia vincit amor*," he said in perfect Latin before he quietly and slowly walked away. The rest of the room watched from afar, seemingly content to let them have their moment.

She turned her attention back to Charlie, who lay on the ground, his chest heaving with every racking sob that worked its way out. She let her hand drift over to his face, her fingers delicately stroking his head. "Shhhh," she whispered. "Being alive is a beautiful thing, isn't it?"

It was, wasn't it? She'd come to realize that, somewhere along the way. Sure, it had taken an unbelievable amount of luck for her to get there—the cascading set of circumstances that had led her to this point were brain-melting, to put it kindly—but she'd gotten there in the end. Life had shown her that it still possessed the capacity to surprise her, and that made all the difference. This was her fresh beginning.

For Alice, that was enough.

Alice would always remember that moment, even years and years on. The words left her mouth, and Charlie, still covering his eyes, coughed a half sob, half laugh. She felt his hand tighten, pulling her slightly closer. Then he began to vigorously nod his head.

And that was when, without rhyme or reason, Alice somehow knew everything was going to be okay.

OUT OF THE DARKNESS . . .

*C*harlie had a headache. It had been a long, long time since he'd been able to say that, and frankly, there was still a sick part of him that enjoyed it. He knew that would wear off soon enough, but for the time being, he welcomed it. He did, however, miss being able to breathe out of his currently swollen nose.

He stood up behind his desk and winced at the lancing pain in his leg. With a slight limp, he began to wander slowly around the room. The space was smaller than he'd expected—he'd envisioned something more Oval Office when in reality it was more modest middle manager. To be fair, he got to keep his other office as well, so square footage wasn't an issue, but still—it was the principle of the thing. A large, if plain, brown desk was positioned in front of the entrance, two comfortable blue chairs facing it. The walls were painted a very pale yellow, a subtle shade without being drab. Several bookcases occupied space along both the back and side walls of the room, but the walls were otherwise bare.

For all Charlie's gripes, however, the presidential office did have one thing that made up for all of its other failings, and then some: a window. To be more specific, it was a massive skylight that took up at least half of the ceiling, placed just where his eyes gravitated to when he settled into his high-backed leather chair. Beyond it was a view of outer space, and from what he understood, it always would be—a perpetual window out across the universe.

He adored it.

As Charlie stood beneath a drifting galaxy, he came to realize that it was the first time he'd really had a chance to study his new office. *Melissa's office.* His brain made the connection automatically, despite his best efforts to keep that gritty reality locked away in some unreachable recess of his mind. She was gone. In one sense, the day-to-day management Charlie had found himself suddenly thrown into was a welcome problem, seeing as it was the perfect distraction from his thoughts. Now, idle for the first time in hours, he felt the memories he'd tried to avoid come rushing back in a torrent.

———————

THEY'D MADE MELISSA comfortable in a spare room adjacent to the one Alice woke up in—a random tidbit Charlie learned after the fact. It was an all-too-familiar scene for Charlie, and to see someone he considered a friend be the center of it was heartbreaking. While it was true that she would have been transferring out anyway, given that she'd voluntarily passed on the presidency to Charlie, from what he'd heard, the presidential transition usually took upward of several weeks. Now, however, her departure time had been greatly accelerated.

He wished he could say she looked perfectly serene, hooked up to the ventilator with its rhythmic *hiss*, but there was a touch of pain around her closed eyes that spoke to the contrary. An examination determined that the bullet had entered from her left side, passed through both her lungs, and exited. How it missed all of her ribs was anyone's guess. That was often the way of it, wasn't it—an eighth of an inch in one direction instead of the other the only difference between still breathing and six feet down. The ventilator was essentially keeping her from asphyxiating, but it was only a matter of time before the internal bleeding proved too much for her body to bear. There was nothing anyone could do.

When the ETD was a few minutes away, the few people who were in the room—the members of the Council and a handful of Melissa's staff—began to pay their final respects. Although those with Ferryman Keys and Council members (who apparently didn't need them, which explained an awful lot) would have been able to see her spirit after she passed on, it was agreed that Charlie would handle it like any other case: alone. Melissa had been an exemplary employee for the Institute, but that didn't guarantee she'd be understanding in death. *Everything for the good of the many*, Charlie remembered thinking bitterly.

The room emptied out, except for Cartwright, who stayed a moment longer.

"It is rather remarkable," he said quietly. "I believe as ageless, undying men and women, we have come to view death through a lens far removed from reality. I will begrudgingly admit to feeling detached, myself. Which is to say, I couldn't understand your feelings when we last spoke out in the desert. It is strange, then, when it impacts one of our own . . . a stark reminder of the deep and profound sense of loss that accompanies death. Maybe that is what makes you such an extraordinary yet ill-equipped Ferryman."

With a stolen glance, Charlie looked over at his mentor. "How so?"

Cartwright put his hand on Charlie's shoulder and patted it gently. "Because maybe for you, every death is like losing one of your own." He returned Charlie's look with earnest, somber eyes. "How could anyone possibly acclimate to that?" Without saying another word, Cartwright squeezed his shoulder, turned, and left the room.

Charlie stood, Cartwright's words heavy in his ears. At this point in his life, he didn't know what to think.

He watched as Melissa's blood pressure continued to drop, bit by bit. Finally, her pulse disappeared. There was no horrific alarm signaling nurses to come in, no doctors with defibrillators. It was a suffocating silence, with only the occasional pump from the ventilator punctuating the room.

Moments later, she was standing before him. They looked at each other, neither particularly moving. Eventually, Melissa looked at her corporeal self with a sad smile. Charlie fingered his Ferryman Key, finding a modicum of solace in its gilded letters and familiar weight. Even now that he was mortal, the key still did its job.

"I'm glad you took me up on this last assignment. It's kind of a tradition, one president passing to the next, even if this transition isn't exactly proceeding normally." Though she was speaking to him, she was still looking down at herself. "I was a little worried you wouldn't."

"Because I wouldn't be able to handle it emotionally?" he asked.

Her eyes lingered for a second more on the woman in the bed before she turned her attention to Charlie. "Yeah, something like that."

Charlie rubbed the back of his head. "Well, I appreciate the honesty."

After they lapsed into silence, Charlie spoke up again. "You knew the whole time what was coming, didn't you?"

She took a few steps away from her bed toward Charlie. "Did I win the Oscar for best female Ferryman in a lead role?" The casual enthusiasm Melissa displayed erased any doubt Charlie had about her mental well-being postlife.

"Sorry," Charlie said, "it went to Meryl Streep again."

Her laughter filled the room. "Jeez, they wouldn't even give it to me posthumously," she said. Charlie must have been wearing his heart on his sleeve, as she immediately remarked: "Come on, Charlie, don't look like that. It's only death."

He snorted and looked away.

"Listen," she said with the familiar managerial tone she used when things needed to get done. "I'm not going to stay here long. The more I draw this out, the harder it's going to be for the both of us. You know it, I know it. So, a few important things. On the back bookshelf, there's a section for some of my own personal books. Wedged in between *The Hitchhiker's Guide to the Galaxy* and *A Dirty Job* is a binder. It's for you. Unfortunately, I don't really get to talk you through some of the things I've learned in my relatively short tenure as president, so I made a primer that will hopefully be an adequate guide to your new role. I'll be honest, it's kind of thrown together, given the short heads-up I had, but I hope it helps all the same. I included a letter addressed to Virgil, and I'd appreciate it if you gave it to him. There's also letters to members of my staff. I put some instructions in there for them, just to get them along, but they're all great, as I'm sure you'll find out. You're also going to need a new vice president, as I imagine Shira—she was mine—will probably want to try her hand at managing. The rest of my staff, you're more than welcome to keep on board. That's up to you."

When Charlie continued to avoid looking at her, she stuck her head into his field of view. "Hey," she said, looking mildly concerned, "you getting all of this?"

"Mmm," Charlie said by way of reply.

Melissa sighed. "You've done this a million times before, Charlie. I'm just the final drop of water in a very full bucket. One more job."

"You don't get it," he blurted out, his voice louder than he meant. "I treated you like crap—always running off, disappearing without telling anyone. You know, just generally making your life miserable."

Melissa eyed him carefully. "Let me ask you a question: Now that you know the truth about me and Virgil, do you honestly think I didn't know where you were? Maybe on a few rare occasions I only had a vague notion, but realistically speaking? I always knew."

"That's not the point. I was always selfish, and you've been nothing but selfless all the way to the end of your life. And now, here I am, standing around like an idiot because there's nothing I can do to repay you. To borrow a phrase, it fucking sucks big, fat donkey balls."

With a measured grace, Melissa took a few steps closer. "So you feel bad because you think you're indebted to me?"

"No." He thrust his Ferryman Key out in front of himself, and turned it hard. A familiar *click* echoed, but there was a sharp grinding undertone that followed it. "I feel bad because you were a friend—a really great one— and not only am I just realizing that, but now I'll never get the chance to show you how much I appreciate it." The invisible door slowly creaked open, revealing the blinding white light of the world beyond.

Melissa's focus was initially on Charlie, but as the door continued to gently slide open, her eyes wandered over. As the outpouring of light formed a veil across her face, Melissa's eyes grew wider.

"Oh God," she whispered. "It's beautiful." She stared at it, un-blinking, for several seconds before she wrested her eyes back. Despite her best efforts, she couldn't help but cast expectant glances in that direction every couple of seconds. Finally, she shook her head, as if forcing a thought from her mind, and steeled her gaze on Charlie.

"Charlie, I didn't do this to make you feel bad, but you are who you are. There's not a whole lot I can say that will change that. But you finally have the chance to be happy now, and after all you've been through, without once complaining to me about how much this was eating you up inside . . . you need to take this chance. This isn't punishment for me. I've been given more years than any person rightly deserves. I've seen it all, and now I get to go home. I'm not scared anymore. And to be perfectly clear, don't you dare think for one second that I didn't like being your manager. If I leave here with one regret, it's that I never got to be a true manager to you and Dirkley. I think that really would have been a blast."

She walked past Charlie and stood in the doorway, her spirit almost completely enveloped by the light. "Can I tell you one thing, as a friend, before I leave?"

Charlie shuffled his feet and tried to look at her—the sheer intensity of the light forced him to shade his eyes with his hand. "Sure," he said dumbly. Melissa seemed to be fading away, as if she was becoming one with the light.

"I'm glad you saved the girl." Her voice sounded distant now, like a person calling out from a moving train. "You want to pay me back for this? Then take good care of her. And Dirkley. And yourself."

He was barely able to make out the last words. He thought he could hear her say something else, but he couldn't quite catch it, and so the words were lost in the space between the world of men and the world beyond. No sooner had she finished speaking, her silhouette now lost in the blinding radiance, than the door swung shut, filling the room with a loud *SLAM*.

Then, something happened that Charlie had never seen before: his key fell to the floor with a clatter. He gingerly picked it up, noticing immediately that something was different. The word *PORTHMEUS*, one of the defining features of the key, was no longer engraved in the shaft. He knew instinctively that it was just another ordinary key now . . . and he was just an ordinary man.

WHEN CHARLIE snapped out of his reverie several minutes later, he found himself standing in front of the bookshelf Melissa had mentioned, the plain black binder she'd made clutched in his hand, half removed from the shelf. He'd had so many other things on his mind—what to do about the still missing Javrouche, how to break Melissa's passing to Dirkley, what to do about *everything* involving the Council and their bazillion secrets—that he'd almost completely forgotten about the primer. Charlie pulled it from the shelf, then returned to his desk, dropping it on top with a meager *thud*. It was thinner than he'd expected, but as Melissa had said, time wasn't exactly on her side when she'd put it together. He eased the cover open.

The first section was a collection of inset folders, each containing several sealed envelopes with names hastily scrawled across them. They were for Melissa's staff, no doubt. Charlie grimaced at the thought of passing those out—*Hey there, I'm your new boss because your old one kicked the bucket just for me. Pleased to meet you.* He decided he'd host a meeting with all of them tomorrow before doing individual meetings—it would probably be easier that way.

The next section, a collection of documents, made up the majority of the binder's contents. Most were typed, but several were clearly copies of much older, handwritten forms. As Charlie continued flipping through, he would occasionally find a sticky note from Melissa affixed to a page. The headers of the documents weren't all that illuminating—titles like "A Treatise on the Nature of the Ferryman Artifacts" and "Notes on the Selection of Ferrymen" didn't exactly reveal much—but Charlie hoped they would after a careful reading.

He reached the final section, and flipped it open. Inside was a plain manila folder inserted freely into the binder, a large note attached to its front. It read:

> Thought you might be interested in this.
> —*Mel*

The memo earned a raised eyebrow. *Well, I am now,* Charlie thought. It wasn't like Melissa to be circumspect. He removed the note and slid out the folder. The first thing he noticed was the stamp hidden underneath, clearly blazoned across the folder's cover: *Office of the President.* The second were the words written on the folder's tab.

Death Record: Elizabeth Crowley Dawson

Charlie stared at the name, his brain slowly piecing together what he was looking at. Then his hands started to tremble, so much so that he had to set the folder down on the desk. The pain in his head, his leg—everywhere really—disappeared instantly. He shrank away from the folder like it was a leper.

His wife . . . It was everything the Institute knew about his wife—including how she died.

When it became clear after his induction into the Ferryman

Institute that Charlie wouldn't be allowed to see Elizabeth again, he'd spent a considerable amount of time trying to find out this very information. What had become of her? For years—decades even—he'd asked around as discreetly as possible. He knew the odds were minuscule—given the sheer number of Ferrymen who existed and their continual turnover, it wasn't so much finding a needle in a haystack as in a forest. Still, Charlie went about his quest undaunted. But as the years passed, either no one he talked to had her case, or no one could remember. After eighty years, his questioning became far less frequent. By ninety, he only asked as an offhand aside every now and then. A hundred years? Maybe he asked once or twice.

And now, lying in front of him, were his answers.

Which, of course, was the exact moment the knock on his door came.

Charlie cleared his throat and replaced the folder in the binder. "Come in," he called.

The door cracked open a bit, then Alice's head poked out from behind it. She looked at him, then took a quick survey of the room from behind the door. Apparently satisfied that it wasn't booby-trapped, she slid in, closing the door behind her. She stood in front of it, both her hands behind her back on the knob still.

"Hey," she said.

Charlie didn't move. He was simply too surprised to see her. "Hey" was all he managed back.

Alice's eyes took to studying his new office. "Nice digs," she said. "Can I sit in one of your fancy chairs?"

Oddly enough, that was what removed Charlie from his stupor. "Sure."

"Thanks," she said, even though she was practically sitting in one before he'd replied. She folded her legs, crisscross, and let her hands fall in her lap. It looked grossly uncomfortable to Charlie, but it seemed to suit Alice just fine.

"So, is *how are you doing* considered classified information nowadays given your fancy new title? I'm dying to know." She grimaced after she spoke. "Really poor choice of words just now. Sorry."

But Charlie waved her concerns away. "No, and fine. Lots of things to keep me busy. In fact, I'm surprised the Council even let you come visit me with everything going on."

"They didn't," Alice replied nonchalantly. "But Cartwright might have strongly hinted at where I'd be able to find you. Besides, it's not like I'll ever be back here, so fuck it. What are they going to do, shoot me?" She let out a mock laugh. "But seriously, please don't let them shoot me. I've had enough guns pointed in my general direction to last a lifetime. Two or three, even."

"I don't know . . . What's in it for me?"

Alice considered that for a moment. "My undying gratitude . . . ?"

"Please. I don't want anything that's undying for the rest of my mortal life."

Mortal life. Now, there was a phrase Charlie hadn't thought he'd ever use again in reference to himself. But it was true . . . he was mortal. Maybe not quite a normal human, per se, but not far off. It was the only thing he'd wanted for so long—not because he wanted to be a regular person, but because he wanted to escape his life as a Ferryman so desperately. So much death, so much pain . . . and now, he could finally leave—say his farewell, bow, and wait for the curtain to fall. For the first time, that was his choice to make.

But he no longer wanted that. The constructs of his life that had been pulling his sanity apart now stood silent. In fact, Charlie was having a tough time understanding it himself. And yet there it was . . . The girl in front of him—this strange, wonderful girl—was his reminder that there was more to living than just watching it end.

"Nothing undying, huh . . ." Alice stood up from the chair and began to stroll around the room. "What about undying love?" She picked a random book from the bookshelf and began to absentmindedly thumb through it.

"Exceptions to every rule." Charlie carefully rose to his feet, barely even wincing this time. He slowly hobbled his way over to where she was standing, book open in her hands. "Do you want to go for a walk with me?" he asked blithely, and for a moment, the past and future simply melted away and he was left to exist in just that moment.

"Around here? Won't you get in trouble for that?" Alice replied.

Charlie shrugged. "You only live once, right?"

Alice laughed, genuinely and fully, at his admittedly awful joke. Her smile seemed, for the very first time, carefree. It was what Charlie knew was lurking there all along, hidden but not forgotten. Later on in his life, he would point to that moment as when he knew things he couldn't possibly have known, but which all managed to come true anyway.

She rolled her eyes. "I swear to God, the absolute cheesiest dork *I have ever met* . . ." She closed the book in her hands and set it aside on his bookshelf. "Sure, I'd love a tour of your office. Lead on."

Charlie held up a single finger and limped back to his desk. "One second," he said as he pulled a pen from the canister on his desk. With a flick, he pulled off a sticky note, scribbled a brief message on it, then opened the binder to the very back and attached it to the folder Melissa had left for him. "All right, good," Charlie said, and he circled back around to the door where Alice was waiting.

As he opened the door, he didn't look back at the universe floating above them in his window, at the stars flickering like lighthouses on a galactic sea, or at the poorly written note he'd left.

Charlie closed the door softly behind them, off to show Alice a glimpse of the world between the living and the dead.

A place they'd both already been.

EPILOGUE
FIVE YEARS LATER

THE REAPER

James stared at the man sitting across from him and beamed. It had been so long since he'd had a chance to interview a potential new recruit, especially one with this remarkable of a background.

"You sure I can't get you anything? Water, coffee, tea?" James asked.

The man sat, eyes glaring, and said nothing.

"Okay. No problem at all. Just perk up if you change your mind." From the top of his desk, James pulled out a small manila folder and opened it, making a show of examining its contents even though he'd just about memorized the file at this point.

For years, James had heard rumors of a rogue Ferryman. Of course, the Institute always denied it—as well they should, given all the headaches that would cause, internally or otherwise—but James had a good nose for these things. Where there was smoke, there was fire, and he'd always gotten a whiff of fumes whenever the topic came up. Now he had confirmation of its truth.

"You know, I have to say, it's really remarkable you found this place. We're not an easy organization to find. To do it in only five years . . ." He whistled appreciatively. It was true. They were a group that could generally only be found when they wanted to be. For this man to seek them out on his own . . . well, it only piqued James's interest that much more. "Let's just say I wouldn't want to find out what it's like to be on your bad side." He rattled with hearty laughter.

For what seemed like the first time since he'd arrived, the man moved, leaning forward in his chair. "No," he said flatly, "you don't."

James smiled brightly, nodding vigorously. "Of course not, of course not." He closed the folder and gently tossed it on his desk. With his legs crossed, he placed his hands on his knees and looked across, grinning. "So what can I do for you today, Mr. Toulouse?"

Toulouse didn't move, instead staring straight ahead. James got the feeling Toulouse was trying to stare *through* him, but he didn't mind. The newbies only ever ignored him in the beginning. They all learned not to with time.

"I'm here to speak with Death," Toulouse said.

"Oh, exciting! Unfortunately, he's unavailable for the foreseeable future. However, I am his second-in-command if you have any questions . . . ?"

Toulouse frowned, but continued anyway. "I'd like to work here. I have . . . business in this industry that needs finishing. And please . . . call me Javrouche."

James's grin somehow stretched even wider at this. It was just as he'd hoped. The former Inspector Javrouche, sitting right in front of him. It looked like James's sources had been right, after all. Sure, James had felt relatively confident about the man's identity after acquiring Javrouche's file from the Institute. But there was no doubt now—he was the real deal. And what a prize this could be! Here was a man who'd not only managed to make contact in only five years—five years!—but had done it all while avoiding capture by the Ferryman Institute. At the risk of gushing a bit too much, the whole thing was downright impressive. Javrouche was *exactly* the sort of recruit James had been looking for, and he'd pretty much fallen right into his lap. Of course, the Inspector undoubtedly had some attitude issues they might need to iron out, but James never had a problem with attitudes for very long.

Javrouche's arrival also meant something James had suspected but could never prove. Now he had his proof: the Ferryman Institute had been lying to him. James *hated* being lied to. He was not the man you tried to cheat, no, sir. But there would be time to deal with that. For now, it was time to settle in his greenhorn.

"Well, that is fantastic news! We're always looking for exciting candidates here, and let me tell you, I think you've got a lot of potential, Mr. Javrouche." James extended a well-manicured hand. "It's a pleasure to meet you. My name is James. Allow me to be the first to welcome you to Death Inc."

INTO THE LIGHT

William Henry Taylor Cartwright IV stood, poised motionlessly on the edge of the cliff. The gentle breeze rustled through his hair and even played with the twirled-in edges of his mustache. The last dying rays of daylight imbued the scorched earth of the canyon walls with the colors of the vanishing sun, and the sky, once a vivid blue, had been transmuted as if by some unseen alchemist into a dazzling selection of pinks and purples. Cartwright saw all this and let the beauty of it wash over him.

Then, he jumped.

As his body plummeted down into the canyon below, his thoughts drifted back to earlier that afternoon.

"I HOPE THE TEA is up to scratch," Charlie said as he set the cup in front of Cartwright. "We don't have any Earl Grey, but I've been told by a reliable source that this is good."

Cartwright sipped from the small cup. It wasn't what he normally went for in the tea department, but he'd be lying if he said he wasn't impressed by the beverage in front of him. "I must say, this tea is actually rather enchanting. It's honey-vanilla chamomile, you say?" he said, before taking another sip. "Not my usual cup of tea, to very literally borrow a phrase, but wonderful all the same."

Charlie took a sip from the bottle of beer he'd just opened. "I could serve you the worst brew of tea you've ever had and you would tell me you find it exotic and interesting."

Though he tried to hide his grin behind the cup of tea, Cartwright doubted he'd succeeded. "I'm afraid I've not even the slightest idea what you're talking about. I'm well known in many of my circles for my brutal honesty." Even years later, it was still a joke they both had a good laugh at.

Cartwright set down his tea and crossed his legs one over the other. They were out on Charlie's deck—Cartwright's favorite spot on the entire property, which he had no shame in saying—and the summer sun filtered through the rustling leaves of the oak trees planted in the backyard. When the chirping of the birds quieted down, which was admittedly rare at that time of the day, he could hear the creek that marked the end of the yard. He had no qualms congratulating Charlie on a job well done. It was a beautiful place for a home.

"So, my good fellow," Cartwright said, "you've officially been our president for five years now . . ."

Charlie choked slightly on his beer at the abrupt change of topic. He coughed and sputtered for nearly half a minute afterward. "Sorry," the former Ferryman said as he pounded his chest, "I didn't know you were here on business."

"I'm not," Cartwright replied, taking a sip of tea in between his statements. "I'm asking as a comrade, not a colleague."

"So as Cartwright, not Virgil?" Charlie asked, a devious grin sneaking onto his face.

Cartwright greeted it with a snort. "Please," he said with a dismissive wave of his hand, "you know my feelings about that name."

"I know. But I've only tormented you over it for a little while." Charlie's smirk deepened as he took another pull from his bottle.

"My question, Charles," Cartwright said as he resumed drinking his tea, "has nothing to do with work. I wanted to ask about you."

Charlie set his bottle down and crossed his arms. "Me, huh?"

"Yes, you. Is that line of questioning off-limits?" Cartwright leaned forward in his chair. "It's not a subject I broach lightly, but I feel it important to ask. Five years is a long time to most men, but not to a man who already has given service for more than two hundred. You know me, old friend—I fear I will be eternally concerned about your well-being."

Charlie didn't answer immediately. Instead, his gaze ventured off into the trees that littered the several acres surrounding the house. The area immediately around the deck was nicely landscaped, but the foliage grew thicker toward the back of the lot. Cartwright watched as Charlie's eyes lost focus, like he was looking for the answer in the trees without actually seeing it.

"Honestly?" he finally said, returning his focus to Cartwright. "I've just been so lucky." Charlie nodded at this, as if he was proud to have found the right answer. "I'm a very lucky guy."

Cartwright had been listening and watching intently, but he needn't have. The words were spoken with such genuine sincerity that he knew it was the truth and nothing but. The sound of a sliding deck door interrupted his further thoughts.

"I'm coming out now, and I'm not covering my ears, so if you're talking about Institute stuff, this is your warning to shut up."

Both Cartwright and Charlie turned to see Alice come waddling out from the kitchen and onto the deck. Her arrival was preceded by the pronounced swell of her pregnant belly, and from what Cartwright remembered from his last visit several weeks ago, she was due in only a handful of weeks. Her wedding band flashed triumphantly in the rays of sun that found their way onto the deck. Though she was still the same Alice he'd met five years prior, her life with Charlie certainly appeared to have been good to her: even before the pregnancy, she had filled out somewhat to a healthier weight, and though her endless sarcasm hadn't left her, it seemed to be counterbalanced by a new sense of optimism.

Cartwright got out of his chair and took her hand, applying a gentle kiss to the back of it. "My dearest Alice, may I say that you look positively radiant. I have a hard time distinguishing what light comes from the sun and what is from your effervescent glow."

Alice snorted and gave the tiniest hint of a curtsy—a greeting specifically for Cartwright that she'd adopted long ago, but found more difficult to do these days, what with a nearly fully formed human being inside her—before easing herself into a deck chair. "You probably can't tell the difference because I'm roughly the same size as the sun. So, if by *radiant* you mean massive, then I can't agree with you enough. Seriously, if my hips get any wider, I'm going to need Charlie to knock down half the walls in the house."

Charlie went to speak, but he apparently thought better of it and instead reached for his beer. Despite his effort, the action didn't escape his wife's notice. "You were going to say something, weren't you?" Charlie vehemently shook his head. Alice rolled her eyes. "You are an absolutely atrocious liar."

Cartwright laughed, and even Charlie couldn't help the half smile that touched his lips. The wind whispered through the trees, adding its own note to the music of the day.

"Do you ever miss it, Charles? Being a Ferryman?" Cartwright asked out of the blue.

Charlie's expression faded to neutral at the question. "The answer in front of my wife? No, of course not, because then Alice and I would never have been able to experience this." He delicately took her hand and gave her a tender look that Cartwright didn't doubt was something the two shared on a fairly frequent basis. "The honest answer, though?"

"Oh boy," Alice said, covering her eyes in mock horror, "here we go."

"The *honest* answer," Charlie said, repeating himself but louder, "is that there's one thing I really miss . . ."

CARTWRIGHT HIT THE GROUND with a magnificent impact. His body lay perfectly still, a disastrous mess of broken limbs and lacerations. But as time passed, his body slowly pulled itself together, until he was able to stand again. With a casual ease, he dusted himself off. It was so odd to him, having watched Charlie do it for so long, to now find himself the one at the bottom of the canyon, clothes shredded and covered in dust.

"Hmph," he said, gazing up at the majestic walls that surrounded him. He was pleasantly surprised at the buoyant rush it had given him. "Maybe Charles was right. Perhaps I have been missing out."

If there was one thing Cartwright had learned, and rather quickly, it was that even a man who'd been around for millennia could still learn a thing or two, apparently.

He made his way over to the rope he'd fixed into the canyon wall and began the slow climb back to the top. There was still enough sunlight left for one more dive, after all.

ACKNOWLEDGMENTS

What follows here is my best attempt at thanking all the wonderful people who contributed to this book in one way or another. I don't think it's possible to list every name here, so to everyone—friends, family, loved ones, complete strangers in line at Duane Reade, etc.—thank you for being a part of this adventure, whether you were knowingly partaking or not. You have my utmost gratitude.

I'd like to thank you, the reader, for being a part of this journey. I imagine you're only reading this section because you're stuck on a Brooklyn-bound F train and that creepy guy across the car is staring at you and the only way to avoid eye contact is to keep reading even though you presumably just finished and now all you have left is this lousy section . . . Whatever the case may be, I'm beyond grateful that you would spend a portion of your limited free time reading this book. I sincerely hope it brought some enjoyment to your life.

The rest is a little personal, so if the creepy guy isn't there anymore, you can stop reading. I promise, there won't be anything good past here. Pinky swear.

I owe enormous thank-yous to the people who are most directly responsible for making this happen: to my agent, Hannah Brown Gordon, not only for being the best champion for this book I could have ever asked for, but also for just being seriously awesome in general; and to my editor, Ed Schlesinger, who did amazing things for this story in both form and content (I mean, seriously, read this sentence. It's like the Great Wall of China. Now imagine a whole book of them) and is one of the most infectiously enthusiastic, fun people I've had the pleasure of speaking with. I've been extraordinarily lucky to have them both in my corner, and this book is miles better thanks to their care and passion. I would also like to sincerely thank Mary Beth Constant for her truly wonderful copyediting expertise. In addition to making it appear as if I actually know how to write proper English (hint: I don't), I learned so many awesome things from her comments that I'm ninety-nine percent sure I will never lose in bar trivia ever again.

I owe a tremendous debt of gratitude to many people for reading various versions of this and offering their feedback. First and foremost, my dad, who's probably read it more times than I have (which may or may not be grounds for institutionalizing), and who not only cheered me along from day one—long before day one, really—but also rode the roller coaster with me the whole way. To my wife, Carly, who really made me believe this had a shot, and who put up with this whole process, including late nights and busted weekends, all with grace. Fortunately, she hasn't noticed she's completely out of my league yet, which has really worked out in my favor (please don't tell her). To my brother, Tim, for his feedback, late-night chats about the craft, and teaching me all there is to know about perseverance. To Tim Walsh, who convinced me to send it to him after several beers, then power-read the whole thing in something like two days. To Garrett Marco, who offered up his expertise to a struggling (and, if I'm honest, whining) Internet stranger, free of charge, and provided some great feedback.

I'm very grateful to my entire family, especially my parents, who both instilled a love of reading in me at a young age. To my mom, who has been an unending well of love and support, even if I unfortunately never inherited her knack for proper grammar and spelling (I still have no idea if the *i* goes before or after the *c*). She's always been my biggest fan, and I will never be able to thank her enough for that and many other things too numerous to list. A thank-you to my sister, Kate, for being such a positive force in my life and for willingly listening to me wax lyrical about life, the universe, and everything. To all my aunts, uncles, and cousins who've asked about the book, thank you all.

I would also like to extend my sincere gratitude to the fine people at Cross Pixel, past and present, who've had to put up with working with me over the years. I'd especially like to thank Alan Pearlstein and Jeff Weitman, whose kindness, support, and understanding during my undertaking of this cannot be overstated, particularly on days when I came into the office looking a little more bleary-eyed than usual.

I want to thank all the magnificent professors and teachers who have shepherded me along the way. Each one of you has contributed to this directly or indirectly. I'd like to particularly thank Rachel Basch, who ran a wonderful writing workshop and made the mistake of complimenting a short story of mine by saying it was funny, which in turn made me think I could actually write (I can't, so please blame her partially for this . . . but seriously, thank you) and Francisco Goldman, who ran a fantastic workshop as well but also introduced me to magic realism and, in particular, *The Master and Margarita*.

A thank-you to all the people who have shared their stories, or parts of them, with me throughout the years, whether in class or over the magic that is the Internet. I've been very fortunate to have shared classrooms with folks far smarter than I, and I am better off for it. To all the people who have crossed paths with me in life and gone on to other things, I'm grateful for all of you, for shaping me into who I am today, and wish you nothing but the best. To the lovely people at NaNoWriMo who inspire would-be authors to dream a little, and from which this novel was born, thank you. To Reddit and Wikipedia, for being invaluable resources and/or wastes of time, depending on the day, thanks and curses to you in equal measure. If there is any junk science or geography, that is all of my own devising.

Thank you and begging of forgiveness to anyone I forgot to mention.